The Fortress

By James McNally

Prologue:
The Followers

James McNally

He woke with a start, as if someone had dumped a bucket of ice water on his head. If he hadn't been alone in the room, he might have thought someone really did try to drown him; his sheets were drenched. A thin sheen of cold sweat covered his body. He groped for the bottle of Poland Spring on the bedside table, brushed it with his fingers, and nearly knocked it to the floor. He managed to catch it and pull it to him. Removing the cap, he took a long, drawn-out swig of the warm — but still refreshing — water then recapped the empty bottle and tossed it aside.

He stood and walked naked into the bathroom. He urinated and washed his hands. He donned a robe and walked down the hall to the living room. The window to the street below was a black rectangle of darkness in an already darkened room.

He shivered, remembering what had awakened him. It was the same dream he'd had for the past several nights, and each night he woke panting and drenched in sweat. In it, he was once again 11 years old and running through a dark and rainy forest. This, he believed, was from a past he barely remembered anymore. He and his brother, Scott, had been kidnapped as children. People had died during the ordeal, but he and Scott had been saved by a friend. That was the extent of what he knew from that time. Most of what he knew were stories he had heard other people tell. He wondered why, after twelve years, were these details of his life resurfacing?

The end of the dream was more disturbing than any memory. In the final minutes, before he woke, nearly screaming, the world — and everyone in it — was dead.

The streets are empty. Cars sit abandoned on the roads with their doors flung open as if the occupants fled too quickly to worry about shutting them. The storefronts, with their windows smashed out, stand empty and untidy—with the shelves picked clean, and unwanted merchandise smashed and disorganized. A strange wind blows through the land, warm and foul-smelling. Then there is a feeling like being sucked through a hose, and the dream takes him miles away from his home, to a structure that looks like nothing he has ever seen before. The front door of the massive structure stands open, and people he doesn't know file inside. As he nears the front of the structure, a man stops and turns to face him.

"It is time," the man says.

"Time for what?" he asks.

The man fixes him with a blank stare. "You are the Chosen One. It is time to pull the True Believers together and prepare. The world is ending and you must make the necessary arrangements." Then the man says something he remembers from his childhood. The non-sequitur has the ability to make his heart skip a beat. The man says: "Don't say ain't, or your mother will faint, and your father will step in a bucket of paint." Then the man turns and walks into the structure with the others.

But that wasn't the end.

He turns away from the structure.

He is now in an old cabin, a memory from his childhood again. There is an old man standing there. He looks like a black Santa Claus. The old man pulls a knife from the sleeve of his baggy shirt and stabs the woman sitting in a chair. He recognizes the woman as his Aunt Virginia. She had been murdered when he and Scott were kidnapped, but doesn't think this is memory. This is a horrific detail of that night he has interpreted from what others have told him.

The dream pulls him away from the violent scene and he is in the forest again, running. He trips on a rotted stump and someone grabs him.

He screams.

This is where the dream ends and he wakes.

He and Scott saw separate psychiatrists to deal with what they had gone through that summer. His own memories were suppressed as a coping mechanism, or so his doctor had said. But what had his brother been through back then? Scott refused to talk about what had happened to him that summer, but it was clear that Scott had endured much worse conditions than Chris. Reports mentioned beatings and mind games. His brother had grown up pretty well-rounded despite all that, though. And Scott was extremely protective of Chris. He thought that this protectiveness was due to the kidnapping; and this was backed up with what he knew of Scott before that summer. Before the horrors of that summer had changed them, Scott had been a disinterested older brother who could be downright mean at times.

But why dwell in the past? He liked who Scott was now, and that was all that mattered. He and Scott had become best friends ever since returning home from the Adirondacks. Even now, Scott lived just a few houses down from him.

He pulled the robe closer around him and tightened the belt as he peered outside. It had rained earlier, but the rain had stopped and now a glistening film covered everything in the glow of the corner streetlamp. But the dull lamplight illuminated more than just the wet surfaces.

Three people stood on the curbside, their faces turned up, looking at his apartment—at *him*. He stepped back. It was happening again. They were there to take him away. His eyes searched the room for a weapon. He considered calling Scott, but a glance at the clock informed him it was only two in the morning. He didn't want to bother Scott and his wife, Kaylan. Besides, he wasn't a helpless 11-year-old boy anymore, and this wasn't the cabin. He was safely locked behind a gate at his own home. The door was bolted.

He returned to the window and saw there were seven people out there now. He stared out, shocked, confused. As he watched, two more people approached to stand in the crowd. In all, over twenty people came to stand on the curb, looking up.

He paced the room. Every time he glanced outside, the people were there, unmoving.

He tried to forget about them — ignore them — but his anxiety rose with every minute they continued to watch him. He checked again, fearful that they were coming for him. He checked that the door was truly locked, and then returned the window, staying in the shadows where he could see them. He watched and he waited. They didn't move. They didn't look at one another. Their eyes didn't waver from his window.

When he could take it no more, he picked up a marble elephant statue, unlocked the door and flew down the steps to the walkway. He stormed out the gate to the roadside. He sprinted down the road and stood facing the crowd. They still didn't move, except to swivel their heads and look at him. He raised the elephant over his head as he drew closer. The group seemed unconcerned with his aggressive stance. They stared at him, unflinchingly still.

"Who are you and what are you doing here? What do you want from me?"

One man stepped forward. He was young, about thirty, clean-shaven, with brown hair.

This was the man from his dream. *It is time…*

Chris took an involuntary step back, raising his weapon with a menacing wave. The man ignored him.

"I am Roger," the man said. "We are True Believers, here to serve you. Tell me: what is your bidding?"

Then the man *bowed*. Others in the crowd did the same. Something else from his memory resurfaced then.

You will bow down before me.

He took a few steps away from the crowd. They didn't look up; they didn't try to follow him. They stayed in the same spot as he scurried away and reentered his apartment. He bolted the deadlock and put the chain in place. He returned to the window. Roger and the others had stood back up and were once again staring up at his window.

The horrors of the dream reverberated in his head until his brain began to ache. He chewed a handful of dry aspirin, and returned to the window. His headache slowly tapered off as he watched the gathering crowd grow ever larger.

He stayed in the shadows watching them until morning. As the sun rose over the park on the other side of the street, he once again headed outside. He did not bring his elephant weapon this time. When he approached the group they once again bowed to him.

"You, Roger, stand."

He stood.

Chris waved the man forward and the man took two steps. Chris took two steps closer as well. When they were standing nearly nose to nose, he spoke softly, looking directly into the man's piercing gray eyes.

"Why are you here?"

"To serve you."

"All of you?"

The man didn't respond. Chris stepped to the side and looked at the others bowing down. "You're all here to serve me?"

There was a monotone chorus of "yes" that reminded Chris of church.

He stepped back in front of Roger and said, "Why are you here to serve me?"

Roger looked confused by the question.

He rephrased it. "Who am I that you would serve me?"

The man still seemed confused, but replied this time. "You are the Chosen One."

That phrase again. Hearing it aloud, coming from this man, caused Chris's heart to stagger, and he had trouble swallowing. He took a calming breath. He closed his eyes, and opened them again, hoping they would be gone. They weren't.

The man spoke again. "What is it you wish from us?"

Throughout the night more people had arrived to stand in the crowd. There were now more than fifty people bowed down. He thought about what the man had said.

He turned away from the crowd. Roger watched him intently. He said: "I *am* the Chosen One, and you *will* bow down before me."

The man didn't respond. These were not questions.

"I do have something I want you to do for me."

"What do you wish, Chosen One? Name it."

"I want you to build something."

Part One: Remembering the Forest

James McNally

Chapter One

1.

Chris stepped out of the limo and walked around to the tinted glass of the front passenger-side door. The motor hummed as the window lowered, revealing the dark, air-conditioned interior—and the driver—who leaned over to see Chris more clearly.

Chris leaned in. "I'll be here a while, so feel free to look around if you want."

"If it's all the same, Sir, I'll just wait out here and catch a nap."

Chris pressed his lips together. "Suit yourself."

He stood and looked to his left, at the rickety old motel, unused, overrun with weeds and in need of paint. He turned toward the fenced-in area in the opposite direction from the motel, inhaling the acrid scent of chlorinated water. It brought back fond memories that threatened to bring tears to his eyes. The pool vibrated with energy and warmth. The sound of shouting and splashing carried on the wind, giving proof that the pool was open for business. Chris quickened his steps, excited to see the old Z-shaped pool again. A sharp whistle cut through the air. One blast: attention. His memory recalled the rules of the pool. One blast was meant for one person, who would be singled out by the lifeguard, and reminded of the safety rules. Two blasts and the entire pool was to stop and look to the lifeguard for instruction. Had there been three blasts, it was a warning for all swimmers to exit the pool, like a water fire drill. Only it usually wasn't a drill. He had almost drowned in this pool back when he was 11, during that same summer his life had changed so dramatically. The near drowning had been the beginning of it all. It was also how he met Brian.

Chris walked through the front gate, an entrance big enough to fit rescue vehicles in to the pool area; something he learned firsthand. He turned right and passed the girl in a pink bathing suit sitting on a metal folding chair. She looked up with shining blue eyes, and smiled at Chris, but didn't speak. He walked past her into the office he remembered as Leah West's. The person behind the desk was not Leah, however. It was someone Chris knew on sight, although the man was much older than he remembered him. There was some gray in his hair and Chris laughed at that.

The man with graying hair looked up, confused at first; but recognition set in, and the man's eyes widened. His mouth dropped open.

"Chris? Is that you?"

Chris laughed. "It's me."

Brian rushed around the side of the desk, bumping his knee. Chris cringed, but Brian seemed not to notice. He took Chris by the shoulders and pulled him into a hug. "You're all grown up. The last time I saw you…"

"I know." Chris was suddenly hit with the realization of it all. He had been an eleven-year-old child the last time he had seen Brian. Now, he was going on thirty-one.

Brian leaned back against his desk. "It's been, what? Twenty years since we last spoke? You're a man now. Honestly, I never thought…"

"…that you'd ever see me again?"

"Exactly." Brian nodded. He rubbed his chin as he studied Chris. "Back in town. Is Scott with you?"

"No. He didn't come."

"I could understand. Why would you want to come back here? The memories…"

"They aren't mine. I have very few memories of this place. Are you busy?"

"I'll make time for you, Chris. Let's take a walk."

Brian allowed Chris to exit the office first, following close behind. They walked side by side to the pool.

"Can you believe I never did learn to swim?"

"No?" Brian looked shocked.

"I better not let Leah know that. She'll force you to finish what you started." Chris laughed at the idea. "Where is she these days?"

Brian stopped walking. Chris turned.

"Leah is no longer with us. She passed away four years ago."

Chris flushed. "I'm sorry to hear that. Was it…?"

"Cancer?" Brian finished Chris's thought. He paused and then continued. "No, she had won that fight. It was her heart."

After a moment, they began walking again.

They came to the area of the pool where Chris had fallen in and almost drown. They stopped again and looked into the water. Chris could feel alternating waves of refreshing coolness and eye-stinging chlorination.

"How is Scott these days?" Brian asked.

"Scott's good. He's married to a nice girl named Kaylan. I asked him to come with me, but when he heard what I have planned he decided he didn't want to participate."

Brian raised an eyebrow. "What *do* you have planned?"

Chris studied Brian, wondering how best to approach the subject. Brian was a straight-forward guy, Chris decided. He would just come out with it. "I plan to visit the cabin."

Brian spoke as he released a long, controlled breath. "The cabin…"

"And the other places from that period of my life. I've had to suppress my curiosity for Scott's sake, but I need to see the places where it all happened. I can't afford to hide from it anymore. And I would like you to tell me any details you remember from that time, if you are willing to share."

Brian stared at Chris. "Why?"

"I have some new…developments in my life. I need to do this."

"You want to know why those people calling themselves Keepers of the Forest took you?" Brian shrugged. "You may never get what you're looking for."

"That's not exactly what I'm doing here. I want to retrace my steps, see it all for myself. I have no memory of those events, and I doubt visiting the places where it happened will jog my memory, but I still have to do it. I can't explain it any better than that."

Brian's head dropped slightly. "I suppose I know what you mean. I'll tell you what I know."

"Thank you."

"When do you want to do this...excursion?"

"No better time than the present."

"OK, but I'm hungry. Can we stop for food?"

"Sure, we can eat."

"Whose car should we take?"

"Mine."

Chris's crooked half-smile caused Brian to raise his head and narrow his eyes.

2.

Sitting in the back of the limo, Chris sipped at a glass of champagne as Brian drank a cola. Brian's eyes flicked from the small refrigerator, to the TV built into the back of the seat in front of him, to the plush leather seats, and back to Chris. The air conditioning put the air at just the right temperature. A mirrored glass separated the back of the limo from the driver.

The fridge was stocked with Chris's favorite foods; one of these being peanut butter and banana sandwiches. Brian pulled a sandwich from the cooler and unwrapped it. "Nice," he said through a mouthful.

Chris stared at his glass of champagne, looking at it from different angles. "I feel like I'm getting away with something, drinking this."

"Looks like you did well for yourself." Brian washed his sandwich down with the last of his soda.

Chris offered him another soda, but he declined. Chris refilled his own glass from the chilled bottle in the bucket between them. The ice sloshed and crackled as he replaced the bottle. "Turns out it's quite lucrative being me."

Brian laughed. "What makes you so special?"

Chris didn't laugh with him. "I think you know the answer to that."

Brian turned and glanced out the window to his left. The sky showed blue with only a few small white clouds. In the distance, Brian saw the large steel structure being built on the shores of Ampersand Lake. He called it an eyesore, but Nancy felt it was much more ominous than that. He turned back to the inside of the limo when Chris continued talking.

"Part of my reason for coming back is to understand who, or more precisely, what I am."

Brian pulled his eyes from Chris's face. "I don't think I'm ready to have this conversation."

Chris took a sip from his fluted champagne glass. "I don't want you to do anything you're not comfortable with. I didn't come here with the intention of drudging up old horrors. I need to know what you know, but not at the expense of your sanity — or our friendship. If you aren't up to talking about it, we can do this another way."

"Do what? You still haven't told me why you're back in town."

"I'm getting to that, but if you can't…"

"It's fine. I can share what I know. Don't worry about that."

Chris sat back. After a moment of silence, he said, "why didn't we keep in touch with each other over the years?"

"That's easy. You were a kid. Your parents asked me not to, and I had no choice but to obey their wishes. Then after so much time had passed I just figured you moved on with your life."

"When you say my parents, you really mean my mother; don't you...or, as she would have preferred, do not you?" Chris huffed. "That doesn't even make sense."

"How is your mother, that old battle axe?"

"She's dead."

"Oh, Chris. I'm sorry."

Chris laughed. "Don't be. It was a long time ago. In fact, both my parents died in a plane crash heading to Australia. It was bound to happen. They were never home with us. Even after what happened she had no trouble leaving me to travel. She wasn't a nice woman." Then he added, "I miss my dad, though."

"Well, I'm sorry I didn't stay in touch."

Chris looked into his eyes and placed a hand on his arm. "It's in the past."

Brian studied Chris's childlike face. *He still has that same crooked half-smile I remember from when he was a kid. He seems so innocent. Why, then, do I feel like he's about to turn my world upside down?*

The limo began to rock and bounce over gravel road. Brian studied Chris's pale, stricken face. They were about to see the cabin where Chris had been kidnapped, and his guardians murdered. Brian didn't speak for the rest of the ride, and they climbed out of the limo when it stopped.

3.

Brian waited as Chris instructed Roger to take the limo back to the end of the road.

"We'll walk back to you when we're finished here, Okay?"

Roger agreed and drove away.

Brian watched the limo until it was out of sight then turned to Chris. "Your staff is very obedient."

"He's are very loyal to me, but Roger isn't my staff."

"What is he then?"

Chris turned back in the direction the limo had gone. He looked at Brian. "He's a friend, but he's even more than that. I can't explain it."

Brian nodded. *And you don't have to.*

Together, Brian and Chris turned toward the cabin.

The property had not been kept up over the years. Grass came up to their waist, and the stone path leading to the front door was choked with weeds. Chris took a deep breath and walked up to the door. Brian tested the knob and the door opened. He held it open for Chris to enter first.

The furniture had been removed. The floor was covered in an inch of dust, and weeds reached up through cracks like nosy little trespassers. "I remember very little of the time I spent here, and most of it is like a foggy snapshot. One thing I do recall is the huge fish tank that was built into the wall here." They both peered through the hole the fish tank had left in the wall looking in on the kitchen. They entered the kitchen and glanced around. Some cupboard doors hung open, and still others had fallen completely away; but there was nothing on the shelves. The sink was rusted over. No water ran from the faucets. Mice had built stray homes in the empty pantry. Brian imagined the food that used to stock those shelves. Aunt Virginia had been a great cook. *Surely, Chris you must remember that.* Brian's heart grew heavy as he recalled the nights eating the dinners she had prepared. "I haven't had venison since that week I came over for dinner. That week before..."

"Before I was kidnapped." Chris and Brian shared a look. "I remember that."

They exited the kitchen.

Chris continued. "What can you tell me about that time?"

"Where should I start?"

"From the beginning. How did you find out I wasn't coming back for swimming lessons?"

Brian stopped walking and Chris stopped to wait for him.

"Well, I guess that was when Sherry came to the pool and posed as your mother. She said you wouldn't be coming back. No one had any reason to doubt her. We didn't know your mother—didn't know much about you, either, for that matter. Leah took her at her word. She had no reason not to." Brian blushed and turned away. He looked back when Chris spoke.

"But you didn't believe her. You knew she wasn't my mother, didn't you?"

"I had no reason to doubt her. I didn't *want* her to be your mother. I guess I wasn't ready for our time together to end. Leah warned me not to get too close. She kept reminding me that you would be leaving eventually. But at that moment it just felt too soon."

Chris didn't speak and waited for Brian to continue.

"But, no. I didn't believe her. Something about her didn't jive with what you had said about your mother. She used contractions, for one thing. There was other stuff, too, but that was the big one. I knew something bad had happened, even if no one else did."

"Thanks for not giving up on me."

Brian took a breath to suppress a swelling in his chest. *I love this kid, still.*

"What happened then?"

"Well, I guess nothing. Not for several weeks. The next big break I got was when Sherry came asking for help to get you and Scott away from the others."

They exited the cabin through the back door, trudging through the high grass to the pair of rusted bird feeder poles standing sentry at the edge of the lawn. Chris stared down at the two wooden crosses hiding in the tall weeds. One read Virginia, and the other read, simply, Ed.

"This is where the investigators found your aunt and uncle. They had been buried in shallow graves. I made the grave markers, and placed them here after the bodies had been removed."

Chris stared at the ground Brian had pointed out as the shallow grave, and he swayed on his legs.

Brian reached for him. *He's going to pass out.*

Chris caught himself. "I'm okay."

When Chris was steady again, they walked around the edge of the tree line until they were back at the front of the cabin. They started down the gravel road toward the limo.

The two walked in silence for several minutes. Chris spoke first. "Scott and Kaylan went to the same college. They were inseparable from the moment they met. She took a liking to me right away, which was good. If she hadn't Scott might have dumped her on the spot."

Chris laughed.

"How could she not. You're very likable." Brian looked at Chris's face, to see how his comment had been received.

Chris blushed and turned away for a moment. He turned back to Brian when his embarrassment eased. "What about you? When did you and Nancy get married?"

Brian pulled at a limb from a tree as they passed under it. He casually stripped the back off the stick as he spoke. "I married Nancy about a year after the last time I saw you. Once the sensationalism of the whole ordeal passed; when we could take a step back and see that we had true feeling for each other, the only natural recourse for me was to marry her."

"I remember Nancy from the days after she helped you rescue Scott, but it's limited. Not like the memories I have of you. I have a fondness for her, but it's nothing compared to what I feel for you. It's like I feel gratitude for what she did. But with you, I feel genuine love. It's a love that stuck with me over the years. I've missed you more than I've ever missed my parents. It was only natural for me to come back and reconnect with you."

Brian struggled to swallow the lump that formed in his throat. He turned and tossed his stick into the bushes.

When the limo came into view Chris stopped Brian. They stared at their feet, kicking at the stones as Chris came up with the words to express what he wanted to say. Finally, he spoke. "How much do you know about the group that took me?"

"I know everything. I read all the police reports on the incident. You might say I was obsessed with the case. I made friends with some of the detectives in charge of the investigation, and learned things the general public wasn't supposed to know. I will tell you everything I know."

"Good to hear," Chris said. They continued toward the limo. "You can tell me all about it when we get where we are going next."

"Where now?" Brian asked.

Chris opened the limo door for Brian. "We're going back to the house in the woods where I was held."

Brian collapsed onto the leather seats in the cool interior of the limo, physically and emotionally drained. He mumbled. "I'm starting to feel like I'm the one being kidnapped."

Chris laughed. "Nice." And he dropped into the seat beside Brian.

4.

Chris walked up the driveway toward the house. He and Scott had been held captive here. A lump formed in his throat as Brian led him to the back door. He glanced back toward the limo, but it was already gone. Roger waited for them further down the road, with the same instructions as before; when they were finished, they would walk back. He reconsidered that directive now, wanting nothing more than to return to town and enjoy good conversation over a relaxing cup of coffee.

He turned toward the house and squared his shoulders. This was his idea, after all. He would finish what he started.

Brian spoke, drawing Chris's attention.

"The house was secretly owned by the group's leader, Crispus Brown." Brian flicked his gaze from the house to glance at Chris. "Ansestry.com confirmed that he was the offspring of Crispus Attucks, one of the first victims in the Boston Massacre during the revolutionary war. From what Sherry was told, the old man's ancestor used to hold British prisoners in the basement. I've been through the house since the police cleared it of evidence, and I have to say the place is creepy."

"Take me inside." Chris's voice was soft, but determined.

The backdoor lock had been broken by vandals and they entered through there. Spray-painted phallic symbols and foul language decorated the walls. Brian led Chris through the kitchen to the dented and beaten metal door leading to the basement. They descended the steps in the dark; but in the basement, enough daylight came through the small windows high up on the walls to allow them to see where they were going. They moved to the end of the row of cells and Brian pointed into the one on the left.

"Scott was held in here."

Chris turned to the wooden door in the far wall of the basement. "What was in there?"

Brian stared at the door but didn't speak until Chris prompted him with a look.

"They buried their mistakes in there."

Chris's body felt suddenly cold and he shivered. He closed his eyes. "Explain."

"The police found the remains of four small boys buried in the earthen floor of that room. It is speculated they were the failed attempts that came before you. The last time I was here the holes were still visible from when the bodies were exhumed. I wouldn't advise going in there without a flashlight. There are no windows. In fact, I would advise not going in there at all."

Chris nodded and they headed back up to the ground floor.

Chris followed Brian up to the second story. They walked halfway down the hall and stopped in front of a door.

"You were kept in here."

Chris reached out slowly, turned the knob and pushed the door open. He stepped inside.

He had vague memories of the room. His dreams had taken him inside this room, and looking at it now, he saw that the dreams had been correct. There had been some guilt for Chris, having been able to sleep in a comfortable bed, in a warm room, while Scott languished in that cell. Scott insisted he had preferred it that way, and had even expressed joy that Chris had been treated to at least that luxury during the ordeal; but still Chris agonized over the terrible things Scott had been through.

Brian led Chris out of the basement to the back yard. They followed a short path to a shed deep inside the woods that surrounded the house. The shed was locked, and they really didn't have any interest in entering it anyway, but Brian told Chris what he knew of the shed.

"They killed a woman in here. Actually, she was just a girl. A nineteen-year-old girl. There seemed to be no reason for the murder. Just a senseless act by a sadistic group of killers. Maybe they were preparing for the act of killing Scott."

"I'm sorry for that girl."

"Chris, you don't blame yourself for all this, do you? You know none of this is your fault, right?" Brian seemed genuinely concerned now.

"They did all this on my behalf. I must be somewhat at fault."

"That's bullshit. You were a kid. You were abducted. You had no control over their actions. None of it was your fault."

"I'm working through those feelings. Deep down I know I'm not to blame for any of this, but how can I not feel some guilt over this, some shame."

Brian stepped forward and gripped Chris by the shoulders and pulled him into a hug. Chris said nothing as Brian led him along the overgrown path to the back yard.

Chris spoke first. "Can you tell me what you know about the members of the cult? The so-called Keepers of the Forest?"

Brian took a breath. "How much are you willing to hear? I know a lot about them. I studied the investigation files extensively." He laughed. "I lied and told them I was thinking of writing a book."

Chris laughed. "You should have written a book." His smile faded. "Tell me everything you know. Don't leave anything out. I'll handle it ok."

"Crispus Brown dropped off the face of the earth in the seventies. He had been arrested several times back then for inciting violent riots and breaking and entering.

"The next in line was Mason Reed. Not much is known about him. He was in and out of jail as a kid but nothing more than breaking and entering. As an adult, he spent some time in Albany County Correctional facility. He met Ted Becker there. Ted and Vincent Don Vito were cell mates. Mason must have met up with Crispus sometime after being released. Mason disappeared after that.

"In the meantime, Ted and Vincent broke out of jail and must have sought out Mason. They were never seen again until they were found dead, here, at this house."

Chris studied the house as Brian spoke. When Brian stopped talking, Chris looked at him.

Brian continued.

"Sherry was the last to join, and the only real believer, other than Crispus, himself. I knew Sherry, spoke to her. I learned a lot about who the Keepers of the Forest were from her."

Chris looked down at his feet. He jammed his hands into the pockets of his jeans. "I would like to say I remember her, but I don't. That whole time has been complete swabbed from my mind. I remember events leading up to it, and stuff directly after, but nothing from the time my family was attacked at the cabin, or when I was in this house."

"Do you want to hear about what happened in there now?"

Chris swallowed hard. When he spoke, his voice was a whisper. "Yes."

Brian closed his eyes. When he opened them again he seemed to be somewhere else, or more precisely, in another time. "The investigator played it out for me as they believed it happened."

Brian walked over to the warped and rotting wooden platform that had been overrun with weeds. "They built this just before the night everything went down. It's believed to be the stage for some kind of ritual that had been planned." Brian turned toward the house and pointed at it. "The first to die that night was Vincent. He was stabbed, presumably by Sherry, as she was trying to get you and Scott out of the house. I don't know why, but she only managed to get Scott out. He was in bad shape. Beaten. Nancy and I took him back to town. Something happened, though. Probably something to do with her run-in with Vincent, but she wasn't able to get you out. She had to go back in for you.

"She didn't make it. The investigator believes Mason found you both trying to escape. He locked you in the wicker thing back there." He pointed to a burned out collapsing structure that looked like the skeletal remains of some ancient beast. "He killed Sherry. He lynched her from that tree branch hanging over the platform. He must not have had permission to do that because Crispus fought with Mason. Crispus won. Mason's body was found here with his head caved in." Brian pointed to a place near one of the platform's legs. Crispus was killed near where Sherry's body was found. He had been shredded. The police believe it was an animal, but I know it wasn't an animal. It was that…thing. It's what dragged you into the lake. Sherry called it a Dryad, but it didn't look anything like the wood nymph she described. When we escaped, Crispus was still alive. He spoke to me. He told me to get you as far away from the house as possible. He wanted the Dryad to bring Sherry back to him. It didn't work. It wanted you. It probably killed the old man just because he was a nuisance. It had no intention of reanimating Sherry. It came after you."

Chris barely breathed as Brian spoke. He released his held breath when Brian stopped talking. After a moment, he asked, "what happened to Ted?"

Brian's face seemed to drain of color. "I can tell you that first hand. The group was using the station wagon once owned by your aunt and uncle like it was their own personal vehicle. When I managed to pull you from the wreckage of that cage, I put you into the station wagon. The keys were in it because Sherry had planned to use it as a getaway car. Ted came out of the house and jumped onto the hood. I drove away with him clinging to the car like a squashed bug. Eventually, he fell off and I ran him over. The Dryad came after us not long after that."

Chris studied Brian's face.

"You know why it wanted me." Chris wasn't asking a question. "You know I'm the Chosen One."

Brian closed his eyes again when he spoke. "I used to have visions of you while you were in this house. I saw you in my dreams and in the world around me. I saw you when no one else could. I thought I was losing my mind; but after what we went through, after I had time to look back on it, I came to the conclusion that: yes, you are the Chosen One. You sent your consciousness to me to keep me focused. Whenever I was in a place where I thought I was wrong about your fate, you kept me from losing faith. You even saved my life."

"I did?" Chris's voice was small, humble. "How?"

Brian turned and faced Chris, fixing him with an intense stare. "You want to go down the rabbit hole, so we might as well go all the way."

"It's what I want."

Brian nodded. "When that thing came after you, that...Dryad, as Sherry called it. It nearly tore me apart. You stepped in front of me and it stopped. It *obeyed* you. If you hadn't stopped that tree creature from tearing me apart, I'd be as dead as the cult leader...and those men they found out in the woods."

Chris's head snapped around to look at Brian. "There were other victims?"

"Yes. Three men on a fishing trip had been torn apart. The authorities assumed the same animal that killed the cult leader killed those men. I'm convinced it was that tree-thing. The Dryad. It was real. I never had any doubts about that."

Chris listened to what Brian said. He had all sorts of questions running through his mind. He brought the focus back to the original conversation. "You accept that I'm the Chosen One?"

"Yes."

"Good. Because I have something to show you that's about to change the world as you know it. If you didn't believe, it would be harder to convince you of what I need you to do."

"And what is that?"

Chris shook his head. "I can't tell you. I have to show you."

"Okay, so show me. Let's get out of here. This place is giving me the creeps."

"Agreed."

Together, Chris and Brian headed back to the limo.

5.

During the ride to the house, Brian said, "Keep in mind that Nancy never had visions of you. She never saw the Dryad, and all the things it could do. She doesn't know you are the Chosen One. To her, you are the kid we almost didn't save. She thinks I revived you that night, after you fell into the lake."

Chris bit at the inside of his lip. Not having seen the things Brian had seen, it would take a lot more effort to convince her of the truth. He could do it, though. He had to. Her life depended on it.

As the limo pulled up in front of the house where Brian and Nancy lived, Chris steeled himself for the task ahead. Chris climbed from the limo and followed Brian into the house.

Nancy glanced up from the recliner and removed her reading glasses. She opened her mouth to speak, but as Chris stepped out from behind Brian, she lost her words. Chris saw her eyes furrow in confusion, then grew wide as recognition hit.

"Chris." The name came out of her in a single, long breath; like the gasp of a person holding their breath for a long time.

"Hi Nancy."

Chris had met Nancy only briefly in the time after that summer's ordeal, but he had been told much about how she helped get Scott the medical attention he needed after he escaped the house. She had risked her own life to help them and Chris appreciated her for that.

Nancy ran to Chris, pulling him into a tight embrace. When she stepped away she turned her head away, not allowing him to see her face. After a moment, she turned and faced him. Though there was a bright smile on her face, her eyes glistened with tears. She blinked them away.

"I'm sorry to be such a basket case," she said. "I just never imagined I'd get to see you again after we parted ways. I've always thought about you and your brother. How is Scott? Is he here, too?" She looked toward the door.

"No, Scott didn't come with me." He didn't intend to tell her the reason. "He's doing very well for himself, though. He's married."

"Married." She sounded happy, but shocked. "I do hope I get to see them. Does your appearance here mean you'll all be coming back into our lives?"

Chris nodded. "It does." He didn't mention his intentions yet. He needed her to be as oblivious as possible. Saying no to his request was just not an option, and he didn't know how to express this sentiment without sounding demanding.

The rest of his visit went well. Chris drank coffee with them and talked about what had been happening with him and Scott over the years. Nancy asked questions to fill in the blanks. Chris told her what he could without mentioning the most recent developments. She seemed satisfied with the info he did provide, however. His visit ended about three hours later with Nancy and Brian seeing him out. Nancy spotted the limo on the street and whistled.

"That's what you've been riding around in? You really are doing well for yourself. What do you do that you can afford that kind of luxurious lifestyle?"

Brian shot Nancy a look that Chris took as a warning, but she ignored her husband. Chris laughed.

"You might say I am the head of a very generous group. Everything is donated to me." He waited to see if this answer satisfied her curiosity.

She shrugged but did not ask him to elaborate.

"Your friend, the limo driver, he didn't have to sit out in the car. You could have invited him in as well."

"He prefers to stay in the limo. Believe me, I've tried to get him to get involved, but he chooses not to. He's very…by-the-book."

Nancy nodded. They stood on the front porch for another moment. As Chris stepped off the porch, Nancy stopped him with a hand on his arm.

"Are you heading back tonight? Can't you stay? We could make up a room for you, and for the driver, too."

"Oh, thank you very much. But we have hotel rooms already. I wouldn't want to impose on you, in any case."

"It wouldn't be an imposition, Chris. Surely, you know this."

Chris hugged her. "I do. I just know Roger, and he will never agree to sleep in your home. He would not leave me here to sleep in the hotel, either. If I stayed here, he would sleep in the limo."

"I understand. We wouldn't want that. Promise I'll see you again, though. Don't run off without coming by again."

"I wouldn't think of it." He hugged her again and headed out to the limo. The tinted glass didn't allow them to see him, but he could see them. Nancy waved and he rolled the window down so he could wave back."

"Back to the hotel, Sir?" Roger asked.

"Yes. Roger, will you ever call me Chris? I think of you as a friend, not a follower, and definitely not an employee. Please call me Chris."

"Okay, Sir. Thank you."

Chris frowned, and raised the mirrored partition as the limo pulled away from the curb.

6.

Chris stared in the mirror as he brushed his teeth. He tried to see if there were any physical changes since he had given in to the role of the Chosen One. There didn't seem to be; he still saw the young face with olive skin. There was no drastic proof of maturity — wrinkles — or anything like that.

He heard Roger's shower running in the adjacent room for exactly five minutes, and then it went quiet again. The man was as quiet as a church mouse. Was Chris taking the identities away from these people who catered to his needs? It wasn't like it was his choice — they came to him, after all — but still he worried.

After Chris finished his nightly routine, and lay in bed, he found he was much too awake to sleep. He tossed and turned for as long as he could before he decided sleep would not come. He stood and rummaged through his suitcase until he found what he was looking for. He tucked the item under his arm and exited his room. He stepped up to the door to the right of his door and tapped three times. Almost as if he had been waiting on the other side of the door, Roger answered the knock.

Roger stood in the doorway, shirtless and barefoot, wearing only a pair of light blue pajama bottoms. He didn't speak. He didn't move to allow Chris into the room.

Chris held the rectangular wooden box out in front of him. "Play chess with me?" He felt a fool for asking.

Roger didn't bother to answer. He took the box from Chris and turned toward the one Cherrywood table in the room. The quiet man busied himself with setting up the chess board. Chris shrugged and entered the room, closing the door behind him. He sat down at the table opposite Roger and waited for the board to be populated with the little black and white plastic figurines. Chris was reminded a time, as a child, he would ask Scott to play board games with him, only to be ridiculed for having such interests. Scott was into video games, and thought Chris was insane for wanting to engage in such primitive activities. The universe had rewarded Chris for all his toils by providing him with a perfect playmate.

"Don't let me win this time, Rog. Letting me win is the equivalent of cheating. You aren't a cheater are you, Roger?"

"No, Sir."

"And Dammit! If you don't start calling me Chris I'm going to walk out that door and you won't know where I went. I'll walk away from all this and disappear. Do you want that?" Chris panted. Where had that anger come from?

Roger stared at him with a blank expression.

"Well, do you?"

"No, S—Chris. I don't want that at all."

"Thank you. I'm sorry to threaten you, but my life has changed so drastically I'll go insane if I don't get some normalcy around me. I need you to be normal. Can you please be normal? For me?"

"Yes, *Chris*. I can be normal." Roger belched.

Chris stared at him a moment, startled. After a long pause, Chris laughed.

Roger won the chess match. Chris never was good at the game.

7.

The limo pulled up in front of Brian and Nancy's place 8 a.m. the next morning. Nancy invited Roger in and, to Chris's surprise, he agreed. In the breakfast nook, they ate sausage patties and scrambled eggs, with toast and orange juice. Afterwards, they retired to the living room and drank coffee. Roger had his first taste of the dark, bitter liquid and decided he didn't like it. Chris was proud of him for trying. When the conversation turned more personal in nature, Roger excused himself and returned to the limo.

"He didn't have to leave," Nancy said.

Chris looked back toward the door where Roger had exited, as if looking to see if he had returned. He turned back to Nancy.

"He knows. He prefers the solitude. I've been working on him." Chris's face took on a faraway look.

Nancy leaned forward. When she spoke, her voice was a whisper. "What is…the relationship between you two?"

Brian turned on her with a look of surprise, and a touch of anger.

Chris laughed. "He appointed himself my personal assistant. That means he's my chauffer, my secretary and my bodyguard. He is also my closest friend. I trust him with my life."

"I didn't mean to pry. It's just that…"

"You don't have to explain. Actually, that's why I'm here. I have some explaining to do of my own."

"You? Why?"

Chris studied her inquisitive face and then turned to Brian. He turned back to Nancy before he spoke again. "Have you heard of the resent deforestation happening over near Ampersand Lake?"

Nancy sat back with a disgusted sigh. "Yes. For the past three years or so there have been close to ten thousand acres torn down."

"Eight thousand," Chris said. "To be exact."

Nancy sat up quickly. Brian turned to Chris now, too. He had their full attention.

"Tell me you have nothing to do with that." Nancy's face turned ashen.

Chris studied her expression of concern and confusion. He looked at Brian and saw something close to fear on his face.

"I am in charge of the project."

Nancy shot to her feet. Chris stayed calm, but Brian stood and prepared to protect Chris from an attack. She turned away instead, and paced. When she sat back down there were tears of anger and frustration in her eyes. "I've been protesting that project. There are fences all around the area, and armed guards keeping the more aggressive protesters away. I've tried and can't come within 1000 feet of the area. Believe me, I've tried. I want to know what they are building out there."

"It's what I'm building out there. And I can do better than tell you what it is. I can take you there. In fact, it's why I'm here. I have some news to tell you that is going to change the way you see the world. When you hear what I have to say, I'm hoping you will understand why."

Nancy's breathing quickened. Her words came out in rapid succession. "I don't know if I want to know. Or if I want to go near that place. I want nothing to do with it."

"Nancy, stop." Brian's voice was hard, authoritative. It reminded Chris of the voice he used at the pool. "This is Chris. We owe it to him to hear what he has to say. Stop being such a hothead."

Nancy turned slowly toward her husband and glared at him. Chris expected her to turn her bitter words on her husband, but she stayed quiet.

"Neither of you owe me anything," Chris said. "If anything, I owe you. Speak freely, Nancy. I want to hear what you have to say."

She turned back to Chris, visibly calmer now. She spoke slowly, enunciating every word clearly. "You declared eminent domain on seven homes. You swooped in and took land away from people who had lived on the same land for generations. Who gave you the right to take their land?"

"All those people involved were generously compensated for what they lost. In most cases people were happy with what they received…"

"I know, for a fact, two families were not happy. I spent a lot of time with them, consoling them. They are friends of mine. They wouldn't take your money."

"The Holmes's and the Lutz's." Chris nodded. "I remember them. Please come with me and see what I'm doing there. I think you will understand why I've done what I've done. There is no way to explain this; you have to see it for yourself."

Nancy sat forward. "You keep saying that. I guess it's time we do go and see what this amazing thing is you have to show us. When do we go?"

"We can go right now."

When no one moved right away, Brian stood and headed for the door. Chris waited for Nancy to move, but when she didn't, he followed Brian to the door. Nancy stared at them in the doorway for a moment, flicked her eyes away, then headed for the closet to grab her jacket.

Brian gently led Chris onto the porch by the arm. He spoke softly, out of Nancy's range of hearing. "Why wouldn't you warn me what you were about to do here? I really could have used a heads-up on this."

"I certainly didn't want to exclude you, but I didn't want to take the chance you'd reveal my plan to her prematurely. I felt it best you both heard about this at the same time."

Chris glanced into the doorway and saw that Nancy was on her way to the door.

"You're right," Brian said. "If I had known about this ahead of time, and didn't tell her, we'd both be getting those death glares."

They were laughing as she exited the house, but stopped at a look from her.

Inside the limo, Brian said, "I can't believe you've been only a few miles away all these years and you only now came around for a visit."

"Actually, I haven't even been to the site yet, myself. This is my first visit, too."

Nancy glared at him but said nothing. Chris ignored her. Brian reached into the fridge and removed a cola. He handed it to Nancy, but she merely turned away. He uncapped it and took a long sip.

The limo turned off route 30, onto Tupper Lake Highway, heading east. The limo turned south on Corey's Road. In another few miles, the limo rumbled over Corey's Road Bridge, and then Ampersand Road took them through a deep wooded area for several miles. Finally, the road turned into a dirt path. As they neared their destination, protesters came into view, blocking the road. Roger honked and slowed down. As the limo moved through the crowd, people outside slammed their fists into the side of the car. They spit at the windows and cursed the people inside. At one point the limo rocked on its wheels, but the threat was minimal. Eventually, the protesters stopped attacking the car, and the limo moved into the section of road patrolled by guards. They rolled up to a massive double-door gate and the start of the fenced area. Roger stopped, spoke briefly to the guards at the gate, and was permitted to enter the area beyond the fences.

They were on their way. The road here was paved and wide enough to permit two large, all-terrain vehicles to ride side by side. The trees were sparser, too. Within minutes there were no more trees at all. In another few minutes, they saw the tower.

Chris stifled a chuckle as he watched the expressions on his friends' faces change. Nancy's mouth dropped in a comical O shape, snapping it shut when she became aware of it. Brian spit his drink onto the window. He used his hand to wipe at the mess, but only managed to smear it around.

"I've seen it at a distance and, sure, I heard the rumors, but this is massive beyond words." Brian continued rubbing at the window, but his eyes were on the structure.

The limo stopped and Nancy clambered out of the back seat. Brian climbed out on the opposite side and they both met at the front of the limo. Chris joined them, smiling. He had to admit it; he was as impressed as they were, but he had the advantage of knowing what to expect.

Nancy took a tentative step toward the structure. She looked up, shielding her eyes from the sun as it shone off the surface of the monolith in front of her. She turned her head down, stumbling. Brian caught her before she toppled. Clinging to each other, they turned to Chris.

He stepped up and led them toward the tower. He spoke in a voice sounding very much like a tour guide. He raised a hand and motioned toward the structure. "The Ark sits on three hundred and fifty square acres of land. There is a rivet and steel skeletal structure underneath, a layer of steel about four inches thick over that, and another two inches of hardened steel, welded together to be completely air tight on the outer hull. It's a half mile wide from corner to corner and a mile up. It can hold over seven thousand families. The inside is completely self-sustainable. There is food and water enough for the families to live comfortably for over a year, quite possibly, forever. There is livestock and hundreds of acres of crops inside the Ark. The ceiling over the plants have ultraviolet bulbs to mimic sunlight. There is a natural spring deep beneath the ground, which is why this location was chosen. The spring has never been in contact with human life. This is an important feature. The Ark is a gigantic clean room. Not even microscopic organisms can penetrate its barriers once the doors are sealed. It's powered by 700 generators that all run on natural gas that's pumped in through underground sources. The ventilation is state of the art. The filters are one way; fumes are pulled out through pumps and not even the smallest microorganism can pass through their filters to get in once the place is sealed up. The generators, though, are not the only power system. The real power of the Ark starts on the surface, with several hundred acres of solar panels that collect energy from the sun, and enters through cables running underground.

"The septic system, too, uses subterraneous pipes, and empties into an underground lake bed. The lake is then processed through a sewage treatment plant. The resulting water reentered the Ark, clean enough to drink, but used in the toilets and as bathing water."

"I didn't think there were that many germophobes in the world," Nancy said.

"You called it the Ark. Are you expecting another flood?" Brian asked.

Chris shook his head. "This is not housing for people afraid to get sick. This is for all of us. There is an extinction level event coming, but it's not a flood this time. It's a disease. The illness will take six months to dissipate. After that time, we will be able to send people out to see if it's safe for the rest of us. Once we know it's safe we can leave the Ark and start to rebuild."

"We?" Nancy said.

'Yes, we. You, me, Brian, Scott, Kaylan, and thousands more. Everyone I can fit in here."

"I'm not living in that." Nancy lifted her chin.

Chris's body went cold, and his voice raised an octave. "You have to. Anyone not inside the Ark when the epidemic hits will die."

"It's ridiculous. A waste of money and space. How can you possibly know this epidemic is coming? Or that this monstrosity will keep it out? Haven't you read The Masque of the Red Death? You can't keep death out."

"I can." Chris's voice echoed his desperation. Softly, he said it again. "I can."

"How *do* you know this epidemic is coming?" Brian asked.

Chris flicked his eyes to Brian. Was he siding with Nancy for show? Surely, Brian planned to go into the Ark with him. He had counted on Brian blindly following him anywhere. "I have visions about it; dreams that tell me everything I need to know about what is coming, and when."

Nancy looked at the structure and then back at Chris. "This is just an elaborate doomsday shelter. You are no different than all those other lunatics out there stocking up for a scenario that will never come about."

"Nancy, how can you stand there and call Chris—my friend—a lunatic? How can you be so disrespectful to him? Why are you so determined to offend him?"

Chris's heart lightened as Brian defended him. His determination strengthened. Chris touched her arm, drawing her attention. "I'm not offended. It's just that I can't fail you, not on this. I have to do everything I can to prove I'm not a crackpot. Your life depends on me convincing you to enter the Ark before it's too late."

"I didn't mean you are a lunatic, Chris. I really didn't mean it that way. It's just that this kind of stuff doesn't happen. There have been so many predictions of this kind all through time. The world was supposed to end at the start of the millennium. It didn't. It was supposed to end in 2012, but it didn't. You'll have to do better than dreams to convince me what you are saying is true."

Chris nodded as he listened to her. "Fair enough. I have one month to convince you to enter the Ark."

Brian choked on his own saliva. "One month? That's when you predict the world will end?"

"The doors will be sealed in one month. The disease will sweep across the planet at any time after the doors close. It could be one day or a month. I don't know the exact time when the world will end. But I do know that the disease will hit soon after the doors are sealed."

"You just proved to me you are guessing. You don't know when the epidemic will hit? What if you sit in that metal death trap for six months and the disease never hits?" Nancy crossed her arms over her chest.

Chris didn't respond. He couldn't. It was very possible that what she said could happen. He just didn't think so. Perhaps the dream to tell him the exact details of the epidemic was still to come, but so far it had not.

Brian spoke up. "What dream did you have that told you the time to close the doors. What if the disease hits before the doors close?"

"The dream was specific to when the doors needed to be closed. I trust the dreams; they've never been wrong."

"Are you still having these dreams?" Brian asked.

"Yes. I hope I have a dream that will show me I've convinced you both to join me. I'd hate to think I won't have you in the new world with me."

"What about Scott?" Nancy asked.

Chris turned to her at the mention of his brother. "What about him?"

"Has he agreed to go into the… the Ark?"

Chris didn't hesitate. "Yes. And so has his wife."

Nancy showed no emotion. "I can't believe you're only giving us a month to decide."

"With all due respect," Chris said. "How much time do you need to decide to live?" He fought to keep the bite from his words, but some bitterness seeped into his comment.

Nancy turned slightly away from Chris.

Chris took a deep breath. "We still have to take a tour of the Ark. Check it out. You might actually like what you see. Some of the residents have already moved in. I think once you see what we are doing, you won't be so…disagreeable."

Nancy barked a humorless laugh. "Nice choice of words."

Chris felt a sense of loss when he looked into her eyes. He feared he would never have the words that would convince her. His only hope was that Brian would do what he had failed to do. He attempted to hide his sorrow and fear with a smile, but he couldn't keep the disappointment out of his voice. "Let's go inside."

Brian and Nancy stepped into line, following him into the structure. Nancy stopped before going in.

"One second. I want to grab my jacket in the limo." She turned and rushed back to the limo and disappeared inside.

Standing next to Chris, Brian spoke very softly and clearly. "Don't worry, buddy. We're with you. I'll convince her."

Chris nodded slowly that he understood. "Thank you."

Nancy returned and they once again started toward the building.

This time Chris stopped them.

"Sorry, there's one thing I wanted to do before we went inside." Chris lifted his watch near his mouth. "Toby, start the countdown."

"Yes, Sir." The tinny voice echoed out of an unseen speaker inside the watch that wasn't a watch. Chris pointed toward the building. Brian and Nancy glanced up. Large red numbers appeared in the steel just above the industrial sized doors. The numbers counted down.

01: 05: 57.

"One month, five days and fifty-seven hours." Chris checked the numbers counting down on his wrist band. The numbers on the band matched exactly the numbers on the wall. The only difference being the wrist band included seconds ticking away as well. "Okay, the countdown has officially begun. Let's go in and see what we can see."

Nancy reached out and took Brian's hand.

I'll convince her, Brian had said. Chris prayed he was right. *When she sees how amazing this place is, she'll have to change her mind, right.*

The three friends entered the Ark.

Chapter Two

1.

The opening led to an enormous warehouse-type chamber. Their footfalls clacked on the floor, and echoed off the steel walls. The sound was deafening to Nancy's ears, and maddening. *If I have to hear that echo for the rest of my life, I'll kill someone.* The mere size of the room caused her vertigo to return, but this time she recovered without assistance.

She saw a man standing near a golf cart, and recognized him as Roger. Behind him, she spotted a large window looking in on a room filled with computers, various other electronics, as well as closed circuit television monitors.

"Is the whole place going to be this bland?" Nancy was startled by the echo of her own voice in the cavernous room. She spoke again, softer this time. "And so…loud? It's just so…antiseptic."

Chris turned to Nancy. "The building was constructed without any real design to speak of. The homes are white, but we can paint your apartment any color you wish before you move in, if that will help relieve your discomfort."

Chris led them through the door near where Roger stood.

"This is the control room." He led them to a console with about twelve computer monitors built into it. The walls in this room were white, with chrome on the control panels, and black table tops. Only two of the twelve screens projected a picture. Nancy recognized the limo on one of the monitors, but the other screen showed a part of the building's façade she didn't recognize. As she watched, the pictures changed, and other images appeared. One camera showed a bird's-eye view of the fence. Two people stood outside the fence using wire cutters to break the links. The man at the console clicked a button and spoke into a mic.

"We have protesters at the east perimeter. They have damaged the fence. If they are unarmed, do not to call the police. Just chase them away." The man at the console swiveled his chair and turned to his visitors. He pushed his thick, plastic framed glasses higher up on his nose.

"Toby, these are my friends I've been raving about all these years. I'm giving them a tour. Nancy, Brian, this is Toby Granger. He's our resident nerd."

"I prefer programmer Chris, if you don't mind." Toby pushed his glasses up on his nose again and stood. He tripped on his chair and fell against Nancy. "Sorry, sorry."

Nancy chuckled, noticing his reddened cheeks. "It's fine. You're fine."

"Nice to meet you." He wiped his sweaty palm on his pantleg and offered the hand to her.

She shook it.

Toby chuckled. "Now I can put a face to the stories. I feel like I know you already."

He then shook hands with Brian.

"We're looking forward to getting to know you better," Brian said.

"Oh, so you've agreed to join us?" Toby pushed his glasses up on his nose again.

Nancy watch a bead of sweat roll down his temple. She spoke up before Brian had a chance to answer. "We haven't quite committed to that yet."

"Oh, well, I hope you do."

She was glad when Chris interrupted them.

"We know you have a lot of work to do, Tobias, so we won't take up any more of your time." Chris nodded to Toby and drew the group's attention to the door.

Toby's chair scraped against the floor as he returned to the monitors.

As the three of them exited the control room, Roger drove up on the golf cart. Nancy waited for Chris and Brian to embark before she, too, climbed on.

Roger drove the length of the cavernous main room, the cart's electric motor humming. Nancy breathed more easily as they left the anxiety-evoking steel cavern behind for a much more natural sized hallway. Her tense muscles relaxed.

The hallway was wide enough to accommodate another golf cart side by side, but they came across no other riders. Some people walked past, and Chris greeted them all by name.

Impressive. Does he know all seven thousand people inside the Ark by name? She had a hard time believing that he did.

The hallway crisscrossed with other halls, and Nancy soon lost track of where they were. *I'll get lost in this massive labyrinth, and won't be found until I'm nothing but a pile of bones.* Nancy tried to count the doors they passed, but soon lost track of those, too.

At the end of the hall, the cart stopped in front of an industrial sized lift. Nancy looked to the left and right, intimidated by the endless halls leading in both directions. Roger drove the cart onto the lift and a mesh gate closed behind them.

"What floor, sir-er, uh Chris?" Roger said.

Chris laughed. "You're learning, Rog. You're doing great." Chris locked eyes with Nancy. "Let's go to the garden. I think we need to see a little color."

Roger tapped a command into the console on the cart's control panel and the lift whirred to life. The cage rose, passing several floors and stopped with a hard bump. The mesh gate opened and Roger backed out and turned left. He drove for several yards, then stopped. When He and Chris stepped off the cart, Brian and Nancy did as well.

Chris led them to a door with a frosted window. The only thing visible through the glass, however, was light and distorted colors. He used the keypad to the right of the door. After hearing a click, he pulled the door open and allowed his guests to enter the room.

It wasn't just a room, though. It was a garden. It was vast, but did not cause her anxiety. She inhaled deeply, taking in the aroma of several different species of flowers. Nancy walked along rows of marigolds, begonias, lilies, and entire color pallets of roses. The rows of plants were immaculate. Her face beamed, unable to hide her enjoyment. She dropped down into the dirt and examined the plants.

"Who handles the weeding? These rows are perfect, and the plants are in immaculate condition."

"There are no weeds, so no need for weeding. There's no need for pesticides or other artificial growth additives. It's the same with our vegetables. We also have animals, for food, as well as for stuff like milk and eggs."

Nancy stood. She turned to Chris. "This place must have cost a small fortune, and I won't ask where you got the money for it—or the governmental support, for that matter—but wasn't there a way to do this to save more people? Seven thousand is not a lot in the grand scheme of things. Seven thousand people isn't enough. If you were really serious about this, you should have tried to save more."

Chris stared at her. After a moment, he responded. "Do you think I wanted all this? That I want so much of the world's population to die? I didn't do this. I didn't plan it. I didn't ask for it; it's been dumped on me." His hands shook, and tears rimmed his eyes.

I didn't mean to strike a nerve.

Chris continued. "Now I have to do what I can to save as many people as I can. The reason this place exists is because the True Believers made it happen. They did this for me, so naturally, they are allowed to come with me into the new world. I'm also offering this to you and Brian. Scott and Kaylan. It's a gift I'm offering to you. It's the perk of being friends with the Chosen One."

Nancy gaped at the name Chris had used to describe himself. She hadn't heard him being referred to as the Chosen One since those horrible people had done it. She stumbled back. When she saw that she had inadvertently trampled a row of azaleas, she dropped down and tried to fix them.

I should tell him I didn't mean to offend him. I should show him some compassion, I know; but God, this is all just so…crazy. I can't deal with this now.

Chris walked past her. "Maybe we should complete this tour another day. I'm sorry. I don't feel well. We'll finish the tour another day."

"Chris…" Brian reached out.

Nancy looked up as Chris shrugged away from Brian's grasp. "Roger will drive you home."

Nancy stood next to Brian, brushing the sod from her hands as they watched Chris leave. He didn't look back. Brian walked out behind him. She soon followed, taking small, slow steps toward the door.

2.

"Honey, he called himself the Chosen One. Doesn't he understand the implications that name has? People died because of that name. His aunt and uncle—" Nancy turned toward the window of the limo. As they neared the street on which they lived, she felt a sense of relief.

"I know," Brian said. "But you have to look at it from his perspective. He's had a lot of time to come to terms with that designation."

Nancy swiveled her head to glare at Brian. "You sound as though you already knew this."

Brian glanced at his hands as they fidgeted with a loose string on his shirt. "I did."

Nancy's eyes grew wide. She drew in a breath as if to let loose with a barrage of insults, but instead exhaled loudly and turned to the window again.

Brian spoke softly, but with a stern tone. "Chris believes he is the Chosen One. The people who follow him believe he is. Whether we do is irrelevant, if it's what they believe. And yes, I will support him no matter what he calls himself. He's still Chris. I see it in his eyes. I see it in his crooked smile. This hasn't changed him."

Nancy barked a sardonic laugh, but didn't turn away from the window.

"He's still Chris, even after the change took him."

Nancy turned to him now. "What are you talking about?"

Brian looked deeply into Nancy's eyes. He narrowed his brow and spoke in a whisper. "Chris died that night."

"I know, and you—"

"No." The word was harsher than Brian had intended. He softened his expression. "I couldn't save him. He died in my arms. There is a lot about that night I never told you, but maybe I should have." He paused and let what he was saying sink in.

"You believe. You believe he's the…what? The Chosen One."

Brian didn't deny it. "I saw things that night that can't be explained. I saw the earth, the trees—everything—rise up to take Chris. The thing got Chris and pulled him into the water. Chris didn't fall in; he was pulled in, by some…I don't know…some tree creature. It drowned him and took over his body. He wasn't revived by me. He was revived by this thing. Call it the Dryad, I don't know. But whatever it was, it gave Chris his life back."

Nancy found it hard to swallow the lump in her throat. She did it somehow and then spoke the words she was afraid to speak. "Does Chris—do you—believe he is some kind of God?"

"No. Not a god—not *the* God. Just a vessel. He is a messenger of the dangers to come. And I've seen enough to believe we should heed his warning."

It took all Nancy's strength not to yank open the door and fall into the street. Tears formed in her eyes, but she didn't know if they were from anger, or sadness. Her world seemed to be falling apart, and it shouldn't be that way. She should be happy. A long-lost friend had come back into her life, and all she could feel was a kind of numb disconnection from all that she knew. It was as if the world had gone crazy and she couldn't go crazy with it. She suddenly felt alone.

And she wished Chris had never come back into their lives.

The limo stopped in front of their house. She climbed out and went into the house without saying anything more. Brian motioned for Roger to roll down his window. When the driver did, Brian reached in and shook his hand.

"Thank you for bringing us home."

"You're very welcome," Roger said.

Brian hovered at the window. He leaned in closer. "Can you tell Chris…" He hesitated, unsure what to say. "Can you just tell him I'm sorry. I want to return soon. Will that be okay?"

"I'm sure it will be," Roger said.

Brian offered an awkward smile to the limo driver. Roger stared with a blank expression on his face.

Brian stood. "Okay, well, thanks again." He stood back as Roger rolled up the window and drove away. He hesitated for a few minutes before entering the house. Nancy had retired to the bedroom, even though it was only 6 pm. Brian tried to stall the confrontation with his wife for as long as he could, but at 9 pm he was tired, and he was unsure if his wife wanted him in the room with her. Finally, he made his way to their bedroom.

He knocked on the door and opened it a crack. "May I come in?"

"Yes." Her voice was soft, sleepy.

He entered the room. She was in a nightie, brushing her hair. When she finished, she climbed into bed. Brian stripped down to his boxers and climbed in next to her. She rolled closer to him. He put his arm around her.

"Hold me," she said.

He held her. She cried against his shoulder. He stroked her hair, kissed her neck. Their lips found each other and they kissed. They made love. Brian dozed off.

"I love you," Nancy said.

"I love you, too." His voice was dreamy.

"I'll go with you, wherever that might be."

Brian had fallen asleep. Nancy followed him down.

3.

Chris's pulse raced as he watched the limo pull up and the passengers climb out. Scott and Kaylan walked hand in hand toward the Ark. Roger stayed behind, leaning against the limo's driver side door. Kaylan stared up at the immense building. She mouthed the word "wow."

Chris laughed. *That's right, she hasn't seen the Ark yet.* Chris's heart swelled at the sight of her. *Her child-like wonder is such a refreshing contrast to Scott, who seems totally unimpressed. Is he hiding his true feelings, or is he really not overwhelmed by what he's seeing?*

"Quite the hut you have here, Christopher," Kaylan said as she walked through the entrance.

Chris laughed. "I'm so happy to see you."

"Good to see you, Bro." Scott gripped Chris in a headlock. When they broke apart, Kaylan took a turn hugging Chris.

They turned in unison when a car approached and parked next to the limo. Brian and Nancy climbed out and took a few tentative steps toward the Ark. Roger motioned for them to follow him and he led them through the large doors.

"I'm happy you came." Chris hugged Brian and turned to Nancy.

She stared at him, hard and long, and when she spoke it was with a note of sarcasm. "How can we resist the Chosen One, right?"

Chris stood unmoving, but relaxed when she reached out and hugged him. He let out a relieved breath and fell into her embrace.

He released her and stepped back. "I have good news. The Holmes and Lutz families are going to join us. I was so worried that they wouldn't accept, but then they just showed up."

Brian spoke up. "My wife had a little something to do with that."

Chris clenched his jaw, confused, and turned to Nancy. "You did it?"

"I did."

"How…?"

Nancy shrugged. "I just told them I thought it would be in their best interest to take you up on your offer."

"Her opinion means a lot to them. She's very convincing."

"It means a lot to me, too. Thank you." *I won't drive her away again. I have to watch what I say, and not get worked up when her opinion opposes mine.* "I just wish more of the displaced families had decided to take me up on my offer."

Nancy's puzzled look caused him to explain.

"They all had the option to join, but took the money instead."

"Oh," she said. "I didn't know."

"What's on the tour agenda today?" Brian asked.

"I'm going to show you where you'll be living for the next few months."

Scott spoke to Brian. "Are you and Nancy moving in today, too?"

Nancy responded. "No. Sadly we have a lot of duties to tend to before we give up our lives. I understand that the going consensus is that the world won't be here when we step out those doors, but I'm a pragmatic girl. I have to take care of the 'what ifs.'"

"Completely understandable," Kaylan said. Then she reached out a hand. "We haven't met. I'm Kaylan Bellinger."

Nancy ignored the hand and pulled Kaylan into a hug. "I'm Nancy Hoat. This here is my big lug, Brian."

Kaylan laughed. "I know who you are. I don't think you know the star quality you two hold in the eyes of these boys. They speak of you with reverence and love, always."

Brian blushed.

Nancy hugged Scott and kissed him on the mouth. "I can't tell you how much I missed you, Scott. I keep thinking about that fifteen-year-old boy, so badly beaten he could barely open his eyes, or speak. I thank the stars you came through it all."

Scott smiled, took one of Nancy's hands in his and pulled it to his mouth so he could kiss it. "I never go to bed at night without saying a little prayer for you. Without you, I probably wouldn't be here today."

Brian pushed his wife out of the way so he could hug Scott next. "Good to see you again, my boy." He stepped back.

Chris cleared his throat. Everyone looked at him, and at Roger standing directly behind him. "Let's get the tour under way then, shall we?"

Roger climbed into the driver's seat of the first of two golf carts waiting for them.

"I got this one." Scott scrambled past Chris and Brian to take the helm of the second.

Kaylan took a seat in the cart driven by Roger.

"Really?" Scott said. "Is my driving that bad?"

Kaylan reluctantly climbed out of the cart she was in and took the seat next to her husband. She looked at the others. "I guess I'm obligated to go into the wall with him. For better or worse, and all that, right?"

Chris laughed at Scott's frowning face.

They stopped on the fiftieth floor.

Roger drove his cart left out of the lift. Scott tried to pass Roger but the carts instead engaged in a race through the hallway when Roger wouldn't relent.

A couple stepped into Scott's way from an intersecting hall. Scott slammed on the breaks, sending the couple scurrying back the way they had come, and Kaylan into the handrail in front of her. She punched Scott's arm when she had recovered.

"Idiot."

"Margaret. Joe, are you guys all right?" Chris said.

Margaret clutched at her throat, her eyes wide.

"Sorry," Scott said.

Joe placed a hand behind his wife's back and comforted her. "You okay dear?"

Margaret took a deep breath and nodded.

"I really am sorry," Scott said again.

When they resumed, Scott remained behind Roger.

When they reached their destination, Scott climbed off his cart and approached Roger. "I totally would have overtaken you if that couple hadn't appeared."

"No, I don't believe so." Roger cracked slit in his lips that would have made the Mona Lisa envious.

"You lost, Scott, honey," Kaylan said. "Deal with it."

"Traitor!" Scott clutched at his heart.

Everyone disembarked as Chris led them to the first door on the right. He punched in a number on the keypad and the door opened.

Chris opened the door and allowed everyone to step inside. "This is just one of the many ballrooms inside the Ark."

Kaylan whistled. She stared in wonder at the sheer size of the room. Red velvet tapestries covered the walls. The floor seemed to be made of glass and the ceiling was mirrored. When Chris flicked a switch, the lights came on and the place sparkled.

"How do you do this?" Kaylan laughed.

"I want to use this room for every party we throw. And I throw a lot of parties."

"Wait till you see the ballroom on the top floor. It's big enough to fit everyone inside the Ark, all at once."

"No shit," Kaylan said. "Let's go see it."

Chris led them back to the waiting golf carts. "Next stop, floor 400. Let's also see where we are going to live for the next few months." After what seemed like an eternity, the lift stopped. "The only floor higher than this one is the roof." Chris laughed. He knew there was no way to get out to the roof. "And just so you know, only we will reside on this floor. There are no other residences up here, and your key will be the only thing that will let you access this floor. We are all alone up here."

They entered the ballroom on that floor. They stood around and just stared at the vast, empty space.

"Not much to look at," Kaylan said and her voice reverberated through the distance. "Big, though."

Chris's voice mixed with Kaylan fading echo. "It's a quarter of a mile wide and nearly a half mile long."

"Needs decorating," Kaylan said. She turned to Nancy. "We can take on that challenge, huh?"

Nancy didn't respond.

Chris led them back to the waiting carts, and they headed around the corner to the living quarters. Chris hopped off and plugged a numerical code into the keypad. He held the door open for Nancy and Brian.

"This is will be your place."

As Nancy looked around, Chris added: "The white walls are only temporary. Say the word and I'll have it painted in any color you wish."

"How do you know the lock code?" Nancy asked.

"What?" Chris was momentarily lost by the question.

"The code to our apartment. Can anyone just come in any time they wish?"

"Not at all. Every lock is defaulted to my birthday. If, or when, you move in you can have it programed it to your specifications."

Chris moved on to the rest of the house. "I'm sorry, but the designers were not very creative. All seven thousand homes are exactly the same in size, diameter and layout."

"Really?" Brian said.

Chris nodded. He led them through the kitchen. The living room is here. There's a bedroom here, in the front." He led them down a hallway. "This is the main bathroom, here." He opened the door across the hall. "This is the master bedroom, and it has a second full bathroom inside." He walked them to the end of the hall. Two swinging doors opened up into the kitchen. A third door led from the kitchen to the dining room. "You're free to cook your own meals, or you can enjoy any one of the myriad restaurants available. Everything is free; there is no charge for anything within the Ark. You simply have to ask, and it's yours."

"Wow," Brian said. "Really?"

Nancy touched his arm to quiet him. She spoke to Chris. "Nothing is free. Once we're locked inside here, we've essentially given up our freedom."

Chris peered into her eyes, and she peered back. *Why does she push so hard to defy me? What did I ever do to her?*

Without further confrontation, Nancy turned away and entered the master bedroom.

She entered the bathroom. And froze in place. She strolled over to the bathtub and sat on the edge of it. She looked into the basin. She was awestruck.

"Yea, we added Jacuzzi bathtubs to make up for the lack of stimulus. It's hoped that the relaxation of the bubbles will help alleviate the monotony of living inside a giant steel box."

After the home was thoroughly examined, Chris, Brian and Nancy walked back out into the hall. The door across the hall was open. Inside, Scott and Kaylan were milling about. Chris led the others into the house. Roger, as normal for him, hovered in the hall.

"This is where you will be staying?" Brian asked Scott.

Scott nodded. "Yes, and my Bro will be in the house directly connected to mine."

"Surprise," Chris said. "We'll be neighbors."

Brian laughed. "I have to say, I'm excited to move in. I think this is going to be the adventure of a lifetime."

Nancy said nothing.

4.

"I wanted to make sure I showed you this room." Chris stepped off the golf cart. He walked up to an electronic door and it whooshed open. The rest followed him in.

"What's this?" Brian asked. "Looks like an internet café."

"There are thirty computers in here. Before we leave, I want everyone to sign up for a skype account. We can skype with each other here inside the Ark, and with people on the outside."

Kaylan said. "I understand that we can skype through an internet link, but if the world ends like you say, won't the internet eventually go down?"

Chris nodded. "Yes. Eventually, the link to the outside world will break and we will be completely cut off. The power grid will eventually shutdown as well. It won't affect us in here, though. We will be 100 percent self-sufficient. We have our own power sources, and even our own internet."

Kaylan began an off-handed tapping at the keyboard of the nearest computer. "I still don't understand. How are we going to know when it's safe to leave the Ark?" She took her finger across the keyboard one long last quick zip and turned to Chris. Her normally playful expression was gone, replaced by a look of dread. "You're saying all those people are going to die, and I don't know how I feel about that. I don't want it to be true, Chris. I don't want people to die like that."

Chris tried to meet her gaze, but it was hard. He felt a lump form in his throat. He struggled for words that could make this easier for her—for all of them—but there just weren't any. "No one wants that, Kaylan." Something from his dream came back to him then. "Not everyone is going to die."

"Say what?" Scott stepped forward, suddenly interested in the conversation.

Everyone turned to Chris. He began slowly but his voice built momentum as he explained what he knew. "The initial infection is going to take time to build, some small pockets here, some there. Eventually, the entire globe is going to feel the impact. People are going to get sick and stay sick. By the time people start dying 80 percent of the world's population is going to be infected. There will be some who are spared, I don't know why these people will not get sick when so many others will. Of the people who are infected, perhaps 10 percent of them will improve and rebound."

"Is that supposed to be good news?"

Chris turned to Nancy when she spoke up. He felt suddenly cornered.

"Nancy." That firm voice from Brian again.

"I want to know. Is 10 percent of the population acceptable to you Chris? How about 15 percent? 20?"

Chris tried not to look toward the door, but his urge was to run through it.

He opened his mouth to speak — to say anything — but Kaylan beat him to it.

"What's the next stop on the tour, Willie Wonka?"

The group turned to Kaylan. Brian laughed, and Scott joined in. Chris shot a cursory glance at Nancy, and when she turned away, he let out a relaxing sigh.

5.

Chris climbed onto the golf cart, but Nancy did not.

"Chris, if you don't mind, I'll forgo the rest of the tour."

Chris climbed back off the cart. "Sure, sure. If that's what you want."

"In fact, I was thinking I'd like to visit the Holmes's, and the Lutz's."

"I think that's a great idea. Hop on. I'll take you there."

"No, if you don't mind, I'd like to make the trip the old-fashioned way. Just point the way and we can be on our way." Nancy hooked her thumb, indicating Brian.

"Oh, you're going, too, Brian?"

Brian's gaze flicked from Nancy to Chris. "Um, I guess…"

Chris cleared his throat. "Okay, great. You can find your friends on floor 210. The Lutz's are in 2111 and the Holmes's are next door to them in 2113. If you take the corridor this way, all the way back to the main lift, then take a right, the personal elevators are at the end of that hallway."

"Thank you, Chris." Nancy walked down the hall in the direction Chris indicated. She walked quickly, but felt a hesitation from Brian as he followed her. When they reached the bank of elevators, Nancy pressed the button.

They waited for the lift to arrive.

"Did you want to go with Chris?" She asked. "Should I have allowed you that option?"

Brian placed an arm around his wife's waist. He leaned down and kissed her. "I'll go where you go."

She placed her head on his chest.

Seconds later, the elevator doors swished open and they entered. The doors closed them in. immediately, a female voice asked, "what floor please?"

Nancy and Brian stared at each other, confused. Nancy recovered first. "Uh, two hundred and ten?" *Chris could have warned us the elevator talked.*

"That's super cool." Brian laughed.

"We have arrived at your destination."

The doors opened and they disembarked.

Nancy scanned her surroundings. *I feel like I'm on the same floor I just left.* She and Brian strode down the hallway, toward the large industrial lift. The three-way intersection looked exactly like the previous floor. Nancy expected to see Chris riding up on the golf cart crying, "gotcha."

She headed down the middle corridor, looking at the small metal etchings riveted to the walls, announcing which homes were down which hallway. She found the etching for apartments 2111 and 2113. She took that hallway, searching the door signs for the numbers she sought. She chose to visit the Holmes's first.

Nancy paused in front of the door, and knocked only after taking a few calming breaths. After a short pause, the door opened a crack, and a single eyeball peered out at her.

"Hi, Derek," she said to the man hiding behind the door.

Derek flung the door wide. He spoke in his usual too-loud voice. "Hi, Nancy, hi."

"Hi." A weight lifted from her heart at the sight of him. "I came to see your new home. Are your parents in?"

"Yea, come on in, Nancy. Mom, Dad, Nancy's here."

"We heard ya." Glenn Holmes grumbled. "We're not deaf. Yet." He turned to Nancy and Brian. "Welcome. Come on in."

"Hi, Glenn." Nancy turned to the woman sitting in a recliner. "Patty, how are you?"

"Oh, I can't complain," Patty said…but she could. And was about to. "Other than this ache in my back that won't slacken. Took everything I can think of for the pain, and still it won't ease up. These apartments are wonderful—state of the art and all that—but they are so darned big. Three times bigger than my house. I need a scooter to get from one end of the room ta th'other." Her laughter turned to a groan and she clutched at her back with a grimace.

Brian said, "Derek, you helping your mother out around here?"

"I sure am, Brian. I sure ta hells am."

Brian laughed.

Derek took Brian by the hand. "Come to my room, Brian. I want to show you my new room."

"Okay, Buddy."

As Brian disappeared into Derek's room, Nancy sat down in a rocker next to Patty. "How was the move? Your sore back isn't because of this place, is it?"

"No." Patty stressed the absurdity of that thought by sitting up. "In fact, I couldn't have asked for a more comfortable place. Better than a nursing home could ever want to be. And that boy— the one who brought us here—"

Nancy provided the name. "Chris."

"Yes. He has been in to see us every day since we moved in. He's a very nice boy."

Nancy agreed. "Yes, he is. And he was very happy that you decided to move in. I'll talk to Chris and see if he might have a wheelchair, or something to help you get around."

Patty's eyes sparkled. "Bless your kind heart, my dear. Don't go to too much trouble. I'm sure Chris has more important tasks to handle. I don't want to be a bother."

"No bother, and I'm sure Chris will be happy to do this little thing for you."

Nancy glanced around the room. She recognized much of the same furniture and decorations that had adorned their house on the lake. Her chest grew heavy as she thought about what these people had given up.

Nancy laid a light palm on Patty's hand. "Are you truly happy here? You can be truthful with me, Patty. I would protect your privacy."

Patty placed a cold, knotted hand over Nancy's hand. She leaned in. "Really, I couldn't be happier. Even grumpy old Glenn loves this place."

Glenn coughed a laugh. "Don't go giving away my secrets, old lady."

"Where are my manners? I should offer you an iced tea, or something to drink." Patty started to get up but Nancy stopped her.

"We can't stay long. We want to visit with the Lutz's before we get going."

"Okay, suit yourself. Are you planning to stay? We'd love for you to visit again."

I haven't made up my mind about this place yet, Patty. She couldn't say that, though. How could she after talking them into living there. "We will visit again. Bet on it."

Brian came out of the bedroom with Derek following behind, showing him a picture book.

"And then in this part, the Goldie Locks girl breaks the chair. She's bratty."

"She sure is, Buddy." Brian was looking at Nancy as he spoke.

Nancy and Brian stayed another fifteen minutes, sharing memories of the old times, before heading to the door. Derek watched closely from a crack in the door as Nancy and Brian knocked on the next door over. He closed the door when they disappeared into the Lutz residence.

6.

Kaylan looked to Scott for an explanation when she exited the skype room, and saw Roger and Chris driving away. "Is the tour over already?"

Scott climbed into the golf cart's driver seat. "He said he needed to go. I guess Brian and Nancy ended the tour early. Chris, I guess, figures we can finish another time."

"Oh." She couldn't help but think something had happened and she missed it. No doubt it had to do with Nancy. The tension between Nancy and Chris was so strong she could taste it on her tongue. She climbed onto the cart and Scott drove away.

He drove the cart back to the entrance and parked it in the row with the others.

"What do we do now?"

Scott walked away without answering. She followed him.

He stepped through the main entrance and approached one of the guards standing there. Kaylan was sure it wasn't a good idea to pester the guards, but Scott didn't have that filter.

"Hello," he said. The guard looked at him but did not respond. "I'm Chris's brother."

"I know who you are." The guard's response had no hint of friendliness in it.

"My name's Scott. I appreciate all you've done to help my brother. I just wanted to say thanks for that."

The guard stood unmoving and silent.

"What's your name, if you don't mind my asking."

The guard shifted the weight from his left foot to his right. His rifle, which was slung on his shoulder, scraped against the metal hull with a dull thud. "Gerard."

"Nice to meet you, Gerard."

Kaylan watched as Gerard's jaw clenched and unclenched repeatedly, and she pulled Scott away from him. When they were no longer in earshot she said, "Probably shouldn't bother the guards. They have a job to do." Then she added in a whisper, "Besides, that one rubs me the wrong way. He gives me the shivers."

When Scott started walking toward the parked cars, Kaylan thought he planned to climb into a vehicle and drive off, but he continued walking past the cars, heading for the fence. She huffed and followed him. *What trouble is he getting into now?*

He stopped just before the fence's gated entrance and stared out at the protesters on the other side of the fence. Kaylan stood beside Scott looking out at them as well.

STOP KILLING TREES, one sign said.

OUR FORESTS ARE PRECIOUS TO US, read another.

One simply stated: YOU HAVE NO RIGHT!

"I don't trust these people," Kaylan said so only Scott could hear her. Those protesters will eat Chris alive if he's wrong about this. She reached out and took Scott's hand. When a protestor slammed her wooden sign into the fence near them, she gripped his hand even tighter. If she was being honest with herself, she wasn't completely convinced that Chris's visions—or dreams, or whatever—were all-together real. But Chris believed, and so Scott believed. And if Scott believed, she would support them no matter what she believed.

Scott started walking forward again and, tethered to him, so did she. As they drew within yards of the fence, she could hear the shouts and taunts from the protesters.

"You should rot in hell for that eyesore you built," a woman said.

As Kaylan approached, a guard motioned for her to stay back. When she refused, he placed himself in front of her to act as a shield.

She stepped aside so she could confront the woman who had cursed her. The guard didn't stop her, but kept an arm out to protect her.

"We're not killing babies in here, goddammit. We're protecting ourselves from the…"

Scott pulled her back.

"You might as well be," the woman said. "You're killing trees and destroying a beautiful skyline. I look out my window and all I see is that thing jutting out of the trees like a giant penis." Then the woman slapped her sign against the fence again, and the links rippled.

"You can't reason with them," Scott said. "Don't try."

"Yea, I guess. Besides, our presence here is aggravating the natives." She turned and headed back to the Ark.

Scott waved and at Gerard as they passed, and although the guard looked at him, he did not wave back.

"Let's try out one of the eateries in here." They stepped through the main entrance and headed for one of the dining halls on the first floor.

Upon entering the restaurant, an old woman with stringy gray hair and gnarled, stick hands approached them. Her eyes were like cruise missiles, and they were locked on Scott.

"You're the brother of the Chosen One," she said.

Scott nodded.

"So nice to have you here. I'm Ethel. If you need anything—anything at all—you just holler 'Ethel!' and I'll come a running. Okay, sweetie?"

"Thank you," Kaylan said. "Aren't you sweet."

Ethel's face clouded as she turned to Kaylan. But then the brightness returned and the old woman walked away.

She wasn't convincing anyone with that fake happiness.

Kaylan giggled. "Some of these people are so creepy."

Scott shushed her.

"Oh, she can't hear me. She probably forgot her hearing aid."

Kaylan and Scott picked up a tray at the beginning of the line and waited their turn to be served. Ethel stood in line seven patrons ahead of them. She looked over at them. She wiggled her fingers in a dainty wave. Scott nodded his head in a casual reply.

When it was their turn to choose a meal, Scott chose a burrito and a bowl of Pasta e Fagioli. Kaylan asked for Chicken Riggies.

"It's true you don't get paid for your services here?" Kaylan kept her eyes on the server as she accepted the bowl of soup.

Scott nudged his wife with his elbow, and she knew he was warning her not to open her big mouth; but she was honestly curious. And the server didn't seem to mind the question. She ignored him.

The woman behind the counter stared at her for a moment before responding. "We are all part of the collective. No need for money. It's just part of being in the community."

Kaylan turned to Scott. "We should help out. I want to be part of the community."

"You are," the woman behind the counter said. Kaylan turned and looked at her with an inquisitive eyebrow, *huh*? The woman continued. "You are here with the blessing of the Chosen One. That makes you part of the community."

"But still, I want to help out. I want to…contribute."

"Get permission from the Chosen One and if he is okay with it, come back here. I can always use some help. Do you know your way around a kitchen?"

Kaylan turned to Scott. She turned back. "I know how to wash dishes."

The woman smiled for the first time. "I'm sure we can find something for you to do that's not so…menial. My name's Sue Kemp."

"I'm…"

"Kaylan, I know. And you're Scott, the Chosen One's brother."

Kaylan turned her head slowly to Scott, her eyes wide. "We're famous here." She relaxed her face and giggled. They turned and faced the rows of tables.

Kaylan carried her tray down one row, but there were no empty tables. She and Scott scanned the quaint little Italian

Trattoria for a place to sit, but all seats were occupied by other patrons. Movement in Kaylan's periphery caught her eye and she turned. She saw Ethel waving them over. Kaylan took one last look around, hoping to spot an empty table. Scott gave up the search and sat with the old woman. Kaylan, head lowered in defeat, followed.

7.

Nancy and Nora sipped tea, sitting in adjacent chairs with a coffee table between them. Brian glanced in at them from the dining room as he drank from the bottled water Tom had offered. *Nancy's been so confrontational about this place. I hope Nora can help her adjust.* He really wanted to move in to the Ark.

"…Brought my own personal supply, and once it's gone, I'm gonna have to dry out for a while, like you."

Brian snapped out of his thought. He nodded and chuckled, hoping he hadn't missed so much of the conversation that Tom would notice.

"I hope that didn't offend you?"

"Not at all," Brian said. "I know I'm a washout." They laughed.

When the laughter died out, Brian broke out the question he had been sitting on since entering the Lutz's place. "How are you and Nora getting along in here? You guys going to stick it out, till the doors close, I mean? You still have to make a break for it."

Brian smiled to try and lessen the severity of his statement.

Tom shrugged. "I guess we will. Nora is determined to stick it out. Honestly, though, how could anyone turn down the opportunity to be a part of this? Even if the world doesn't end, when I took one look at this place I knew I wanted to see what it was all about."

Brian let out a low grumbling sound. He hated the thought of the world as they knew it coming to an end. He knew Nancy still didn't fully believe any of this was true. Brian wished it wouldn't, but he knew too much about what Chris had done to think the guy was a crackpot. If Chris was crazy, then Brian was crazy, too. He'd seen things that couldn't be explained away; and sure, Brian could take the easy road and just say he had imagined all the bizarre things he'd seen, but he knew he'd only be trying to fool himself if he did that. The tree-thing that had dragged Chris into the water when the boy was 11 years old had been as real as the soda he was holding.

"My '68 Ford pickup truck."

Brian returned to the present at the sound of Tom's voice.

"Right. Nice piece of machinery." He didn't know what else to say.

"It's a classic," Tom said with his chest puffed out with pride, but then the good feeling faded. "Think it'll be ok when we get out of here?"

"I'm sure it will. It's a plague we're hiding from, not a flood."

Tom rubbed at the graying stubble on his chin. "I get that, but when the shit hits the fan out there, and people are desperate, what if they break into the garage where I'm storing it and vandalize it."

Brian shifted in his seat. "You think it'll get that bad?"

"It's a possibility."

"Never really thought about the implications of what would happen on the outside. I guess I was trying to stay neutral, for Nancy."

"Can I be frank with you, my boy, without stepping on your toes? I don't mean to offend or anything, but I've made an observation and wanted to run it by you, if I could."

Brian leaned forward in his chair. "Of course, you won't offend me."

"Sounds like you're committed to joining us in here even if Nancy doesn't?"

"That's really still up to Nancy. But yeah, I want to move in. Don't get me wrong, though. I wouldn't enter the Ark and leave her behind. If she says no, then I stay out and face the future with her. I have no other option. It's both, or neither of us."

"I'm sure she will, and I hope you do, too. I would appreciate the company. A lot of strangers in here. And Nora would love having Nancy around. Oh, I know she's against all the deforestation, and the displacement, but hell; if I can overlook all that—after all, it was my land they took—she can let that go."

Brian took a sip of his drink.

As the conversations winded down, Brian and Nancy said their goodbyes and exited the Ark. They headed out to the car and climbed in, Brian in the driver's seat. He pulled up to the gate and waited for it to open. Guards moved into place to keep protesters from rushing through. Brian drove out the gate and moved into the midst of the thick cluster of bodies. The protesters parted as the car moved through them. No one attacked the car, but some muffled curses and threats passed through the glass. The car's occupants ignored this. When the car cleared the majority of people Brian picked up speed. They did not speak right away.

Once they were a couple of blocks from home he broke the silence.

"The visit went well, I think. The families are really settling into their new homes. Even after the place is sealed, I think they'll be ok. We'll be okay, too, if we decide to move in. I think it'll be a good decision. What do you think?"

Nancy looked at him. She seemed tired. "I haven't made up my mind. I still have time. I can't be rushed, and I can't be swayed. You'll just have to be patient."

"Okay. Okay, no problem. Not rushing you to decide. But just so you know, I'm okay with this. I'm looking forward to it, in fact. But if you decide to not move into the Ark, I'll understand. I will respect that decision and I'll stand by you, no matter what comes."

"I can't help but think they've all lost their minds. There is no way the world is going to end in some apocalyptic plague sweeping across the land. How is this any different than the cult that kidnapped Chris?"

"It isn't the same…"

"Something happened to him, Brian. Something happened to Chris. Although he might not remember—at least he says he doesn't—what happened to him when he was kidnapped, it clearly affected his judgement. And don't get me started on this crazy group of people following him, like he's some kind of God, or something. Giving him millions to build this goddamned monstrosity. Honestly, if I weren't close to Chris, I would be right there on the picket line, protesting this organization. If I decide to move into the Ark, and let's face it, I probably will, because I know how much it means to you, I'll feel like the kidnapped person. I'm trying to wrap my head around this Brian, for you, for Chris…but it's not easy for me."

Brian had pulled up to the front of the house while Nancy talked. He stopped the car and stared at his wife as though he didn't know who he was seeing. She was an imposter, a doppelganger. This wasn't his Nancy. He fought back tears. She stared straight ahead when he turned to look at her. He realized his mouth was hanging open and closed it with a snap.

He stepped out of the car and headed into the house. He was in the kitchen when he finally heard her entering the house. They didn't talk for the rest of the night. The silence between them stretched into the next day as well.

Chapter Three

1.

August 29th, Sixty-eight hours till lockdown.

As Chris exited the Ark, the heat of the sun beat down on him like an oppressive mother. He came out every day after making his rounds, to look for Brian and Nancy. There had been no word from them since their visit to the skype room. The thought of them not returning plagued him. Had he offended her beyond repair? Did she truly feel her beliefs so strongly that she would risk, not only her own life, but that of her husbands? As he approached Gerard, the guard, he waved. Gerard readjusted his rifle strap, but did not respond to the greeting. Chris hated guns. He had never played with toy guns as a child, and dreaded holding real guns as an adult. He understood the use of them to control the crowds of protesters was necessary, but still, he didn't like them. There were more guards with guns posted out by the gate, and several armed guards who patrolled the perimeter. The guns were a deterrent. Mostly. Though no shots had been fired, the butt of a gun was used to beat down a protester who was found scaling the fence. The protests, so far, were not aggressive. Chris was thankful for that. He dreaded the idea of a guard having to shoot a citizen.

Chris raised a hand to his forehead to block the sun from his eyes. He peered out at the gate in the distance.

No cars approached.

But still he watched…and he waited.

2.

August 29th, Sixty-two hours till lockdown.

The rumble of primitive drums pounded out a staccato rhythm through the air, and wax plants and vines decorated the surrounding area. Dull lighting imitated the shade of a canopy of leaves in the jungle-themed restaurant. Wild cats snarled and growled, and howler monkeys cackled. Chris picked at his food as he looked around at other diners in the hall. He spotted a man talking with his hands, a glob of food dangled from a fork in one of the hands. At another table a woman fed her small child, a girl of about two years of age. At still another table a man and woman sat seriously close to one another, laughing and talking loud enough to be heard over the background sounds.

Chris's attention returned to his own table when Kaylan spoke.

"I think this is my favorite place. I want to come here every night to eat."

Scott took a bite of his food, chewed, swallowed. "Why aren't you eating, Bro?"

Chris looked at his plate. Mashed potatoes and gravy, roasted asparagus and caramelized lamb. Good stuff. But Chris wasn't hungry. And his throat felt constricted. *I can't eat because the people who saved us when we were kids are going to die, which means I wasn't convincing enough to save them.* "I had a big lunch."

He managed to eat his food with great effort, and after dinner they gathered in the game room. Roger was there playing chess with Adam Greenberg.

Chris took a seat at Roger's left. Roger didn't look up. *He has such strong skills of concentration, and his resolve is unbreakable. Look how he barely blinked as his queen took out Adam's knight.* Adam's queen rested at the outer edge of the board, already fallen victim to Roger's ruthless strategy.

In contrast to Roger's calm exterior, Adam fidgeted in his seat. Sweat dripped from his brow, and he whimpered like a whipped dog.

"I've seen the sharp edge of this man's wit, myself," Chris said.

Roger glanced at him with a raised eyebrow.

"What?" Chris said. "I did. After I threatened you." He turned to Adam. "He was letting me win."

Adam wasn't listening. He reached out to touch his rook, thought better of it and pulled his hand back. He reached out again; this time intending to move the bishop, but pulled back once again. Finally, he moved the rook.

Once he pulled his hand back, he saw the mistake.

Roger moved the queen into place and called out in a soft, casual voice. "Check and mate."

Adam huffed and pushed away from the table.

As Adam walked away, Roger turned to Chris. "Care to play?"

"Not right now." Chris moved in to whisper into Roger's ear. "I was thinking of going on a road trip."

Roger nodded. "To acquire the friends…Brian, and his wife."

"You read me like a book." Chris sat back and folded his arms over his chest, his whispering pretense forgotten.

"I have to say this is a bad idea. What if you can't convince them to come even then?"

"What are you getting at?"

"I think you should wait for them to decide. Otherwise, you risk angering the woman. The man will follow where she goes."

"You're right. I feel it in my gut, but in my heart, I want to do everything I can to get them in here. Do you have any ideas? I'm desperate."

"I'm afraid I have no advice to offer."

Chris closed his eyes, and took a deep breath, hoping to calm his racing heart. He tried to push all the thoughts pressing in on him, away from him. When he opened his eyes again, Roger was gone.

3.

August 30, forty-eight hours till lockdown.

Chris picked at his breakfast and dropped the food into the disposal after having eaten only a few bites. He considered calling Brian, but decided to send a text instead, and remind him of the deadline. The response was curt: Will get back to you soon. How could it possibly take so long to decide to live?

Chris dressed and started his rounds. He started at the floor below, and worked his way down. He went door to do, greeting the residents, and asking if they needed anything. If they did, he jotted it down in his notebook. His visits were short but effective, and it ate up a lot of his day, leaving him little time to worry about Brian and Nancy.

When he reached floor 200, his mind turned to the two families on that level who knew Brian and Nancy personally.

Nancy had gone to see the Lutz's and the Holmes's that last day they came to the Ark, had insisted on it. *Maybe Nancy had told them something I could use as a clue to their plans. Maybe Nora or Tom, or Patty, or Glenn, knew something about what Nancy was thinking.*

Chris knocked on the Holmes's door and Derek answered. "Hi, Christopher. Mom, Christopher is here."

"Did you invite him in?" Patty's muffled voice carried from somewhere beyond the door.

Derek turned back to face Chris. "Won't you come in?"

"Thank you, Derek," Chris said. Patty used her cane to stand and greet Chris. He rushed to her aid. They hugged.

"Christopher, I'm sure you have a million things to do around here and still you stop by just about every day."

Chris helped Patty back into her chair. He sat adjacent to her, and leaned forward so he didn't have to shout to be heard. "How has the Ark been for you so far? Do you find you're living comfortably here?"

"Oh, yes. The people are so nice to us. We have been very comfortable." Chris noticed Patty opened her mouth to say something more, but then closed it again.

"What is it?"

Patty grimaced. "It's not that I'm complaining, you understand."

"No, Patty, whatever it is you have to say, feel free. What's on your mind?"

"It's just that Nancy mentioned something about getting me a wheelchair. Did she say anything to you?"

In fact, she hadn't. But Chris would never mention that.

"As a matter of fact, she did. It must have slipped my mind. I'll get you a chair right away. I'm sorry that I wasn't on top of this for you."

Patty waved a withered, age-spotted hand at him. "Nothing to forgive. I know you have a lot to do, getting ready to seal up the place, and all."

"I'll have a chair for you right away so you can get out and smell the fresh air before the doors are closed. You wish to go outside, don't you? Get some fresh air? We only have about forty-seven hours of freedom left."

"Fresh air's overrated." Patty chuckled. "Besides, the air's not so stale in here."

Chris chuckled. "We have recycled air flowing through the entire building at all times. The air inside the Ark is as clean and fresh as anything outside these walls."

"And it shows. My asthma hasn't acted up since I've been here." Patty rattled on about a few aches and pains. Her conversation deviated to something about washing dishes, and then came around to Nancy again.

"By any chance, did Nancy say anything to you about her plans? She and Brian haven't returned to the Ark yet."

Patty tilted her head slightly, thinking. "No, not that I recall. Nothing rings a bell."

"I was just hoping she might have shown an interest in visiting you again."

"As a matter of fact, Nancy did say she would definitely see me again."

"They haven't returned yet, and the doors will be sealed soon. I guess I'm getting a little nervous."

"Oh, I'm sure they will come. They have to, don't they? Didn't you say there was a plague coming? We're safer in here?"

"Yes, that's all true, but not everyone believes. I've been having trouble getting Nancy to take this seriously."

"She'll take it seriously. I wouldn't worry about that."

"She told you as much?" Chris asked. He turned to see Glenn stumble out of the hallway from the direction of their bedroom wearing a white muscle shirt and boxers. He mumbled his hello as he plopped down in an adjacent recliner. Chris gaped at the tufts of gray hair on the old man's shoulders.

Patty spoke, pulling Chris's attention back to her. "They actually didn't spend too much time here. They spent the majority of their time next door. You might want to ask them."

"I'll see them after I've spent time with you."

Patty touched his hand and smiled. "You're a good boy."

"Thank you," Chris said.

Chris stayed long enough to have a slice of homemade banana bread and tea. He said goodbye and headed out. He knocked on the Lutz's door and waited. Without turning his head, he said, "Hi again, Derek." When Chris turned toward the eyeball peering through the crack in the Holmes's door, Derek ducked back inside and closed the door.

Tom answered Chris's knock and invited him in.

"Good to see you again, my boy." He invited Chris to sit and then sat opposite him. "Any particular reason for the visit?"

He could be blunt with Tom. "I'm here because I'm worried that Brian and Nancy might not be joining us, and I'm wondering if their last visit to you left you with any insight on the matter." He paused and then added, "and to tell you we are about 46 hours from lockdown."

"That lockdown is fast approaching, ain't it? And as for Brian and Nancy, I wouldn't worry about them. If I know Nancy, she's busy closing bank accounts and saying her goodbyes to all her wonderful friends. They have plenty of time."

I wish I shared your confidence. "I guess I'm having last minute jitters." His nervous laugh was unconvincing, but Tom didn't seem to notice.

Tom continued. "If Nancy was preparing for a long absence, it makes sense she would get everything in order first. She didn't seem completely sure the world was ending. She'd have to make sure the mortgage is paid, and the electricity is turned off."

"I get that. I've been so stupid to worry."

"Now don't go putting yourself down. You care, that's all. I hope I put your mind at ease."

"You did, thank you." Chris glanced around. "Where is Nora?"

"She's gone outside for a walk. We know the lockdown is coming and she wanted one last look at the trees and the grass and the sky. She's going to miss the outdoors."

"It won't be long before we are able to go back out again."

"I know that, and she does, too; but she's still going to miss it when we are locked in. She likes to walk barefoot in the grass."

"I'll be sure to show her the greenhouse. There are patches of grass in there and she can walk around barefoot."

"Sounds lovely. I'm sure she'll be happy."

"In any case, I'd like to talk to Nora. I'll swing by again later."

"I'll let her know."

"Will you and Nora be there when the doors seal? I hear some people are making an event out of it."

"I'm not sure. Maybe. Perhaps we'll see you there."

4.

August 31. Twenty-four hours till lock down.

At least the weather is cooler today than yesterday. Chris walked up to the guards surrounding the fence, and addressed the lead guard. "It's Rick, right? Your name?"

The guard nodded.

"Hi Rick. I want to start pulling people back toward the Ark. Select three guards to head back. Keep three here with you to deter the more aggressive protesters from trying anything reckless."

"Will do," Rick said.

The guard didn't divert his attention back to the fence. *He's got something more on his mind.* "What is it, Rick. You seem like you have something to say. Feel free to speak your mind."

The guard shifted his rifle. He cleared his throat. "I don't want to tell you how to do your job, or anything; but should you be wandering around so dangerously close to the aggressors? I fear for your safety."

"I like the hands-on approach. I trust I'm well protected. Thank you for your concern, though."

Rick selected the three guards—two men and a woman—and instructed them to walk back with Chris.

Chris skipped lunch, but was dragged to dinner with Scott and Kaylan. Chris's heart leapt at the sight of the Jungle Café, as he and Kaylan had begun calling it. He liked it as much as Kaylan did, apparently. Only he hadn't known it until he entered it again. Soft jungle sounds accompanied their voices as they talked.

Chris's eye snagged on the girl taking the order at the next table. As the man told her what he wanted, the girl glanced over at Chris. She diverted her gaze quickly. She scribbled the man's order onto her pad. The man's female companion ordered next. Chris's knack for putting names to faces helped him to remember the man's name was Jeffrey, and the woman was…Monica, he believed. When Jeffrey spotted him, Chris also remembered that Jeffrey was strangely afraid of him. He seemed to be the only resident in the Ark who was. Jeffrey had come to Chris asking if he could move his stuff into Monica's place. A strange request, as the people of the Ark were free to do as they wished in such regards, and asking permission was not even necessary.

Chris's eyes followed the server as she approached his table. She didn't look at him.

"Can I take your order, please?" Her voice was soft, soothing, but not so low that she couldn't be heard over the jungle noises.

"You are…Carrie, right?"

She nodded, still not looking at him.

"I'd like the soup du jour, and grilled ham and cheese sandwiches." Kaylan drummed her fingers on the table. "Sorry, Chris. But I'm hungry. Socialize later."

Chris's forehead heated up. He sat back.

"I'll have the smoked salmon dinner." Scott tapped the menu with an excited finger.

Carrie turned her body in Chris's direction, but didn't look up from her pad.

"I'll have a plate of the ravioli."

Carrie walked away without another word.

Scott and Kaylan stood and walked over to the drinks, which were self-serve. They returned and sat down, sipping at their drinks.

"You seem more like yourself today, Chris," Kaylan said.

"I feel more like myself today."

"You heard from Brian, then?" Scott asked.

"No, but that's fine. I know they are just getting their lives in order before coming back. We all did it: sold stuff we wouldn't need, closed accounts and prepared for the long absence. They are doing that as we speak."

"But you haven't actually heard from them."

Chris felt his small hairs tingle at Scott's words.

Chris shook his head. "No, but that doesn't worry me. They'll be here."

When the food arrived, Chris accepted his plate, happy for the distraction from the current conversation. He took a bite of his ravioli and chewed.

After dinner, they went to the theatre and watched a stage performance of Our Town. It felt less like a Broadway production and more like a high school play, but Chris enjoyed it. He laughed louder than anyone else, and hoped people couldn't see the concern racing through his veins like ice water.

Chris invited Scott and Kaylan to his room after the show. He didn't want to be alone. Being alone meant he had to think, and he had been doing so well not thinking about Brian and Nancy, that he wanted the distraction to continue.

After drinking tea, something interesting happened. Chris felt tired. He hadn't slept in days, so when his eyes started to droop, he wasn't sure what to make of it.

His eyes closed but he could still hear.

Kaylan's voice: "Your brother's sleeping. Should we let ourselves out?"

Scott: "Give him a couple more minutes. If he wakes back up, I don't want him to be alone."

A lightness entered Chris's heart at his brother's words. He would have smiled if his muscles would work.

"What do you think?" Kaylan asked Scott.

"About what?"

"Good thing you're cute. About Brian and Nancy?"

"Just cute? I'd at least like to think I'm handsome…maybe even hot."

"I'm serious."

"I don't think they are coming back."

A sigh from Kaylan. "It's going to break his heart. Don't they understand that?"

"It's not Brian; it's Nancy. He's just staying back for her."

"They only have eight more hours to show up. I really hope they do."

A yawn, Scott. "Me, too."

The voices grew farther and farther away until there were no more voices. Chris thought maybe they had let themselves out after all, but it didn't matter.

He was asleep.

5.

September 1. Two hours till Lockdown.

Chris heard the alarm on his wrist band go off and bolted awake. Somehow, he had gotten to bed last night. He overslept. He looked at the band. The alarm was a proximity alert. For the next two hours, the band would count down the half hour till Lockdown.

Chris showered quickly and was on his way down in the elevator when the next half hour chime sounded. There had been no announcement that Brian and Nancy had entered the building. He headed for the door and stood next to Scott and Kaylan.

Kaylan hugged him as he approached. She didn't speak, but her support was there just the same.

All the perimeter guards had been pulled in. The only guard Chris saw near the gate was Rick. Beyond the fences, intermingled with the protesters, news crews had begun to set up. *Vultures. They're hoping things go bad, I know it.* They pointed their cameras at the protesters, they took footage of the Ark.

The protesters shouted so loud, Chris could hear them over the distance. *Please don't do anything to cause guns to be drawn.* That would give the film crew plenty of fodder for the 6 o'clock news, wouldn't it. Time ticked by. Chris watched the gate for movement. The only thing left to do was to admit Brian and Nancy through, then Rick would fall back. The doors were on a timer that no one could control. He couldn't hold them open if Brian and Nancy didn't make it in time. The timer had been installed for just such scenarios. The human element had to be removed from the equation. Once the doors were closed, they could not be opened again without Chris's permission.

He looked down at the counter on his band.

One hour till lockdown.

He looked at the gate.

Those people are going to tear down that gate the minute the guns are removed. He expected people to try and tear down the walls. An impossible feat, but they would still try.

Something moved near the fence, drawing Chris's attention. But it was only the protesters. They were shaking it, trying to bring it down with their combined weight. People tried climbing it but Rick used the butt of his gun to knock them off.

The final chime rang in Chris's ears like a death knell.

Chris felt dizzy with grief. He swayed but Kaylan was there to steady him. Roger was there, too now, and he brought Chris a bottle of water. Chris took a sip and handed it back to Roger, who held onto it at the ready if Chris wanted more.

Fifteen minutes till lockdown. Chris turned around and scanned the crowd gathered behind him. Nora was there. She waved to him. His throat was tightened, and his spit turned as thick as grammar school paste.

Why? Why was this supposed to happen? Why was the world supposed to end? It wasn't fair. All those people were going to die. He suddenly mourned for them all, wished he had room for everyone inside the Ark.

The simple fact was he didn't have room for them all.

But there is room for two more.

Movement in the distance drew Chris's attention to the fence. The gate slid slowly open. Rick was there with his gun drawn. When people moved to enter, the guard fired a warning shot that echoed over the distance like a rolling boom of thunder.

He's going to get overrun.

But the crowd didn't charge forward. Instead, they *separated*. Brian's car emerged from the throng of protesters, moving slowly. Five minutes. Plenty of time. The gates closed again, and Rick rode up on a jeep, side by side with Brian's car.

Brian's car.

Chris's body felt suddenly as light as wind. *This is what people are talking about when they say they are walking on air.*

The vehicles stopped inches from the doors. Rick jumped off the Jeep and rushed through the doors.

Brian and Nancy exited the car, Brian from the driver's seat. They ran toward the doors.

One minute till lockdown and they were practically inside. The wait was over. Chris hurried them in.

Chris hugged Brian. He turned to Nancy. She seemed distracted, unhappy. *She'll learn to love it here.* He reached out to hug her as well.

As Chris stepped back, he saw two young people that must have slipped through the gates as they closed. As they ran up to the Ark, Gerard fought with them, trying to force them back. He reached for his gun. Chris rushed over to the scuffle and pulled the couple into the Ark. He motioned for Gerard to put the gun away. The claxon started and the doors began to close. More people had made it past the gate and were running for the Ark but they would never make it in time. The heavy steel doors inched closer together. They came within a foot of each other. The crowd moved closer still, but were no threat.

Nine inches apart now.

Chris turned back to Brian and Nancy when the threat to the strangers had been neutralized.

Nancy stepped up to Brian and kissed him on the lips. She seemed distracted. He seemed confused. Chris was confused, too. She turned and ran through the closing doors. She barely made it before the doors grew too close together for a human to fit through. Brian screamed and rushed forward to pull her back in. Chris, Scott and Roger stopped him. Brian nearly lost a hand.

Two inches apart, and Chris peered out at Nancy. Tears streaked down her face. She said, "I'm sorry."

The doors came together with an echoing clang. The sound of suction sealed the doors against the smallest microbe.

Brian screamed and slammed his fists against the steel. Chris tried to pull him away but Brian shrugged him off.

What happened? Why had Nancy exited the Ark at the last minute? He wanted to comfort his friend but so much was happening that demanded Chris's attention. Behind them, the gathered crowd erupted in a cluster of shouts and cries of alarm.

A girl sobbed near him.

Chris turned toward the girl and the boy cowering beneath Gerard's rifle.

"We're sorry," the boy said. "We're not protesters. We're not here to cause trouble. We were just curious, that's all. We wanted to know what was going on. We wanted to know who you are. We didn't mean to…"

Chris didn't know what to do. He turned to Gerard. "Take them to my office. I'll figure out what to do with them later."

Gerard nodded and motioned for the two intruders to go with him.

As they stood and the three started to walk away, Chris called out. "Gerard."

The guard turned. The intruders stopped and waited for further guidance.

"Be nice. They are just scared."

Gerard nodded.

Chris turned to Brian. He had stopped slamming his fists into the steel, and now sat slumped against the wall with his head on his knees. Chris walked over and placed a hand on Brian's back. He didn't know what he could do to comfort his friend.

Or did he?

"We can still see her," Chris said.

Brian looked up. "What?"

"Come with me."

Chris led Brian to the control room. Chris motioned for Toby to evacuate his seat and Brian sat down in his place. All twelve monitors were now on, and each showed a black and white image of the surrounding perimeter. The monitor directly in front of the main doors showed an image of Nancy standing just outside. Brian placed a hand to the monitor and touched her image. She stood unmoving for several minutes. People crowded around her, brushed past her, and pounded on the structure's façade. They ignored her and pounded on the steel walls.

Nancy swayed on her feet, turned and walked away.

6.

Chris led Brian to a soft chair and helped him into it. Creeping dread filled Chris as he watched Brian sloop forward and stare blankly into space. *He's in shock.*

"Can you get Dr. Jacobson to coma and look in on Brian?"

The intern nodded and ran off.

Brian stepped out of the control room and addressed the rumbling crowd.

The mass of nervous, scared and confused faces turn toward him. When the mumbling quieted down and he could be heard, Chris spoke.

"We knew the sealing of the doors would be an event, but all and all, things went well. We had a couple of last minute arrivals, and an unexpected departure, but no one got hurt. It's over now. We are safe. Our new lives begin now."

As the crowd slowly dispersed, Chris headed back through the control room to his office.

Gerard stood over the couple as they cowered together on the sofa, holding each other in a death grip. The girl had calmed down, but she was still wary of the gun.

"Are you going to make us drink the Kool-aid now?" she asked, and the boy nudged her.

"Shh." The boy narrowed his eyes at the girl, flicking a cautionary look at Gerard. "Don't anger the guy with the gun, huh?" He showed the guard his most winning grin.

They sat quietly for a moment.

The boy said. "So, what's this place all about? What did we get ourselves into here?"

"I'm Chris."

"I'm Eric and this is Cindy."

"Happy to meet you, Eric and Cindy." Chris shook their hands. "Welcome to the Ark."

"Ark? As in Noah's?" Eric asked.

"That was the inspiration, yes."

"Are we in trouble?" Eric peered up with obvious fear in his eyes.

Chris laughed. "No, you're not in trouble. You're actually in a good position. Do you know why this place was built?"

"Something about hiding from an end of the world scenario?" Eric said. "People in town think you're all going to die in here. That you're some kind of doomsday cult. Like Jim Jones, or the Heaven's Door people."

"It's actually the opposite. We're in here because a plague is coming that's going to wipe out 99 percent of the world's population. We're protected from that in here."

Chris turned to Gerard. "Take them to apartment 2411. Jeffrey Moore moved in with Monica a floor up. I'll let him know we're using his old place. If Monica kicks him out, I'll find someplace else for him."

Chris turned back to the young couple. "Go with Gerard. He'll show you where you'll be living for the next few months. I'll be by later and explain the way things work around here."

The couple stood and Gerard herded them toward the door.

"Gerard."

The guard stopped in the threshold and turned back to Chris.

"After you finish with our guests, I want you to gather up all the guns and put them in the armory. We won't need them in here."

Gerard turned and led the two charges through the control room and out of sight.

Now, back to helping Brian deal with his grief.

7.

The two strangers walked hand in hand down the hall, Gerard walked behind them, pointing the way. They reached a door at the end of the hall, and Gerard tapped in a code. The door whooshed open.

The boy examined the room. His eyes darted around at the boxes piled up all around, and the shelves lined up like the aisles in a bulk products store. "What's this place? I thought you were taking us to an apartment?"

Gerard said nothing, but led the boy and his girl to an open area in the room where there were no boxes and shelves. The boy and the girl looked around, confused.

After another few minutes of silence from the guard the boy turned to his girlfriend. He shrugged. When he turned back to the guard, a bullet took him in the forehead just above the right eye. The girl's scream filled the room, mixed with the echo of the gunshot. The dead boy slumped to the ground and the girl ran for the door.

The bullet took her in the back of the head and lifted her off the floor. Brain matter and bone sprayed out from her forehead as the bullet exited, and she slumped to the floor. Her blonde hair turned red with blood

Gerard holstered his pistol and glanced around. He spotted the large, floor-model freezer and dragged the dead boy over to it. He lifted the lid and looked in. It was empty, so he slid the corpse in. He then collected the girl's corpse and dropped her in with the boy. There was a key dangling from the locking mechanism, so he used it to lock the freezer. He dropped the key into his pocket. There was very little of the boy's blood to clean up, and after collecting the bullet and cleaning up the bits of bone from the girl, he exited the storage room.

As Chris had instructed, Gerard collected the guns from the guards and stowed the weapons in the armory. Guns would no longer be necessary, after all.

Part Two: The Ark

James McNally

Chapter Four

1.

September 3.

Brian pressed the send button and the computer screen showed an image of himself staring into the camera. After a few seconds, Nancy's face came up on the computer screen, replacing his. The first thing he noticed was how tired she looked.

"Hi," he said.

She turned away from the screen and looked back. "Hi."

"I've been trying to get you since that first day."

"I know. I saw the skype account app blinking. I just wasn't ready to talk to you yet."

"That's fine. We don't have to talk about anything unless you want to. I just wanted to see you again."

"I want to explain, that's why I answered the call."

"Okay."

She hesitated. After taking deep, cleansing breaths, she spoke. "I didn't feel like I belonged there. I couldn't rightly stay inside that place feeling like an imposter. And as much as it killed me to do it, I had to let you stay. I knew how much it meant to you, and to Chris, to have you inside when the doors closed. I'm sorry I did it, but it felt like the right thing to do at the time. I may regret it, but what's done is done."

"I would have stayed there with you." His own voice sounded heavy in his ears. Emotion clogged his throat.

"I know. That's why I did it this way."

There was silence for a time, and then Brian cleared his throat. "How did you get back to the house. You didn't take the car."

"No. There were too many people who'd broken through the fence. I walked back through the crowds of angry protesters to Ampersand Road. After an exhausting trek over wooded land, I made it to Tupper Lake Highway. A passing car with a woman driving stopped, and asked if I needed a ride. She took me back into town and I walked home from there."

"I'm glad you're safe." He dreaded asking it, but he felt compelled to. "Have there been any…?"

"Outbreaks?"

"Yea, any sign of the impending doom."

"Nothing yet, and no sign of the world coming to an end."

"Good to know, I guess."

"What do you mean, you guess? This is great news. This means Chris's prediction that millions of people will die isn't true."

"It means it hasn't happened yet."

"I don't want to argue."

No, he didn't want to argue either.

"The Ryans were asking about you. Joel wanted to know if you were going to return the weed whacker you borrowed." She offered a humorless laugh. "I told him you were out of town, and gave him back his tool. I figured you wouldn't mind."

No, I don't mind. And I don't want to talk about the neighbors. "I want to know how you are doing. Are you going to be okay alone? Do you need anything?"

"I'm going to be okay. You know me. I'm a survivor."

"Yea." It was either laugh or cry, and he wouldn't do either in front of her. "That you are."

"I think we should end the session now. I have errands to run."

They said "I love you" to one another—and meant it—then signed off.

Brian sat in the chair staring at the black screen for a moment. After a while he looked around. People in other seats were still talking to their loved ones. People were laughing and talking cheerfully. Brian could imagine he wasn't trapped inside a giant steel box. He wanted to believe he was travelling out of town, just like she told Joel Ryan, and he was in an internet café.

But all the imagination in the world couldn't change the truth. Nancy was out there where people were in danger of getting sick. These people sitting around him now, talking to their loved ones without a care in the world, either didn't grasp this concept, or had come to terms with the truth of it.

Brian stood and walked to the exit. The doors swished open and he stepped into the hall. He walked down the left corridor to the control room. People in here wore headsets, and typed away on keyboards. Toby monitored the cameras mounted on the outside of the building. Toby glanced up at Brian turned his attention back to the displays.

Brian peaked into Chris's office, but he wasn't in there.

He returned to the room he would have shared with Nancy, but without her, the place seemed somehow desolate. For the past few nights, Brian had been crashing on Chris's couch. He couldn't, with any honesty, say he was sleeping on Chris's couch; he hadn't slept since Nancy left the Ark, but he appreciated his friend's generosity.

He had gone in search of Chris, but it was Roger who rode up beside him on a golf cart. The cart was pulling a wagon full of household supplies—cleaning agents, bulk rolls of paper towels. The cart slowed to Brian's pace.

"Need a ride somewhere?" Roger asked.

Brian stopped moving, and so did the cart.

Brian climbed on. "I'll go wherever you're going."

"I'm just making a supply run. Nothing exciting."

"Let me help you. I have nothing to do and I'm feeling useless."

Roger shrugged and started the cart rolling again. He delivered supplies to the Jungle Room Café and Brian helped him unload. They headed down the hall to the freight elevator and rode it to the ground floor.

"Thanks for letting me tag along. You're a life saver."

Roger lowered his gaze. "You're welcome."

They rode through the halls and down the southwest corridor to a supply room. The room was set up with several metal shelving units lined up in rows, and some of the items Roger had requested he retrieve were on high shelves where Brian couldn't reach.

Brian walked up and stood beside Roger. "I need a ladder."

Roger didn't turn away from what he was looking at. "Over there." He pointed.

Brian followed his finger to the corner of the room, and a stepladder folded up and leaning against the wall.

"Oh, okay. Thanks."

Brian didn't walk away right off. He studied Roger's expression of concentration.

"What are you looking at?"

"The freezer."

"It's a freezer, yes."

"It's a *locked* freezer."

"I'm still not sure what the big deal is."

"That freezer is empty—or should be—and shouldn't be locked. If someone is storing something in there that they didn't want anyone else to touch, they should have come to me first."

"Where is the key?"

"I don't know. I should know, but I don't know."

Brian shrugged. "My guess is someone put something in there they needed frozen, but didn't want anyone else to touch."

"And that's fine, but they should have come to me, or Chris."

"Maybe they did go to Chris and he forgot to tell you."

"Unlikely, but I'll ask him." Roger turned back to the task of supply gathering.

2.

September 4. 9 a.m.

Brian clicked the call button and initiated a video skype session with Nancy. She answered with her hair tied up and makeup applied. She looked beautiful. His heart soared with love for her. She looked *healthy*.

"You looked well rested," he said. "You look really good today."

"Our talk yesterday did wonders for me. I feel like a massive weight was lifted. Thank you for not giving up on me."

"I'll never give up."

"That's so reassuring to hear."

"I have a job now." Brian puffed out his chest.

Nancy laughed. Her eyes brightened. "That's great. What is it?"

"I'm helping Roger with deliveries. It's not much of a task, but it keeps me busy."

"So, great. I want to hear more about it, but I have an appointment soon, so I can't talk long. Can we get together again tonight? I want to see you before going to bed. It relaxes me."

"Sure, you got it. When should I call you?"

"How does 8:30 sound?"

"It's perfect. See you then."

Nancy signed off and Brian sat back, his image filled the computer screen. After a moment, he reached out and turned off the monitor. The screen went dark.

He stood and exited. He met up with Roger after breakfast for the morning supply run. He hopped onto the cart and rode to the supply room with Roger.

The man didn't speak, and when Brian tried to spark a conversation, he was only met with one word responses. *I won't give up, though. Nope. I'll wear him down until I have him talking my ear off.*

Brian laughed at his thought, and this caused Roger to glance over at him, briefly.

At the storeroom, they climbed off the cart. Roger waved a hand in front of the sensor and the doors swished open. Brian gathered up the items from his list and tossed them into the wagon hitched to the back of the cart. He moved quickly, working up a sweat. Roger didn't even seem to be slightly winded, even though he moved quicker than Brian, and with better efficiency.

They made their deliveries and ate lunch together. When their deliveries were completed, Roger headed off to do whatever he did when not working, and Brian returned to his apartment to shower and prepare for dinner.

He found Chris, Scott and Kaylan at the jungle café, and they ate dinner together. Brian filled them in on his day's events, and he listened to what they had to say.

"I've been working in the kitchen with Sue, and she's been very patient with me. She'll have me learning how to cook in no time." Kaylan took a bite of her salad.

Brian recalled Kaylan mentioning an interest in working at the small buffet-style restaurant. "That's the Sue Kemp place?" He nodded. "We deliver to her."

"She mostly has me watching water boil, but little by little I've been adding to my tasks. Before long, I might be as good a cook as she is."

When Scott laughed at this comment, she punched him.

After dinner, Brian relaxed in the lounge near the skype room. At 8:30 he took a seat in front of a computer and dialed up Nancy's account.

"Hello, my love." She had a smile for him and he exhaled, releasing the tension in his shoulders.

"Hi. How was your day?"

"Busy." She relayed her days' events to him, and he concentrated on her voice. He memorized the nuances and mannerisms. She stopped after a few minutes. "I'm monopolizing the conversation. What was your day like?"

"Not nearly as interesting as yours. The best I can do is my new responsibilities put me in touch with a lot of new people. I've been working to get Roger to open up and say more than just 'yes, sir' and 'no, sir.'" He chuckled. "Oh, and Kaylan is learning how to cook."

"Good for her. I'm happy for all of you. Give everyone my love."

"I will. Nora misses you. She wanted me to convey that. I try to check in on them every day, as well as the Holmes's."

"Tell her I miss her, too. And give my love to our old friends. Have they been adjusting well?"

"I think so. They say they are happy."

"Good to hear." They talked for another half hour, until Nancy stifled a yawn. "I'm exhausted. Talk to me again tomorrow?"

"Bet on it."

They logged off and Brian headed up the elevator. He entered his apartment and dressed into the sweats he liked to sleep in, then headed out and knocked on Chris's door.

"Come on in," Chris said upon answering. "I made coffee if you want some."

"Sure." Brian stepped through the door and took his usual place on the end of the couch.

Chris poured two cups of coffee, walked them into the living room, and handed one to Brian. Brian took the cup and sipped at the hot liquid. Chris sat in the adjacent chair.

"How's Nancy?" Chris lifted the cup to his lips and peered over the rim at Brian.

"She's fine. She sends her love."

"I send mine to her, too." Chris took a sip from his cup and set it down.

Brian set his cup on the table, too.

"How do you like helping Roger? I think he's thrilled that you're willing to help."

"How can you tell? I'm sure he doesn't rave about me."

Chris laughed. "That's true. I ask him about you and I'm lucky if I get him to string two words together. But I know him well enough now to know when he's excited about something, even if no one else can see it."

"I was feeling lazy sitting around. Staying busy helps keep the gloom away. Normally, Nancy is there to neutralize the bad times, but Roger has his unique charm. I've enjoyed spending time with him."

They finished their coffee. Chris placed the cups in the kitchen, and they continued talking until they couldn't stop yawning. After an extensive yawn, Chris spoke. "Excuse me. I feel rude, but I have to head to bed. Feel free to crash on my couch."

"Thanks, as usual."

Chris pulled a pillow and blanket from the linen closet and placed them on the couch for Brian. He then entered his room and closed the door.

Brian set up the couch for sleep, but he wasn't tired. He could have blamed it on the coffee, but that wasn't it. Not really. Nights were hard for him. It was the only time of day there was nothing there to distract him from his missing other half. He sat in the dark for some time, and eventually curled up. The couch was comfortable, and he did fall asleep.

3.

September 5.

Brian woke when Chris was in the shower and slipped into the hall. He entered his own place and showered. He spent a half hour Skyping with Nancy and then found Roger. The list of supplies was short so they finished their task early.

"So, what do you want to do now?" Brian asked.

Roger looked at him with a question on his face. "Do?"

Brian slapped him on the back. "Yeah, let's go do something. Surely you do more than just deliver stuff all day."

"I…eat."

"Great, let's go get something to eat together."

"Okay."

Brian took Roger to the Eighties Café for lunch. Girls Just Want To Have Fun bellowed from the juke box. The room was bright—too bright—and the white walls seemed to glow. Brian laughed when he saw that Roger was looking down at the black and white checkered floor, and was only stepping in the black squares.

They took a seat in a booth in the back and after a minute the waitress came to take their order. Brian ordered a double cheeseburger and a root beer.

"What do you want, Bud? Don't worry about the bill. Food's on me." Brian laughed, but clearly Roger didn't get the joke.

The Cyndi Lauper song ended and Cherry Bomb took its place.

"I'll have a cheeseburger, too."

"Okay, cool. You like cheeseburgers?"

"I've never had one."

Brian's mouth dropped open. "What? You honestly never had a cheeseburger before?"

"No."

"How could that be? You never had one at a picnic as a kid, not at all?"

"I grew up alone with my mother. She was a vegan. When she died, I continued to follow her dietary restrictions."

Brian felt a strange rush of heat through his body. Something magical was happening here. Roger had opened up to him. That was no small thing. He suddenly wished he had an audio recorder on him. He needed proof of this.

"So, you're a vegan. Why are you eating meat now, then?"

"I'm not a vegan; my mother was. I simply continued with her meal plans. But I am willing to eat meat. I never had the opportunity, or desire, to eat a cheeseburger, until now."

I opened the floodgates. He won't shut up about himself. "I appreciate your candor, Rog. Thanks for opening up to me." *I always thought you might be a robot.*

Roger's blank stare communicated to Brian that the man had no idea something remarkable had just happened.

Brian sat with this hands clasped on the table in front of him, and his feet tapped to the music playing. "I like this restaurant. It's like someplace I would visit in the real world. In here, I can forget I'm inside a big tin can."

Roger frowned. "You don't like it inside the Ark?"

Brian's feet stopped tapping. "I like the people. But I'm stuck in here while my wife is out in the real world. I'm afraid she might die. I want to be out there, dealing with the same shit she's dealing with. I feel like the ultimate prank was played on me."

"But she chose to leave. It's her fault she's out there, and not a result your actions."

Brian's face heated, and he restrained himself from reaching across the table. *Watch it, buddy. That's my wife you're talking about.* "That's beside the point. I'm saying I want to be with her."

"But you're safer in here."

Brian took a deep breath. When the heat left his head, he responded. "Your own safety is not a concern when someone you care about is in danger. I guess I won't be able to make you understand if you haven't experienced this amount of love for another person."

"I think I understand."

Brian laughed. "I don't think you do, but let's not get into that conundrum, thanks."

Roger didn't respond.

"I'm glad we were able to have this little chat; but I told you things I wouldn't dare say to Chris, and I'd appreciate if you didn't say anything to him either."

"I won't repeat what you said to him, or to anyone else."

"Thank you."

"You're welcome."

Another song started as their food arrived. Brian wasted no time. He grabbed a handful of fries and shoved them into his mouth. As he chewed, he watched Roger stare at his sandwich as if he had no clue how to eat it.

"Use your hands."

Roger looked up at him, then back at the burger. He picked it up between both hands and brought it to his mouth. He took a bite, chewed.

As Brian watched Roger eat his first burger, and feeling encouraged by Roger's sudden willingness to share details of his life, Brian dared to ask the question that was on his mind. "Roger, what made you a True Believer?"

Roger took another bite of his burger. He chewed several times before swallowing. When his mouth was free of food, he responded. "When I was a child, I was walking home from the store. A man came up to me and said, 'one day you will bow down to me.' He scared me so bad that I ran home and hid in my room. Throughout my life, I had visions of that man regularly. After mother died, I dedicated my life to finding out who that man was. Years later I had a dream, and I saw a multitude of people bowing down to the man who had spoken to me as a child, I knew it was real when I met others with the same devotion. The man was Chris, but as you see him today. The others helped me to understand who the Chosen One was, and why we were devoted to him."

"I, too, had visions of Chris, so I know what you're talking about. It was during his time with the Keepers of the Forest. Were you a part of that group."

"No. That was an abomination."

"I'm glad to hear you say that."

"But we all owe their leader a great deal of gratitude."

"What?" Brian coughed up a chunk of burger.

Roger paused as Brian recovered.

"It was Crispus who found the Chosen One."

"But he killed people."

"His methods were deplorable, but his outcome was a success. Without him we might not have found Chris in time."

The food in Brian's stomach roiled, threatening to come back on him. "Forgive me, but it sounds like you are impressed by that murderer." Was Nancy correct? Were these people nothing more than doomsday cultists?

Roger stared at his burger for a moment, and turned back to Brian. "No, I have no respect for that group, or its leader. I merely feel gratitude that Chris was identified by them."

"Have you spoken to Chris about any of this?"

Roger's brow furrowed. His look caused Brian to feel foolish, but he wasn't sure why.

"He has never asked. I don't speak to the Chosen One, unless spoken to. I wouldn't presume to express my beliefs or opinion to Chris unless he asks. He never has."

Brian watched Roger eat. What a complex individual Roger was. "Why are you willing to express your opinions and beliefs to me then?"

Roger chewed and swallowed the last bit of cheeseburger. "You are not the Chosen One." Roger dabbed his mouth with the napkin. "And you are wrong, you know."

"About what."

"I know how it feels to care so much about the well-being of another that you would risk your own safety for them."

"Oh? Why is that?"

"I would die for Chris."

4.

Chris knocked on the door. Derek cracked the door and peeked out. When Derek saw Chris, he yanked the door open. "It's Chris. Chris is here."

"I come baring gifts." He pushed the wheelchair in that he had brought with him and placed it in front of Patty.

"Sorry I haven't been around in a while," Chris said and sat down next to Patty's chair.

"Be quiet." She waved his concern away. "You come around much too often as it is."

"Well, I'm hoping your world is about to get a whole lot bigger after today."

Derek examined the wheelchair. "For Momma."

"Can you push your mother around in this thing, being sure to be careful?"

"Yes, I can." Derek laughed.

"What do you say? Want to take it for a spin?" Chris asked.

"Lead the way," Patty stood and swiveled her body, and Chris helped her sink into the wheelchair.

Derek pushed his mother down the hall, following Chris to the elevators.

"Where do you want to go?" Chris asked.

"I heard there's a garden. I want to go there."

Chris led the way, and Patty climbed out of the chair to walk the few steps toward the budding plants. She smelled a tulip and then moved down to the marigolds. She collapsed into the dirt. Chris rushed to her, but she was laughing. She scooped up a handful of dirt and let it sift through her fingers.

"I could spend all day here," she said.

"I'll leave you to it then." Chris pointed to the others in the garden. "If you need help someone here will be glad to help you. If you need me, send word and I'll come running."

"Thank you so much," Patty said and fought against tears. "You don't know how much this means to me."

Chris kneeled down next to her and took her dirty hand in his. He kissed a clean spot and placed it in her lap. He stood and walked over to a tool station. He collected a watering can, a claw, pruning shears and a small hand spade. He set them down next to Patty.

"Feel free to take some flowers back to your place if you want."

Patty thanked Chris again. He walked away, smiling.

5.

September 5. 10 p.m.

Brian had been so flabbergasted by what Roger had said at dinner that he hadn't had the words to respond. But the discussion hadn't left his mind. It was there in the back of his head, even while he skyped with Nancy. Now, as he lay in the dark on Chris's sofa, he understood what he had wanted to say in reply.

What Roger felt for Chris was nothing like what Brian was talking about. Brian was referring to a human need to protect your own. Family. What Roger was referring to was more from a sense of duty. It was why men and women from the secret service put their lives on the line for the president. There was no real love there, just honor.

But then, how could Brian assume Roger didn't feel love for Chris? This caused another notion to occur to Brian.

Did Roger believe Chris was a god?

Brian yawned. He closed his eyes. In the morning, he meant to ask Roger that very question.

6.

September 10.

Kaylan took a seat in the booth facing away from the door. When a shadow fell over her, she turned around, and groaned inside. "Hello Ethel."

"We have to stop meeting like this." Ethel laughed.

Scott waved at the old woman. He motioned for Ethel to take a seat. She accepted.

Don't encourage her, Scott. Why was she here? Was she following them? Creepy. The background jungle sounds suddenly turned ominous. Kaylan glanced around and saw plenty of empty seats. Dare she insist Ethel find her own seat? Scott wouldn't forgive her if she insulted the old woman like that. Surely Ethel knew Kaylan's feelings for her.

Of course, she did. She's doing this to torture me, I'm sure of it.

Kaylan met Ethel's eyes. The older woman smiled. *There's no humor in that smile, only malice. I'm sure of it.*

"Thank you for letting me sit with you. I would have been so lonely sitting alone."

"How long have you been coming here to eat?"

Ethel glanced at Kaylan. "This is my first time, actually."

I thought as much. A sideways glance at Scott let Kaylan know her true feelings for Ethel were transparent, and he was not happy with her conduct.

Carrie arrived to take their order. Ethel ordered soup.

Scott leaned forward. "I'd like the lamb dinner."

Carrie turned to Kaylan.

"I'll take the chef's salad with vinaigrette dressing."

Carrie walked away.

"You're too skinny, dear. Salad's not enough. You should eat like your husband. Put some meat on your bones. We'll need fertile woman if we're going to repopulate the earth."

Kaylan turned to Scott and giggled.

"I'm serious. The world is going to be extremely depopulated. We'll need young people like you to build up the population again."

"What is your contribution to the world, Ethel?" Kaylan asked and Scott nudged her. "I'm just curious. You can't help repopulate the earth, so why are you being spared when so many other younger, child bearing women are going to die?"

Ethel stared Kaylan down. Kaylan met her gaze without flinching. Finally, Ethel's expression softened.

"I have other uses, dear. I have knowledge."

"I'm sorry if she offended you, Ethel. She has a wicked mouth."

"I'm not offended. I appreciate a vigorous discussion." Ethel laughed a little too loud.

The discussions for the rest of the meal did not have the same temperature and seemed forced at times. Kaylan felt the tension leave her shoulders when Ethel finished her soup and excused herself.

"Don't you think that was a little unnecessary?" Scott asked after Ethel had gone out of earshot.

"I didn't like her telling me how to eat. And don't apologize for me."

"She didn't mean anything by it. That's just how old people are. They feel the need to spread their wisdom."

"Well, there's something about her I don't like. I don't want her telling me what to do. I don't think any wisdom she has to offer is going to help the world, either."

Scott kissed the corner of his wife's mouth. "That mouth of yours is going to make this stay inside the Ark feel a lot longer than it needs to be."

"My mouth isn't doing that, Ethel is." Kaylan bit into a carrot from her salad.

7.

September 12.

Brian had been distracted during his call with Nancy, but she didn't seem to notice, and he was glad for that. Nancy ended the session—she always ended the sessions, because Brian could never bring himself to do it—and the screen went dark. Brian exited the room and sought out Roger.

When Brian arrived, Roger was already filling the wagon.

"Sorry I'm late."

Roger stopped and held a six pack of toilet paper under his arm like a football. "No need to apologize."

"You're the best boss I ever had, and before I married a rich girl I had a lot of bosses."

"I'm not your boss."

Brian laughed, amused by the other man's naiveté. *He has no sense of humor. He doesn't know when someone's joking with him.*

"You're an exceptional person, Roger, and I love you."

"Thank you."

Their day ended at twelve thirty. "Will you have lunch with me today?"

"Okay." Roger walked beside Brian.

As they entered the jungle room, Brian took a second to adjust to how empty it was. He'd seen the tables at least half full every time he entered. Today there were only two other diners sitting at two separate tables.

When Carrie came to their table, Brian greeted her.

"Looks like a slow day today."

Carrie looked at the other customers. "Yea, it happens."

Brian placed his order, and Roger ordered. Carrie walked away.

"I've been thinking about our last conversation. I have unanswered questions. You really opened a door with the things you were saying. I'm hoping you can help clarify my perception of the things you said."

"I'll do what I can."

Brian studied Roger's expression. The man was impossible to read. He couldn't tell if Roger was annoyed, or bored, or just tired. Brian clasped his hands in front of himself on the table. *Let's just get to it then.*

"Do you think Chris is a god?"

"A god? No. He's not a god. He's human, and he's vulnerable. I worry that he's not safe. I trust he's safe in here; I don't know of any True Believer who would harm the Chosen One, but outside the Ark? People will see him as the cause of all the trouble and will want to see him dead."

Brian hadn't thought of that. Roger was right. Chris would be in serious danger if he came across survivors of the coming plague. They all would, for that matter.

"You said you would die to protect Chris. I would die to protect him, too. But I've known him for years. I protected him when he was in danger from the Keepers of the Forest. I would die to protect him because of the love I feel for him. Why would you feel that way about Chris?"

The food arrived, and Roger sniffed it. He took a bite of his sandwich chewed, swallowed. He looked up at Brian.

"I love Chris, too. He isn't just the Chosen One to me. He's my friend, too. He has been helping me to be a better person. I've never had someone take such an interest in me. I appointed myself his personal assistant because I sensed something in him. He genuinely cares about me. No one has cared about me since my mother. For that I would give my life to protect him.

Brian didn't speak. He couldn't. The lump in his throat refused to be swallowed down. He reached across the table and placed a hand on Roger's hand.

"I believe you would give your life for Chris. I commend you for your commitment to him."

Brian pulled back. They finished their lunch in silence.

8.

September 15, 8 a.m.

Chris knocked on door 2411. He hadn't had an opportunity to visit until now. He knocked again when no one answered. *Wake up you people inside. Wake up and answer the door, damn it.*

Nothing.

Chris took the elevator one floor up. He approached Monica's door and knocked. After a minute or two, Monica answered wearing a robe. She smiled at Chris.

"What can I do for you?"

"Good morning, Monica. I'm sorry to bother you so early but is Jeffrey here?"

"He is. And no bother at all. Please come in."

Chris stepped inside and she led him to a chair. He sat.

"He's in the bedroom. I'll send him out. Do you want something while you wait? Coffee, Danish?"

"No, thank you. I'm fine." He chuckled politely.

She disappeared into the room and moments later Jeffrey came hopping out, shirtless and still struggling to pull on a pair of jeans.

"What did I do?" Jeffrey bit his nails, and flicked his eyes around as if looking for an escape route. His comical reaction made Chris laugh.

"You didn't do anything wrong. I'm sorry to bother you, but I was wondering if you've been downstairs since moving in here?"

"No, I never even entered that apartment. Why? Am I being kicked out of here?"

"Not at all. You can stay for as long as you want, and as long as Monica will have you. I'm just concerned for the newcomers that I assigned to your old place. I haven't seen them since they arrived when the lockdown took effect."

"I haven't seen them. I haven't been near the place."

Chris stood. "Thank you, Jeff. Sorry for intruding. Tell Monica I send my regards."

"Will do."

Chris exited the residence and returned to 2411. He knocked one more time. When five minutes passed with no response he tapped his wristband.

"What-up Boss?" Toby sounded exceptionally cheerful.

"Hi, Toby. Can you do me a favor and reset the lock to residence 2411. I need to get in there and see what's going on."

"Sure thing."

After a minute, Chris heard a click from the door in front of him.

"All set," Toby said.

"Thank you."

Chris tapped his birthday into the key pad, the default setting, and the door responded with a beep. He opened the door and stepped inside. The room was dark so he hit the light switch. The room lit up.

"Hello," Chris said. "Sorry to intrude, but…"

He stopped. Something about the place didn't seem right. It didn't seem…*lived in.* He walked into the kitchen. There were the usual dishes in the cupboards, but there was no food. The cupboards and the fridge were empty. This wasn't shocking, since most people ate in the various cafés and restaurants. He checked the bedroom. The bed was made, the sheets turned down. A mint rested on each of the two pillows. No heads had slept on these pillows.

Chris exited the residence and headed down the hall to the elevators, his mind racing. Nothing was making any sense. Did he imagine the couple who entered the ark just as the doors were closing? No, of course not. Gerard had been there. He knew they existed.

Chris entered the control room.

Toby looked up and turned away. He did a double take. "Chris? What are you doing here?"

"I'm looking for Gerard."

Toby turned to a monitor not being used for surveillance and tapped at a keyboard. A few more taps and then a roster popped up. "He's not scheduled for duty today."

"Oh, of course." Chris exited the control room. "If you see him, or if someone sees him and you learn about it, can you let him know I'm looking for him?"

"Can I ask why?"

"He's the only person I know of who saw the two last minute guests we received. The day the doors were sealed. I want to know that he escorted them to the apartment I assigned them to."

9.

September 15, 9 p.m.

Chris approached the door to residence 4211 and slowed his pace when he saw the note taped to the door. He stared at the note for a moment, perplexed. He reached up and tore it off the door. He turned it over in his hands. His name was scrawled on one side of the folded piece of paper. The handwriting was decidedly masculine, he deduced. He unfolded the paper and examined the hand-written words, then read what was there.

Dear Chris,

We understand you have been looking for us. We didn't mean to cause you so much trouble. Cindy and I decided not to stay in this apartment. You see, we met some friends here and they decided to take us in. We hope we will get to meet up with you at some point during our stay inside the Ark, but I wanted to make sure you didn't continue to worry about us. Just know that we are being taken care of quite well by our friends (who wish to remain anonymous), and that everything is fine.

Thanks again for everything.

Sincerely,
Eric.

Chris folded the paper and crammed it into his pocket.

10.

September 15.

Gerard stood in the darkened room and stared at the figure shrouded in shadow. The figure shifted in the seat but did not stand. Gerard finally broke the silence. "The Chosen One is getting closer to the truth. We have to act now while we still have the upper hand."

"No." The shrouded figure's gruff voice echoed in the room. "I have distracted him. He will not look for them again for a while. I have bought us some time."

"But how much? How long before he starts looking for them again?"

"Keep in mind that you caused this mess. You should not have acted so rashly and killed the Nobodies. I am doing what I can to clean up your mess."

"I'm sorry." Gerard lowered his head. "It's just that I couldn't stand to sit back and watch as two more non-believers took part in what we have here."

"Be patient, Son. Soon all the non-believers that bleeding-heart Chosen One brought into the Ark will be eliminated. After all, they are not the ones who will inherit the earth. Only we chosen few will be around to walk out those doors when the new world order is restored. All the non-believers—including those closest to the Chosen One—will never see the sun again."

Gerard mumbled a goodbye and turned. He bumped a stand, and nearly sent a vase of tulips crashing to the floor. He caught the vase, however, and righted it. He cleared his throat, trying to mask his embarrassment, and then stepped into the lighted hall, leaving the shadowed figure alone in the dark.

Chapter Five

1.

October 6.

Margaret Polk's husband did not believe. He refused to join her inside the Ark. Against his wishes, she cleaned out their savings, five hundred thousand dollars, and handed it over to Chris. She also gave him a 3-million-dollar inheritance fund that was all hers. It was small ripple in a 20-billion-dollar pond, but every bit helped. Her husband fought her, taking her to court for the money—even threatened to kill her if she went through with it—but in the end, Chris's lawyers won out, and Margaret escaped her overbearing husband.

She moved into residence 5523 the day the Ark opened and hadn't looked back. Her husband was out there, now, in the world, and she couldn't wait to kick his bloated corpse after the plague got him.

Chris visited Margaret on occasion and she cherished his visits. He had been by an hour ago, and she cooked him dinner. She imagined he received a lot of dinners, lunches, and breakfasts from the appreciative followers; as well as all sorts of deserts and other treats. It was a wonder he didn't weigh a ton. He couldn't possibly take up everyone on their offers of food, but he did accept hers, and she loved him for it.

She had heard from Paul Morris that he planned to marry off one of his daughters to Chris. Paul ran the restaurant with the jungle theme, and his two daughters, Margot and Carrie, had come with him into the Ark and helped him run the place.

Margaret thought it was silly that Paul would presume Chris, the Chosen One himself, would choose one of his daughters to take as a bride. The thought was ludicrous really, but everyone had their fantasies, she supposed. Paul was a dreamer, and he had high hopes. But Margaret doubted very highly Chris would go for such a plan.

2.

October 10, 9:23 p.m.

"The news is calling Chris a crackpot," Nancy said. "They are reporting that the people in the Ark have closed themselves off from the rest of the world so they can commit whatever crimes against man and nature they want without the prying eyes of the civilized world. They think the Ark is going to end with one of the biggest mass suicide tragedies the world has seen since Guyana. It doesn't help that they got wind of what Chris went through as a child. The media is drawing the line between the Keepers of the Forest and what's happening now, sensationalizing it."

I pray they didn't draw that line with your help. The thought caused Brian to cringe. How could he even entertain something so vile about the person he loved.

"They can say whatever they like. It's not true," Brian said. "They are only saying that because there's no way to refute it."

"People on the street are saying you're all just a bunch of crazies in there, locking yourselves away from the rest of the world and that you're all going to die. People are expecting the doors to open and there will be thousands of corpses inside. People are saying…"

"Why are you listening to what people are saying?" He thought about adding: *they're all going to be dead soon, anyway.* But what he would really be saying was *you'll* all be dead and he didn't want to think about Nancy that way.

"It's been over a month and still not a single illness reported. Well, none that would alarm. Flu season's about to start and people are getting the sniffles. We should start to consider the possibility that Chris's plague isn't coming."

"It's too early to come to that conclusion just yet."

"I guess so." Nancy yawned. "Let's call it a night, okay? I'm tired. I love you."

"Good night," Brian said. "I love you, too."

Brian signed off, but he wasn't tired. He entered the lounge area attached to the skype room. He saw a flyer advertising the various programs and sites available. His eye landed on one listing in particular. Apparently, there was gym. He headed to the there. He walked in and glanced around. In the center of the floor a multitude of weight machines, exercise bikes and treadmills waited to be used. Around the perimeter of the room was about a quarter mile of track. He saw two people in shorts running on the track, and recognized one of them as the guard, Gerard. He didn't recognize the other man with Gerard. He waved, but Gerard did not appear to see him.

Brian entered the locker room. In a corner of the locker room, Brian found storage bins filled with brand new gym clothes; gym shorts, sweat pants, tee shirts and sneakers. He picked through the bins until he found clothes that fit him and dressed in the athletic wear. He stepped out of the locker room and looked around. Gerard and the other guy had stopped running and were walking and talking in hushed tones. *Doing a cool-down routine.* Brian started out on a treadmill for cardio for a half hour, switched to weight training. He was proud of himself for being able to lift 150 pounds. When he was thoroughly soaked in sweat, he retired to the locker room. He tossed his wet and stinky clothes into a plastic bag and showered. After exiting the showers, he took a complimentary towel off the shelf and dried off. As he slipped back into his clothes, Gerard and the stranger entered the locker room. Gerard locked eyes with Brian but showed no sign of recognition.

The stranger walked up to Brian, smiling. "Hi there. I'm Rick. You're Brian, right? Chris's friend."

Brian shook Rick's hand. "That's right. Nice to meet you."

"I'm one of the guards here. Feels foolish saying I'm a guard." Rick chuckled. "Nothing to guard in here, right?"

Gerard acknowledged Brian's presence now with a slight nod of his head.

"Do you ever smile?" Brian asked Gerard. The tall guard pulled back his upper lip until his front teeth were exposed. It looked more like a grimace, or a snarl.

Rick turned to Gerard and then back to Brian. "Don't mind him. He can be a bit gruff. He's a good guy, though."

Brian wasn't so sure about that. Something about the tall, silent guard made Brian cringe. He ignored the feeling and concentrated on what Rick was saying.

"I'm always looking for a gym partner, so if you ever want someone to work out with let me know. This clown is not always available."

"I certainly will." Brian's words were intended for Rick but his eyes were locked on Gerard. "Thank you."

"Great," Rick said.

"Great," Brian said, mimicking Rick's enthusiasm. "And we can even let the clown tag along if he wants." Brian pointed at Gerard behind his hand as if trying not to let the other man see what he was doing.

Rick laughed. "Sure, why not?"

As Rick and Gerard headed for the showers, Brian exited the gym. He still wasn't tired, but he supposed a visit with Chris would be just what he needed to get his mind to wind down. He wouldn't tell Chris what Nancy had reported. Chris didn't need that burden on top of everything else the kid was trying to accomplish.

Besides, he probably already knew. Surely, Chris was monitoring the media outside the Ark.

3.

October 31, 7 p.m.

Brian studied the decorated doors as he strode down one hall, and then another. *Halloween appears to be the favorite holiday for*

True Believers. Children dressed up and went door to door, and for the adults, some of the restaurants threw Halloween parties.

Brian entered the Jungle Café, where a Halloween party was in full swing. He felt pretty good, considering.

Considering he was apparently struggling with non-24. Though the disorder was typically associated with the blind, a disruption in the sleeping pattern of a person who cannot tell the different between night and day, Brian had been diagnosed with the disorder. Dr. Jacobson prescribed him a sleeping agent, and gave him a night mask.

"To block out any light while you're sleeping," she had said.

And the regimen seemed to be working. He was sleeping again. He would start to wean himself off the sleeping pills next. *See if I can sleep without them.*

As he strode through the café, he passed many well-crafted disguises, all animal-themed to stick with the jungle motif. He found Kaylan, Chris and Scott. Kaylan wore a black cat costume, and Scott sported a tiger mask. Brian had gone with snake makeup on his face and a shiny green suit. Chris was a monkey. The party-goers sported some really outlandish costumes. One person wore a gorilla suit that could not have been comfortable. Not only did it look hot, but heavy as well. It had to be a chore to lug all that fur around.

One man wore a leopard loin cloth. He beat his chest, and bellowed out a jungle call. Several critics mocked his terrible Tarzan caterwaul. The man merely laughed with them.

Paul, the proprietor of the establishment, lingered in the background as Brian made his rounds. Everyone he passed complimented him on his makeup. He stood near the snack table and surveyed the room.

Kaylan stopped at the table and poured herself a glass of punch. "Looking good, snake man."

Brian felt his face heat up. *My makeup is going to run off with the sweat.*

"That tight snakeskin suit is accentuating all your best features."

What was she trying to do to him? He fidgeted. When his discomfort grew to the point that he couldn't stay still any longer, he took a single step away from her.

She laughed.

"I'm just joking around. No need to get all flustered."

"What would Scott think about you flirting with me?"

She laughed again. "How cute that you think I was flirting with you."

Brian's previous exhilaration deflated, like a party balloon with a slow leak.

"Way to crush a man's spirit."

"Awe, I'm sorry." She reached up and kissed him on the cheek, which caused his face to heat up again. She walked away, leaving him to ponder what had just happened.

When Roger approached the snack table, Brian chuckled. Roger's idea of a costume was a pair of cat ears.

"You put a lot of thought into that costume." Brian's sarcasm was lost on the man.

Roger pulled the ears off his head and looked at them. "They were given to me."

Brian handed Roger a drink. "I'm glad you came. I want Chris to hear one of our extensive conversations. He'll never believe that you can carry on a conversation unless he hears it for himself."

Roger sipped his drink and said nothing.

Don't clam up now. Brian motioned for Chris to join them. Kaylan and Scott walked over with him.

"Who knew fanatic cultists could throw such a raging party." Kaylan spoke with a cockney accent.

Scott rolled his eyes.

She turned to Roger and spoke normally. "No offense. I don't think you're all cultists."

Brian pulled Chris by the arm, closer to him and Roger.

"It's just that this is the first non-alcoholic party I've been to. I think it's interesting so many people think they can have a good time without a drop of booze in them." Kaylan shrugged.

Someone at the front of the room announced it was time to judge the best costumes. The nominees were the Jackal, the hyena, the lion—another hairy and elaborate costume—and the gorilla. Many people in the room started to chant Tarzan, so he was brought up to the front of the room as well. Cheers ensued.

"The winner will be chosen by applause," the announcer said.

Each contestant stepped forward. Their applause was rated by a panel of judges.

"I believe we have a tie between the gorilla and Tarzan." Paul moved these two contestants to the front of the line. "Who thinks Gorilla is the best." More cheering filled the room. "And who thinks Tarzan should take the prize?"

The cheers multiplied. Kaylan placed her pinky fingers in the corners of her mouth and blew a high-pitched whistle. The applause became a sustained roar.

"Looks like we have a winner."

The skimpy, breechclout clad swinger posed for his adoring fans.

The man inside the gorilla costume removed his head. Sweat dripped down his chubby face. He took a deep breath, grateful to have the heavy costume off at last.

The room returned to a dull roar as the applause faded and conversations resumed.

Brian opened his mouth to speak, but when Paul walked over to the group, the moment was lost once again. Brian threw his hands up and leaned against the wall.

"I'd like you to meet my daughter," Paul said.

The girl stepped forward, smiling shyly.

"Hi." Chris shook her delicate hand. "Would you like some punch?"

"Thank you," she said.

Chris poured her a cup of punch and then picked up his own cup. They sipped at their drinks and looked around. Neither talked to the other. If their eyes met, they would smile politely and then look away.

After an eternity of awkward silence, Carrie said, "I should get going. It was a pleasure meeting you."

"Oh, yeah. You, too. A pleasure meeting you."

"I'm sorry about my dad. He was excited to introduce us."

"Oh, I'm glad he did."

"Okay, well bye then." Carrie turned and walked through the cluster of masqueraders.

"Bye." Chris watched as she disappeared into the crowd and then turned to Scott. "I think he just tried to hook me up with his daughter."

"She's cute." Scott brushed his shoulder against Chris's.

"Yea, I guess she is." Chris laughed.

"Go for it. What's it hurt to go on a date with her?"

"What's the big deal if she's cute or not?" Kaylan asked. "She might be a good person even if she's not a knock-out."

Scott shrugged. "Being cute is still a great plus."

"Still, that shouldn't be the first thing you use to decide if you should date her, Chris. That's all I have to say about it."

"I don't think we hit it off. We just stood there and didn't even talk to each other. I don't think it'll work out."

"If it's any help, Nancy and I were friends for years before I finally opened my eyes and saw what was right in front of me. Start out as friends, and see where it goes. No pressure."

Chris nodded. "Yea, I see what you're saying."

"Roger." Brian pulled the man out from the shadows. "Do you have anything to add to this conversation?"

Chris glanced at Roger, but the man simply stared at him. Before anything was said, a woman came out of the crowd and stood in front of Chris.

Brian clenched his hands into fists. *I can't believe this. I should have known I wouldn't get five minutes alone with someone as popular as Chris.*

Roger walked away.

"Hi, Chris?" the woman said. "My name's Margot. You met my sister, Carrie?"

"Yes, I met her. She's nice…"

"I came to see if you would have dinner with her tomorrow night."

"Sure, sounds great."

"Okay, good. Meet her here tomorrow night at 6 p.m. and I'll show you kids a night of fine dining you won't forget for a very long time."

"Are you the master chef who cooks the great food here every day? My friends and I are addicted to your culinary masterpieces."

"Yea," Margot said. "The date is with my sister, not me. So back off Chuck."

Brian chuckled.

Chris lowered his eyes and turned his head away. Margot spun around and walked away.

"Looks like you're not all-powerful Chris in everyone's eyes in this place." Brian walked away, still laughing.

Chapter Six

1.

November 1, 5:58 p.m.

Chris read the sign on the door of the Jungle Café: Closed early for a private matter. *Should I knock, or just go in?* He knocked on the door. The door opened and Margot stood in front of him, looking him over. She seemed to approve, and allowed him to enter. Margot's hair was pulled back, and ringlets lined her face. She wore a form-fitting black dress. *She cooked in that?* The mess from the previous night's celebration had already been cleaned up and the place looked spotless. *They worked fast here.* The place was sparsely lit, with candles at every table, but only one table was dressed up for the occasion.

He followed her to a single table with two chairs. On it was a red-checkered tablecloth, with a single red rose in an elegant vase and two place settings, complete with silverware and ice water. Margot held out the chair to the right, and he took a seat.

"She'll be right with you," Margot said and exited through the kitchen door.

A few minutes later, the door opened again, and Carrie stepped out. She was beautiful. If Margot had worked on the ensemble, she had outdone herself. Carrie's red dress sparkled in the candlelight, her lips were the perfect shade of red to accentuate the dress, and the makeup was flawless. Her hair, too, framed her face with tight ringlets. Chris stumbled to his feet and held the chair out for her.

"Thank you." Carrie's voice was small, but clear.

Chris sat. He tried to make eye contact with her, but she shied away from his direct gaze.

"I'm kind of nervous. I'm not used to this. The place looks nice." *What's wrong with you, Chris.* He quickly added, "You look nice. Am I rambling? I feel like I'm rambling." Chris played with his silverware and hit his water glass, knocking it over. The water rolled across the plastic-coated table dressing toward Carrie. "Oh, shit. Damn, oh; sorry, I didn't mean that. I don't usually curse this much." He tried to mop up the water, but it was too much liquid for the thin paper serviette.

Carrie reached across the table to help. She laughed, unable to help it. "Don't worry. It's just water."

Chris used the palm of his hand to brush the rest of the spilled water onto the floor. He wiped his wet hand on his pants and stopped trying to clean it up. *Act natural, Chris. Ignore the heat in your cheeks. Maybe your olive skin will hide your embarrassment.* But it was no good. Carrie hid her smile behind one hand.

Her fingers are so delicate. He fought back the urge to take her hand and feel its gentle touch, its soft skin.

Margot came from the kitchen pushing a serving cart. Her black dress was covered with a white apron. She uncovered their meal—a cucumber, tomato and kale salad in a red wine vinaigrette. She saw the puddle and glared at Chris. He offered a nervous half smile that would have left most people absolutely mushy with compassion, but not her.

"This is supposed to be a romantic dinner. I feel like a waitress at Chuck-E-Cheeses." Margot set the salads down in front of them.

"Sorry." Chris picked up the wrong fork for salad. Margot took it from him and handed him the correct fork.

She huffed and pushed the cart back to the kitchen.

"She's just trying to help. She doesn't mean to be offensive." Carrie picked at her salad.

You don't have to apologize for your sister. He couldn't say that out loud. But the truth was, Margot's attitude was easier for Chris to understand, and to deal with. *It's your shyness that flusters me.*

"The food is good." Chris's mouth was full of food. *Dummy, wait till your mouth is empty.* He reached for his napkin, wiped his mouth. He finished chewing and started again. "The food is good."

Carrie nodded.

The second course was roasted asparagus with cranberries. As they ate, Margot removed their plates. She brought Chris a new glass of water. The main course was tuxedo sesame crusted chicken with avocado slaw and veggie kabobs.

"Your sister can really cook."

Carrie nodded again. "It's her calling. I try to help her but the best I can do is hand her the ingredients. The cooking is all her."

Until that string of words, I thought I was on a date with Roger. He chuckled, but after a look from Carrie he stopped.

Chris picked at the slaw, naming off the ingredients in his head: chunks of avocado, slivers of carrot, shredded Bok Choy, chunks of walnut. He ate the salad with the correct fork. He watched as Carrie picked a fork to eat her asparagus and copied her. When the meal was over, Margot brought out baklava and strawberry cheesecake for desert. Chris ate what Carrie didn't.

"I ate too much," Chris said when the silence between them began to linger. "Would you mind going for a walk? I need to work off all this food."

"That would be nice."

Chris stood and tried to help her with her chair, but she stood too quickly. She stepped around the table and joined him. They started by walking down the hall together. They walked slowly, waving to the other people they met.

"Tonight was fun."

"Yes," Chris said. "Fun." Although he was thinking it was anything but. "It was the best meal I've had in all my life, I think."

"Mmm," Carrie said.

Chris cringed inside. *She knows how good a cook her sister is, Chris. No need to keep reminding her.* They rode the elevator to the floor she lived on and they walked down the hall to her door. She tapped her code into the keypad and the door unlocked.

"Thank you for walking me to my door, Chris. You've been very good company."

Carrie started to push the door open but Chris touched her arm, stopping her. He pulled back quickly, suddenly unsure why he had done it.

"I had a nice time."

"Me too," she said in one short breath.

Chris leaned in but as his lips neared hers, she turned her head. He placed the kiss on her cheek. As he pulled away, she slipped through the door and was gone. Chris stared at the door a moment and then headed back down the hall to the elevator. He returned to the restaurant. Margot placed the last of the dishes on her cart, look up…and scowled.

"What are you doing back here?"

"I came to see if you needed any help."

"I don't." Margot turned back to the task at hand.

Chris sauntered over to the table and dropped down into his chair, sagging.

"I made a mess tonight."

"No worries," she said. "I cleaned it up." When he didn't respond, she sat down across from him. "Oh, you mean with Carrie. I wouldn't worry about it. She's shy. I'm shocked she was even willing to meet with you."

"She didn't like me," he said. "I was awkward and silly. She was probably embarrassed to be seen with me."

Margot kicked the table. A jolt of fear ripped through his spine.

"Stop feeling sorry for yourself. She likes you just fine. I told you, she's shy." This time she kicked his shin. "And stop slouching, you're not a forlorn teenager. You're an adult; act like one."

Chris sat up in the chair, scowling. "That was uncalled for."

"Trust me, sweetie. It was very called for. Trust me, she likes you just fine. She'd be a fool not to. You're sweet, handsome…and you're the Chosen One."

"Why do you say it like that?"

"Say what, like what?"

"When you say the Chosen One, it's like a joke. You put that sarcastic twist on it."

"Noticed that, did you?" She laughed. "I'm not like the other True Believers in here. I won't worship the ground you walk on. If you want my respect you have to earn it."

"How do I do that?"

"You start by realizing you're not a kid anymore and grow up." She mimicked his maudlin vocal pattern. "'She didn't like me.'" Her voice went back to normal. "Why should she like you? You're like a kid in a grown-up's body. Grow up."

You're mean. He laughed. He'd never say that aloud. Besides, she was right.

"Why didn't he pick you?" Chris said.

"What?"

"Your dad. Why didn't he pick you to set me up with?"

She leaned back in her chair. "Who says he didn't, and I turned you down."

Chris laughed. "Didn't think of that."

She looked away. After a moment—perhaps collecting her thoughts—she turned back to him. "Besides, I'm not right for you. You and Carrie are a better fit."

"Maybe," Chris said. Did he see a slight change in her demeanor? Was she disappointed that he would think Carrie was the better choice? He couldn't be sure; because whatever he had seen was gone in an instant. "But then maybe not."

Her stoic face gave up nothing.

"How is this for the ultimate brushoff; she turned away when I tried to give her a good night kiss."

"That was rude of her."

"It was my fault. I wouldn't shut up about how good of a cook you were."

"Ha." Margot got control of her pleasure. "I mean, oh, you did?"

He chuckled. "Yeah."

"You should go. I have dishes to do and you have stuff to do as well, I'm sure."

"I could help you do the dishes."

"I'd rather you didn't. I've had about enough of you tonight. I'll get this shit done faster on my own, no offense. It's been a long day. I'm sure it has been for you, too."

"For me it's not over."

"Exactly, so you run off and do what *Chosen Ones* do."

I love how she says that.

"I'll see you around. Okay?" She stood.

"Fine." He heard the childish lilt to his voice. He tried again. "Have a good night."

She waved him off and pushed the loaded cart to the kitchen. When she was out of sight, he left the restaurant. He headed down the hall to the elevator and took it to the first floor. On his way to the control room, he wondered how he could get Carrie to open up to him. *Too bad she's not more like Margot.*

Wow, where did that come from?

Chris spotted a man up ahead, shuffling toward the main doors wearing pajamas and a robe. *A sleepwalker?* One of the man's slippers came off his feet. The man ignored it, and continued heading for the main hangar doors.

"Excuse me, Bill? Bill Thomlinson, is that you?"

The man stopped and did a slow turn to face Chris. The man's expression was dull, emotionless. The man took a few tentative steps toward Chris. He could see now that he had been correct. The man was Bill.

"Bill, you dropped a slipper. These floors must be cold on your bare foot." He offered Bill a hand. What was it the experts said? Don't wake a sleepwalker? Or was it you should wake a sleepwalker?

"Open the doors," Bill said.

"No, Bill. Come with me. I'll get you back to your apartment." Chris had known Bill's mental state had been dodgy, but he was harmless enough.

"We're going to die in here."

The inflection in Bill's voice caused prickles of gooseflesh to break out all over Chris's body. He reached tentatively for the monitor on his wrist. The man stepped forward again. Chris took a deep breath and dropped his hand away from his panic button. *He just needs help back to his apartment.*

Bill spoke again. There was a new edge to his voice, as if he was explaining how the universe worked. "There's nothing wrong outside. No one's getting sick. We shouldn't have locked ourselves in here." The man's demeanor changed once again, and this time, his voice grew *thicker* somehow. Chris thought Bill's voice turned angry, predatory. "Come out of this place, or I'll come in here and kill you all."

Bill pulled his arm out from the folds in his robe's sleeve, and a butcher's knife, one you would see in a chef's kitchen, materialized. He raised it over his head and ran forward. Chris hit the panic button on his wristband and stumbled backward.

Within seconds three guards charged from the control room, and careered toward Bill. Bill turned to face the new threat. Chris shouted for them to stop. The guards stopped, batons in hand.

Chris circled around to stand with the guards. He put a placating hand out, hoping to still the distraught man. "Please, Bill. Put the knife down. We can talk about this."

"No." The voice coming from Bill did not sound like Bill at all, Chris realized. "No talk. Die. All of you must die. You don't belong here."

Before Chris could do or say anything more, Bill—or whoever had control of Bill—dragged the sharp edge of the blade across his own throat. Blood bubbled from the wound in a crimson wave that soaked the front of Bill's robe. The man lost a river of blood in seconds and crumpled to the floor.

2.

November 1. 9:50 p.m.

Chris stared dumbly at the body in front of him. He had a crazy thought: *he's (it's) going to get up and come at me.* The guards surrounded Chris. He moved past the body and started down the hall at nearly a run. Two guards followed him.

He reached the end of the hall and turned left. He took this hall to the end and entered the infirmary. Dr. Hellen Jacobson looked up as Chris entered. Her smile faded.

"Chris, what's wrong?"

"We have a problem. Can you grab a gurney and follow me? If you have something like a sheet, bring that, too."

"Of course." Hellen pulled a clean white sheet from a tin linen closet in the corner, and grabbed a folded portable cot and pushed it toward the door. "What's happened?"

"There's been...an accident." Chris helped her pull the cot down the hall. The guards ran alongside them.

"Should I have grabbed a first aid kit?"

"It's too late for that, unfortunately."

As Chris stopped at the intersection and headed down the south corridor, and back toward Bill, he caught a glimpse of Hellen's concerned face. *I should warn her what she's about to see, but I don't have the words.*

"Bill Thomlinson killed himself."

The cot jerked as Hellen stopped momentarily. She recovered from the shock of Chris's words and pushed the cot in front of her again.

As they reached the body, they stopped. Chris watched as Hellen assessed the scene. She unhinged the cot and opened it. She pulled a pair of purple rubber gloves from her pocket and put them on. She pulled a second pair of gloves from her pocket and handed them to the nearest guard. She directed the guard to stand at the feet of the corpse.

I should be doing this. I should be helping to lift the body. But Chris couldn't bring himself to step up.

When Hellen unfolded the sheet, Chris helped her lay it out flat on the floor. She directed the guard to lift the feet, and she took the body under the shoulders. They carried Bill to the waiting sheet and placed him gently in the center of it. She tucked the sheet tightly around the body and they lifted the form onto the cot. She lifted rails on both sides of the gurney and clicked them into place. Blood quickly soaked through the white sheet.

Chris stared down at the puddle of blood on the floor. He felt cold, his skin felt clammy. *I'm going to pass out. Oh god, I'm going to pass out.* He shook off the panic settling into him and turned to Hellen. "What will we do with the body?"

She thought on the question for a moment before answering. "In the infirmary, I have a pharmacy. In the back is a separate room for cold storage. We can store him in there for now."

"But for how long?"

"Until such time that we can take him outside again, and bury him."

Chris felt that cold hand of panic reaching for his throat. He swallowed hard. *I'm not prepared for this. I didn't account for this happening. I can't…*

"How long can we hold him in there?"

"The body should be okay in there until the doors open again."

The body. She called him the body. She already doesn't see a human being anymore. I have to be clinical, too. It's no longer Bill. It's (something else) *just a body now.*

A dead body.

Chris remembered first meeting Bill. The old man was quirky, and a bit unbalanced, but he had been a harmless and friendly old man. Chris choked back a sob.

He glanced down and saw the man's slipper that had fallen off before the incident had taken place. He picked it up and set it on the gurney with him. The other slipper had fallen off after, and now sat in the puddle of blood. Chris looked up at the guard moving toward him, pushing a rolling bucket and a mop. Water sloshed from the bucket as the guard came to a stop.

They all have this under control. I have nothing to worry about. We'll get through this we'll…

Chris rushed to the nearest bathroom and threw up.

After cleaning himself up, Chris headed to his office inside the control room and sat in the cushioned chair. He couldn't sleep, not after that. Maybe not ever again.

Brian and Roger came to him when they had been told of the news. *I should tell them what I believe, what I saw – that it hadn't been Bill talking to him, but someone (something) else – but I just don't know how.*

So, he stayed quiet.

The voice that had come from Bill was not human. It had been guttural and savage. It was the voice of something *supernatural.* That was the only way to describe the voice Chris had heard. They will say Bill went stir crazy and was not in his right mind. He was speaking gibberish. *They will say I was in shock. They will treat me differently.*

But to Chris it wasn't gibberish at all. What Bill said was a definitive threat. And the threat wasn't over.

"I've been making my rounds in the hopes that something like this wouldn't happen. I missed his visit the past couple of days. Otherwise, maybe I would have seen this coming."

"This isn't your fault, Chris." Brian dropped down beside him. "You need to stop putting so much pressure on yourself. It's not your fault."

"Maybe not, but how do we prevent it from happening again? And what if it happens on a massive scale? We'd never be able to deal with a threat like that."

"This was a fluke," Roger said.

"We need to enact a new rule. We are going to institute a series of town hall meetings. Everyone must attend." Chris turned to Roger. "I want to know who we have with a background in mental health assessment. We're going to start monitoring everyone. What good is surviving the plague if we all go crazy in the end?"

Chris called Gerard to him. The big guard stood over Chris. "I'm giving you complete access to the Ark. I want to set up mental health stations on every floor. I want people to report anything out of the ordinary. If they are having trouble sleeping, I want to know about it."

"Setting up a gathering of this size is not going to be easy." Gerard folded his arms.

"I don't care, no matter what the complications are, I want it to happen. I can't…" He tried again. "We can't lose any more people the way we lost Bill."

When everyone filed out of the office, and only Brian and Chris were left, Brian sat in a chair next to him. Chris looked at him, knowing he had something to say and waiting for him to say it. Brian stared at Chris for a moment before speaking.

"I just want you to face the possibility that this type of thing can't be avoided. It can't be helped if people decide they can't take the isolation anymore. It's a risk one takes in a situation like this. I don't want you to drive yourself crazy trying to control something that is out of your control. Do you hear what I'm saying?"

"I do. And I understand. But…" Chris considered telling Brian what he believed.

"What has you so scared, Chris. I see it in your eyes. You're not telling me something."

Chris looked at the door. It was closed. They were alone. Brian would understand.

"Something was in Bill."

"Yeah, it's insanity. He was ill."

"Maybe, but there was something else. Something sinister. It spoke through Bill. Whatever it was, it didn't like that we trapped ourselves in here. It said it wanted to kill us all. I want to make sure it doesn't have the chance to get in again."

"Whatever Bill said, whatever he had planned to do with that knife, he's gone now. He's no longer a threat."

He doesn't understand what I'm saying. Or he doesn't want to hear.

Brian put an arm around him. Chris saw the concern in his friend's eyes. He saw compassion there. What he didn't see was understanding. *I'm alone with this.* Chris leaned into Brian's shoulder. He was suddenly very tired.

Chris sat up and looked into Brian's gaze. "What if Nancy did the right thing by not staying? What if we, here in the Ark, are the ones who are doomed to be exterminated?"

"You're exhausted. You're in shock. You just witnessed a horrific thing, and now your imagination is getting away from you. Come with me. I'm going to take care of you for a change. We're going to see Dr. Jacobson and she's going to prescribe you something to help you sleep. You'll feel better in the morning, I promise."

Chris let Brian lead him out of the office, and he suddenly felt every bit the child Margot had accused him of being.

3.

November 2.

Gerard stood in a darkened room. The figure in the recliner sat unmoving. "The Chosen One's plan concerns me. He will know there are people missing. We have to stop this from happening."

"Chris gave you the keys to the kingdom, my boy. What could possibly be worrying you?"

"The plan. He plans to account for very person within the Ark."

"A plan like this takes time to develop," the stony voice said. "If and when the truth about the two intruders is revealed, it will already be too late. We will have completed our goal."

"How much longer before we can put our own plan into action?" Gerard asked.

"Be patient. Do not act rash again. When the time is right you will know. I will know, and I will then tell you. Do not act without my permission again."

"I won't." Gerard's tone was obedient but with a touch of defiance.

"Now go. I want to be alone with my thoughts so I can figure out where we go from here."

Gerard turned and headed out of the dark room. In the hallway, he headed left to the elevators. He took the lift to the main floor.

Gerard relieved Rick as front guard of the control room.

"Meet me in the gym at six?" Rick asked him.

Gerard stared at rick for a moment. He had no time or interest in going to the gym that night. He had more pressing matters to contend with. "I can't make it."

"Okay. I'll see if Brian wants a workout partner."

Gerard glared at the other guard. After a moment, he said, "You do that."

4.

November 12.

Chris looked up from his desk as Gerard entered the room. The guard pushed a utility cart in front of him. On the cart were the thousands of paper files on every member of the Ark, excluding of course, Chris's family members.

The size of the project facing him caused his heart to palpitate. *I have to go through every file and look for signs of mental illness on each member of the Ark.* During the planning stage of the Ark's construction, Chris had considered putting all this info on computers, but he had no idea if there would be power in the new world. He collected files on every member, from jobs they had as teenager, down to their most recent doctor's appointments.

"Thank you, Gerard. You can just leave the cart where it is." Chris picked up a handful of manila folders and tossed them down on his desk.

Gerard exited the office without speaking.

Chris skimmed through the files on his desk; paper after paper, with the list of names for every person within the Ark. He knew most of the people in those files very well, some not so much. Bill had been well known to Chris, and still he fell victim to…whatever it was that happened to him. Chris's shoulders sagged. He felt the strain of his monumental task in his neck, and he rubbed at the pain.

Chris glanced over at Roger sitting in the recliner. "I need you to do something."

"Of course, what is it?" Roger stood.

"Sort these files by floors. There are two hundred floors with roughly thirty to forty people on each floor. I want someone on each floor to meet with each resident on that floor." He spoke quickly. "We're going to ask them a series of questions, looking for anyone with stressors or signs of depression. If they're suffering from cabin fever, I'll weed it out and combat it, one at a time if I have to. I need to find anyone who has a background in psychology to get us started."

Chris turned to Roger suddenly and stared at the man. Roger stopped moving, waiting for Chris to speak.

"A party."

"A party, Chris?"

Chris turned back to the files. He stared down at them as if they were the enemy. "A party. Everyone's invited. Nothing chases away the blues like a party."

"You wish to host a party for all six thousand plus residents of the Ark?"

Chris's head swiveled to face Roger. "Don't sound so shocked. We can do it."

5.

November 30.

Chris stood just inside of the gigantic ballroom on the top floor. Brian stood to his left, and Scott to his right. He knew they were looking at him, waiting for him to explain why they were there, but he didn't oblige them just yet.

"When I first had the dream of everyone in the world dying, I refused to believe it. Couldn't be true, I said." Chris looked at Brian. He walked a few paces away and turned, facing them. "I thought I was going crazy when the dream persisted. And then when I heard the voice in my head telling me to prepare, I didn't think it anymore—I *knew* I was crazy." Chris looked down at his feet. "Not long after that, the people started showing up. At first there were just a few. Roger was one of the first. After that there were hundreds. They kept asking what I needed them to do. I knew the answer. I had a dream telling me all the specifics of the Ark. I didn't understand what I was seeing, so I asked for architects. There were hundreds of architects and engineers at my command. I was not crazy after all. Everything I had envisioned began to come true. The workers did as I asked, and I pointed out what needed to be changed if they strayed off track. The money came pouring in. Everyone gave every cent they had to make what I envisioned a reality. No one ever questioned, even once, why I was doing this, or how it would benefit them. When the Ark was finished, they just started moving in. This has been my life for so long, I stopped questioning it."

Scott raised a hand to ask a question. "So, why are you telling us this…I mean, why now?"

Chris looked at him. "I want to know where you stand—"

Scott answered immediately. "With you, Chris. Always."

Brian nodded agreement.

Chris released a long-held breath. "I'm happy to hear that. But what I'm really asking is how much of what I've been doing do you stand behind? I need to know if you can indulge me a little longer?"

"How much farther do we need to take this?" Brian looked at Scott and back at Chris. "I'm here all the way."

"Me, too, Brother," Scott said.

"Why do I feel like you're about to tell us something that just might blow our minds?" Brian chuckled.

"It just might." Chris turned and looked down the length of the giant banquet hall. He backed up until he was once again standing between the others. "I'm going to try and get every resident of the Ark up here in this room."

The others said nothing for a long time.

Finally, Scott said, "Kaylan is going to freak if you don't let her decorate."

They walked out of the room together. Chris followed them down the hall, but as Scott and Brian headed around the corner to the right, toward the apartments, Chris continued going straight, toward the elevators.

Chris headed down to the Holmes's residence and knocked. When Derek answered the door, he immediately reached out and grabbed Chris by the hand. He shook it vigorously and then pulled him in. He closed the door behind them.

Patty worked the wheels of her chair, meeting Chris half way.

"Look at you, getting around on your own." Chris squatted down so Patty didn't have to look up.

"We were just on our way to the hydroponic garden."

"Great. I won't keep you then. I just wanted to know if you had any party supplies I could borrow?"

"What kind of party supplies?"

"I guess it's going to be a New Year's Eve party."

She motioned to her son. "Derek, take Chris into the room and show him where they are."

Chris stood and followed Derek into the master bedroom. Derek walked over to an object in the corner of the room that looked like a low table with a lacy white cloth covering it. When

Derek removed the cloth, Chris saw that the object was not a table but a chest. Derek flipped the latches and lifted the lid. Inside, Derek began removing boxes until he found what he was looking for.

One box was marked with a Christmas tree, and one was marked with a birthday cake. He set those aside and pulled out a box marked with streamers and party favors.

"Is this what you're looking for?" Derek's loud voice echoed in the room.

Chris opened the cardboard box and saw streamers and balloons in every color. "It's perfect, Derek. Thank you."

"Is it enough?" he asked.

Chris laughed. "I'm hoping there will be others with a few supplies as well. I have a lot of space to decorate."

"These will make the party look pretty."

"Yes, they will." Chris closed the box and lifted it off the floor.

Derek placed the rest of the boxes back in the chest and closed it. He replaced the lacy cloth and walked Chris back to the living room.

"Will those suit your needs?" Patty asked.

"Yes, they're perfect. Thank you."

Chris walked with them to the elevator. They took the first one down and he took the following elevator back to the top floor. He set the box down inside the ballroom.

I'll send Roger out to collect more decorations.

His stomach growled.

He headed for the elevators and took it down to the Jungle Café.

Some of Margot's cooking would really hit the spot right about now.

He entered the café. Drums beat a soft rhythm in the background. He walked past a table with a couple sitting across from each other, eating quietly. *She looks mad about something, and he looks bored.* He sat near the door to the kitchen. A moment later Carrie came out to take his order. She didn't look at him.

"What can I get you?" she asked.

"How are you, Carrie? I've been meaning to…"

"I've been good. Thanks for asking. What can I get you?"

Okay, then. No small talk it is. "I guess I'll have a burger and fries."

Carrie turned and scurried into the kitchen.

Chris glanced around at the other diners. An older couple near the entrance seemed especially jovial, leaning toward each other, and laughing like teenagers on a date. *Good for them.*

Carrie returned with his food and he thanked her. "Is Margot cooking?"

"No, my dad cooked it. But he taught her so it should be good."

"I'm sure it is." When Carrie turned to leave, Chris spoke again. "I didn't mean it that way. I was just wondering where she was, that's all."

Carrie shifted her weight. "I wouldn't know where she is."

"Have a seat with me. I'll share my fries."

"I have other guests to…"

"There is hardly anyone in here, and they already have their food. You can spare a moment to sit with me."

Carrie looked around. *She's looking for an excuse.* After a moment, she sat. His smile was not reciprocated.

"I never thought you were like that," she said.

"Like what?" Chris's smile faded.

"Bossy."

"I'm not bossy…am I?" He had never meant to give her that impression. "I didn't mean to offend you."

"I'm not offended."

"Why don't you like me. What did I do to offend you?"

"I like you just fine." She glanced at him, but when his eyes met hers, she turned away. "I have nothing against you."

"Something about me bothers you, what is it?"

Carrie took a deep breath and exhaled slowly. "It actually has nothing to do with you, and everything to do with my father. I have a boyfriend. I love him with all my heart, and he was not allowed to come. I am offended that the real love of my life is out there and might be dead soon because my father didn't approve of him."

Chris tried to swallow the lump that formed in his throat. He had invited Scott, Kaylan, Brian and Nancy—not to mention the two other families—into the Ark. *She hates me because I used my privileges to protect those I love, while she has to watch her boyfriend die. I'm a monster.* "I would have demanded he be allowed in. I wish I had known."

Carrie reached across the table and took Chris's hand. "I don't blame you. You couldn't have known."

"What is his name, your boyfriend?"

"Jeremy Ferguson."

A moment of quiet passed between them before Chris asked his next question. "Do you stay in contact with him?"

Carrie stared at him a moment before responding. "How would I do that? And is it a good idea. I mean, people are going to die, right?"

"If you love him, you should want to see him, no matter what his fate might be. But it is possible that not everyone will die."

"Still, how would we stay in touch with each other if he's out there and I'm in here?"

"I'll work out the details."

Carrie stood. Chris went back to his meal, excited about the prospect of helping reunite Carrie with her lost love.

6.

Chris entered the kitchen. He reached into the fridge and pulled out a carton of orange juice, poured himself a glass and gulped it down.

Brian entered the kitchen yawning and scratching his face. "Hey," he said to Chris.

"Hey."

Brian dumped cereal into a bowl and poured milk over it. He scooped up a spoonful and crammed it into his mouth. He dropped down into a chair, holding the bowl under his chin.

Chris drank the rest of his juice and put the glass in the dishwasher. He sat down next to Brian.

"I need a favor."

"Shoot." Brian struggled to keep his mouthful of cereal from spraying out.

"From Nancy."

Brian stopped chewing. "What?"

"I found out last night that Carrie left a boyfriend out in the world. I want to know if Nancy would find him and help him set up a skype account."

"I'll ask her. What happened? Date didn't go well?"

Chris laughed, a soundless chuckle that was less humor and more disdain. "You could say that. But it wasn't going to work out. I knew that. Then I found out about the boyfriend. I want to try and get them reunited, since I wasn't able to get him into the Ark with us."

"I don't understand. You could have brought him in?"

"No, I never knew he existed."

"So then why is it your fault?"

Chris exhaled. "It's not."

Brian shrugged. "Whatever. I'll talk to Nancy about it today. I'm sure there's some way for her to get in touch with him. Maybe if he's not too far away she can visit."

"That would be great."

"No promises."

Chris put his hands up in supplication. "Of course, not."

Brian stared at him. He shook his head, smiling. "You're really something. You know that?"

Chris stood and headed for the door. "I know."

Chapter Seven

1.

December 2. Six-fifteen p.m., Crimean time.

The boy kicked the soccer ball down the street to his home. He looked up the street toward the west, and shielded his eyes from the setting sun. He saw a military vehicle parked there. He turned toward the house, where his mother had stepped out onto the front stoop. She saw the vehicle, too, and when she spoke there was a touch of urgency in her voice.

"Vremya, chtoby priyti na uzhin, Piter." *Time to come in for dinner, Peter.*

"Chto u nas na uzhin, mat'?" *What is for dinner, Mother?* He did not turn away from the military vehicle as he spoke.

The mother replied, but Peter didn't hear what she said. He was too curious about the lone soldier on his street.

Peter picked up his ball and started toward the house. Peter's mother sighed with relief and dipped back inside. She did not see when Peter dropped his ball near the steps and walked back out to the road. He headed east, toward the jeep. He stopped at the driver's side door and looked in at the man slumped over the wheel.

The man was wearing the uniform of a Russian soldier. Peter was a Crimean resident, and he was used to seeing Russian soldiers, but not alone. And this one appeared to be…sick. He knocked on the glass. The soldier sat up but only looked straight ahead. Peter knocked on the glass again. The soldier's head turned slowly, and the man's glassy eyes searched for the source of the sound that had awakened him. When he spotted the boy standing outside his vehicle, the man rolled down the window. He seemed to have trouble holding his head up.

Peter asked, "dyaden'ka, ty v poryadke?" *Mister, are you okay?*

136

The soldier, head swaying, stared at the boy for a long time before speaking. "Idi domoy." *Go home.*

Peter didn't move. He thought he should get a medic for the soldier. The man did not look well at all. He turned toward his house, wondering if his mother would help the soldier. She had a secret hatred for the Russian soldiers. She was not one of the sympathizers of the Russian occupation. Although she and her family, as well as many of her Crimean brethren, spoke Russian, they did not want to be considered Russian. She was Ukrainian, and would always feel that way. She explained all this to Peter, then told him to be wary of Russian soldiers.

But Peter was inquisitive, and he believed all of mankind should be tolerant of one another. He had made up his mind to ask the Russian soldier to follow him to his house, but when he turned back to tell the man his mother could help him, the soldier coughed. Droplets of sputum rolled down Peter's face. He wiped it away.

"Idi domoy," the man said again and rolled the window back up.

Peter turned away from the jeep and walked back to his house.

As he entered, his mother asked him what took him so long. Peter didn't reply. He didn't need to. His mother had already moved on to serving some kind of hot, steaming soup into a bowl. She placed the bowl in front of Peter, but tsked him when he reached for the spoon.

"Moyte ruki pervyye." *Wash your hands first.*

Peter ran off to the bathroom and washed his hands. When he returned, he jumped back into his seat and lifted his spoon. He sniffed the food, and wrinkled his nose. "Mamochki, yeda plokho pakhnet." *Momma, the food smells bad.*

Peter then coughed into his bowl.

His mother turned away from the sink. She looked at Peter and thought he seemed ill. She walked over and placed a hand to his forehead. He felt hot.

"Yeda plokho." *The food is bad.*

His mother tested the soup. It tasted fine to her. She told him to go to his room and lay down. He jumped off his seat but stopped and swayed on his legs, afraid they would give out under him. When he felt steady again he took a step toward his room.

He stopped again, leaned forward, and vomited.

2.

December 2.

Eleven-fifteen a.m., Eastern Standard Time.

Carrie looked up from the table she was clearing and saw Chris enter the café. His friend, Brian, followed close behind. They both wore broad smiles on their faces. The hairs on the back of her neck tingled. *Why can't he just leave me alone, and let me suffer through my misery in peace?* Chris moved in front of her cart and blocked her from pushing it back to the kitchen.

"Excuse me," she said.

"Would be willing to do me a favor?" Chris said.

Her hairs stood up again. This time a chill crawled on her skin, accompanying the hairs. *No, actually, I don't want to do you a favor.* "What kind of favor?"

"It's the good kind," he said.

"Okay, but what is it?"

"I want you to go with Brian."

"Go? I can't go. I have to…and the…" She struggled to come up with an excuse, but nothing was coming to mind.

"Don't worry about work. I'll cover for you," Chris said.

Carrie glanced toward the kitchen door. *Come on, Dad. Pop out and tell me you need me to do something for you, urgently.* But she knew he was fine on his own in there, and would not be coming to her rescue. Reluctantly, she removed her apron and handed it to Chris. "I can't be gone long. Are you sure you can handle serving if I'm not back before the lunch crowd shows up? It can get pretty hectic."

"I'm sure I can handle it. Just go."

Carrie followed Brian out of the restaurant, wary but obedient. They took the elevator down to the first floor. *Thank you, Brian, for not trying to engage in small talk.* She followed him to a door that opened automatically as they stepped in front of it.

"This is known as the skype room." He led her down an aisle to a monitor that was already loaded up. He motioned for her to sit, and she did looking at him. He pointed to the screen.

She glanced at the screen. "What am I looking at, I mean besides my own image on a computer monitor?"

Brian didn't answer. Instead, he used the mouse to click the button labelled CALL. After a moment, the image of Carrie was replaced by a blur of movement on the screen. When the pixels reformed themselves, a new face appeared on the monitor.

It was Jeremy.

A hand flew up to Carrie's mouth.

"Hi, Babe," he said.

She tried to speak but her voice caught in her throat like a chicken bone. She felt a rush of heat throughout her body and her eyes grew wet, blurring her vision.

She grinned.

"It's really you?" she said when she had gained control of her voice again.

"It's me. I've missed you so much. How is your adventure going? I'm not sure where you went, or why, but I miss you. Will you be coming back soon?"

She looked at Brian, confused. *He doesn't know.*

Carrie wiped at her eyes. *He doesn't know and I can't tell him.* "My dad brought us to a place where we could help people. It was last minute, and he gave us no time to prepare. I'm sorry."

"Like a missionary?"

"Yes," she said. "Exactly. We'll be gone for a few months. I hope to return to you very soon, though. I've missed you so much. You don't know what it means to me to get to see you again. I've been so depressed without you here. I wish you could have come, too."

"Me, too, Babe. I'd go to the ends of the earth with you." He laughed. *Oh, how I've missed that laugh.*

Carrie's heart beat a rapid thump/thump in her chest, and her mind turned giddy. She longed to feel his rough hands on her skin, and his bristly facial hair on her cheek. The man had five o'clock shadow no matter how close he shaved. She wanted to kiss him.

"How did you…" She tried again.

"Where…when…How did they find you?"

"The man who's there with you, Brian? He did it. Him and his wife looked me up. She came right to my house and told me to get a skype account. I said I wouldn't until they told me what it was all about. Once I knew what was going on I didn't hesitate. I miss you so much, Care. Nancy helped me set up the account, and Brian—and some guy named Chris—came on and told me they were there with you, but that your location was a secret. They said something about a jungle? I always knew you had a thing for animals. Have you been able to see any in the wild?"

Tears threatened to spring to her eyes but she kept them back. "No, not yet. Right now, I spend all my time feeding the natives." She laughed at her own choice of words. She wasn't happy about deceiving him, but there was plenty of time later for the truth. She didn't want to sully this moment with questions she didn't know how to—or couldn't—answer. She just wanted to look at him, and hear his voice. She was lost in his smile, his words. She let him talk and talk. When he asked her a question, she provided a curt, polite response and asked him a question in return. He could talk, that boy, and she was happy to listen. Then the time moved on and she had been skyping for nearly two hours, she sadly explained that she would have to go.

"Will you be back on tomorrow?" he asked.

"I will," she said. "Is the same time good for you?"

"Yes, absolutely. I'll look for you."

"I'll see you tomorrow then. I love you."

"I love you."

She clicked the end call and pushed away from the table. She stood and turned to Brian.

But he wasn't there. She hadn't noticed when he left, but clearly, he had done so to give her privacy.

I agreed to see him again tomorrow, but I don't know if Chris will be able to cover for me. Her foolishness caused heat to rise in her cheeks.

She rushed back to the café where Chris was placing a plate of food in front of a woman diner. As he turned to walk away from the table, she rushed into his arms and hugged him. She pulled the apron off him and tied it onto herself. "I agreed to skype with him again, if you can cover the shift again." She wiped nervous sweat from her hands onto her apron.

"As often as you need me." Chris grinned up at her as she stood over him. She rushed into the kitchen.

Margot stepped though the entrance and approached Carrie and Chris. "Okay, what's going on? My mopey sister is *smiling*."

"I just skyped with Jeremy. We are going to do it again tomorrow. Think Daddy will freak when he finds out?"

Margot nodded. "I won't tell him. I don't remember when I've seen you so happy."

"Chris set this all up. I owe him so much for this. He is such a great guy."

"Yeah, he's such a nice guy."

Carrie rushed through the kitchen door to finish her shift.

3.

December 8.

Scott watched as Kaylan struggled to hang a streamer over her head. He chuckled under his breath. *I should help, but I can't stop looking at that cute butt.*

"Do you need help?"

She turned and looked at him. The look caused him to cringe. He backed away.

"Maybe if you used a chair, you wouldn't have to struggle so hard."

"I have this. Why don't you find something else to do for now?"

"I want to help."

"Sweetie, don't take this the wrong way, but if you left, that would be a big help."

"You sure?"

"I'm sure."

Scott pulled a chair over to where she was struggling to decorate. She huffed, but allowed him to help her onto the chair. He held the chair as she stood on her toes reaching up. Scott had a perfect view of her behind from where he stood, and couldn't help himself from reaching up and cupping one firm buttock.

"Stop that." She swiped at his hand.

Laughing, Scott reached up higher, moving toward her stomach. She squirmed, anticipating the tickle, and the chair wobbled and Kaylan fell.

Scott caught her and carried her to a table and sat her down. He stood between her legs and leaned in, kissed her.

"You're going to make this task impossible to finish." She teased his neck with her lips.

His breath caught in his throat, and he pushed harder against her, his erection a throbbing heat in his groin. He pressed his lips to hers, and lowered her head to the table. As she lay across the table on her back, legs dangling off the edge, Scott lifted himself onto the table and straddled her.

Kaylan squirmed under him. "You're going to break the table." Her voice was a soft whisper in his ear.

He ignored her complaint and unfastened his jeans. He did the same for her. She stopped protesting and helped him push her slacks down her thighs. He nudged his waistband down, cherishing the quick intake of breath she made as he entered her. He thrust against her hips, causing the table to scrape against the floor. He pressed his face into her hair, struggling to keep from laughing.

Her fingernails dug into his back. The pain took the giggles away and he gasped. As their passion intensified, the table shook. Kaylan cried out. Scott concentrated on the act of his lovemaking, wanting it to last, but feeling the buildup of his excitement reaching its peak.

He cried out arching his back. Kaylan whimpered and moaned beneath him.

Something cracked, and the table lurched. Kaylan cried out. Scott collapsed and lay motionless on top of her.

The table dipped on one side, unwilling to bear their weight any longer. They dropped, sliding toward the floor where the legs had buckled.

They lay entangled in each other's limbs, laughing and breathless

After redressing, Kaylan dragged Scott to the door.

"But I want to stay."

She opened the door and shoved him through it.

As she closed the door, he put a hand in the way. "Do you realize what we did?"

"You mean breaking a perfectly good table, that we will now have to explain?"

"Besides, that."

"What did we do?" She moved into the doorframe, preventing him from reentering.

He glanced around himself, not looking at anything in particular, then back at her. "This floor is about a mile up in the sky, right?"

She waited, not answering.

"We just joined the mile-high club."

She leaned toward him, smiling. "Great." She kissed him. "Now, go." She closed the door, shutting him out.

Well, I'm *impressed with us.*

He walked down to the elevators and pressed the button. The doors opened and he stepped in. He ordered the lift to take him to the bottom floor. He walked to the control room, looking for Chris. Instead, he found Brian.

As Brian sat in a chair next to Toby, studying one of the many monitors, Scott leaned against the console. "Seen Chris around? I'm bored, and Kaylan kicked me off the decoration committee."

"I have no idea where Chris is, but Roger's looking for help. He's in the main storage room at the end of the west hall."

Scott glanced over the monitors. He saw protesters on the camera outside the fence. Though there was no sound, there was clearly people shouting out there. The protesters were looking toward the cameras and shaking their fists.

How long before they find a way to tear those cameras down?

"What are you doing? I thought you usually helped Roger?"

"Today I'm learning how to monitor the control room."

Scott walked out and headed down the west hall. At the end, he entered the storage room door to the left of the hall. He stopped, just inside the door and glanced around. Roger struggled with a large bag of something in the middle aisle. Scott rushed over and helped him lift it.

"Thank you," Roger said.

They lowered the sack into a wagon hitched to the back of a golf cart.

"Need help with anything?"

"I need this delivered."

Scott glanced at the contents of the wagon. He saw spades and shovels. The bag he had helped Roger with was fertilizer. "To the hydroponic garden?"

"Yes. You know where it is?"

"Yep." Scott dropped into the driver's seat of the golf cart.

Scott drove the cart and attached wagon to the garden. He helped the garden's attendant there unload the fifty pound bags of fertilizer, and other supplies.

"Good to see you're hard at work, young man."

Scott turned around. Ethel stood wearing a pair of gardening gloves, holding a hand spade in one hand, and a pair of pruning shears in the other. At her feet was a basket with a few snipped flowers laying in it. She looked down.

"I like to add fresh tulips to my home. Adds a splash of color."

Those tools look more like weapons in her hands. He stifled a bout of giggles at the thought. *Luckily, her only casualties are those flowers.*

"Where is your sweet wife?" Her expression was pleasant enough, but he wasn't buying it.

Scott lifted his chin. "She's off doing her own thing."

"I haven't seen you in the restaurant lately. I got used to sitting with you."

"We eat at odd times. I'll let Kaylan know you asked about her."

"Oh, that would be nice."

Scott couldn't be sure—as dense as he was when it came to social situations—but her reply seemed to drip with sarcasm. Was she seriously being condescending, or was she just that inept when it came to every day conversations?

He smiled at her and walked away.

He rode the golf cart back to the storage room for a new task. He felt a moment of discouragement when he saw that Roger wasn't there.

Scott unhooked the empty wagon from the golf cart and drove it out of the storage room, down the hall, and stopped at the infirmary. Inside, the resident doctor looked up at Scott from her desk.

"Ah, my first patient of the day," Doctor Hellen Jacobson said. She was a psychiatrist, but with her medical training was more useful as a doctor in the infirmary.

"I'm afraid not, Doc," Scott said. "I'm just looking for something to do. I was wondering if you had a task you've been too busy to complete, or an errand that needed running."

Hellen laced her fingers together and placed them on her desk. "I'm afraid not. There is very little for a doctor to do inside the Ark. We are cursed with uncommonly healthy residents." Dr. Jacobson laughed. "The most effective use of my facilities has been as the morgue for Bill."

Gruesome thought, but okay.

"If I come up with something I'll flag you down."

"That would be great. Thank you."

Scott exited the Infirmary. He drove the cart back toward the control room, and found Roger.

"What's next?" Scott asked.

Roger sighed. "I have nothing. Come back tomorrow if you wish."

Scott hopped off the cart and allowed Roger to drive it back to the storage room.

Brian exited the control room. He glanced up at Scott. "Did Roger find something for you to do?"

"Yea, but now I'm right back where I started."

"I'm headed to the gym," Brian said. "feel free to join me. An extra workout partner is always welcome."

"That would be great, But I'd have to go all the way up to my place to get a change of clothes."

Brian laughed. "Not here. There are clean workout clothes at the gym. You should be able to find something that fits you.

"Really?" Scott chuckled. "This place is amazing."

"It's paradise."

Brian led Scott to the gym. "I met friends there and have been working out with them on occasion, but it'll be nice to be with a *real* friend for a change, if you know what I mean. The one guy, Gerard, is a cold fish."

"I think I've met him. He's the guard, right?"

"Yes, and he takes his job seriously. I catch him looking at me and it's like he's plotting something, or waiting for me to plot something so he can take me down. I don't trust him."

"Have you mentioned this to Chris?"

"Nah, it's not that serious. It's me, actually. I've been feeling paranoid lately. Some people seem to not like us 'non-believers' being here."

Scott laughed at the mocking tone as Brian said non-believers. "Sorry. Actually, I've been feeling that way, too. And so has Kaylan, I think."

"I just thought you might want to know, in case we run into them. The other guy is Rick. He's cool. A bit of a talker, but that's not such a bad thing."

As they entered the gym, they discovered Gerard wasn't there. Nor was Rick. In fact, for the duration of their workout, Scott and Brian had the gym to themselves.

4.

December 10.

Doctor Stephen Bartlett stepped through the plastic lining, and into the tent. There were fifty cots with a patient on each one. There were more patients sitting in chairs toward the back of the tent. Inside the protective hazmat suit, his breath sounded foreign to him; as if someone behind him was breathing in his ear, and it was not his own breath at all. But he was a doctor with the World Health Origination, and was used to wearing such bulky, uncomfortable—and cumbersome—suits. It came with the territory, he supposed.

He spent some time looking over the charts, but there was nothing on them that would help him understand the situation. He walked past the cots, and past the people sitting in chairs. Some people reached out, begging for help. He avoided their groping hands and moved into the very back of the tent. He gulped as he passed through the flap and looked around.

There were hundreds of bodies piled up back here; dead bodies of those who had already succumbed to the illness. He exited the tent through the long tube that ran from the tent to the makeshift operation headquarters. He unzipped the flap at the end of the clear plastic tunnel and stepped through to a smaller tent. He zipped the flap back up and walked over to a small square, wooden box painted bright orange and stepped in. He tugged on the cord and a warm, soapy liquid sprayed down on him from above. He stayed under the spray, lifting his arms and turning around and around, for the required five-minute duration, ensuring that no microorganisms escaped the quarantine zone. When the spray ended, he stepped out of the second tent and stripped out of his hazmat suit.

"Who's in charge here?" His English accent revealed that he was of Northern English origins, most likely from the Whitfield area.

"That would be me, sir." The Belorussian man in green fatigues stepped forward. His Russian accent was thick, but he spoke English well enough.

"What is your name?" Dr. Bartlett asked.

"National Guard Commander, Vladimir Konstantinov."

The doctor glanced at the man, twice. "Thank you, Vlad. May I call you that?"

The man nodded.

"Can you tell me how many PUIs are in this camp?"

Vlad stared blankly at the doctor. "PUIs?"

"Patients under investigation." Dr. Bartlett sighed. "Is there someone with medical training I can talk to?"

Commander Vladimir waved at another soldier, and a woman in a white lab coat was brought forward. Dr. Bartlett shook her hand. She introduced herself as Dr. Malvina Alkaev.

"Can you tell me what's going on here?"

"Yes, we have been bringing in the sick from the surrounding villages to this place. The illness hits fast, and kills even faster. We cannot understand how to stop the disease's progression."

"What is the incubation period, and how long after symptoms appear do the affected expire?" Bartlett asked.

"It appears that the incubation period is alarmingly short, we surmise that, within minutes of exposure, the patient is infected.

Ten days after the patient presents with symptoms, the patient dies. It's fast, no? Too fast."

"Not really," Bartlett said. "The Ebola virus tends to kill very quickly."

"It's not Ebola."

"What?" Dr. Bartlett looked at her, incredulous, as if he were talking to an idiot child.

"The patients show symptoms of Ebola, but test negative. The illness appears to be bacterial in nature, although no known antibiotics seem to be effective."

"You don't say…" Bartlett looked around, hoping for someone else to speak to.

"It's uncanny that we cannot pinpoint how and when the infection is spread. Two patients who have no known ties to one another, in two separate and remote locations, will come down with the illness at the same time."

"That makes no sense."

"I agree. It defies explanation." Malvina called for her notes, and when she received them, she handed them over to Dr. Bartlett. The notes consisted of lists of names, locations and symptoms presented. There was chart after chart of tests that had been run and the results. Nothing seemed to make sense to Bartlett.

"Your notes are thorough, but one detail isn't listed. What is the survival rate?" He handed the notes back to Malvina.

She didn't bother checking her notes. "Zero."

"What?" Dr. Bartlett couldn't have heard her correctly.

"As of this moment," she said in a hushed tone, as if this was the best kept secret. "Every patient who contracted the disease, has died."

Bartlett looked around at the people in the encampment. He wondered how many of them would get sick. Surely, they couldn't contain this illness forever. He casually coughed into his hand. Ten days later, he died.

5.

December 15.

Kaylan placed a balloon on the nozzle of the helium tank and released the gas. The balloon slowly expanded to the size she wanted, and she stopped the release. With dexterous fingers, she tied the balloon off without losing any of the gas. She tied a string around the knot and let it float to the ceiling. In all, about one hundred multicolored balloons bobbled and swayed above her head, their strings dangling like colorful tails.

Word had gotten around that the disease Chris had predicted had begun to infect the earth. News reports put the latest cases in Eastern Europe. Hundreds of thousands, dead.

Kaylan didn't feel in the mood to party anymore. In her heart, she had always thought Chris was wrong about the disease, and their stay in the Ark would just be an elaborate vacation. She had a mother and father out there. She had a sister. She asked them to come with her, but when they refused, she didn't push it. Why didn't she push it? Her hands shook as she lifted another balloon to the nozzle. Without any relish, she filled another balloon. It floated up and joined the others.

The feeling of being in a perpetual party had been replaced by a feeling of being trapped in a hellish prison…or a tomb. She dropped the deflated balloon and pushed the helium tank away. "I can't do this anymore."

"The balloons? Are your fingers getting sore?" Carrie walked over to Kaylan.

Carrie and Margot had agreed to help with the decorating and had joined her after their shift at the restaurant ended.

Kaylan looked up at her. "I can't do any of it. I can't pretend I'm not upset about people dying while we sit safely inside our steel cage."

"This isn't new news, Kaylan. We planned for this. If you didn't believe it would really happen, why did you agree to come to the Ark in the first place?"

"I'm always up for the next good time. It promised to be mad fun. And besides, Scott insisted on supporting Chris, and I go where he goes."

"If I'm being honest, I'm only here because my father insisted I come. Margot, too, I think. After hearing about the deaths in Europe, I'm glad I'm here."

"I guess so am I, but I have friends out there, family, too. They're in danger and I can't help them."

Kaylan mentally kicked herself.

"I'm sorry. I'm acting like I'm the only one with problems. Jeremy is out there, too, I know."

Carrie pulled a seat over and sat down next to Kaylan. "Yea, someone I love deeply is out there. But we can't beat ourselves up for being the fortunate ones. We can only make the most of what time we have, and be grateful when we wake up in the morning. Jeremy has no idea what's coming and I want to keep it that way. I feel horrible enough leaving him behind, I'm not going to corrupt whatever time he might have left stressing over the future. It might be selfish of me not to warn him—and believe me, if there was anything he could do to protect himself, I'd tell him to do it— but warning him will do no good."

"I believe that, too. That's why I've cut all ties. I can't skype with my folks. I'll take one look at them and start crying. They'll know something is up right away. Oh sure, they won't believe— not at first—but I'll know the truth."

"We're just going to have to get through this together. We'll have each other."

"I'm so happy to hear you say that," Kaylan said. "I've been feeling like an outsider looking in. You just made me feel like I'm a part of the inside."

Carrie smiled. "Well, to be honest, I feel like any outsider myself. I'm not a True Believer. That's my father. But we can be outsiders looking in together."

"Sounds good to me."

Kaylan leaned over and hugged Carrie. Carrie reciprocated. As they pulled back, Margot glanced over at them.

"She's going to wonder why we stopped decorating."

Kaylan glanced at Margot, but her mind was still circling around the plague. "I can't believe Chris is still going to go through with this party, knowing what's happening out there. It just doesn't feel right to me."

Carrie turned to Kaylan. The slight smile on her face faded. "Now more than ever the people need this party. They need to forget about what's happening out there, or we might all go insane. It is terrible, the world suffering like this, but there is nothing we can do to stop it."

"I understand all that, but in my head, it still feels wrong."

Carrie didn't speak. Kaylan knew there was nothing else to say. Carrie had pretty much said it all. Kaylan felt better having spoken to her. She still wasn't in the partying mood, but she no longer felt angry about it. This party was to celebrate the people who were going to live.

The door opened behind them. Kaylan turned and saw Chris walking toward them.

Margot walked over, too.

"These two insubordinates have been slacking off for the last fifteen minutes."

"I think I can forgive them this one time. They are working for free after all."

Chris glanced at Kaylan. There was concern in his eyes. "Are you doing okay?"

"Yeah." Kaylan glanced briefly at Carrie, turned back to Chris. "Yeah, I'm doing okay."

Chris looked into her eyes for a moment longer. When she smiled, and lifted her chin, he seemed satisfied that she really was okay, and he walked away.

6.

December 16.

Brian hit the call button and waited. Nancy took an especially long time to respond, and that worried him. When she finally did come onto the screen, he had to force himself to look upbeat. *She's not buying it, but it's all I got.*

She looked tired. Her eyes were hollow sockets, and her skin was waxy, pallid. Even the grainy pixels of the computer monitor couldn't hide her sickly complexion. His smile must have faltered, or she simply saw through his pathetic attempt to mask his shock. *I never could hide what I was thinking from her.*

"Don't look at me like that," she said. "I'm not sick, just tired."

"What are you talking about? This is how I look when I'm happy to see you."

She grimaced, clearly not buying it.

"I miss you."

"I miss you, too, my love. Of course, I do." Now it was her turn to fake her happiness.

"Have you been getting any sleep? You look tired." Brian was afraid she might find offense in the criticism of her appearance, but she only shrugged.

"I get sleep when I can, but I see so much panic around that it's hard to concentrate on sleep. The media doesn't help. I try not to watch the news anymore. I wish other people would do the same. Fake news is rampant. What I have been able to confirm as true, is that the illness is a pandemic. They are calling it the Ebolic Plague, or Ebolic Fever. The news, real news, says it mimics the Ebola virus, but it's a bacterial infection. Apparently, though, antibiotics can't touch it. There are no known cases in America yet, but it's already claimed most of Europe and Asia. It's working its way across Africa as well. All flights in and out of America have been suspended, but people fear it's already too late. There is a belief that it's already in America."

He didn't want to hear about that. Not from her, anyway. He wanted to know she was doing all right.

"How are your classes going?"

She groaned. "Fewer and fewer kids attend these days. People walk around wearing masks, like that's going to help. I try to tell them that wearing a mask only protects me from what they have. It's not going to keep them from getting sick. Wearing a mask is as useless as holding your breath. They want to believe they are doing something to protect themselves, I guess. I can't blame them. People are scared, and they should be." She leaned closer to the camera and whispered. "Chris was right all along."

Brian didn't know how to respond to that. It wasn't a contest. Chris didn't *win*. Brian knew that something had happened to Chris. In Brian's mind, there had been no doubt that he was right. There was so much about Chris Brian had never told Nancy. Now, thinking back on it, he wondered if she would have left the Ark had he told her.

Chris drowned, Nancy. He was dead. Dead, dead, dead; and I didn't bring him back. It did. It. The dryad. I don't know what happened to him when he drowned; maybe he was replaced by something else. There seems to be something of Chris left in there, but I don't know. All I know is that something higher than us humans makes Chris tick, so if he says the world is ending, I believe him.

No, he wouldn't have been able to convince her. She would have thrown him into the looney bin.

"You're thinking so hard I can see smoke pouring out your ears. And I know why. You're wishing I hadn't backed out of the Ark. Quite frankly, so am I. We can't change that now, though. I'm out here now, and I have to take my chances with the rest of the world."

I'm sorry. He couldn't say it, but he could think it. He couldn't say it, because she wouldn't understand what he was sorry about. He didn't even know. He thought maybe he was sorry that he hadn't been able to convince her to believe. He was sorry that she had to face this alone. But mostly, he was sorry because he was happy that he had stayed in the Ark.

"Do you ever wonder if Chris was right about the Ark being protected from the plague?"

Brian's mind snapped back to the present conversation in time to understand her question. "If he was right about the plague, it goes to reason that he would be right about that too."

Silence followed.

"I miss lying next to you," she said at last. "I miss touching you, kissing you." Her voice softened to a whisper again. "I don't want to die."

Brian felt the sick tug of despair in his heart. His breath caught in his throat. She needed him, and he wasn't there.

"You're not going to die." He surprised himself by the strength of his words. If she believed nothing else, she could believe in this. "You're not going to die. You're going to live; do you hear me? Board yourself up in your house. Do it now, before it's too late. Don't go outside, and don't let anyone in. You can survive this. Chris even agreed; there are going to be survivors. We'll search you out once the crisis is over. I'll come for you. Do you hear me? I'll come for you. Don't lose hope."

"I love you," she said and wiped at her eyes.

"I love you, too."

7.

December 19.

Brian clicked off the computer. Nancy was feeling better, sleeping, and he was relieved. He stood and pushed the chair in. He exited the skype room.

He headed down the corridor to the end. From down another hall, he heard voices. As he drew closer he recognized Kaylan's voice. At the industrial lift, he turned and looked left. He could see the Kaylan now, clearly. He also saw a man he did not recognize. He couldn't tell who was the aggressor; Kaylan was clearly giving as much as she was taking. As Brian arrived on the scene, the man backed down.

"What's going on here?" Brian turned to the man. "Sir, what's your name?"

"His name is Jerry Moynihan, and he just flipped out on me." Kaylan's chest heaved as she spoke, her nostrils flared like an angry bull in an arena.

Jerry Moynihan stared down at his feet. After a moment, as if a switch was flipped, he looked up and flew at Brian.

"You don't belong here." Jerry's face contorted into an angry scowl. He pointed a finger in Brian's face. The finger was so close Brian could see dirt under the cuticle. He said it again. "You don't belong here." Jerry turned on Kaylan again. "Neither does she."

Brian put a hand out to silence Kaylan, who hadn't said anything yet, but he knew her well enough to know she was about to. And what she would say could only make matters worse.

Brian spoke in a soothing, natural voice. "No one here wants any trouble, right? I know I don't. Kaylan doesn't. Do you, Jerry? Do you want trouble?"

The man looked at Brian as if he wasn't even sure where he was anymore.

There's something more going on here than just a bully trying to pick a fight. This guy is genuinely confused. Cabin fever? Maybe, but Brian didn't think so. Jerry looked scared. He looked…

Possessed.

Brian motioned for Kaylan to come with him, and they walked away from Jerry. The man did not follow them, but he continued to stare after them as they walked away. Brian checked behind them to ensure Jerry wasn't following. When they reached the elevators, Brian realized he had been holding Kaylan's hand. He released it with a sheepish grin.

"We should tell Chris about this. He needs to know the natives are restless."

"The last time I saw him he was with Roger. I don't know where they went, though."

"Where were you headed when you ran into good ole Jerry, anyway?" He laughed, hoping her aggressive posture would loosen up. It did, a little, he supposed.

"I was at the infirmary getting a first aid kit. Scott cut himself, and I wanted to be prepared when he did it again. I left there, and was heading back to the elevators when he saw me. He actually changed his direction so he could confront me—what an asshole." She was breathing heavy again.

"Forget him. Go back to whatever it was you were doing. I'll find Chris."

He sent her off in the elevator, but he stayed behind. He expected to see Jerry again, but he made it to the intersecting hall without incident. He headed down the central corridor to the control room. He passed the milk processing plant, and glanced through the large sliding glass doors at the rows of cows. He triggered the automatic sensor, and the doors slid open. A gush of manure and stray wafted out at him. Cows bawled as they were milked, and machinery whirred and clanked as the milk was first drawn, and then sent through the machinery to be pasteurized. He was suddenly struck with a thirst for a tall glass of cold milk.

Chris and Roger were in the back office. He knocked on the door and Chris waved him in. He entered and gave Roger a cursory nod of greeting and turned to Chris.

"I'm coming to inform you of a little scuffle I came across a moment ago, that I think you should know about."

"What happened?" Chris set aside the folders he was looking at. He turned his full attention to Brian.

"To get the full story, you'll have to talk to Kaylan. What I witnessed was a man named Jerry Moynihan arguing with her. When I approached, he looked to me like a raging wild dog. His eyes were bloodshot, and I think I even saw a little foam forming around the corners of his mouth. He looked furious. He was screaming that she didn't belong here."

Chris dropped into the chair behind him. "Are you sure she didn't say anything to set him off?"

"I am not. And it's quite possible she did. She has that effect on me sometimes. But I don't think that's the case here. He said the same about me when all I was doing was trying to calm him down."

Chris rifled through the folders on his desk. When he found the one he was looking for, he pulled it out and opened it up.

Chris has files on all these people. Of course, he did. He's very thorough. But does he have one on me? The thought smacked of conspiracy, so he quickly brushed it away. *That's how Nancy thinks, not me.*

Chris looked back up at Brian. "I don't see anything here that would indicate he's any kind of threat. I'll have a talk with him and see what's bothering him. I'll see Kaylan, too. Get her side of things."

Brian saw something troubling then. Chris turned and gave Roger a look. It was a knowing look. Roger gave it right back to him. *They know something the rest of us don't. what are they hiding?* There was that old conspiracy theorist rearing its ugly head again. *But still, just because you're paranoid, it doesn't mean you're not being followed.*

"What are you two keeping from me?"

Chris's head swiveled around to look at Brian. His eyes looked wide, like a deer caught in headlights.

Chris closed the file and set it aside. He stood and came around the side of the desk. He leaned against the front of the desk, crossing his arms and his legs. "I've been concerned that some people inside the Ark are having trouble…adapting to isolation. Although it's an extreme case, I worry that another incident like Bill could happen again. It's not likely, but if it does, I want to prevent it if I can."

"Are we in danger?" Brian's stomach flip-flopped. *What if that old bastard had a knife, and tried to stab me? Or Kaylan?*

"The chances that another incident like Bill are super remote. And I'd appreciate it if you didn't run off and start telling everybody what I just told you."

"I think you know me better than that. Otherwise, you would never have told me, right?"

"Right." Chris clapped his hands together and stood up. "Anyway, this party to ring in the new year is going to reset everyone's clocks back to zero-zero. Fresh as daisies in the spring. Everyone will become shiny, happy people again. You'll see."

Brian wanted to believe that.

He did.

8.

December 19.

Chris opens his eyes. He is lying in his bed, but he's not in his room. He's outside. There is a slight breeze blowing, and it ruffles his hair. He stands up and he sees that he is among the clouds. The wind whips all around him. The clouds are so close he can reach out and put his hand through them. He takes a few steps, but stops suddenly. He is standing on the top of the Ark. He is so close to the edge now, that he feels he will topple over the side if the winds blow any harder. When he looks down, he sees the wall, only the wall, going down into nothing. He can't even see the ground below because clouds hide the view. He turns away from the edge. Behind him, he sees a group of shadowy people standing there. The people seem ominous from the start. He's afraid of them. He tries to side step around the people but one of them rushes out. He hears a voice say, 'you don't belong here,' and the figure pushes him. He back peddles, tries to stop himself, but he can't; and he topples off the roof, falling down, down, down. Clouds swirl around him as he feels the ground rushing up to meet him. At the instant he hits the ground, Chris wakes with a gasp.

Chris sat up in bed and looked around. He was not outside. He was in his room. He took a few calming breaths to still his rapidly beating heart. He had a headache from his head hitting the imaginary ground. He walked to his bathroom and chewed on a couple of aspirin. He grimaced at the bitterness, but it was his preferred way to take the pills. He wanted the medicine to enter his bloodstream as soon as possible.

The bedside clock said it was 6 a.m.

He walked out to the living room. Brian slept on the sofa, a soft rhythmic snore filled the dark room. He returned to his bedroom and prepared the shower. His mind kept turning back to the dream that had awakened him.

It was the first dream he remembered having since the doors sealed, and it was a portentous nightmare.

Not a good sign.

By the time Chris finished his shower and dressed, Brian had awakened and was also taking a shower. Chris made his way to the elevator and headed down, all the way down to the bottom floor. He entered the control room.

Chris sat down in the chair next to Toby. The monitors showed that the protesters still lingered, but they had diminished greatly. A light snow fell that clung to the coats of the protesters, and flakes falling closer to the camera looked like the feathers of a giant bird. Toby glanced over at Chris, smiled and turned back to the monitors.

"I'd like to speak to you, if I can," Chris said.

Toby turned back to Chris. "Absolutely."

Chris looked around the control room. There was no one in earshot. He turned back to Toby. "You're a devout True Believer, right?"

Toby nodded. "Yes. I thought you knew that..."

Chris cut him off. "Yes, I do. It's why I'm coming to you. But do you hold any animosity with the people I've allowed into the Ark with me? Do you believe Brian, Scott, Kaylan, the Lutz's or the Holmes's don't belong here?"

"No, I believe they do belong here. They are your invited guests. They have more right to be here than any of us. We are here because we asked to be; they are here because you willed it so. I don't understand why you're asking me this."

"I've been thinking that there are some among us who, not only don't think my friends are welcome, but might also do them harm?" Chris looked around again, but they were still alone. "Who relieves you?"

"John Renault."

"Do you trust him?"

"I do."

"I ask because the person on these controls have complete control over everything in the Ark. I wonder if you can gage his behavior. Is he opening doors that shouldn't be opening? Does he speak disparagingly about my guests? Even if he doesn't think you're listening, I want to know what you hear. Be alert to anything suspicious."

"I can do that, of course. But I trust John with my life. I think you and your friends can, too."

"I hope you are right. It gives me great pain and sorrow to believe anyone inside this Ark would betray me."

"I must say I'm shocked. I can't believe anyone would do what you say. If I may ask, what causes you to believe something like this could be true?"

"I had a dream. In the dream, I was murdered. I heard the phrase 'you don't belong here' muttered in the last moments of the dream. There have been instances when people here, inside the Ark, have uttered those same words, and they were referring to my friends."

"I have been gullible. I thought everyone was safe in here, but that may not be the case. Until I know the truth, though, I plan to move the Lutz's and the Holmes's to the top floor with me where I can keep a better watch over them."

"Won't moving them alert the traitors that you're onto them?"

Chris nodded. "It will, but what choice do I have? They are potential targets right now, and I can't risk leaving them open to harm. I'll tell them—and everyone—that it's what I should have done from the beginning. And Patty should be up there, so she doesn't have as far to go when we have the New Years' Eve bash. I will make it look like the move was planned from the beginning."

"I hope that works," Toby said.

9.

December 24.

Gerard paced floor. His partner sat stolidly in the recliner, shadowed in the darkened room like a wraith. Gerard kicked the stand holding the vase of tulips, not caring if it toppled or not. The vase did not fall; it wobbled precariously for a second and then righted itself.

"They know." Gerard turned toward the shadowy figure. "I'm sure they know. I've received word they are moving the others to the top floor. We don't have access to that floor. We'll never finish what we started now."

"Calm down," the gravelly voice said. "I have a plan."

10.

December 25.

Chris, Brian, Scott and Kaylan spent Christmas morning in each other's company, exchanging small gifts each made for the others. Chris gave Roger a handmade Chess game. Roger had nothing to give to Chris, but that was okay. Roger's voice quivered with uncharacteristic emotion when he thanked Chris. Roger carried the game with him everywhere, playing with anyone he could get to compete with him. He was an excellent player and too few were willing to take him on. Some did, though.

Brian excused himself and went to the skype room to connect with Nancy.

At first, he didn't think she would answer his call, but eventually she did. His eyes lit up, relieved to see her.

"Merry Christmas," he said.

"Merry Christmas to you."

"How are you?"

She glanced away, and then returned her gaze to the screen. "I'm lonely, I guess. Missing you."

"I miss you, too. Always."

"They think there have been some cases of Ebolic fever in America. I guess we couldn't avoid that shoe from dropping forever."

"No, but you are prepared for this. You finished blocking off the house, right? The plastic is up, and the boards are in place?"

"Yes, but there's no guarantee that will work. I'm sure others have tried it."

"It will work." Brian's voice was stern. "It will work."

She nodded. "Yes."

Brian looked over the monitors and saw Carrie a few seats away talking to Jeremy.

"I'm so happy that Carrie and Jeremy had the opportunity to connect. That was a good thing you did."

"What *we* did. You were instrumental in making that work."

He nodded, smiling.

"Does he know the truth about where you are yet? Does he still believe the lie?"

Brian's expression was grave. "I think so. We prefer not to call it a lie, though."

"You call it what you want. But the truth is that family left him behind to die."

Brian wanted to say, *he has a chance*; but she was right. Even if he lived through the plague, he would still have to live with the truth that they did leave him behind. Better he died not knowing the truth. When would be the right time to tell him the truth, anyway?

"How was your morning. Did you all exchange gifts yet?".

"Yep," Brian said and lifted his foot to the desk so she could see the argyle sock on his foot. "These were from Kaylan."

She laughed. "Are they handmade?"

"I think so, yes."

"I'm sorry, but they're hideous. What did you give them?" she asked.

"I secretly learned woodworking, and made each of them a wooden gift. Scott got a wooden horse statue, and Kaylan received a little Chinese woman. I made Chris and Roger wooden chess set, carving each of the little figurines meticulously by hand."

"Really? Now *that* I'll have to see." She giggled.

Brian was happy to see her smile. At the start of the conversation she was so sad and tired looking that it broke his heart. "They aren't masterpieces, but I did pretty good. Chris painted me a picture of a pool, with swimmers and a lifeguard standing in a high chair. He's an amazing artist."

Brian said their goodbye and they disconnected. As he stood, Carrie turned and they waved to each other. Brian headed out and sought out Chris. He learned from Toby that Chris and Roger were in the infirmary.

Chris looked up as Brian entered the infirmary. He thought Chris had that guilty look in his eyes again. *What are they doing here, anyway?*

"What's going on?" Brian asked. "Is someone hurt?"

"No, nothing like that."

"What then?"

Chris flicked his eyes to Roger. *Why? For an excuse?* They shared a look and then Chris returned his gaze to Brian. "I…I mean we were going to examine Bill's body."

"What would you be looking for?" Brian wasn't sure he wanted any part of this.

Chris studied Brian intently. "I need your word that what we discuss here stays here, between us. I don't want anyone to learn about what I'm doing."

Brian stepped closer to Chris. "You have it."

"I'm concerned that there may be people here, inside the Ark, who mean us harm. We're going to examine Bill's body for any sign that he may have had contact with someone else here in the Ark. We are trying to discern if there may be others who could pose a threat to us."

"I've asked this before. I'll ask it again. I would like an answer. Are we in danger?"

Chris took a deep breath. He looked at Roger, then at Hellen. Finally, he returned his gaze to Brian. He raised his hands in a placating gesture.

"I just don't know."

11.

December 29.

Jenna Mac Numara watched as people walked down the street wearing full-body hazard suits and masks; the kind that covered the entire head, with three round protrusions on the bottom jaw — the kind she had only seen, until now, in horror movies. She adjusted her own blue face mask more tightly on her mouth and stepped through the door of the grocery store. She would be quick, in and out, and then get back home before anyone could get her sick.

She avoided the coughing woman in aisle seven. She rushed down aisle eight and tossed her needed items into the basket on her arm. When she had everything she had come for, she headed for the checkout lane. No one talked to her and she talked to no one. Everyone wore a mask of some type. Some of the people looked so sick they should have been in the hospital. Hospitals had stopped taking new patients so people were just going about their lives.

Jenna stepped over the dead person laying across the sidewalk and scurried faster to her apartment. She felt the eyes of strangers on her, studying her. She entered her apartment and quickly shut the door. She dropped her bags to the floor at her feet. Her hands moved over the three separate locks she had installed, locking each one in turn, and only felt at safe once the last one was engaged. After a moment of hesitation, and no one seemed to have followed her, she picked up her bags and headed to the kitchen.

She unpacked her groceries.

She had just finished and was stowing the plastic bag in a drawer for future use when she heard the first stirrings outside her door. Jenna froze. From other apartments, she heard pounding, cracking wood and screams. She heard the sound of flesh being struck. Struck by fists, and struck by more unyielding objects.

Something pounded on her own door.

She gripped the counter and tried to steady her legs. She had survived other raids, and she would survive this one. She had three bolts on her door; no one was getting in.

Something heavy — heavier than a fist — struck her door. Jenna started to cry. She tried to move toward the back of the room but when she took a step her legs threatened to buckle. She clung to the counter and waited.

The heavy object hit the door again. And again.

She heard the crack of wood breaking.

"Go away." She screamed the words, but the door cracked some more.

With another strike of the heavy object against the door, the wood finally gave up the fight and split. A sledgehammer crashed into the door a final time and splinters of wood blew inward. The door was gone.

Jenna found the strength to move. She rushed to the window where the fire escape led to the alley below. She struggled to open the window as three intruders entered her apartment. The two flanking intruders rummaged through cupboards as the middle intruder headed straight for Jenna. She screamed and fought to climb through the window but the muscular man with the sledgehammer wrapped an anaconda-like arm around her waist and pulled her back into the apartment. She struggled to break loose from the arm but it only tightened around her, squeezing her until she couldn't breathe. Tears streamed down her face as the arm released her and she dropped to the carpeted floor of her living room. She looked up at the man standing over her.

He was sick; she could see that right away. He was sweating and his skin had a pale blue tinge to it. His eyes were black orbs in sunken sockets. Acral necrosis sores covered his nose, black flesh that festered and stunk like rotten hamburger. On his bare chest, she saw swollen lymph nodes around her shoulder blades.

She sobbed and begged but it did her no good. Even through the blur of tears, she could see him lifting the sledgehammer over his head.

She screamed and the hammer came down, aimed at her face.

12.

December 31.

Toby's voice boomed through the speakers installed in every hallway and in every residence inside the Ark. "Please make your way up to the top floor. The ballroom is now open for festivities. There is a party on floor 400. If you wish to take part in the festivities, please make your way up to the top floor. Guards on each floor are positioned to assist. Please see the nearest guard if you need assistance."

Each guard carried with him—or her—a two-way communicator. They could speak directly with Toby, or with Chris.

The people on every floor moved with military precision. No one argued, no one grumbled. The floors cleared one by one, with people moving in single file, fast enough to keep the line moving at a steady clip, but without looking like a wild, rushing crowd. The elevators whirred and moved with sturdy and superior construction.

Chris stood near the doorway as people filed into the ballroom. Along the walls, tables had been set up with snacks and hors d'oeuvres. The people entering the room milled about, gawking at the beautiful decoration, and headed for the food.

Phillis Reinhardt spotted Chris and shuffled out of the crowd to talk to him. "Ah, so here is the mastermind behind this wonderful party. Will this room hold so many people?"

Chris giggled. "The room can hold six *hundred* thousand people." He shouted the last. "It's a big room."

"Yes, but is it…strong enough? Will the floor not give out? I guess, is what I'm asking. You are, after all, putting us all in one place. If the floor gave out below us, we'd all perish. That would be the end of this little exercise." Phillis stifled a nervous little laugh behind her hand.

"The Ark was built for strength and longevity. The Ark will be able to hold twenty times its present capacity—including this room. This room will hold out okay, Phillis. No need to worry. You'll be here in the Ark for years to come."

"Hush your mouth." Phillis giggled. "I want to see the sun again before I die."

Chris laughed. "I'm talking hypothetical. Of course, we'll open the doors again."

"Soon, I hope."

Chris continued to smile as Phillis turned and walked away. The smile was beginning to hurt his face. *No one is meant to be this fake for this long.* But he would continue, and he would show no weakness. His mind swam with the knowledge of the sickness spreading across the land. He had planned, and he had acted, an in the process, he had saved thousands of lives. But still, he couldn't stop thinking about the millions more he wasn't able to save. He thought of Nancy. He thought of Jeremy, and he thought of the thousands of others who would perish and leave these residents of the Ark to deal with that loss. This party was one last chance to know happiness before the cataclysmic fall that was sure to come. These partiers didn't understand just yet what awaited them when the doors did finally open.

They were a resilient bunch, he concluded. There was nothing they couldn't overcome. They were survivors.

The total time taken to emigrate from their homes to this massive gathering place was two hours and forty-five minutes. It was an impressive feat, and Chris was proud of them. No injuries reported, and no fights. So far, so good.

But the night was young.

Chris walked among the revelers, wishing them all a Happy New Year. Some stopped him, wanting to toast, and he picked up a glass of punch to honor their wishes. Then he would move on.

"Having a good time?" he asked Patty.

She looked up from her wheelchair. "It is the best time I've had in a long time. I'm enjoying the opportunity to get to know so many new people. I can't believe how many people are here."

"People are treating you kindly, I hope." Chris was also referring to Derek, as he stood protectively near his mother.

"I made lots of new friends." Derek spoke in his loud voice, which was needed in order for Chris to hear him over the dull roar of a thousand conversations going on at once. "My new friend Ethel said I make her laugh."

Chris remembered Scott and Kaylan's aversion to the old woman, and he was thankful Derek didn't understand sarcasm. "I'll bet you do."

Patty reached back and patted her son's hand as it rested on the handle of the wheelchair. Her face beamed with pride as she craned her neck around to smile up at him. "You're a good boy. Momma loves you."

Chris bade them goodbye and turned to survey the rest of the occupants of the ballroom. He saw Paul and Carrie standing near a refreshment table. Not far from them, Margot saw him and waved. His smile took on a new form as he waved back at Margot; his face no longer hurt. *Well, this is refreshing. A real, honest-to-god expression of happiness. Feels good to have a reason to laugh again.* Their eyes lingered on one another for a moment, as if they were the only two in the room. But someone bumped into him and the moment was gone.

"Oh, sorry, Chris. So sorry."

"Hello, Annette." The name came to him the minute he spoke it, and he knew right away it was correct. *One of those quirky talents of mine that make me the perfect Chosen One, I guess.* He could never explain the gift he had for names, he just heard the name once and it stuck. He shook her hand. "Enjoying the gathering?"

Annette's smile faltered.

"What's wrong?" He sensed it in her then, the inner turmoil she felt.

"Can I speak openly with you?" she asked.

Chris spotted two empty chairs and led her over to them. "I wouldn't have it any other way. What's on your mind?" They sat facing each other. He took her hands.

"I've been having horrible dreams. But the dreams aren't the only problem." She stopped, and seemed too nervous to go on.

"Whatever it is you can speak to me. I want to help."

She took a deep breath. "I was afraid to come. I was leery about being around all these people. I finally forced myself to do it, afraid that if I didn't, I wouldn't be able to overcome what's been happening to me lately."

"What's been happening to you?"

"It starts with the dream. The same dream every night. I'm surrounded by a bunch of people at a party. I'm having fun, but something in the dream is warning me I'm not safe. When I look around, I see a man looking in my direction. His face is shrouded in shadow, so I can't see who he is. Until, that is, he pulls the scythe out from behind his back and starts swinging it. He is moving through the crowd cutting off heads, cutting some people in half. He's moving straight toward me. I wake up screaming." Annette seemed too breathless to continue. Her hands shook, lips quivered.

Chris quickly poured her a cup of water from a nearby pitcher on a table, and helped her hold it to her lips. She took the cup and sipped. When she pushed it away, he placed the cup on the edge of the table.

She's shivering.

"Thank you."

"You're very welcome."

She took a deep breath and continued. "I was afraid to come, afraid I'd see a faceless man out to kill me."

"I'm glad you did come. And I assure you, no one here is out to hurt you. Do you believe me?"

She nodded. "Yes, of course. But there's more."

Chris felt a chill pass through him, though the room was warm.

Annette said, "I think I'm going mad. I'm having hallucinations. I'm afraid to leave my house because of them."

"Can you tell me about them?"

She nodded again. "When I'm walking down the hallway, the hall will start to stretch. It *turns*, as if it's being twisted. I stumble to catch my balance. The floor seems to drop out from below me, and I have to lean against the wall until the feeling passes. It's been happening so often that I've stopped leaving my apartment. I fear going back because most recently, I've been having trouble inside the home as well. The mirrors seem to *ripple*."

Bill Thomlinson. The name echoed in his head, and Chris couldn't help but wonder if the old man had had similar issues before his meltdown.

"This sounds to me like perfectly ordinary fears." The lie sounded convincing enough to his own ears. He hoped she would buy into it as well. "You stay as long as you feel comfortable. If things get too difficult for you, head on home. Let me know you're leaving and I'll have someone walk with you if you wish. Tomorrow, I'll have Dr. Jacobson swing by your place and talk with you. I don't want you to feel alone in this ever again. I'm here for you. I'll take care of you."

"Thank you, Chris." Her voice was choked with emotion.

He squeezed her hand gently, kissed her cheek and stood.

Chris spotted Brian sitting alone.

"Why are you just sitting here, Bri?" Chris stood over his maudlin friend, staring down. "Get up. Mingle."

Brian looked up and tried to smile but failed. Chris sat down next to him.

"Is it because Nancy's not here?"

"Mostly, but it's also something she said."

"Tell me about it."

"When I spoke to her this morning I mentioned this party. She was pissed that we planned to have a party while people on the outside were dying. The plague hit the US. People in Florida and California are rioting in the street. We've lost contact with most of Europe and Asia. Africa is being ravaged by the disease. She's disgusted, and I can't help but feel she's right."

Chris felt his jaw clench, and he took in a long breath of air to clear his head, and cool the heat rising in his face.

"What right does she have to judge us?" *Clearly, I didn't wait long enough before speaking. Hopefully, he'll still respect me after I say what is on my mind.* "This isn't something that we caused. It's something that I warned everyone about. The people in the Ark do not deserve to grieve just because they chose to live. They prepared for this; they sacrificed everything they had so they could live. Nancy has no right to sit out there and judge. I'm sorry she's out there where people are dying, but she was given the opportunity to join us and chose to suffer. Please don't infect the others with her poisonous attitude. Don't allow her to infect you with it, either. You shouldn't feel guilty just because you chose to live. She had her chance. Perhaps, if she had stayed, and chose to boycott this party, I'd sympathize with her plight. Hell, there are people in here—who sacrificed everything to be here—that chose to stay away from the party. I commend them for their choice. But this party is for the people that wanted to live. No one is allowed to feel guilty here."

"I don't think guilt is what she's striving for. It's respect for those who are dying that she wants us consider."

"This gathering isn't about disrespect, either. Why does she feel the need to dampen our spirits with these negative vibes? We can have respect—and not feel guilt—and still celebrate our own lives. This party has nothing to do with what's going on outside. This is about starting a new life, in a new world, and at the start of a new year. My advice to you is eat, drink and be merry, my friend; we live in a utopia now, and that could only happen by destroying the old world as we knew it. Outside those huge metal doors is a new Eden, and we will all be able to enjoy it soon. Nothing happening here is anything we should feel guilty about."

Chris stood and walked away before Brian had a chance to respond.

13.

December 31.

Brian watched his friend walk away. Chris was right, of course. But he could also see Nancy's point of view as well. Truthfully, Brian wasn't feeling guilt over being one of the survivors; his unease stemmed from the pressure of walking a tightrope between two strong-willed *frenemies*. He was worried for his wife. He wanted her to live through this cataclysm so he could see her again. That was all he wanted out of this.

But he didn't want Chris to be angry with him, either.

Brian stood and looked over the food trays. He fixed a plate of Chicken Riggies—a specialty food of the Utica area—and buttered a slice of Italian bread. He asked to sit with Patty, Glenn and Derek. They were happy to have him.

"Hi, Brian." Derek's overly loud voice was easily heard over the din of the other partiers. He laughed and Brian laughed, too. When Chris looked over at them, Brian waved. Chris waved back.

Brian felt a great weight lift from his chest.

The room was a sea of people. Brian didn't think he had ever been anywhere with so many people in the same place at once. Somewhere much farther on Brian could hear music playing, even over the din of a multitude of voices all talking at once.

After Brian finished eating he stood and walked around. The room was not as crowded as he might have thought; there was room for another one hundred thousand people, and this thought caused him to recall another of Nancy's issues. The Ark was big enough to hold much more people than were allowed in. The residences were grandiose, and if they had been built smaller, twice as many people could have been allowed to survive.

Brian forced these thoughts from his mind, though. The Ark was what it was, and thinking any further into what already was could be as pointless as screaming at the gods for allowing this disaster to happen in the first place.

Brian found a troupe of dancers and stopped to watch as they twirled and pranced across the floor. He lost himself in the dance, mystified by the talented people who were called to join Chris in the new world. When the dance ended and the others clapped, Brian clapped, too.

He glanced around and spotted the large black rectangle hanging from the north wall. The red digital numbers counted down to the new year.

10:32:15.

10:32:16.

10:32:17.

He turned away from the clock; because, for him, it was only ticking away the remaining time those outside the walls of the Ark had left. He turned and watched the face-painting area for a while. He watched a little blonde girl get a butterfly painted on her cheek. He saw that she was looking at him, and she wanted to smile, but she knew the movement might disrupt the artwork being applied to her face. Her eyes twinkled with delight.

Brian looked around and studied the faces of the people enjoying the festivities. None of them were thinking of the horrors being visited upon the people outside, and he envied them for it. He forced his face to remain pleasing, even as tears threatened to spring to his eyes.

He blinked them away and turned and watched a puppet show. He laughed as the puppets bounced, and their mouths flapped—not so in sync in with the words, necessarily—to the story of Cinderella. He laughed out loud when the conclusion of the story had the raggedy Cinderella eating the glass slipper instead of trying it on.

Brian moved around and through the crowd until he reached the music. At the moment, a country tune, sung by a male artist, pumped from the speakers. It sounded familiar, but he wasn't a fan of country music and couldn't name the song, or the singer.

He laughed out loud as an enthusiastic group of dancers performed a country line dance, some even wearing cowboy hats and boots. To his surprise, he saw Kaylan dancing in the line as well. She was amazingly proficient; kicking, tapping her heel with her hand and then turning, all in sync with the people around her. Brian clapped when the song ended and the dance concluded.

Kaylan ran up to him and threw her arms around his neck.

"God, I forgot how fun that could be." Her breath was a hot, sweet cloud near his ear. She backed away from him, and turned shyly away.

"You were very good."

"Thank you." She glanced around. "Have you seen Scott?"

"No, not yet. I saw Chris over by the food. Maybe Scott is with him?"

Yes, food. That's a very safe bet with Scott." They started through the crowd to the tables. As they passed a table with a cake as the centerpiece, Ethel looked up at them. She turned back to the table and scanned the surface.

"Has anyone seen the knife for cutting the cake? I can't find the knife."

Kaylan spotted the triangular spatula and picked it up. "Use this." Kaylan turned the spatula sideways and cut out a wedge of the chocolate cake. She placed it on a plate and handed it to the woman.

"Thank you." Ethel giggled.

Kaylan and Brian walked on, scanning the crowd for Scott.

Chris came up to them, walked with them.

"We're looking for Scott, have you seen him?" Kaylan side-stepped a line of people holding paper plates and waiting for their turn at the food. Brian followed her through the line, and then Chris did the same.

"I have not," Chris said when the three of them were through the barrier of people. "And it's almost impossible to find someone in this crowd."

"We separated when I wanted to check out the country line dancing and he wanted to eat. I was sure he would be here somewhere."

"I think you'll have better luck if you stop looking for him and run into him by accident," Brian said and laughed.

"You're probably right." Kaylan frowned. "Lost another husband."

Angry shouts drew their attention from their search for Scott, and they turned in unison in the direction of the noise. Two men had gotten into each other's faces and their eyes burned with anger. Chris quickly ran to them. Brian reached out to stop him, but missed. He didn't want Chris getting involved but, of course, he would. *Don't, Chris. It's not your fight.* He recognized one of the men as Jerry Moynihan, the man who had confronted Kaylan and him in the north corridor, and it sent a cold chill down his back.

Kaylan tugged on Brian's sleeve; she, apparently, saw Moynihan, too.

I should jump in there, not Chris. But confrontations are his skill set. He'll calm them down if anyone can. Brian would jump in only if necessary. He didn't want to agitate Jerry further with his presence. He would hang back and only get involved if the situation became more than Chris could handle.

People moved past the two angry men, some were oblivious to the conflict. Brian lost track of the action for a moment, but focused in again as soon as the way cleared. He moved closer. Brian saw Jerry turn to Chris. Brian could see Chris talking, but couldn't hear the words. Jerry's posture changed, and he was no longer hostile. Brian grinned; Chris's talent for diplomacy was amazing.

But the second man did not calm down. He swung a roundhouse at Jerry, but the targeted man ducked, and Chris took the fist in the face. Brian bolted forward, catching his friend even as he fell backward. The man who'd thrown the punch looked confused, staring at his own fist as if it belonged to someone else.

Brian expected Jerry to grow angry again when they locked eyes, but Jerry didn't even seem to recognize him.

"I'm sorry," the man who'd thrown the punch said. He flexed his fingers, splaying them. He dropped his hand to his side.

Brian focused all his attention on Chris. "You okay, Man?"

Chris nodded. He rubbed his jaw where the fist had struck as Brian helped him back to his feet. The two men had dispersed, disappearing into the crowd.

"What happened?" Brian asked.

Kaylan stood beside Brian. She studied Chris's face.

"I'm okay." Chris brushed her questing hands away.

"Can we get some ice over here?" Kaylan motioned for someone near the drink table to assist. Someone filled a linen napkin with ice and brought it over. Kaylan took it and arranged the ice to sit comfortably on Chris's face over the bruise. Chris took the compress and held it gingerly on his cheek. When he tried to remove it, she forced him to put it back.

"Thanks," he said to her.

"What happened?" Brian asked again.

"I don't know. Jerry and Mark were arguing over something, but neither man could say what it was about. When I asked Jerry to explain he looked at me confused, like he didn't even know where he was. He acted like he had just woken up from a dream."

"Strange," Kaylan said.

Chris tried to stand but Brian lowered him into a chair. "You should rest."

The expression on Chris's face bothered Brian more than the scene that had just played out moments ago. Chris's eyes darted around the room as though seeking out an enemy he couldn't see. Brian gripped Chris's shoulder, pulling his friends gaze to him. As Chris focused on Brian, and their eyes met, Brian saw irrational fear swimming in the brown pools.

"Chris, what is wrong?"

"Why would it choose me and then abandon me like this?"

"Chris, what are you talking about?" Brian felt a tingle of real dread stirring in his guts. Chris wasn't making sense. Brian glanced around. "Is there a doctor nearby? He sounds confused. There might be a concussion."

Chris whispered into Brian's ear. "It's not a concussion. It's the Dryad. It's trying to destroy us all. It's coming through and reaching us inside the Ark. It's killing everyone outside, and now it's trying to destroy us from the inside. Why?"

"I don't think…"

"It's true." Chris shook his head vigorously. He would not be dissuaded. "It has *spoken* to me. It spoke to me through Bill. I wasn't sure at first—I suspected—but now I'm sure. The Dryad entered Bill, told me it would destroy us all, and then killed Bill. It wasn't suicide. Now it is infecting everyone with an anger that will threaten to unravel the harmony inside the Ark."

Brian didn't know what to say. He said the only thing he could think of. "I'll help you in any way I can."

Chris's sad eyes met Brian's. A sense of determination sparked in Chris, and his mood lightened.

Roger arrived and studied Chris's face. "Who did this?"

"It was an accident," Chris said and forced Roger's arms down.

Roger huffed, unsure, and ready to exact justice for the outrage. After another moment, he let the fight go out of him. "This is my fault."

Chris turned a stern look in his direction. "Why?"

"I should have been here. I should have protected you."

Chris laughed. "You're not my bodyguard. I'm completely capable of taking care of myself. There was an argument and I got caught in the middle of it. If it's any consolation to you, Mark looked hopelessly distraught for what he did."

"Mark Hammond did this?"

"How did you know it was Hammond? He's not the only Mark in here." Chris smirked, clearly amazed by Roger's powers of deduction.

Roger didn't answer the question. "He should know better than to fight in your presence."

"I don't think Mark was completely in control of his own actions." Chris glanced over at Brian, and they shared a look. The look seemed to say, *how much should I say about my theory?*

But Roger didn't seem to be concerned with Chris's assessment of the situation. "I'm staying by your side for the rest of the night."

Brian relaxed and the burning fear that had been in the pit of his stomach slackened. Roger's presence seemed to help Chris feel less stressed. Chris seemed to have forgotten, for the moment anyway, about his fears of the Dryad's intentions.

Brian decided to stay close to Chris as well.

14.

December 31. Thirty minutes from midnight.

Chris worked his jaw. There was pain, but nothing seemed broken. When he glanced over at Mark, the man turned crimson, and averted his eyes. *He's ashamed. He knows he hit me, but does he remember?* If Chris's theory was correct, Mark hadn't been in control when he took the swing. But why? Why would the Dryad lead me to build this protection around us, just to threaten us once we did? It didn't make sense.

Large numbers of people began to gather around the countdown clock, clearly wanting an unencumbered view of it for the final few minutes. Chris warded off a few more people wanting to know if he was okay, and worked his way through the crowd. The festivities were winding down and the music became a low buzz somewhere far off. The dancing had ceased completely. The youngest children had been sent to bed by their attentive parents. The older generation, too, retired early.

Chris spotted Patty and Derek sitting near the countdown clock. "You guys are still up." He tried not to sound shocked, but he failed.

"We want to see in the new year with everyone else," Patty said.

Derek, unusually quiet, only yawned.

Chris sat down with them. Roger and Brian, who were determined to shadow Chris no matter where he went, sat down, too.

When Chris saw Paul, Carrie and Margot cleaning up their station, he excused himself from the table and approached.

Margot smirked. "I was wondering when we'd see you."

"What do you mean?" Chris piled dirty dishes into a large pan of water sitting on their cart.

"You can't walk by someone in need without offering to help, is all I mean. Don't get offended, oh holy one."

"Don't mind her," Carrie said. "She's happy to see you."

"Enough chatter," Paul said. "Finish up." He pushed the cart of leftovers through the maze of people, heading for the door.

When their table was clear, Chris and Margot carried it over to an unused corner, opening up more space for people to stand. Carrie pushed her cart toward the door, but Margot stopped her. "I got this. You two go enjoy the festivities."

"Are you coming back?" Chris asked Margot.

"I'll think about it." Margot shoved the cart through the doors and disappeared down the hall.

"Want to sit with us?" Chris asked Carrie. She nodded and he led her to the table. He held out her seat. Carrie thanked him. If he had done that for Margot she would have complained. The thought made him smile.

Tom and Nora Lutz joined Chris's group at the table. The talk was casual and subdued. At five minutes till midnight Margot returned and Chris made room for her.

He looked around. "Where is Paul?"

"Not coming," Margot said, but didn't explain further.

The red numbers on the clock began to flash.

Four minutes till the new year.

Chris glanced around at the other tables. The talk had dropped to a whisper. Young children yawned, and pointed at the clock when they noticed the numbers were flashing. Some seemed to know what all the excitement was all about, but some were too young to truly understand. Some had already fallen asleep with their heads on the table. Fathers carried their young ones out and took them back to their homes. The number of people in the room had thinned. Not everyone would see the new year in.

Chris turned his attention back to the group around his table. Two minutes till midnight.

The closer the clock drew toward midnight, the more he felt an acidy burn in his stomach. He couldn't shake the dread the new year brought with it. Thankfully, no one else seemed to feel what he did. *Come on, Chris. This is a good thing.*

One minute to the new year, and the clock flashed even faster.

Kaylan shushed everyone. "Time to count down."

All heads turned to the clock; fifty-five seconds.

At twenty seconds to midnight, the numbers disappeared and the room lights went out. People gasped in surprise. The room had gone completely dark. After another few seconds a large red ten appeared, lighting the faces around him with an eerie red glow that reminded Chris of blood. The revelers counted down as the numbers appeared and disappeared.

"Ten."
"Nine."
"Eight."
"Seven."
"Six."
"Five."
"Four."
"Three."
"Two."
"One."

The clock now lit up with the words HAPPY NEW YEAR! The lights began to strobe and the DJ played Auld Lang Syne. The room filled with revelers singing the words to the song. Chris glanced over as Patty and Glenn kissed. She kissed Derek on the cheek.

Nora and Tom kissed.

Scott kissed Kaylan. Kaylan then leaned over and kissed Roger. Roger saw Chris looking and shrugged. Chris laughed.

Chris turned to the left side of the table, and saw Brian kiss Carrie. She smiled and blushed.

Chris wasn't expecting it when Margot leaned in and kissed him, full and strong, on the lips. Initially, he was too shocked to do anything. But when she didn't pull back right away, he kissed her back.

Margot pulled away from the kiss and sat back. Chris—stunned, confused—stayed in position for several seconds. He felt a rush of excitement racing through his body. The room seemed to go silent. There was no one else in the room but Margot. He tried to meet her gaze, but she avoided his eyes.

After the momentary awkwardness passed, Chris relaxed. The room was full of people again.

Patty yawned. She turned to Derek. "What do you say, Honey? Take me back to the apartment?"

Derek nodded vigorously.

"So soon?" Glenn asked. "The night's still young."

She rubbed his arm. "If I had my druthers, I'd stay up all night long. But these tired bones aren't what they used to be. You stay. Have fun. I'll see you in the morning."

As Derek disengaged the breaks on her wheelchair, Glenn leaned down and kissed Patty again. "I love you, Momma."

"I love you, Papa." They took hands and held them until Derek pulled them apart.

Glenn watched as his son and wife disappeared into the hallway beyond the doors. He turned back to the group. Chris was touched by their genuine affection for each other, and loved them for it. Glenn stood and headed to the table for a cup of punch.

Kaylan and Scott excused themselves and headed toward the DJ. Brian sat back and closed his eyes. Carrie watched him.

"Tired?" she asked.

"Mmmm," he said without opening his eyes.is

"Why don't you head off to bed?"

Brian opened his eyes and sat up. "I'm okay. I'm not ready to sleep yet." He shook off the sleepiness. "Besides, as soon as I lay down I'm instantly wide awake."

"You should see if Doctor Jacobson has something to help you sleep." Chris said.

Brian shook his head. "No. I don't want any more sleeping aids. When I sleep, I want it to be because my body allowed it."

"There is nothing wrong with getting a little help once in a while. I take Benadryl when I can't sleep. It's just to kick-start my own sleep schedule. It's worse for you to go on not sleeping, Brian. How long have you been going without sleep?"

"I sleep. I nod off for about a half hour each night."

"It's not enough." Chris couldn't hide his alarm. "Going without sleep like that causes psychosis. Brian, haven't you heard anything I've been saying? This is exactly the kind of thing I've been trying to fight. We all have to take care of each other or we can forget about ever making it out of this ordeal alive. We'll all go crazy and kill each other long before the plague will get us."

Brian leaned forward and placed a hand on Chris's arm to calm him down. "I'm sorry. Tomorrow I'll go see the Doc."

Chris relaxed, but he glared at Brian through narrowed eyes. "You better."

Chris turned. Margot had been staring at him intently, but when she realized he had spotted her, she looked away quickly. *She looks nervous. Why is she suddenly do nervous?*

Chris moved closer to her. "Thanks for the mercy kiss."

"Huh?" She turned to face him.

"If you didn't kiss me, I would have been the only one not kissing someone when the new year was ushered in. So, you know, thank you."

"Oh." She shrugged off his thanks. "I did it because I wouldn't have been kissing anyone either. I couldn't have that. I grabbed the first loser not kissing someone so I didn't look like a fool. Don't go flattering yourself, or anything."

Chris laughed. "Right."

She stood and walked away.

Nora drew Chris's attention away from Margot with a long, loud yawn. She tried to stifle it, but it was no use.

"Sorry," she said. "I guess I'm not as young as I used to be. I think it's past my bedtime. I don't think I can stay to usher in the dawn like I used to."

"It was nice of you to join us," Chris said. "I'll see you in the morning."

Nora smiled. She looked up at the clock, which now just continued to flash the happy new year message. "We made it to the new year. We're nearly free." Tears welled in her eyes. "We're nearly…"

Nora dropped her face into her hands and cried. Chris quickly moved to sit next to her. He held her around the shoulders as her body shook with the effort of her sobs.

"Nora, what's wrong?" He kept his tone gentle, comforting.

When she had control of her tears, she wiped her eyes and turned to him. "It's almost over, isn't it? We can go outside again, soon. Right? Please tell me we're not trapped inside this place forever. I couldn't stand it if I never got to see the sky again."

"It's almost over, Nora. Soon the doors will open and we'll all be free to come and go as we please. Sure—at first—we'll have to stay close to the Ark. There will be a lot of cleanup to do; but eventually, we will be able to go back to our old lives."

"I don't care about my old life. I just want to see the sky, feel a light breeze on my face, hear birds singing in the trees."

"We have birds," Chris reminded her. "There are birds all over the place in the hydroponic garden. Have you seen them?"

184

"Yes, but it's not the same. I just feel so...cooped up. I want this to be over already. That's all. I'm sorry. I didn't mean to...it's been such a wonderful night. I've ruined it."

"You haven't ruined anything. You're just saying what we are all thinking and feeling. Go back to your place and get some sleep. You'll feel so much better in the morning."

She offered a brave smile. "You're right. I'm just overtired. I'll forget all about this silly outburst after I've gotten some sleep. I hope *you* will, too." She laughed and Chris laughed with her. He helped her to stand and Tom came to stand next to her.

Nora hugged Chris, kissed him warmly on the cheek, and allowed Tom to walk her out of the room. They turned right at the intersecting hallway, and headed down the central corridor to the apartments.

Even as she was leaving, Chris began to formulate a plan to make the rest of their stay inside the Ark a little more bearable. He was thinking sun lamps and water. He was thinking picnics in the sand. He would build a room with a beach in it. It was time for some fun in the sand. It wouldn't be that hard at all. They could fill one of the empty warehouse rooms with sand from the hydroponics room, hollow out a deep hole and fill it with water. People could even go swimming. He thought he could have it up and running in a couple of weeks. His mind spun with ideas. He would get Brian to teach swimming lessons. In fact, Brian still owed him a lesson.

When he returned to the table he was grinning madly.

Margot scowled at him. "What's going on in that devious little mind of yours?"

Chris laughed. "It's a secret. I'll tell you all about it in the morning."

"It is morning." Brian smirked.

"Still, you have to wait."

The DJ played slow, soft music. People danced. People spoke in soft tones. The party went on.

Chapter Eight

1.

He sat in the dining room, shirtless and still. On the table in front of him, lying on a white towel, Gerard examined the pieces of his Smith and Wesson pistol. He fit the parts together with dexterity and skill. Once the weapon was back in working order, he slapped the clip into place and tested its weight. Oh, how good it felt in his hand, like caressing a lover.

He picked up the last piece of hardware and screwed it into place on the muzzle of the gun. This was a silencer. Gerard knew that, despite the name, silencers were not silent at all. There would still be gunshots, loud ones, but the silencer did stifle the sound enough to protect the user's ears from damage in a confined space. He wasn't at all concerned about the sound being heard, no; on the contrary, he wanted everyone to know he was coming.

2.

January 1. 2 a.m.

Tom kicked off his shoes and flopped down in his favorite chair. He enjoyed the festivities, but was glad to finally relax and unwind. Nora had gone into the master bathroom to change and get cleaned up. When she returned, she wore a light blue night gown and fuzzy blue slippers. She sat in the soft chair next to her husband. They reached across the gap between the chairs and clasped hands.

"How are you feeling?" Tom's voice was compassionate. "You were upset at the party. Has your mood improved?"

"I was being silly. I know we're in a better place here. The alternative is being out there where people are dying. I'm honored to have this opportunity."

"You will feel the sun on your face again, my love."

"I was just overreacting. It was the moment. As the clock turned to midnight, and the lights dimmed—then the music started—I just felt an overwhelming sense of loss. That's really what the tears were about. I can't stop thinking about all the people outside. When the doors finally do open, they will all be gone. I'm not sure I want to see that."

Tom leaned over and kissed her.

"I love you," he said.

She smiled and touched his face. "And I, you."

"How about a nice hot cup of tea to help us relax?"

"Sounds great."

Tom stood and headed to the kitchen as Nora picked up the novel she'd been reading and placed her bookmark aside.

Tom filled the kettle and placed it on the burner. He pulled two cups with saucers from the cupboard and set them on the counter. As the water boiled, he placed two slices of bread in the toaster and pushed the button down. He liked toast with his tea. He stood and watched as the coils inside the toaster glowed red.

He turned and looked around the kitchen. This wasn't their home. He would never tell Nora, had no idea if she felt the same way, but he felt like a squatter in someone else's home. He almost wished he had done what Nancy had done. He totally understood why she risked her life to preserve her way of life. Nora had told Chris she didn't care about her old life. Tom didn't agree with that sentiment. He did miss his old life. There were moments when he wished he hadn't given up his home so easily. If he had fought harder, he might have been able to save his home; the place he earned with his own money. He might even have won.

But that was crazy dreaming on his part. Chris had the government backing him up. Chris would have destroyed him in court.

And what would have been the alternative? Would he have prevented the Ark from being built? Maybe not, but he certainly could have postponed the construction until it was too late to be finished before the plague struck.

But the truth of the matter came down to one simple fact: Chris was right to do what he did.

In the end, Tom made the right choice, but that didn't stop Tom from feeling out of place.

As the tea kettle started to whistle, Tom had another thought. *They built this place on my land, dammit. I do have a right to be here. I'm no squatter, so stop with that nonsense.*

Tom poured the tea, buttered his toast and carried the tea cups (balancing his toast on his cup of tea) into the living room. Nora set her book aside and accepted her cup of tea. She placed the tea bag on the saucer and sipped at her tea.

"Thank you," Nora said.

"You're so welcome."

They sat quietly drinking their tea for a time. Tom thought of what they might have been doing had the Ark never been built. *Just what we're doing now. Only, I would be watching the television.* Nora had no use for the TV, but Tom missed it.

He turned to his wife, and she met his gaze with a smile. He could tell she was tired — he could see it in her eyes — but she was clearly unwilling to give up the night. Tom, himself, was not sure what the future held for them, but at least they would face it together.

He and Nora had been married twenty-five years ago. They had never had children, but still their lives together had felt complete. She was all he needed. He hoped he was all she needed as well. The thought was spoken before he had a chance to stop himself.

"Do you regret never having children?"

Nora's cup stopped halfway to her lips and she turned to him. "Where did that come from?"

"I've been contemplating our lives up to this point. With all that's going on in the world, I can't think of a better time to ask. Do you regret that we never had children?"

Nora placed her cup on the table next to her chair and turned her full concentration to her husband. "I regret nothing of our lives together. When we made the decision not to have kids, it was the right choice. Once the opportunity slipped past us, I never once had second thoughts about our decision. No I don't regret not having children."

She studied him a moment longer, and once she was sure he seemed satisfied with her answer, she picked up her cup and sipped her tea.

Tom, too, sipped his tea. It had turned cold but he didn't mind. He hadn't touched his toast, he realized. He took a bite and thought it dry, unfulfilling. He swallowed it and set the rest of the toast back with the other, untouched slice. He started to rise, intending to throw his toast away, when the knock on their door stopped him

3.

January 1. 2:15 a.m.

Gerard threw his gray shirt over his arms and buttoned it up. He tucked it into his pants and picked up the gun. He walked to the front door.

The door directly across from the Holmes's place cracked open. Gerard stepped into the corridor and glanced to his left. There was no one else in the hallway with him. He quietly closed the door to the empty apartment in which he had been hiding for the past several days.

Gerard had learned the default key code to all unoccupied apartments was the Chosen One's own birthday. The elevator code to enter the top floor was the same code. The Chosen one had been foolish to use such a weak security code. Gerard walked past the Holmes's door and stopped at the next door to the left. This was where the Lutz's were living.

From his left pocket, he pulled out the Beretta 9mm. From his right pocket he pulled out the silencer and screwed it into place on the muzzle of the gun. He knew silencers weren't truly silent — he'd shot test shots before, and they are still quite loud — but he

189

didn't need total silence. He figured the apartment next door could possibly hear the shots, but they were old, and their dullard adult child was no threat to him. Gerard simply needed to stifle the sound enough to prevent partiers from hearing the noise.

He tilted his neck until it cracked, tilted the other way; it cracked again.

Then Gerard reached up and knocked on the door.

4.

January 1. 2:15 a.m.

Derek helped Momma into bed and returned to the living room to wait for Papa to return from the party. He liked being at the party, but couldn't go back and enjoy it some more because he had to stay and look after Momma. What if she needed him and he wasn't here? That would be bad. Very bad. He wasn't a bad boy, not like that. He took good care of his Momma.

He colored in his coloring book instead. He liked to color. And he was good at it, too. He stayed in the lines, just like Momma showed him. His favorite book was the one with farm animals. He had been on a farm once. He saw cows and chickens, ducks and cats. The cats were not friendly at all and that made him sad. He wanted to pet the cats, but they hissed and ran away.

He petted the cows instead. They mooed when he touched them and that made him laugh. He liked the farm. He fed the ducks at the pond. Momma worried that he would fall in, but Derek was a big boy. He could swim if he fell in. But he didn't fall in. When the ducks were fed, and all nice and fat, he watched Auntie Florence collect the eggs from the chickens. He ate the eggs for breakfast. Uncle Larry shot and killed a deer, and so they had deer meat for dinner. Uncle Larry called it Vent-a-sin. Ventasin was good to eat. He even had seconds.

Thinking of the farm, Auntie Florence and Uncle Larry made him sad; because Momma said the world was going to end, and so they would perish with all the other people of the world. He didn't

190

want them to perish. To perish meant to die, like the deer died. But no one was going to eat them. That was good. Derek didn't want his Auntie and Uncle to be eaten.

When He finished coloring, he put his book and the crayons away. He remembered to do it this time. Momma would be proud of him.

He entered the kitchen and opened the fridge. He took a grape soda and opened it. He took a swig and set it on the table. He looked through the cupboards for a snack. He liked Twinkies, but they didn't have any of those. The food was delivered on a weekly schedule and they could only get the stuff on the list. There were no stores inside the Ark, Momma told him; and so, they had to make do with what was in storage.

Derek chose a box of crackers and went to the living room with the crackers and the soda. Momma wouldn't want him eating too many sweets. The soda was ok because he was allowed one soda a night. He took another sip.

He yawned. It was late at night, he knew, and he had been up for a long time; but he didn't want to go to bed until Papa returned, so he walked around to keep from falling asleep. He looked at the clock. The numbers said 2:26. He wondered what that meant.

It means it's late, dummy. He scolded himself. That is what it meant. *It's two twenty-six late.* Papa would be home soon. Then he could climb into bed and sleep. *Hurry up, Papa.* His thoughts were more urgent than he meant them to be. "Sorry, Papa." He spoke the words aloud, he realized, when he heard his voice reverberating in the room. He slapped his hand over his mouth. Oops, he meant to say that inside his head.

"Derek." Momma's voice carried out to the living room.

Great, he thought. *Now you went and woke Momma.*

He hurried into the room. Momma was sitting up, or trying to. He helped her.

"Can you do Momma a big favor and get her a glass of water. I have a screaming backache and need to take a pill."

"Sure, Momma. Sure."

He headed to the kitchen to fetch a glass of water. He returned it to her and helped her lift the glass to her lips. When he took the glass back from her, he helped her lay back down.

Derek took the glass to the sink and returned to the living room to wait for Papa. He sat in his chair and tapped his fingers impatiently on the arm. He stared at a single point on the wall until his mind went blank. He sat like that until he heard movement in the hall outside the apartment.

Thinking his Papa had come home, Derek stood and walked to the door. He opened the door a crack and peered out.

It was not Papa in the hall. A man—a stranger—stood at the door to the Lutz's apartment. Did the stranger know who lived there? Nora lived there. She was so nice. She baked cookies for him. Nora was always looking in on Momma, especially since Momma had hurt her back falling down the stairs last fall.

Derek watched as the man pulled something out of his pocket. *Looks like a gun.* The thought made him shiver. *A toy…just a toy.*

The man knocked on the door to the Lutz's.

Derek stayed quiet, watching, and waited to see what would happen next. Tom answered the door. Derek couldn't see him but he heard Tom voice say: "Hello, may I help you?"

Derek flinched when he heard a sound like the cracking of a whip through cotton-stuffed ears. Tom slumped to the floor.

Derek heard a woman scream. Nora. He heard that sound again, twice—thwack, thwack—and Nora's scream stopped as suddenly as it began. When the man stepped into the apartment, Derek stepped into the hall. He saw Tom's body in the doorway. There was blood.

Tom was dead. He watched as the man gripped Tom's body by the legs and pulled him into the apartment. Derek felt a warm wetness hit his leg. His hands shook. Derek slipped back into his apartment and carefully closed the door. He locked it and then stood with his back pressed against it.

Not a toy at all. Derek's eyes were blurry, so he wiped away the wetness there.

He killed them, Derek knew. That man had killed his neighbors.

And now he'll be coming for me and Momma.

Derek raced toward Momma's room. He looked around the room for a safe place for them to hide. He thought about the closet.

No, the man was sure to look for them there.

Then Derek spotted the chest. It was big enough for Momma, but Derek was a big boy, and much too big to fit in there.

Derek dropped down in front of the chest and pulled the lacy tablecloth off. He opened the chest and pulled out all the stuff stored in there. He crammed the junk from the chest under the bed and then went to where Momma lay sleeping under the blanket. He shook her awake.

"Momma, he's coming for us."

Momma came slowly awake. She was groggy, and angry. She didn't want to be woken up. "Derek, what in the hell are you doing?"

"Momma. The man is coming." Derek tried to lift her, but Momma struggled against him.

"What are you talking about? What man?"

"The hunter."

The words stopped Momma's struggles. Derek lifted her easily now and carried her to the open chest. Stay in here, Momma. And stay quiet. I will get him to go away."

Derek lowered Momma into the trunk and closed it. She didn't struggle. He placed the cloth back over the chest and made sure it looked pretty. Once he believed Momma was safe, Derek went to the closet to hide.

5.

Gerard moved the bodies into the bedroom then exited the apartment, closing the door behind him. He peered to the right, to the end of the hallway where his help waited for him to finish. He nodded once to inform the person at the end of the hall that the first apartment was clear. Then he turned to the next door. He splayed the fingers of his right hand, flexing. He switched the gun to that hand, and flexed the fingers of his left hand. He gripped the gun in his left hand and knocked on the door. When no one answered, he tried the knob. The door was locked. Gerard took a step back and kicked the door near the jamb. There was a crack of breaking wood and the door caved in like cardboard. The door flew along its arc and crashed into the wall. It slowly began the journey back to its original position. Gerard pushed it aside and stepped into the apartment.

He saw no one. He moved slowly through the apartment, first checking the bedroom attached to the living room. There was a bed and a dresser, but nowhere for someone to hide. He moved on to the first bathroom. He checked behind the shower curtain but saw nothing.

He came out of the bathroom and looked around. He saw no one trying to make a break for the broken front door. There was a nasty surprise waiting for them out there if they did. Gerard turned to the right and entered the dining room. He moved silently through the darkened room, lifting the table linen and looking under the table. Nothing there. He moved through the swinging French doors to the kitchen. He checked the pantry and the broom closet then moved back into the hallway from the kitchen entrance.

The back bedroom was unused, except for storage and a cursory scan of the room convinced him it was empty. He moved some boxes out of the way and looked deeper, just to be sure. He exited the room and returned to the hall.

There was only the master bedroom left to check.

Gerard stepped into the doorway and hesitated. He listened. Without making a sound, Gerard crossed the room to the master bathroom. He looked behind this shower curtain as well. He stepped back into the room. He listened. He heard breathing. He smelled urine.

Gerard moved toward the closet at the other end of the room. He stood outside and sniffed again. The smell was stronger here. He put his ear to the wood. He heard the heavy breathing inside. He stepped back and smiled. He raised the gun.

The door swung open so fast it nearly knocked the gun from his hand. Gerard stumbled back. The big dumb oaf son bolted out of the room and ran down the hall toward the front door. Gerard considered giving chase, but stopped.

He still heard breathing.

The old woman was in here somewhere. He stood, unmoving, listening. The breathing sounded muffled, as if from behind a thick barrier. He checked under the bed but only saw junk under there. he looked around for another place to hide.

His eyes passed over the chest pushed up against the wall but on the return scan of the room, he spotted it. He stood motionless for another breath. He heard the breathing and knew where it was coming from now.

Gerard smiled.

He kneeled down and placed his ear to the trunk lid. He definitely heard the labored breathing of someone who was having trouble taking a breath. She was scared, and he could hear her sobs as well. He stood and stepped back.

He raised the gun. He aimed it in the area of the trunk where he believed the old woman's heart would be and then pulled the trigger.

Thwack, thwack, thwack.

6.

Derek listened, trying to control his breathing, but it was impossible. He was just too scared. He waited, and when he sensed the man on the other side of the door, and he could see the man's shadow at the gap under the door, Derek made his move. He screamed and burst through the door. The effect was successful. He caught the man off guard and made it out of the room without getting shot. Derek cried as he ran to the door.

In the hall, Derek ran to the right. Papa was at the party, with the others, and that was to the right. Derek ran down the hall to the end and turned the corner.

He ran into the person standing there.

Derek stopped and stared in shocked confusion at the person standing there. After a moment, he recognized who was there.

"Miss Ethel, please help us. There's a man with a gun. Momma's in trouble. Please help."

"Hush child. You're talking gibberish," Ethel said. "Start over. What are you saying?"

Derek turned back toward the apartments. "There is a man with a…"

He stopped as he felt something painful in the front of him. He looked down at his round belly. A knife protruded from his stomach, just above his belly button. The knife was caked with frosting. A hand held the handle of the knife. Derek followed the arm up to the face of his attacker. Ethel stared back at him with a look that was equal parts compassion and disgust. She pulled the knife free and stabbed again. She pulled the knife out of his stomach and blood sprayed over her shoes.

"Ow." Derek growled and reached out with both hands. He took Ethel by the throat and pinned her to the wall. He squeezed until her eyes bulged. Her mouth opened in an O and her tongue poked out. Drool dripped from the corner of her mouth.

Her hands went slack.

7.

Ethel tried to scream out but all she could manage was a kind of gurgling cough. She couldn't believe what was happening. *I'm dying*, oh god *I'm dying. I can't die. I have more to do. I have to finish this. I have a mission to save Chris from himself. Don't let it end like this.* Faces floated in front of her eyes, taunting her. She saw the old man; she saw Brian and Scott. She saw the bitch Kaylan. She couldn't die; they had to die, them. Not her.

196

Not her.

Tears trickled from her eyes, but she didn't think she was crying. She was *leaking.* The pressure on her head as the bastard squeezed her neck tighter and tighter caused her face to burn and tears to flow from her eyes.

Where was he getting all this strength? She had stabbed him twice already. She had no strength to hold the knife and it dropped to the floor. The most that she could muster was to slap harmlessly at his massive arms. Her body convulsed in his hands, and he slammed her head into the wall behind her. Her vision, blurry from the tears, now started to darken. Soon, her vision became a mere pinprick of bright white light in a wall of utter blackness.

A flurry of movement caused the pressure on her throat to slacken and she was able to suck in a gasping breath. Her vision returned. She watched as her son, Gerard, walked up to the dummy and put the gun to his temple. Gerard squeezed the trigger and the hands disappeared from her neck completely.

She gasped. And gasped. She bent over and used the wall to brace herself as the burning oxygen pierced her lungs. She felt a moment of dizziness and then she was able to stand up straight. She took a few normal breaths and then slapped Gerard on the arm.

"Where the hell were you?" Her voice was a hoarse whisper. "That retard almost killed me."

"I had to find the old woman."

"I trust you took care of it?"

"I did." Gerard slapped a fresh clip into the Beretta.

"Good." Ethel picked the knife up off the floor. "Now let's go crash a party."

8.

January 1. 3:10 a.m.

Chris felt an odd, roiling pang in his stomach, and his mind kept turning to beyond the party. It wasn't hunger he felt; it was dread. His uneasiness must have been apparent, because Brian turned to him with a smile that quickly faded, and asked: "what's wrong?"

"I don't know. I just have this general sense of unease, like I left the stove on, or something. I feel like I forgot something."

"Did you forget to leave the stove on?" Brian asked.

Chris laughed, but his unease did not abate. "No. I'm sure that's not it. I don't even know if the feeling is real, or just me worrying about nothing."

"It's not like there isn't a lot to worry about. Least of which is the death of everyone in the world outside."

"That's out of my control. Whatever is bothering me—if it's real at all—is something I could be doing, or doing differently, to resolve. I don't want to alarm anyone, or ruin anyone's good time. I'll figure out what it is later."

Brian nodded and turned back to the music and the Celtic folk dancers. The men wore thick tartan shirts, kilts, and heavy boots. The women wore chunky reel shoes and frilly dresses. The troop spun and twirled, stomped and shuffled in a dizzying display of skill and talent.

The dance ended and the crowd applauded.

Chris clapped as well, but his eyes wandered, and he spotted his brother and Kaylan in an area where people were playing charades. He made is way over to them. Kaylan danced around and acted like an ape, which made Chris laugh. Scott looked up at his brother from his seat.

"Want to play?"

Chris put a hand up. "No, I'll just watch if that's okay."

"Cool," Scott said. "Cool."

Scott turned back as Kaylan pretended to swing from vines.

"Scott said, "Tarzan."

Kaylan shook her head. No. She jumped into Scott's face, scratching under her armpits. She seemed to be pleading with him to understand. Chris laughed again, but they ignored him.

198

"King Kong." Scott nearly jumped out of his seat with excitement.

But that was wrong, too.

Chris said, "Planet of the Apes."

"Yes." Kaylan stopped her mimicry.

"I thought you weren't playing?" Scott asked.

"I can still guess, can't I?" he said.

"I guess so, but now you won. You have to do the next charade."

"You can take my turn."

"That's not how the game is played. You have to pick the next category and act it out."

"Can't you do it?"

"Nope. Pick the name out of the bowl and act it out. You can do it."

"Yeah, you can do it." Kaylan grabbed the bowl and held it out to Chris. After a moment of hesitation, he reached in and pulled out a piece of paper. He read what was written there in disbelief. He folded the paper back up and tossed it into the bowl.

The paper had Grim Reaper written on it. Chris felt like the Grim Reaper, himself. Reaping the death of everyone on the planet. He shoved the bowl away and sat back down.

"I don't know what I'm doing. Scott, take my place."

The other players looked around at each other in confusion.

"Is the game over then?" Fiona asked looking at Chris for an answer.

"I didn't mean to get involved. If you all still want to play, feel free. I can't play."

Martin Foley threw his hands up. "I'm good if we want to quit. I haven't won a single game." Martin walked away.

"Same here," Fiona said. I'm getting tired. I think I'll watch the dancers for a couple of minutes, and then head to bed."

"It's getting late," Kaylan said. "How much longer is this party going to last?"

"Until everyone leaves, I guess," Chris said. "I'm not going to chase anyone out. As soon as the last people leave we'll be finished here."

"What about the performers? Are there going to be performers the entire time? Maybe we don't have to chase them out. Just stop giving them reasons to stay." Kaylan looked around at all the stunned faces staring at her. "What? I'm just looking out for Chris. He looks wasted. He's clearly worn down."

"I'm fine, Kaylan. Thanks for thinking of me, though."

Another troop of dancers began warming up for another dance. Kaylan said, "Do you think they are wearing anything under those kilts?"

"I believe they are not," Roger said.

Chris turned to Roger, astonished. "Was that a joke?"

"Not at all. I helped them set up during practice. They are traditional performers, and completely naked under those kilts."

"I'm going to be there when you tell a joke," Chris said.

Roger gave only the hint of a smile. He turned toward the dancers as they stretched.

The music stopped, and Chris heard bits and pieces of the various conversations around the table. Chris turned toward the people standing to his right. They looked at him with dire expressions on their faces. He felt that strange sense of dread in his stomach again. He focused on the woman named Fiona. She stared at him, studying him. He didn't turn away from her stare. *She's got a knife and she's going to…*

There were a little over a hundred people still left in the ballroom.

Fiona nodded a polite greeting at him when she caught him looking at her. He smiled back but it felt more like a grimace. His stomach roiled. *I'm going to throw up.*

Fiona's face darkened as she glimpsed something behind Chris.

Chris stood and looked behind him.

200

The room burst into a flurry of confused movement and shouts. Gerard stepped into the ballroom and lifted the gun over his head. He pulled the trigger and a bullet whumped from the gun. The slug slammed into the ceiling, causing plaster to drift down.

Someone screamed, then the room grew silent except for gasps of alarm, and crying from frightened people. The crowd moved into a tight clump, with Chris at the center. Slowly, they cycled him toward the back. Roger stuck by Chris's side, holding him back as he tried to move back toward the front.

Chris spotted Ethel standing next to Gerard. He glanced at the knife in her hand and moaned softly as he realized there was blood dripping from it.

"Please stay calm," Gerard said and held the gun out in a non-threatening manner. "I won't hurt you if you do as I say."

"We want the non-believers, that's all," Ethel said. "Send them out so we can do what we have to do. Then everyone else can go back to enjoying the party. We only want the non-believers."

The stunned crowd stopped moving. Chris broke through the front of the group, but Roger stayed with him.

"What have you done?" Chris asked.

Gerard ignored him, but Ethel turned to him and laughed.

Chris glared at her, unafraid.

"We did what needed doing." Ethel's knife hand twitched.

Glenn stepped forward, exiting the crowd, but when Chris saw him moving toward the two aggressors, he gripped Glenn's forearm and stopped him. Roger helped Chris keep Glenn from approaching the armed pair.

"What have you done, you crazy fucks?" Tears turned his eyes red and puffy, and spittle flew from his lips. He muscled out of Chris and Roger's grip, but did not approach further.

They did not answer his question.

"That's right. The old man is one." Ethel waved the knife evocatively. "We want them all. Bring them all forward. You know who you are. Brian, where are you? Scott? Kaylan, you little bitch; get out here."

Kaylan stepped forward, exiting the crowd. Scott held her hand. Brian stepped into place behind them.

Now the crowd, once protective and courageous, moved in an arc away from the six clustered in front of them. No one wanted to be shot accidentally, it would seem. Chris didn't blame them. He didn't want anyone getting hurt, but he would minimize the casualties as much as possible if something did go wrong.

Chris stepped forward. He stopped and held up his hands when Gerard pointed the gun at him. "Gerard, please. Don't do this. There's no reason to harm anyone. Everyone here has a purpose. Everyone. I chose these people. So, whether they are true believers or not, they have just as much right to be here as anyone else. Why can't you—"

"What gives you the right to make those decisions?" It was Ethel speaking now. "We are here because we heard the call and answered it. We heard it even before you were made the Chosen One, some of us. I heard the call as a young girl. I joined the fight long before you were born. Gerard, my son, heard it as a young boy. We have been preparing for years."

Chris took another step.

"Stop right there," Gerard said.

Ethel continued speaking to Chris without regard to Gerard's command. "You are the Chosen One, but there is nothing in the calling which tells me you have the right to pick people—who did not hear the call—to come into the new world. Gerard and I took it upon ourselves to correct that mistake."

Ethel stepped forward. She gave a sideways glance at Gerard and the gun.

"I want the Bitch, Kaylan, to come with me. The others go with my son."

Chris took a defensive stance in front of Kaylan. Roger moved into place at Chris's left, and Scott stood to the right. Brian and Glenn stood between Kaylan and Chris. Some of the others in the crowd began to filter up and move out of the pack. Among those who stepped forward, Chris noticed Jerry and Mark. For a second, he wondered if he would have to protect Kaylan from more than one direction.

"There has to be a better way to settle this," Chris said. He didn't move, and his hands were still up, but he turned his head slightly toward Jerry. He tried to get a sense of Jerry's intentions, but the man's face was stoic.

Ethel waved her knife again. "It's already settled."

"Enough talk." Gerard lifted the gun and pointed it at Scott. "Move over to the wall and turn around. All of you. I promise to make it quick and painless."

Ethel smiled and looked through the protective men to Kaylan. "I can't make the same promise for you."

Kaylan pushed through the group to stand unprotected in the front of the line. Scott reached for her but she brushed his hand away.

"That's right," Ethel said. "Come get what's due."

"I'm not afraid of you." Kaylan took a defiant step toward the old woman. "Let's do this."

Chris grabbed her by the waist and pulled her back. She didn't resist. "You're not helping matters," Chris said into Kaylan's ear. He swung her around, and into Scott's arms. She allowed her husband to hold her, and she didn't try to confront Ethel again, but continued to boldly glare at the woman.

Chris turned his attention back to the trouble, back to the gun.

"No one is going to die tonight," Chris said.

"Too late for that." Ethel held up the knife.

Chris didn't look at the weapon; he focused squarely on Ethel's face. "I don't know what you've done, but I assure you that if you drop your weapons, you'll be treated fairly."

Gerard lifted the gun again. "I'm not going to tell you again."

He pointed the gun at Brian, took aim. Brian raised his hands in front of his chest and slowly moved toward the wall.

"Turn around."

Brian turned and faced the wall.

Scott moved to the wall and stood next to Brian. Scott, too, turned to face the wall.

Glenn didn't move at first but Gerard fired a warning shot at his feet. The bullet pinged off the tiled floor and echoed through the vast room. Screams erupted and combined with the ringing of the gunshot's fading blast. Glenn moved slowly and deliberately to the wall and stood next to Scott. Glenn did not take his eyes off Gerard once, and did not turn to face the wall. Gerard didn't force him.

Ethel motioned for Kaylan to come to her, but Chris pushed her behind him. Roger helped block her in.

"I'm sorry ma'am," Jerry said. Chris turned to see what he was planning to do. "I didn't mean those things I said to you in the hallway. I don't know what got into me." Jerry smiled at her and then rushed toward Ethel. Before she could react, Jerry slapped the knife from her hand and it clattered to the floor, spinning and sliding out of reach, across the tile.

Gerard turned on Jerry and shot. The bullet caught him in the throat and he fell to his knees, clutching his torn neck as blood poured through his fingers.

Chris stepped forward, wanting to help the fallen man.

Gerard turned the gun on Chris. He pulled the trigger.

The bullet thumped into Roger's chest as the man stepped in front of Chris. As Roger sagged, Chris caught him.

Chris followed Roger to the floor, cradling the man in his arms. Chris watched through the blur of tears as the red blossom spread across Roger's shirt.

Roger looked up and touched Chris's cheek. He wiped away Chris's tear. Roger grimaced as pain seared his chest. Then he spoke. "Knight takes pawn."

Chris stopped crying. He stared down at Roger, who had begun to *laugh*.

"You told a joke?" Chris said, stunned. "Now, you tell a joke?"

Roger laughed again, and coughed. Blood sprayed from his mouth. His body went limp. Chris held him, rocking the limp form. He laid Roger on the floor. He stared into the man's unblinking stare. *No, this can't be. I have so much more to do with you. Don't leave me. Don't leave…*

9.

The remaining crowd of people rushed forward, pouring past Chris as he cradled Roger's body. Some of the people broke off the main group and went after Ethel. They pinned her down, not allowing her to move. She struggled, but to no avail.

Gerard wasn't treated so kindly. As the rest of the crowd rushed him, he fired randomly into the mob. Someone went down, someone was hit in the arm by a stray bullet, but the rest of the people continued forward. They reached him and knocked the gun from his hand. Gerard was punched and kicked until he was forced to one knee. When he tried to stand, the mob pushed him down. Anyone close enough to reach him, hit him, kicked him.

Glenn took control of the situation, and broke off a thick wooden leg from one of the tables. He forced his way through the crowd. Standing in front of Gerard, Glenn raised the table leg over his head. The leg came crashing down and cracked Gerard's skull. The man fell sideways, blood gushing from the lacerated scalp. People backed away. He hit him again. Gerard's body twitched, and brain matter leaked onto the floor. From where she sat, Ethel screamed her rage and frustration as she watched her son die in front of her. When she tried to go to him, the people guarding her forced her back down.

Glenn dropped the wooden club and raced out of the room.

10.

Chris was bumped by someone, and he looked up. He saw the crowd of people and remembered what had happened…what was still happening.

Chris followed the man out the door. They turned to the right at the intersection. The older man was too far ahead for Chris to catch up and stop him, and Glenn disappeared around the next corner.

As Chris made the turn, he spotted the man crouched on the floor, leaning over something. Brian and Scott reached Chris and they stopped, too. Slowly, the three approached him. The man wept and held his son's hand to his mouth. Chris knelt down beside him. He removed Derek's hand from Glenn's grasp and helped the distraught man to his feet. Glenn leaned against Chris, still crying.

Glenn's head popped up. "My wife."

The man pulled out of Chris's arms and raced toward the apartment.

The three entered the apartment through the broken door behind Glenn. The older man ran through his house calling his wife's name. Chris rushed to him, stopped the older man and led him to a chair. Chris took an adjacent chair and stayed by his side. Glenn stared ahead. Chris didn't know what to do so he simply sat there, allowing the man to grieve.

"We're looking for her." Chris took his hand. "We'll find her. She's hiding somewhere, that all."

Please let her just be hiding. I can't take much more of this. Please, let her…

Scott emerged from the hallway. Brian followed close behind. Chris and Glenn both looked up as they approached. Brian carried Patty's limp and lifeless form.

"No." Glenn wailed. He sprung from his seat ran to Patty. He took her from Brian and carried her to the sofa.

Chris turned to Brian and Scott. "I'm going to stay here with him until he's ready to allow us to move her. You go check on the Lutz's and see how far this tragedy goes. I only pray they were left unharmed."

Even as he said it, Chris knew the truth.

11.

January 1 8:30 a.m.

A streak of blood spread across the living room floor, but there was no other sign of trouble. When Brian entered the Lutz's bedroom, and found them laid out on their bed, he thought they were just sleeping. A closer inspection revealed the truth of the matter, however. Behind him, Scott choked on a sob.

These are my friends. I spent the last several years sharing stories with them, helping them and being helped by them. How could this be happening?

12.

Chris insisted that Gerard's body not be stored next to the others in the cooler, so he was shoved off in a corner alone, a sheet covering him so Chris didn't have to look at him.

Chris stood over the other bodies looking down at them with anger and frustration clouding his judgement.

I could kill her. But no, he couldn't. Not really. He didn't have it in him to kill anyone. Not even her. But if he had it in him…

Ethel had been handcuffed in the next room over, imprisoned, for the time being, in an exam room at the infirmary. He couldn't bear to look at her. He had been avoiding seeing her since the incident.

Chris put thoughts of Ethel out of his mind for the moment, so he could concentrate on mourning his friends.

Seeing Nora affected Chris hardest of all. He had promised her she would see the sky and hear birds singing in the trees as a summer breeze blew back her hair. He would never get the chance to fulfill that promise.

Chris didn't feel it was right to keep the killer in close proximity to his victims, but he had little choice. There was simply nowhere else to store Gerard.

Chris went from gurney to gurney covering each face of his friends with the sheet over their bodies. He said a silent little goodbye to each one. His throat felt clogged with a dirty rag that he couldn't choke back up, or swallow down.

I'm sorry. I let you all down, and I'll never forgive myself for that.

Once the last face was covered, Chris turned and exited the cooler. He passed through the pharmacy, nodding a solemn greeting to Hank, the pharmacist, as he headed to the exit. He passed through the automatic doors to the main room of the infirmary. This rectangular room served as the reception area. Dr. Jacobson kept a desk at the far end of the room, near the three remaining exam rooms. She had patched up the gunshot victims, who had survived the early morning shooting spree, and was in one of the exam rooms now, assisting someone.

The fourth exam room, the one that was now Ethel's prison, waited for him. He took a deep breath and pulled the door open, stepped inside.

All the exam rooms were identical. Ethel had a cot, a table and one folding chair. There was also a bathroom in there, but it was a small half bath with only a sink and a toilet, used primarily for collecting samples of urine. She would need to sponge bathe from the sink if she wanted to stay clean. Chris hadn't decided yet if he would allow her shower privileges.

"The Respectable One visits the mean old lady." She clasped her hands together on the table with a rattle of the chains.

Chris stood in front of the door and glared at her. He made no move to sit at the table across from her. Quite frankly, he wasn't willing to be within strangling distance of her, for fear that he would wrap his hands around her neck and squeeze.

"Why did you do this? Why would you kill all those people? It doesn't make sense."

Ethel's smug smile faded from her lips and her eyes clouded over. "You monsters killed my boy. I would say we're even."

"We're not even, not by a long shot."

She sniffed and sat back. Her chains clattered as they rolled off the table.

"I've been conducting interviews, and the consensus is you and Gerard were acting alone. Is this true? Do I have to worry about this happening again?"

Ethel giggled, looking every bit the harmless old lady. "Whatever do you mean? I didn't hurt a fly." She shifted in her seat. "Well, there was the Dummy. But I didn't kill him, either; Gerard did that one, too. So, it looks like you're holding me illegally. I didn't kill anybody. I guess you'll have to let me go."

Chris shifted his weight. "Gerard acted on your behalf. That's good enough for me."

"I demand a trial."

"That's not going to happen. In fact, we'll be making new rules and regulations to deal with killers like you. You will be the first criminal to be held accountable for your actions here inside the Ark."

"Will I be getting a lawyer?"

"No," Chris said. "It's not a democracy. We are holding a ballot, and everyone will cast their voice to decide your fate. There are only three choices: innocence, exile, or death."

Ethel's smile faded. "And if it's death? Who will do the deed, you?"

"Yes." He showed no hesitation.

Ethel stared at Chris. He could see she was searching for something that might give her hope, that if it came down to it, he wouldn't be able go through with the sentence. She must not have seen what she was looking for because her confidence did not return.

"When does this…lottery take place? When can I learn my fate?"

Chris shook his head. "You won't get any say in the matter. When we hold the hearing on your fate, you won't know until the verdict is read."

"What about that bastard who killed my boy? He's a killer now, too. He should have the same fate as me."

"We already held a vote on that. It was unanimous that he was innocent of his actions."

"Isn't that just special?" She yanked on her chains, but the steel bar holding her in place was immovable. She looked around, as if finally realizing this was her home now.

A twinge of guilt passed through Chris as he watched her. "I'll tell you that from what I'm hearing, it's very likely your verdict will be exile."

"Exile is as good as death. You might as well kill me."

"If after the votes are cast, and you are exiled, and you still want me to kill you, I will."

Ethel squirmed in her seat. "I don't believe that. You're no killer."

"But it's true. I do believe you should die for what you did. I will cast my vote for death." Chris did not blink as he spoke. He did not turn away.

Ethel stared at him for a long time. After a while, she slowly let a smile creep across her face. "If you truly think I killed your friends, you have every right to hate me. But to wish me dead? That's not in you." She tried to look at him, but then looked away.

"I don't hate you."

She glanced sideways at him. "Come now. Don't start lying now."

"I don't hate you. I'd have to feel an emotion for you to hate you. I have no emotion when it comes to you. I don't feel hate for you, nor pity. Not even disappointment. You targeted everyone I ever loved for death. I should feel something for you, but I don't. When I walk out that door, I won't give you a second thought."

Her smile was sly, arrogant. "Are you sure about that? Did you find the key?"

Chris froze. His voice was a hard whisper. "What key? A key to what?"

"Did you find the key that Gerard had on him? Go get the key. It opens a freezer in the storeroom. You still have one big surprise waiting for you."

Chris's mouth went dry. He turned and rushed out of the room; her cackling laugh followed him into the main room of the infirmary, and beyond.

13.

January 2.

Nancy listened as Brian told her about the Lutz's and the Holmes's. She was, at first, confused. No, it couldn't be. He was lying. Her next emotion was anger. The place hadn't been safe after all. She had led her friends to the slaughter. They should never have entered that death trap.

No, she couldn't do that. Chris had no way of knowing what the future would hold.

He's been too trusting. He should have known there would be danger. She took a deep breath. It was unfair of her to blame Chris. She couldn't think like that.

"How is Glenn? Could I speak to him?"

"I'll see if he's up for a skype session, but right now he's not talking to anyone."

"It's understandable. I'll wait for him."

Brian shifted in his seat, but said nothing.

"Is Chris available? I'd like to speak to him."

Brian stood up, and all she could see was his torso, then he sat back down. "He's actually at one of the other monitors. There were a lot of people who needed to be consoled today. He wanted to speak to everyone personally." Brian stood up after a few minutes, and Chris appeared in view of the computer's camera. Brian backed off, and Chris took the seat.

"Hi, Nancy. How are you?" Chris said.

"I'm fine. Thanks for asking. I wanted to give you my condolences for Roger. I know he meant a lot to you."

Chris eyes clouded over with the fog of memory and then he focused on her again. "He saved my life. I'm going to miss him. I'm going to miss all of them. My last conversation with Nora was about the outdoors, and how excited she was to feel a fresh breeze on her face again. She wanted to feel sand in her toes, the sun on her face, and hear birdsong on the wind. I've decided to create a room in her honor. There will be trees, and birds, and a place where people can go swimming. Brian agreed to be head lifeguard."

"It's right up his alley." Nancy offered a grim, thin-lipped smile. It's the best she could do. "It's a nice thing you're doing in Nora's memory."

"I'm calling it Nora's Pond."

"That sounds wonderful. I hope to see it one day."

"I hope so, too."

"I asked to speak with Glenn, but no rush. He needs his time I know. But, how is he? I mean, is he doing okay?"

"I have him staying with me and Brian for now. I didn't want to move him into a module alone. I wanted to keep a closer eye on him."

"I'm glad to hear that."

There was a pause, where neither of them spoke.

"Okay, I'll let your husband come back and say good bye."

"Thank you for talking to me. I know you have much to do."

"It was nice talking to you. I hope we get another chance really soon, okay?"

"Me too."

Chris moved off and Brian sat back down, filling the screen.

"Do you finally have time for me?" Brian asked.

Nancy offered a tired half-smile. It was a struggle to show any kind of happiness. "I'll always have time for the love of my life."

"Bad joke. Sorry."

"I love your bad jokes."

Brian looked shocked. "You mean they really are bad? I was just joking about that."

"Afraid so love." They stopped the banter. Then Nancy said, "I hear you'll be a lifeguard again soon. At Nora's Pond?" Even through the blurry, disrupted connection Nancy saw Brian's face light up with excitement at the prospect of lifeguarding again.

"I'm so excited about that. I'm going to put a posting up for teenagers who want to learn how to lifeguard."

"Just like old times."

He nodded. "But right now, I just want to talk to you. We don't have to end our session. Let's talk all day."

"As tempting as that sounds, you're too important there to waste all your time talking to me. I'm going to let you go now, my love. And we'll talk again tonight, okay?"

"Yes, tonight." Brian kissed his fingers and placed them on the camera lens. She copied the gesture and then signed off.

She stood and walked toward the window. She had been hearing someone out there but had been ignoring them until she could get off the computer. As a plank of wood dropped in at her, a face, sickly and deranged stared in at her. The man smiled, but it was short-lived. Nancy picked up the shotgun next to the window, took aim, and shot the man in the face. A quick glance around outside let her know there were no other invaders in the yard.

She pounded the board back into place.

14.

January 2. 1 p.m.

Carrie placed the plate of ham, mashed potatoes and green beans on the rolling tray and placed a stainless-steel dome cover over the plate. She filled a glass with milk and placed it next to the covered plate. She then pushed the rolling cart out of the kitchen and through the dining area. She rolled the cart into the corridor, moved down the right, and then right again, and pressed the elevator button. When the elevator arrived, she pushed the cart into the carriage.

"What floor, please?" the metallic female voice asked.

"Floor one, please."

The elevator dropped to the first floor. She exited when the doors whooshed open and headed down the corridor, past the freight elevator to the north corridor. She followed the corridor to the infirmary and stopped. She pushed through the door.

Dr. Jacobson stood up from her desk, rubbed her eyes and came to Carrie. She lifted the lid and looked inside.

"Lunch time at the zoo?" Dr. Jacobson said.

Carrie didn't reply.

"Is this what you're serving at the restaurant? I'm starving. Will you be okay on your own while I go get something to eat?" The doctor replaced the lid.

"I guess so." This was Carrie's first time bringing food to the prisoner. She didn't know what to expect.

Dr. Jacobson rolled her eyes. "I wish they could have found another place to store the criminal element. I don't like having her here."

"I'd be more freaked out by the dead bodies in the cooler," Carrie said.

Hellen chuckled. "I'm okay with the dead, it's the living that perplexes me. I'm not prepared to take care of a living prisoner. I'm not the warden. When it comes to the dead, I know exactly what to do."

"I'm sure it's only temporary," Carrie said. "Has she been much trouble?"

"Surprisingly, no. I hardly know she's there. But if we get more criminal-types in here, I'm going to have to question if I made the right choice allowing her to be kept here. What if I have patients and she escapes and harms them? I don't know. I think she should be kept somewhere else."

"Have you mentioned it to Chris?"

"No. I'll wait until the tenderness of the incident slackens before I bring it up."

Carrie nodded, understanding the logic. She pushed the cart on to the room where Ethel resided. She opened the door and rolled the cart in. She tried not to look at the woman sitting on the bed.

Carrie stopped at the table and began transferring the food onto it. She had been told to stay on the opposite side of the table from Ethel. Ethel's chain could not reach past the table. But still, she was counselled not to allow the woman to touch her.

"What's for lunch?" Ethel stayed on the bed until the food had been placed on the table.

"Ham and potatoes," Carrie said. She was uncomfortable talking to the woman, but she didn't want to be rude. *Just serve the food and get out, not hard at all.*

"You know, I'm not the monster they are making me out to be."

"I wouldn't know. I wasn't there."

"Well, you can believe me. I didn't kill anybody. My son did all the killing. You can even ask Chris."

"I believe you."

"Are you afraid of me? I don't want you to be afraid. I'd never hurt you."

Carrie stepped away from the table but didn't leave right away. "I'm not."

"Really? I don't believe you."

Carrie finished transferring the food to the table and backed away. Ethel took a seat at the table and lifted the lid. She closed her eyes, leaned over the plate and smelled the food. She let a hint of a smile play on her face.

"I'm only here because we — my family, that is — pulled the long straw and earned the right to be your meal supplier."

Ethel contemplated Carrie's words, but most of her attention was on the food. "What a polite way to say you lost the bet."

Carrie felt her face getting hot. *Deliver the food; don't talk to the prisoner.* She chanted the mantra over and over in her head. *Don't get caught up in a conversation, Carrie. Chris warned you against this. Just drop off the food and leave.*

Ethel chewed a mouthful of the meat and moaned with pleasure. "My compliments to the chef."

Carrie should have walked out, but found herself staring at the woman instead.

Ethel glanced over at her. "Have a seat. I'd love the company, and I already expressed to you I have no interest in showing you any harm."

Almost as if against her will, Carrie grabbed the back of the chair on her side of the table and dragged it back. When she believed it was far enough from the table to be safe, she sat.

"I wanted my boyfriend to join us, but my father refused to allow him in. My boyfriend is going to die because of my father's decision."

"Your father is a smart man. If Chris had been as smart as your father, we could have avoided all this mess."

"So, what you're saying is if my boyfriend had been allowed in, you would have targeted him for death?"

Ethel stopped eating. She placed her plastic utensils down, staring at Carrie intently while sucking at her teeth. After a moment, she stopped cleaning her teeth and spoke. "I've angered you. I didn't mean to do that. You are the first person who's been willing to talk to me since Chris threatened to have me killed. I don't want you to be angry with me."

"I'm not angry," Carrie said.

Ethel smiled. "You're crossing your arms and you're tapping your foot. You're closed off and agitated. You're also clenching your jaw. You're clearly angry and afraid. I don't want you to be."

Carrie dropped her hands to her sides, stopped clenching her teeth, and stopped tapping. "There is word going around that two bodies were found stuffed into a freezer. You're work?"

Ethel shrugged. "Anyway, whatever I did—or didn't do—is in the past. I was stopped before any more deaths had occurred. It's all over now, right?"

When Carrie didn't answer, Ethel started eating again. When the food was finished, Ethel downed the glass of milk and returned to the bed.

"I'm done," Ethel said. "Take the trays away."

Carrie stood and returned to the table. She placed the plate on the cart and reached for the dome lid.

Ethel jumped up and scurried to the table, chain jingling as she moved. The old woman grabbed Carrie's hand before she had time to pull away. Ethel held Carrie's hand in place for several seconds. Without saying a word, Ethel released Carrie's hand. Carrie pulled away, and pushed the cart out of the room, leaving the lid and the milk cup behind.

Carrie scurried through the infirmary, down the corridor to the elevators. She passed the doctor along the way.

"How did the visit go?" The doctor stopped and turned to her.

"Fine," Carrie said. She didn't stop. She entered the elevator and said, "Floor twenty-five," even before the automated voice could ask her where she wanted to go. The elevator obeyed her command and delivered her to the floor where her father's restaurant was. She returned the tray to the kitchen.

Kaylan was there, helping with her shift, so she headed to the skype room and called Jeremy. He answered quickly.

Jeremy smiled. "Hi, nice to see you again. Twice in one day." He noticed the dire look on her face and his mood dropped. "What's wrong?"

Carrie caught her breath before she spoke.

"There's been a terrible incident here, where I am."

"At the jungle refugee camp? What kind of trouble?"

"Jeremy, we're not in the jungle. We're not even out of New York State. We've been lying to you. I'm in the tower on Ampersand Lake. Have you heard of it?"

Jeremy nodded. "Yes, it was in the news. The tower that was built to protect a select few from the disease that's ravaging the planet. You're in there?"

"Yes. We would have brought you but my father denied you entry. You're trapped out there where people are dying because of my father."

Jeremy stared at her for a long time. She grew panicked that he was angry at her.

"Please," Carrie said. "I'm sorry. Please don't hate me. I'm sorry."

Jeremy smiled. "Hate you? Carrie, I'm happy. I know now that you're going to be safe. You are safe in there, right?"

She hesitated, but then nodded.

"But you said there was trouble. What kind of trouble. Are you okay?"

"I'm okay, but some people here were murdered. A man and his mother marked a bunch of people as unworthy and murdered them. The man was killed but his mother is being held at the infirmary, in a makeshift prison. I just came from there. I delivered her food."

"Did she hurt you? Is that why you're upset?"

"No, she didn't hurt me. She just touched my hand. I was kind of freaked out at first, but I think I know why she did it."

"Why?"

"She was given strict instructions not to go near me. I am to report to Chris if she did."

"Are you going to tell him?"

"That's what I'm getting at. She's testing me. She's risking the possibility of death to see if I will tell Chris. Maybe she's testing him, too. I don't think he will have her executed."

"Are you going to tell him?"

"I don't know. I don't think I will. I think she has something to say, and I want to be the one to hear it. Many people in here want her dead. Most don't care one way or the other what happens to her. I think I'm going to keep going back, to hear what she has to say. I was freaked out when she touched me, but I think I have to do this. I have to go back."

Jeremy studied her face. "I am so happy to know you're safe. I trust that you know what you're doing. But be careful. I still plan on seeing you in person again one day."

15.

January 2, 6 p.m.

Carrie delivered dinner to Ethel. The woman was already sitting at the table, waiting for her. Carrie showed no sign of distress as she approached the table and set out Ethel's food. Carrie sat down across from Ethel without trying to move away. Ethel offered her some food but she declined. Ethel shrugged and commenced eating the meal.

"I'm going to assume you didn't say anything to Chris about my breach of conduct since you've returned, and he's not with you." Ethel chewed, swallowed.

Carrie didn't respond.

"So why are you so calm about visiting me? Do you no longer see me as a threat?" Ethel took another bite of food.

"Oh, I know you're a threat—and I think you are extremely dangerous—but I think you have a lot to say, and since I'm the only one willing to listen, I think you'll tell me."

Ethel smiled. "How could you ever trust anything I have to say?"

"That's the catch, isn't it? I don't have to believe anything you say. I will just listen. If you want to spout out lies, well, that's your business, isn't it?"

"Well said."

"I know that when you touched me, you were testing me."

"Testing you." It wasn't a question; she was merely repeating what Carrie had said, as if tasting the words.

"I'm going to trust you to behave yourself when I'm here. In return, you can trust me to listen and not to judge. Be honest with me. You won't gain anything by lying to me."

"You can trust me. I won't try to hurt you. Now, what do you want to know?" Ethel cleaned her teeth in that annoying way of sucking through her teeth.

"What caused you to be a True Believer, for one thing. I want to understand what that means. My father is one, but he doesn't talk about it."

Ethel stopped eating and put her plastic utensils down. She sucked through her teeth again. *That's going to get on my nerves before long, I know.*

"You want to know why I'm a believer?"

"I want to see if I can understand my father a little bit, by understanding you. I believe my father is as murderous as you—leaving my boyfriend out there to die proves it—and I want to know why he thinks that's okay. Look at it this way: I wanted to be an anthropologist, and you are now my case study."

Ethel sat quietly thinking before responding. "Your father's reasoning for doing this thing could be completely different than why I would do it; do you understand? Just as his reason for becoming a True Believer could be drastically different from my own reasons."

"Just humor me. Never mind why I want to know. Just answer the questions or I will change my mind and tell Chris about your indiscretions." Carrie crossed her arms again.

Ethel opened her mouth wide and laughed. "Blackmail. I knew I liked you for a reason."

Carrie said nothing.

When Ethel had finished laughing, she smiled. She studied Carrie for a minute before speaking.

"I first heard the calling when I was a little girl. I used to sneak off to the forest near my house almost every day. I always returned home for supper so my mother and father never thought anything of my disappearances. One night I didn't return home. The police were called and a search party was formed. The officers and volunteers from town combed through the forest where I was last seen. They hadn't have bothered. I wasn't lost. I was listening to the trees. They were telling me that a Chosen One would come, and that when I was called upon to follow, I was to do whatever was necessary to assist. When the dreams came to me, I knew the call had been made, and I had no compunctions about what I had to do. I sold all my husband's stocks and all the proceeds went to

Chris. I didn't know why I was doing it until Chris told me why. He told me about the plague."

"How did you know Chris was the Chosen One?"

"The dreams, my dear. Everything I needed to know was in the dreams. It's hard to argue with a dream that tells you who the Chosen One is, where to find him; and when you follow the dream to its end, and you see that it was all true, there is no alternative but to believe. Everything I believed was real. It's a glorious feeling when that happens."

"My father spoke often of the dreams. I don't know if he ever went off into the woods to talk to trees, but he did have the dreams. He said Chris was in them. He believed Chris was a new-age Adam, looking for his Eve. My father wanted me to be that for Chris. I didn't have any such dreams. I have no proof that any of this is real. I only have your word, and his."

"It's not surprising that you have doubts. Gerard did not have the dreams, either; but I trained him from a young age to follow me and my beliefs. He was a True Believer, just as I am, but for a different reason."

"You brainwashed him."

Ethel dismissed her claim with a fluttering hand. "He was just an obedient son, let's leave it at that." She turned away until her emotions were under control. She turned back to Carrie. "But it's clear your father didn't have the same goals as me. He is not the murderer you think his is. He's just a realist who wanted to do what was best for his daughter. He didn't murder anyone; he is simply letting nature take its course. Your boyfriend wasn't meant to be in the new world, that's all."

"Okay, then; now let's talk about why you think it's okay to murder innocent people for a cause that even your own 'Chosen One' didn't condone."

Ethel stared at Carrie for a long time. When Ethel spoke, Carrie felt chills at her words.

"No one is innocent," Ethel said. "We are all marked for death. It's our willingness to do what must be done to survive that prevents our death. I will kill whomever I must to see that the ultimate plan is fulfilled, even if the Chosen One, himself, does not see the truth of it. He's blind to the fact that there is more involved in this than just him. There is more to the story."

"What do you mean?"

Ethel leaned forward. "In all of nature there are two sides to everything: positive and negative, yin and yang, he and she, god and the devil. Everything has an opposite number. Even Chris."

"What are you saying? That you are Chris's enemy?"

Ethel threw herself back in her chair. "No, not me."

"I don't know what you're saying."

"I'm saying, my dear girl, that Chris doesn't have all the information he needs to be an effective leader. We are all in danger if Chris doesn't come into the knowledge of how to lead us into the new world."

Carrie shivered as a chill passed through her.

"Then you have an obligation to him tell him."

"No, I don't have any such obligation. He should be willing to learn on his own. Instead of chaining me up, he should be allowing me to teach him what he needs to know."

Carrie felt frustration at the woman's mysterious words clouding her judgement. "How did you obtain this knowledge then?"

Ethel smiled politely. "I just know. Leave it at that. But know that even Chris must die if his death means the plan will be fulfilled. He is not the new Adam. Your father was wrong on that count. Chris's safety is not the end goal."

Carrie swallowed hard. In a tender voice, she asked, "What is the end goal?"

"It's to stop Chris's opposite. Stop him before *his* plan is fulfilled."

"And what is his plan? Chris's enemy?"

Ethel's eyes widened until the whites seemed to glow with their own inner light. Her mouth stretched slowly into a thin-lipped smile. She looked around the room, as if checking for eavesdroppers.

"It's the complete annihilation of the human race."

16.

January 6.

"How are you doing, my dear?" Glenn mustered the strength to sound cheerful. He even smiled.

"I'm well, Glenn," Nancy said from the computer screen. "You are so sweet for asking. But it's really you, I'm worried about. I'm so sorry for your loss."

Glenn pressed his lips tightly together, fighting back tears. "I thank you, my dear."

Nancy sat quietly, letting Glenn have a moment. "I'm all alone." His voice cracked.

"No." Nancy squirmed in her seat. "No, you're not. You have Brian, and you have Chris. Kaylan and Scott are there for you as well. And so am I. I'm here for you, too."

"Perhaps we would have been better off if we had never come to the Ark," he said.

"No," she said. "Glenn, it's so horrible out here. There are riots, people being dragged from their homes and beaten—or shot—and raped. A group of rioters attacked my house but they didn't have the strength to bust down the door. I think they are still out there. I think the illness took them. Their bodies are still out on my porch. It was good of Chris to offer you his sanctuary. He had no control over what happened to your family, or the Lutz's. I hope you don't blame him."

"No, I don't blame him."

Nor did he. But there was still a part of Glenn that didn't trust anyone anymore. He hadn't wanted it to happen, but he had become a bit of a recluse. When he heard Nancy wanted to talk to him, he jumped at the chance to speak to someone he still trusted one hundred percent.

Nancy lowered her voice. Glenn could see that what she was about to say next was hard for her. "I shouldn't have left the Ark. I was wrong. I would gladly die inside the Ark than face the death that's waiting for me out here."

"It's getting bad then, out in the real world?" Glenn said.

"It is. The television has gone silent, but it's just as well. They have nothing good to report. It's all bad. I don't want you to think about that, though. Take care of yourself, Glenn. I pray we'll see each other in person again. I love you."

"As do I, my sweet girl. Take care of yourself. Until we meet again then?"

Nancy nodded. Glenn walked away. He motioned for Brian—who had slipped away to give them privacy—to return to the computer.

Glenn stepped out to the hall and looked both directions. He saw a group of people walking through the hall to his right. He waited until they disappeared around the corner to start toward the elevators. He headed down the hall behind them. At the end, he glanced to the left and saw no one. To the right, he saw the group of people entering the elevator. Once they had disappeared behind the doors, he started down toward the elevators, himself. He hit the button and stepped aside. The doors opened and he glanced in. Empty. He stepped in and the doors closed behind him.

"What floor, please."

That voice always freaked him out.

"Uh, floor four hundred?"

The lift began to move up.

Glenn stepped off the elevator and walked down the hall to the turn. He walked to the first intersecting hallway and turned left, toward Chris's apartment. He refused to look farther down the hall toward the hallway leading to…

He quickened his pace. He entered the apartment and returned to the room off the living room. His room now. He picked up his picture albums and sat on the bed.

Glenn had been, more and more, finding himself sitting on the edge of the bed, looking at photographs of his family. The photo albums, in fact, were the only possessions Glenn wanted from the old apartment. He ordered everything else to be sent to the incinerators. He would have liked to have kept Patty's dishes, and Derek's toys, but he had no practical use for them, and they would only rot away in storage. So, he allowed them to be destroyed. He only needed the pictures.

Glenn very rarely left his room, except to go into the kitchen and fix a snack, or to use the bathroom. He sometimes exited the room in the night and found Brian sitting up on the sofa, just staring at the wall. Sometimes they acknowledged each other, but mostly, Glenn just went about his business, and Brian went on staring at nothing.

Glenn didn't expect his self-imposed seclusion to last long. He encouraged himself to at least join them in the living room in the evenings.

For now, he stayed in the room looking at the pictures, memories and family, that had been lost to him.

17.

January 6.

Chris entered the control room and sat down next to Toby. Toby glanced over and smiled. They turned toward the computer monitors and looked at what the cameras near the outside entrance showed them.

Several people, clearly sick with the plague, pounded on the doors to be let into the Ark. One man used an acetylene torch on the steel outer hull, attempting to cut his way in. Sparks flew off in a spray that caused others gathered at the door to keep their distance.

Chris turned to Toby. "He can't get in that way, can he?"

Toby shook his head. "Not a chance. That torch is too small, and the steel is too thick. He won't even make a scratch."

Chris thought he hear a touch of "I hope" at the end of Toby's reply.

Chris counted at least one hundred people who had climbed the fence and were now pressing up against the hull of the Ark. Some noticed the camera about twenty-five feet above their heads and were looking into the lens. Their hands reaching out in supplication.

On another monitor, where the camera pointed at the people gathered around the gate, Chris saw even more people along the perimeter of the fence, clinging to the mesh. They either hadn't made the effort, or didn't possess the necessary strength, to climb the fence.

Some had collapsed to the ground and were too weak to get back to their feet. Or perhaps they were already dead. In any case, no one around assisted these fallen few. Chris supposed civilization had collapsed to the point that there would be no law enforcement officers to assist, and no ambulances would be coming to take them back to wherever it was they came from. These people had reached their final resting place. How sad, Chris thought, that these people believed coming here in their last few hours would do them any good.

"Keep me posted. If things get any worse, let me know."

"Will do, Boss," Toby said.

Chris stood and headed down the main corridor to the lift. He turned right and headed for the elevators. He heard the sound of the cart rolling up behind him, but didn't stop or turn around. When he reached the elevator bay, he pressed the button for the upper floors. A hand touched him on the shoulder. Only then did he turn around. He saw Carrie standing there.

"Hi," he said.

She smiled. "How are you doing?"

"I've been managing. Thanks for asking." He glanced at her and turned back to the elevators.

She moved the cart into view, as if she were reminding him of its presence.

He stepped into the elevator when it arrived. She followed with her cart.

"What floor, please?"

Chris allowed her to give her destination first. "Floor twenty-five."

"Floor Four hundred."

The lift started to rise.

"I was just delivering lunch to Ethel," she said.

Yes, I know very well where you're coming from. "I figured. How is that going? She's not too much trouble, is she?"

"No. It's going just fine." She was turned away from him, but she faced him abruptly as the lift rose toward her destination. "Chris, I know I'm not supposed to be talking to her, but she actually has some interesting things to say about why she did what she did. She knows something that she's not telling you. Something to do with you and a force that is controlling you. I really think you should talk to her about it."

Chris closed his eyes. He didn't want to sound angry with her because he wasn't. He opened his eyes and turned to look at her. He spoke in a soft tone.

"If I want any information she might have to give regarding what happened I'll go to her. I don't want you to feel like you have to be a go-between for her and me. And I have no problem with you talking to her, but watch yourself. She's dangerous, and I worry for your safety."

She nodded and turned back to the doors.

She thinks I'm reprimanding her, but that's not what's happening here. When the elevator reached the twenty-fifth floor, and the doors opened, Carrie rolled her cart off the elevator and the doors closed, sealing Chris inside the cab alone.

Chris tapped his wristband and Toby's tinny voice said, "Hi Boss, long time no see. What can I do for you?"

"I want you to post a round-the-clock guard on Ethel, Toby. And I want a guard scheduled to go with Carrie when she serves our resident prisoner her meals. I don't want Carrie alone with Ethel, ever."

18.

January 7.

Carrie knotted her brow in confusion when the guard approached her on the way to delivering breakfast to Ethel. When she asked why he was accompanying her, he simply answered, "Orders."

She was doubly confused when she arrived at the infirmary and found a guard standing outside the door to Ethel's room.

"Let me guess," she said. "Orders?"

The guard nodded but said nothing.

Carrie entered the room expecting to see another guard inside, but there wasn't one there. Ethel glanced at the guard as he entered behind Carrie.

"Who's your friend?" Ethel asked.

"Apparently, Chris doesn't trust us." Carrie pushed the cart to the table and started transferring the food, sitting it in front of Ethel.

Ethel shrugged and commenced eating. "No matter."

"Well, it matters to me. It says he doesn't trust me."

"I'm sure it's not you he doesn't trust. Or he might think I'm brainwashing you."

"He doesn't trust me. I talked to him last night, and he clearly was angry that we are talking. Otherwise the one guard outside the door would be enough. This guy—" Carrie hooked her thumb behind her. "Followed me from the restaurant."

"There are two guards?"

Carrie nodded.

Ethel sat back. "He's serious."

Carrie turned and faced the guard. "What's your name?"

The guard looked around. When he realized Carrie was talking to him, he answered. "Name's Steve."

"Hi, Steve. Are you my guard for the duration?"

Steve took a deep breath and released it in a long sigh. "I guess I am."

Carrie turned back to Ethel. "I spoke to Chris about what you said…that there was stuff you knew that he should know. I tried to get him to come see you. I think he believes we're conspiring. I didn't want to lose his trust, but if what you have to say is really important, he should come and talk to you."

Ethel smiled. "Dear, sweet girl. I doubt anything I have to say will interest him. Not after what I've done to his friends. You might want to cut your losses and send someone else here with my food. There is no reason for you to get involved in all this. Go back to serving the good customers and leave me here to endure my punishment. It's for the best."

Carrie shook her head, violently. "No, I won't just give up like that. Besides, it's too late. I'm already in it. In time, I think Chris will come to his senses and visit you. He'll listen to what you have to say. I'm sure of it. We just have to give him time."

Ethel took a bite of her food. She chewed slowly, and after she swallowed, she responded. "Time is something we might not have very much of."

"What does that mean?"

Ethel looked at the guard and then back at her. "Chris's enemy is close. I don't know how close yet, but time is on the side of Chris's opposite."

Carrie placed Ethel's food on the table and took a seat. She didn't say anything else. She didn't know what else to say. *I have to remember there is the possibility she's just toying with me, not being truthful.* When Ethel finished eating, Carrie cleaned up the dishes. As she headed out of the cell room she brushed by the guard. "Sorry Steve," she said.

"No problem, miss," he said.

Steve fell into step behind her and they headed back to the elevators. Steve's responsibility ended when she had returned to the restaurant. She waved to him and he saluted a goodbye. She watched him walk away. When he was out of sight she pushed the cart into the kitchen and headed back out, leaving the dirty dishes for Margot.

She entered the corridor and scurried to the elevators. She took it to the first floor and headed to the control room. She sped past Toby, who looked up but, made no move to stop her as she entered Chris's office. He looked up at her from his chair. His brow furrowed.

She locked the door.

"What are you doing?" Chris asked.

"I want you to listen to me."

"Unlock my door."

"Not until you hear me out." She took the seat on the opposite side of his desk.

He crossed his arms. "What's to stop me from getting up and unlocking the door myself?"

She grinned. "Nothing at all. And if you want to unlock it go ahead. I'll leave. But I got your attention. That's all I wanted. I'm trying to tell you how important it is for you to talk to Ethel. Hear her out. Don't you want to know why she did what she did? She is convinced there is something more to what's happening here than what you know."

"I'll be honest with you. I don't know anything. I just think that Ethel will try and fill my head with a whole lot of lies in order to save her own skin. I won't be swayed."

"I don't think that's what she's trying to do. I think she has real information to share with you."

Chris laced his finger over his desk. "I understand that you have some kind of connection to her. That's fine. I trust you not to be taken in by her grandmotherly ways. But you have to understand how dangerous she is. I didn't post those guards to keep an eye on you. I posted them to keep an eye on *her*. I'm afraid for your safety. I don't want anything to happen to you."

"She won't hurt me."

Chris stood. He walked over to the door and unlocked it. He turned to her and she stood up.

"I'll go talk to her. For you, I'll do it. But you have to do something for me."

Carrie stepped over to him and kissed his cheek. "Anything. What?"

"Be careful around her. Don't listen to what she has to say anymore. I'll talk to her, but she has nothing more to say to you. Can you promise me to stop having these little over-dinner discussions with her?"

"Yes, and I'll be careful." Carrie seemed satisfied with his answer as she walked out of his office.

19.

January 26.

Chris had promised to see Ethel, but didn't specify *when* he would go see her. He had more important issues to deal with first. The biggest of which was the final touches on Nora's Pond.

The pond was created using sand, and water from the underground source. It was the first use of the filtered water from the sewage plant beneath the Ark. The water was fresh, clear and clean. Chris tested it himself, and proclaimed it potable.

Brian hired teenagers from the Ark as lifeguards, and trained them himself. Chris watched as Brian trained them in the art of water safety. Memories surfaced of his own experience — short as it was — when he had been learning to swim from Brian. It occurred to him that he never finished those lessons. He hadn't been in water deeper than a bathtub ever since, so completing those lessons had never been an issue. He thought that he might finish them now.

The water in Nora's Pond sparkled like liquid crystal, and a light chlorinated scent wafted off the water. The pond was basically a pool with sand lining the pool instead of cement. At the base of the pond a plug could be maneuvered automatically, and the water drained out and fresh water would be pumped in to replace the old. The water was perfectly PH balanced to the smallest degree with computerized controls. The pond would be the cleanest, safest recreational activity in the Ark.

The last of the lifeguards in training exited the water, dried off, and exited the pool area. They waved to Brian as they headed out. Brian stood next to Chris.

"I was just thinking, we never finished our lessens. Ready to give it a go?"

Chris laughed.

"I'm happy to finish those lessons, whenever you want."

"I don't think I'll be needing to go in the water any time soon. But thanks for the offer."

"If you change your mind, don't hesitate to ask. I'll make you look like an Olympic swimmer."

Feeling a change of subject was in order, Chris merely nodded. "How has Nancy been doing? I haven't had a chance to check in with you in a while. I was wondering how she's been."

Brian looked toward the entrance, then turned back to Chris. "She's been in seclusion for so long she's begun to get confused about the days, and she's been missing some skyping sessions. I spoke to her last about three days ago. She apologizes but she doesn't seem interested in talking."

"How does she look?" Chris was almost afraid to ask the question.

"She looks tired. She hasn't been bathing and her hair is always a mess. That's not like her, but who can say what she's supposed to be like these days? On a brighter note, she's stopped fighting off looters, and she doesn't look sick. So that's something to be happy for."

"I still think she'll be okay. She just has to hold out a little longer. I think the pandemic is running its course and will fade out soon. Two more months and I think we'll even be able to open the hatch and send people out to run tests on the air. I have a hunch that once this is done, it's done and we can start picking up the pieces again."

"You've always been an optimist. I loved that about you. The way you stuck by Scott no matter how he treated you when you were kids showed me you always knew he had it in him to be the man he is now. I use that as a guide on how to judge people. Ever since meeting you I give everyone the benefit of the doubt."

"That's great."

Brian excused himself and slipped a pair of jeans over his bathing suit, and pulled a button-down shirt over his arms. He slipped into a pair of loafers, after shaking the sand out of them, then returned to Chris.

"I'm about to go get something to eat. I was thinking at the Jungle Café; do you care to join me?"

"Thanks, but I'm not hungry. I think I'll hang around for a while if you don't mind."

Brian laughed. "You're the Chosen One. You do whatever you wish."

Chris placed a hand on his heart. "I promise I won't go in the water without a lifeguard on duty."

Brian laughed. "You remember the rules, outstanding." Brian headed out.

Chris glanced around. He watched the birds in the trees, and listened to their song. *Nora would have loved her pond.* He kicked off his tennis shoes and dropped down into the sand at the water's edge. He placed his feet in the pool, thinking it breeched his promise to Brian, but only a little.

The water was warmer than he expected it to be, but it still felt refreshing on his aching feet. He needed this moment to unplug and be a part of something that demanded nothing from him.

He closed his eyes, and he might have fallen asleep for a moment—he wasn't sure—but when he opened his eyes again, Margot was walking toward him. He sat up with his feet still in the water.

"Hi." She sat down next to him and removed her own shoes. Her feet went into the water as well.

"Hi." Chris smiled at her. "What brings you here?"

233

"I was just getting off shift and Brian mentioned you were here. He said he wanted someone here with you, afraid of you being here alone, I guess."

"Ah." Chris nodded his head slowly.

"I volunteered to check up on you."

"Thank you. But his concerns are unfounded; as you can see, I'm quite safe."

"Yes, you are. Do you want me to go?"

"No, stay. I don't need rescuing, but I could use the company."

"Great." Margot splashed her feet playfully.

"How have you been?"

"Oh, you know. The same as everyone else trapped in a giant tower. Feeling a little stir crazy and antsy."

Chris laughed. "I hear you."

Margot reached out and touched the water with her hand. "And what's up with you and Carrie? She is not pleased with you right now."

"It's a long story."

"Ha. That's what she said when I asked her."

He thought about it for a moment. "I guess I just feel she's spending too much time with the suspect we are holding for that massacre. It's dangerous for her to be spending so much time with Ethel."

"I agree. I don't even know what the fascination is for Carrie."

Margot turned her head and looked at Chris. When he realized she was staring, he glanced sideways at her. "What?"

She shook her head. "You look tired, is all. I guess you have a lot on your plate. I'm sorry about that. I wish I could make it easier for you."

Chris turned his head and looked at her. He smiled. "Thank you."

Margot glanced around. "You should have invested in an ice cream stand. That and a hot dog cart."

Chris nodded. "We could probably do that. It's a really cool idea."

He leaned closer to her. She dropped her chin to her chest and turned slightly to face him. He looked into her eyes. He wasn't sure why, but he was unable to look away from her.

She leaned in and kissed him.

As she leaned back, Chris sat motionless for a moment, just staring at her. Then he leaned in and kissed her back. She took his hand and guided him to her blouse. He unbuttoned the shirt while continuing to kiss her. She shrugged out of the blouse and discarded it without losing his lips. They parted only long enough for Chris to slip his shirt up over his head and they were kissing again. Margot laughed against his mouth as Chris fought to slip out of his shorts without looking to see what he was doing. She assisted, and then she removed her own shorts.

They entwined in each other's naked embrace and made love while half in and half out of the water.

20.

January 30.

Chris sat in his office. He was smiling. He was looking at the files on the desk in front of him, but his mind had wandered back to the moment he and Margot met on the sand of Nora's Pond. He could still feel her lips on his.

His escapade with Margot started out with nervous fumbling, and that initial coupling had lasted a whole three seconds. He had collapsed against her, apologizing, but she only giggled into his ear. After five minutes of cuddling, Chris was ready to go again. His second attempt lasted several minutes longer, and although she said it had been nice for her, he couldn't help but feel he had been inadequate. She had to help him with everything.

But he didn't doubt she liked lying naked next to him. He surely enjoyed lying next to her.

They had gotten together every night since that first time at Nora's Pond. She usually met him at the elevators when she finished work, and he took her up to his place. Glenn still wasn't venturing out of his room very often, so he wasn't much of a bother. Brian spent the mornings with Scott running errands, and overseeing Nora's Pond in the afternoons. They usually had the place to themselves.

Now, his mind was on Margot, but his duties kept him far from her, and Chris could not be distracted from his daily duties. He stood and walked out of his office. He stopped at the monitors stared at the screen showing the gate. The crowds seemed to be getting bigger, not smaller as he had hoped. Many of them were so sick they just clung to the fence looking in. Some people were still trying to damage the outer hull of the Ark, but the majority of them had tapered off. There were bodies littered all over the ground around the Ark, inside the fenced in area, as well as beyond it. Why did they keep coming here?

"If people start breaking in again, I want to know." Chris squeezed Toby's shoulder reassuringly and Toby gave a stern nod. Chris walked away.

When Chris found his way back to the elevators, he was disappointed to see Margot was not there. He checked the restaurant, where Carrie informed him Margot had left at her usual time and their father had taken over kitchen duty. Chris could see the question in Carrie's eyes — *did you go see Ethel, yet?* — and he walked away before she could speak the words.

Chris returned to the elevators and pressed the button to go up. He rode the elevator to the floor Margot lived on and knocked. No one answered. If she was home she wasn't willing to see him. Had he done something to upset her? He couldn't remember.

He returned to the elevator and headed for Nora's Pond. Brian was there with two of his new lifeguards, and at least thirty swimmers. Chris's chest swelled with pride at the sight of all those people splashing and having fun. *Oh, if only Nora could have seen this too.*

Brian and Chris waved to each other, but Chris didn't want to bother him. He turned and headed out to the hall. A strong and sudden longing for Roger caused Chris to stagger as he walked back toward the elevators. He stopped and used the wall to steady himself before continuing on. Roger had been such a fixture in Chris's life for so long that his absence had a profound impact on Chris's livelihood. Being away from Margot was compounding the feeling of loss.

As the doors to the elevators opened, Chris looked up and saw Margot standing inside the lift's car. She took a step forward but stopped when she glanced up and saw him. He stepped aside so she could exit.

She rolled her eyes at the sight of him. "Hello."

"Hi." His voice sounded hopeful. "I was looking for you."

"Oh?" She didn't sound shocked. "I was home."

"I knocked."

She smiled. "You probably got me while I was in the shower."

"Oh." He didn't sound convinced. "I thought you were avoiding me."

Margot looked shocked for a moment. When it dawned on her why he had looked unhappy, she laughed. "Oh, sweetie. I thought you would know me better by now. If I had a problem with you, I'd tell you about it." She kissed the corner of his mouth.

"I know. I was being needy, sorry."

"Don't let it happen again." She took his hand.

"Not me. Nope." He laughed.

"Hungry?"

"Starving. The jungle?"

Margot wrinkled her nose. "No." She dragged him to the Tiki Club, a restaurant which offered thatched roof stations with stools instead of booths. The place was decorated with bamboo walls and tiki torches to give it a Hawaiian atmosphere. The Hawaiian woman wearing the traditional grass skirt, bikini top, and a flower lei around her neck stopped at their station. She provided Margot and Chris with their own leis, which they donned, and then they ordered drinks.

While they waited for their drinks to arrive, the couple examined the menu. When the waitress returned with their drinks, Margot ordered a pineapple salad and Chris ordered a Hawaiian burger. It was a thick steak burger, with lettuce, tomato and onion, and a slice of pineapple. The order came with steak fries and coleslaw.

They sat across from each other. Chris sat staring at Margot and she sat with her fingers laced together on the table in front of them. Chris took a sip of his drink as he waited for Margot to start the conversation. When the food arrived, they didn't touch it right away. Margot picked up her fork and gingerly jabbed at the salad in front of her. Chris waited patiently to hear what she had to say.

Finally, she spoke.

"So, you were looking for me?"

"Yeah. I see you when I close my eyes. I want to spend all my time with you."

"Woah, slow down, cowboy. We just started this thing. You need time to adjust."

"Adjust to what?"

"I'm your first, aren't I?"

"My first?"

She laughed. "You were a virgin before me, Chris." Her eyes softened. "And I am honored. But you have to make sure you don't lose yourself. We need time apart, as well as time together."

He wanted to tell her she was wrong. He wanted to tell everyone they were together, but he couldn't do that. He knew she was right. They had to slow it down.

"That doesn't mean the time we do spend together can't be hot. I've cherished the time we've spent together. I want to wake up wrapped in your arms. But you also have responsibilities, and you have to stay focused on them as well. Hear what I'm saying?"

Chris nodded. "Yes, of course. I'm a grown man, and I know what I want. I want to be with you."

"And I want you to want that. But at the same time, we need to be sure. It's good that we haven't told anyone about us yet. We can walk away from this and no one but us will ever be the wiser that it ever happened."

Chris took a bite of his burger. He chewed, but he couldn't seem to swallow the food. After much work, he managed to empty his mouth. "Are you saying we should break up?"

Margot scowled. "No, you crazy kid. I just said I want to wake up with you beside me. But at the same time, we have to be realistic. If things don't work out, we won't have people poking their noses in our picnic baskets. I'm also saying you make me vulnerable to get hurt. It's hard for me to get to that place, but once I get there, there's no going back. So, don't hurt me, jerk."

"I'd never hurt you."

"I believe you. Now eat your food."

Chris leaned over and kissed her. They finished eating and they left the Tiki Club. They returned to Chris's room and made love. Afterward, they fell asleep, wrapped in each other's arms.

Chapter Nine

1.

February 1.

Brian leaned toward the monitor. He wanted to see Nancy better. *Damn these grainy pictures.* "You look really good. You must be eating again. I'm really happy with how well you're doing. You look *healthy*."

"I feel healthier," Nancy said. "I'm not fighting off marauders anymore, and that's a plus. But there are bodies all over the place outside the house. I can't deny it; they freak me out."

"Don't think about them. You know they are out there, but that doesn't mean you have to think about them being out there. Just block them out."

"That's easier said than done."

"But you can do it. I know you can. How are you doing on food?"

"I stocked up before things got really bad. I'm doing well. I have the freezer stocked with frozen meats, I have loads of canned foods. I'm using condensed and powdered milk in place of fresh. I've got hardy fruits, like oranges, and lots of bottled water. I'm eating like a queen. And my appetite came back full force."

"I'm so happy to hear that. I think you can beat this. I'll be seeing you soon."

"You should go. People are going to want the pond opened on time."

"They'll wait."

"Yes, they will. But they shouldn't have to. Go. We'll talk again soon." She blew him a kiss and signed off.

Brian took his time shutting down the computer. He had Nancy on his mind as he strode down the hall to the pond.

The doors to Nora's Pond swished open automatically, and Brian entered. Jackie Phelps and Tommy Blake entered soon after him. He waved to the two teenagers. They were exceptional learners, and were excellent lifeguards. He trudged through the sand in bare feet. He took the chair on the left, Jackie took the far chair, and Tommy took the chair on the right. Each chair had a walkie talkie at it for communicating without shouting across the water. They were in their chairs for about five minutes when the first group of swimmers began to arrive.

The lifeguards he trained were capable of handling the pond by themselves, but he liked to be on-hand, just in case an issue arrived that they might not be qualified to handle alone. After a few months of experience, he might decide to let them handle the pond without him.

The radio crackled and Jackie said, "looks like an early crowd today. Over."

Brian responded. "Yes, already ten people this morning. I think that's the most we had all day yesterday. Over."

Tommy entered the conversation. "I've been spreading the word. You wouldn't believe how many people aren't even aware of this place. Over."

"Right." Brian scanned the swimmers. Everyone seemed to be doing okay. "That makes me think I should have Chris make an announcement. Maybe that would get people to come. Over."

Jackie laughed loud enough to be heard over the distance. "What if doing that caused us to have hundreds of swimmers. We'd be outnumbered. Over."

"Good point," Brian said. "We would need rules. A capacity limit. I'll work out the details with Chris before having him make any kind of announcement. For now, let's just keep it to word-of-mouth. Over."

"Okay," Jackie said. "Over."

"Will do," Tommy said. "Over."

"Now let's stop with the chatter and pay attention to the swimmers," Brian said. "Over and out."

The walkie talkies went quiet, and the three lifeguards focused on the people in the water. When Brian looked over at Jackie, he saw her climb down from her post and walk to the edge of the water. She spoke to someone there and then climbed back up onto her chair. She was a true leader. He had no doubt she could make head lifeguard, and if he ever started up swimming lessons, she would be his first Water Safety Instructor. If she was willing, he would teach her everything he knew.

As the day wore on, more and more people came to swim. By lunchtime, there were nearly fifty swimmers at one time. Brian was relieved when people started to leave, and the newcomers began to taper off. By four o'clock, the place had emptied out and Brian sent his lifeguards off to eat dinner. From four to five o'clock, Brian alone watched over the pond. It was no difficult task since there were only four people in the water. At five o'clock, he chased the last two people out. He slipped on a pair of sweatpants over his swim trunks and donned a shirt.

Chris met him at the Jungle Café for dinner.

Carrie served them.

"How is Nancy doing?"

Brian stopped with his fork mid-way up to his mouth. He lowered the fork back to his plate. *Chris always sounds like he's probing for info when he mentions her.*

"She's having trouble sleeping because of all the dead bodies outside on her lawn, but other than that she's been good. She's in high spirits, and eating well. She's not sick." *That's really what you're looking for, isn't it?*

"Oh, good." Chris took a bite of food.

"How about the protesters? Are they still trying to break into the Ark?"

Chris shrugged. "They wouldn't be able to, no matter how hard they try. They aren't a real concern."

Brian glanced over at Carrie. "What about Jeremy? Has she mentioned how he's doing?"

Chris glanced over at her, but when she spotted him, he turned away quickly. "We haven't spoken much lately, but I'm going to assume he's doing okay. I would hope whatever negative

242

feelings she holds toward me she would still come to me if there was a problem."

"You're fighting?"

Chris set his fork down and clasped his hands together. "I wouldn't call it fighting, really? But she wants me to have a sit down with Ethel, and I'm not ready to face that bitch yet."

Brian choked on his mouthful of food. "Wow, I don't think I've ever heard you cuss before. Is that your first time?"

Chris smiled. "That's just one of many new habits I've acquired lately."

2.

February 2.

"Do you think the groundhog saw his shadow this morning?" Margot rolled closer to Chris in the bed, and wrapped an arm around his bare chest. *He's so warm and soft. He feels so good.*

Chris turned to face her. "Hardly matters to us what the weather is like outside." He kissed her neck and she giggled.

She pushed him away, wanting to be taken seriously. "Still, I'd like to know there is some bit of normal life going on out there."

"Unfortunately, I don't think the survivors are concerning themselves over a bit of folklore from a time gone by."

She kissed him on the mouth. "Promise me you'll make sure the tradition is kept alive in the new world."

"*We* will keep it alive, together."

"Okay." She smiled. She hugged him, snuggling closer to his naked body. They dozed for another few minutes like that. Eventually, Chris stood and walked to the bathroom to shower. She joined him.

They dressed and headed out of the room.

As Margot stepped into the hallway, Glenn exited the bathroom. For a moment, they stood face to face.

"Good morning," Margot said.

"Morning." Glenn nodded a greeting and walked past her to his room.

Margot and Chris turned and shared a glance. They laughed and headed for the kitchen.

They weren't necessarily keeping their relationship a secret, but they hadn't plan on telling people until after they had a chance to talk it over first. She didn't expect Glenn to go rushing off to tell everyone what he saw, anyway.

Margot wanted to tell Carrie before anyone else. She knew there was bad blood between Carrie and Chris, and though she didn't have all the details, she didn't think it had gotten to outright hatred yet. She thought that whatever was causing the rift between them might be resolved when the doors to the Ark opened. *That'll cheer all of us up.*

Their bare feet slapped at the linoleum floor as they made breakfast. Chris scrambled eggs and Margot made toast. She also poured two glasses of orange juice. Chris wasn't a coffee drinker, but Margot was. She'd have to wait until she got to the restaurant, though, since he didn't have a coffee maker at his place. She'd have to change that.

They sat at the kitchen table and ate off one plate. After eating, Chris washed the dishes. Margot dried them. As she stood with the last glass in her hand, she turned to Chris. "I'm thinking I'll tell Carrie about us today. Do you mind?"

Chris dried his hands off and replaced the towel on the rack. "No, I don't mind." He frowned. "But do you want me to be there when you do?"

"That's not necessary. Unless you want to be there?"

"No." He answered quickly. Maybe a little too quickly. He seemed to realize her concern and added, "it just sounds like something you can do on your own."

"That's what I was thinking, too. I'll let you know what she says, though."

Chris nodded. "Okay."

Margot arrived at work at 11 a.m. and immediately poured a cup of coffee. *Oh, sweet, black gold.* She made a mental note to get a

244

coffee maker for Chris's place. She greeted her father as he exited the kitchen. She immediately got to work making the day's specials. Most of the morning patrons had received their food. She just needed to handle the lunch crowd, which consisted of a few sandwiches or a bowl of soup. The dinner throng would have their choice for a main dish of home-made macaroni and cheese, scalloped potatoes, or rice with mushrooms. For a protein, they could request roasted chicken, turkey breast, or chopped steak. For a vegetable, they could request roasted carrots, asparagus, or steamed green beans. For the kids, there was always hamburgers or hotdogs with French fries and ketchup.

Margot's homemade macaroni and cheese was a crowd favorite. She remembered it was what she cooked when she met Chris.

There was a lull in diners around 2 p.m., and Carrie fixed a plate to take to the prisoner. She was usually gone for about an hour, and a guard had begun to accompany her to the cell. Margot hadn't seen this cell, but understood it was just a room in the infirmary with a bathroom, a cot and a table. The prisoner was chained up so she could move freely from the three locations inside the room, but couldn't leave. And even though this prisoner was just a little old lady, Margot was glad her sister had the escort. She wasn't sure if it had been her father who requested the guard, or if Chris had made the decision, but she was glad Carrie had the protection.

When Carrie returned, she and Margot fixed themselves a plate and ate in the dining area. They were alone. Margot glanced up several times, trying to gage Carrie's mood. Her sister seemed to be relaxed. Usually, Carrie seemed uptight and agitated all the time. Margot thought this would be the only time they would get to talk.

"How is Jeremy doing?" Margot asked, thinking it best to start off talking about her.

"He seems in good spirits, considering he was abandoned to die."

Okay, so maybe bringing up the boyfriend who could quite possibly die wasn't a good idea. Margot searched her memory of her sister for some topic that wouldn't put the girl on edge. It occurred to her that she didn't know Carrie at all.

"What have you been doing to keep busy these days?"

Carrie stopped eating and looked at Margot. "I play bingo in the parlor when they have it, and I croquet after that."

Margot rolled her eyes. "Sounds fun."

Carrie looked back at her food. "You asked."

"I know." Margot placed a hand on Carrie's arm. "I'm happy if it's what you think is fun. But there are a lot of other things to do besides little-old-lady activities. Why don't you come swimming with me at Nora's pond some time? I've been meaning to go since it opened, and I don't want to go alone."

"I'm not sure if that's a good idea."

"Why not?"

"It's a long story."

"I'm your sister, Carrie. I have my entire life to hear your long stories." Margot's mouth became a stern line.

Carrie laid her head on Margot's shoulder. Margot brushed a hand over her hair.

"I'd like to go," Carrie said. "I just don't know if it would be such a good idea. I'm not sure Chris would want me there."

"That's crazy. He wants everyone to go. It's why he created it. I'm not sure what caused this rift between you and Chris, but I know for a fact he holds no ill will toward you."

"Okay, let's do it. And just out of curiosity, how long have you two been sleeping together?"

Margot choked on her mouthful of food.

Carrie laughed. "I suspected that's what you really wanted to talk about."

"How did you…? When…?"

"It's a small world inside the Ark. If you have your eyes open, you can see a lot."

"And you don't mind?"

Carrie smiled. "Why would I mind? I'm happy for the both of you. Besides, it's not me you need to get the blessing from."

Margot waited for her sister to explain. At last she did.

"It's Dad."

3.

February 5.

"How are things going with the pond?" Chris asked as he walked beside Brian.

Brian was shirtless, barefoot, and wore only a pair of swim trunks. He carried a towel draped over one arm. "It's been going great. People seem to be really excited about having something else to do besides bingo and card games. Every day, the number of swimmers grows."

"That's good news, right? You seem to be getting in late these days. I don't hear you coming in."

"Yeah, I've been finishing up late at the pond, heading to the gym for a light workout and a shower, and not making it back until well after eleven p.m., or so. I'm not waking you up, am I?"

"Waking me up?"

"Yeah, you seem to be asleep already when I come home, and you're gone by the time I get up."

"No. You're doing fine." *I'm trying to get a clue from you whether or not you know about Margot, but you're not making this easy. Do I have to come right out and ask you?* "How about me? Am I waking you up when I leave?" *In other words, do you hear Margot and I leaving together in the morning?*

Brian turned and gave Chris an inquisitive look. "No. Why? How much noise do you make in the morning? And I should warn you, a bomb could go off, and I wouldn't hear it. When I sleep, I'm impossible to wake up. Ask Nancy." Brian laughed.

Chris laughed, too. Relief flooded over him. Then he thought of something else.

"Have you talked to Glenn lately?"

Brian shrugged. "No, not really. I mean I've passed him in the hall a couple of times, on the way to the kitchen or bathroom, but other than the usual pleasantries, we haven't talked much."

When Chris's obvious relief showed on his face, Brian frowned at him. "What's going on?"

"Nothing."

"I feel like you're fishing for something. Why would you even care if you wake me up? It's your place. You could have a big band orchestra playing if you want. If I didn't like it, I could move out. Is there something you're doing you don't want me to hear? Do you want me to move out?"

"Not at all. You're fine, really. And you're right. There's something I'm hiding from you. Something you would know about if you were to wake up as I'm leaving in the morning."

"I'm heading to the skype room. Come along and tell me what you clearly have to say, but aren't."

They walked in silence for a time, and Brian continually glanced over at Chris. His eyes said what his mouth didn't: *Go on, tell me.*

When they reached the skype room, Chris finally spoke. "I've been seeing someone…physically and emotionally. If you know what I mean."

Brian smiled. "You dog. Who is it?"

Chris paused. *Why can't I just say her name? This isn't the big deal I'm making it out to be.* "It's…"

"It's my sister."

The two men turned abruptly to see Carrie standing behind them. She brushed past them and into the room. Brian and Chris exchanged loud, nervous laughs before entering the room behind her.

"Margot? Wow."

"Don't sound so shocked."

They headed over to the computers.

Brian booted up his skype account and connected to Nancy's. She answered after a few minutes. Chris was shocked by Nancy's appearance, but Brian didn't seem the least bit concerned. Chris remembered Brian saying she looked better than she had in days, and wondered what she had looked like previously. She did not look sick, and that was good, but she did look tired—exhausted, really—and undernourished. Chris didn't say anything about the appearance, though.

After the initial hellos, Brian said, "Nancy, Chris has a girlfriend."

"Really? Who is she?" Nancy offered a tired, half-smile. "Tell me about her."

"Her name is Margot. She's Carrie's sister."

"Carrie is the girl we reunited with her boyfriend?" Nancy's voice was hoarse, as if she hadn't used it in a while…or she had been screaming incessantly.

"Yes, that's her."

"I'm happy for you." Nancy closed her eyes for a moment.

Chris waited for her to open them again. "Thank you." *I want to know how you're doing, Nancy; but I don't want you to feel like I'm counting down the days till you get sick.*

"Really, Chris. This is such good news. I'm looking forward to meeting her."

"I look forward to that, too." *I hope I sounded convincing that I believe this is a possibility.* "I'm going to let you have time alone with Brian while I go speak with Carrie and Jeremy. Take care of yourself, Nancy. Bye."

Chris stood and Brian took his seat. As Brian and Nancy resumed their conversation, Chris walked down the row of computers and headed over to the row where Carrie and Jeremy were skyping.

She looked up at him. On the screen, Jeremy's eyes lit up when he saw Chris. *He's genuinely happy to see me. I never get a reaction like that from Nancy.*

"I hope I'm not intruding."

"Not at all," Jeremy said. "Carrie, are you okay with Chris being here?"

"Yes. I'm fine with it."

Chris felt her eyes on him, studying him. Chris pulled a seat over to the computer. Carrie continued to eye him, and it made him squirm in his seat.

"Hello, Jeremy." Chris moved an open palm in greeting. "It's good to see you again."

"Always a pleasure, Chris."

"Have you had much trouble with looters?" Chris asked.

"Not lately. They seem to have tapered off."

Chris leaned forward to be clearly heard. "You did as we suggested, right? And created a barrier of plastic over the windows and doors?"

"Yes."

"How is your food supply? You have enough to last you?"

"I might have misjudged how much food I would need, but my appetite has tapered off the last couple of days, so that should help strengthen the supply, right?" Jeremy smiled.

Chris tried not to let his alarm show. "Right." Chris turned to Carrie and they shared a look. "How long have you been without an appetite?"

"About two days. Yea, two days."

"How are you feeling otherwise?"

Carrie turned to Chris as he asked this question, unable to hid her own concern. He used his eyes to silence her concern. *I'll explain later, for now, don't let on that something is wrong.* He hoped she understood the look.

"Well, my throat has been scratchy. I have a cough. But other than that, I feel fine." He seemed nervous. "I'm okay, right? It's just a stomach bug or something?"

"Yeah," Chris eyes lit up. "I'm sure it's nothing. Give it another day and you'll be fine."

Jeremy relaxed. "Oh, good. You had me worried there for a moment." He laughed loudly, and Chris matched his frenzied tone.

When they stopped, Chris spoke. "Well, I'll let you have time with Carrie. I'll catch you again soon."

"Take care, Chris." Jeremy coughed, and it sounded alarmingly wet. He dropped out of sight of the camera for a few seconds.

Chris stood out of camera range and waited for Carrie to say her goodbyes. He averted his eyes until she turned the computer off and stood.

Worry etched her face. "Tell me he's not..." She couldn't finish.

Chris hugged her. "I'm sure it's not the plague. There are still other illnesses out there. He could just have a normal cold."

"But those questions you were asking him. You sounded like a doctor examining a patient. I think you freaked him out."

"I'm sorry. It's not what I intended. It's just that our biggest concern right now is him surviving the next couple of months. The plague should be running its course. Soon, there will be no more carriers, and the disease will kill itself out. Do you understand?"

"I understand that you are telling me the disease dies when all the people who have it die."

Chris didn't respond. She was correct.

"Do you really think he just has a cold, or something?"

"It's possible. Just remember that."

"That's not what I asked you. Do you think he has the flu, or some other mild illness, and not the Ebolic Plague?"

Chris sighed. "No. I think he has the plague. He will be dead in ten days."

"If his symptoms started two days ago, like you seem to think, he only has eight days."

4.

February 8.

Trevor Morris owned a small charter helicopter that he sometimes used to get his friends to nearby functions. He also used it to make a little cash flying clients who had no other way of getting around to their destinations; like now. Five people, who were desperate to reach the tower off the coast of Ampersand Lake, paid him five grand each to fly them. They believed it was a sanctuary for those who were not sick. Trevor didn't know if it was or not, but the clients paid him a lot of money to be flown there, so he would fly them wherever they wished to go. He finished loading them in, ensured everyone was buckled up, then walked around the back of the chopper. He coughed into his hand quietly. He didn't know why he couldn't shake flu — or whatever it was (it certainly couldn't be the Ebolic Plague) — but he didn't plan to let his clients know he was sick. He didn't want them backing out just because he had a little tickle in his throat for the past ten days.

Okay, so it was a little more than that. He sometimes found it hard to breathe, and he — truth be told — felt dizzy to the point of passing out. But he was okay now. He would make this trip without problems and be back in time to take a second trip. He could make a fortune doing this.

Trevor slid into the cockpit seat and slipped on his headphones. He flicked the ignition switch and the rotors above him began to whir to life. He gripped the collective in his left hand and the cyclic in his right. He worked the throttle on the collective until the bird began to lift in the air. Using the pedals on the floor, he worked the tail rotors into action. Using the cyclic, he moved the copter forward, toward the looming shape of the huge building in the distance.

Sweat dripped into his eyes. He could feel his fever coming back. He listened to the nervous chatter coming from behind him, but couldn't quite hear what they were saying over the noise. He didn't think they had caught on to his well-being, though. He concentrated on his flying.

He struggled to hold the cyclic firmly with the sweat coming off his palms. And he felt so goddamned weak all of a sudden. How could he have felt fine one minute and turn so miserable the next? He shivered as the sweats have him the chills. His head throbbed as if something thick and hard was pushing its way out of his forehead. He released the collective for a second, in order to use both hands on the cyclic.

Someone touched his shoulder and he turned his head slightly. They spoke to him but he couldn't hear what they were saying. He motioned for the man to put on the copilot headgear, and speak into the microphone.

The man did.

"What's wrong?" the man asked into the headset so Trevor could hear him. "The thing is swerving all over the place. What is going on?"

"Nothing at all. It's all part of flying. Haven't you people ever flown in a helicopter before? These things are all over the place."

The man shook his head, unconvinced. "Feels erratic, like you don't know what you're doing. Maybe you should set us down. We're close. We can walk from here. Please set us down."

"Nah." Trevor grinned broadly, showing a crooked row of yellowed teeth. "We're practically there already."

The man looked into Trevor's watery, reddened eyes.

"My God," the man said. He covered his mouth. "Are you sick?"

5.

February 8.

Chris's wrist communicator blinked and he lifted it to his ear. Toby's tinny voice came through the speaker. "Boss, I think I have something you need to see. Better come quick."

Chris moved the communicator to his mouth. "On my way."

He had been on his way down to the ground floor, and in three minutes, the doors opened and he stepped off the elevator. He rushed down the hall and then turned to the left and headed down the main corridor toward the control room. Scott pulled up beside him in a golf cart.

"Give me a lift to the control room?" Chris asked.

"Sure." Scott grinned. "Hop on."

The cart moved only slightly faster than Chris could walk, but it would save on his legs, so he rode. He jumped off at the control room and Scott continued on to wherever he had been headed.

Chris entered the control room and took a seat next to Toby.

"What are we looking at?" Chris asked.

Toby only pointed at the screen of the cameras showing the outside. The camera's point of view gave a bird's eye view of the front of the Ark. The ground was littered with people who had collapsed near the fence. It had been determined that these people were most likely dead. But this wasn't what Toby had indicated.

It was the helicopter coming in at a steady clip.

"Is that thing coming here?"

"I think so," Toby said. "Hell if I know why, though."

Chris watched as the chopper dipped and steadied. It whipped erratically to the left and right, and lifted abruptly into the air.

"Doesn't look like they are very good at controlling the thing." Chris's brow furrowed as the aircraft steadily grew bigger on the screen. "He's still rising higher. He doesn't think he can go over the Ark, does he?"

"Not unless he's stupid, and bad at flying. He needs to start dropping his speed."

"He needs to come down as well." Chris's heart thudded against his ribcage. "He's too high up."

Chris and Toby looked at another monitor that showed the people milling around, stepping over the bodies of the fallen. The chopper would have trouble finding a place to land with all the people gathered in the yard. Like on the other side of the fence, dead bodies sprawled out on the ground. Hundreds of bodies. There was no way the helicopter could land without crushing bodies beneath it. Chris shivered at the thought. He was sure he could feel Toby shivering beside him, coming to the same conclusion.

"What are they thinking?" Chris looked toward the sealed doors. "They can't possibly think we can let them in. Why are they coming here?"

"I wish I knew."

Chris struggled against the gorge rising in his throat, and forced it back down. He gulped to clear his esophagus. They stared in shock and awe as the helicopter continued its approach.

Chris wasn't sure what he was seeing when he saw the nose of the helicopter dip drastically. It wasn't how he had ever pictured a helicopter landing. Then, as if the pilot had just woken up, the nose of the aircraft righted itself. Now it was even closer. Much too close, in fact.

Chris felt a clenching in his throat and in his groin when he realized the impact was imminent. Toby cried out beside him.

The helicopter hit blades first into the side of the Ark, just above the camera's view. Next the cockpit crumpled as it hit the wall. In another instant, an explosion that they could not hear, but could feel, rocked them in their seats, obliterating the aircraft, along with one of the cameras.

As well as anyone who might have been inside.

And those below.

From another camera view, Chris watched as large chunks of debris rained down on those milling about in the yard. He covered his mouth in horror as a rotor blade spun crazily out of control and cut a man in half. Others were crushed beneath the falling helicopter parts. Fuel ignited and people caught on fire, running around like human torches.

Chris turned away. He could watch no more.

Once he had his composure, he turned to Toby. "Did the impact damage the Ark's integrity?"

"I don't think so. The walls are thick. A nuclear bomb couldn't damage this thing. We are built to last."

"I hope you're right." Chris thought he heard some doubt in Toby's voice.

Chris took one last look at the screen, and wished he hadn't when he saw someone without legs crawling from a large piece of wreckage.

Toby clicked a switch and the camera turned off; the screen blinked into darkness.

Chris stood and paced. Toby swiveled his chair to face Chris.

"There was nothing we could do." Toby's voice had regained its composure, and Chris took comfort from its strength.

Chris stopped pacing. "I know." He rubbed a shaky hand across his brow to remove a bead of sweat that had formed there. He repeated the words like a mantra. "I know."

6.

February 13.

As Chris entered the skype room, Brian was saying goodbye to Nancy. He stayed back until Brian shut down the link to their skype session. He nodded a hello to Brian, but his eyes sought out Carrie. When he spotted her, he headed in her direction. She looked up as Chris approached, and there was so much sorrow in her eyes that Chris's throat clenched. He sat down next to her and looked at the screen.

Jeremy smiled when he saw Chris, but it was a challenge. He had lost all energy, and laid his head down on his arm so that he was facing the camera in a prone position across the desk.

"Having trouble shaking this cold," Jeremy said with a weak cough.

Chris nodded. "That's okay, Buddy. Just hang in there. It'll get better."

Carrie spun on Chris with a look of contempt on her face, but said nothing. *Jeremy doesn't have much longer to live. I simply want him to slip away with hope still on his mind.* Carrie seemed to understand his motives and her features softened.

Jeremy, apparently, knew his fate, however. "I think I'm done for." He took a soft inhalation of breath. "I'm tired."

"We'll let you go then, Love," Carrie said. "We'll let you rest."

"Please, don't go." He lifted his head slightly, but had trouble keeping it up and placed it back on his arm. "I'm so lonely. Everyone I've known is dead. I'm afraid to be alone. Please stay with me."

"I'll stay," Carrie said. Her voice was thick with emotion. "I'll stay for as long as you need me."

"Thank you." Jeremy closed his eyes, but opened them again quickly. "I don't want to fall asleep."

Carrie didn't know what to say. She looked at Chris for help.

Chris pulled a seat up to the monitor and sat down. "Sleep could be good for you, Buddy. Maybe you should sleep."

"I'm afraid I won't wake up."

Next to Chris, Carrie made a low, strangled whimpering sound; he doubted it carried over the internet. Even if it had, Jeremy was too far gone to notice. Chris lightly squeezed Carrie's hand. *Be brave.*

"I must not have kept the sickness out. I have what's killing everyone. I'm dying." Jeremy's words were not spoken in distress. He could have been telling them he was hungry; the words were calm and matter-of-fact. Tears formed in Carrie's eyes but she wouldn't let them fall. They clung to her eyelashes. Chris's heart ached for her loss.

They watched Jeremy for a time. His eyes were trained on the camera, but he couldn't hold the gaze for long. The lids closed slightly and his chest heaved. He exhaled.

He breathed in.

He exhaled.

His chest didn't rise again. His eyes seemed fixed, glazed.

Carrie let loose with tears and cried. She sobbed loudly. She called out for Jeremy to talk to her—just talk to her—but Chris knew it was over. He pulled her into his shoulder and she accepted his comforting embrace. She cried openly against him. He glanced at Jeremy's still form one more time.

And then he flicked off the monitor.

7.

February 13.

Chris took Carrie back to the apartment and stayed with her as she slept. When he explained the situation to Kaylan, she agreed to take over Carrie's duties at the restaurant, which included, unfortunately, taking food to Ethel.

She served breakfast to the customers that morning as Margot cooked. She took a break around eleven and ate lunch with Margot. As they ate, they talked.

"The prisoner missed her breakfast." Margot took a bite of her meal.

"I don't care." Kaylan showed no sign of remorse.

"Did you hear about the helicopter that crashed into the side of the Ark?"

"Yes, but Chris insists the integrity of the structure is still intact. We're not in any danger."

"I hope you're right. I don't want to die like those people out there…like Jeremy. It's awful."

Kaylan shivered just thinking about the death happening out there. *I don't dare speak of it, or I might bring it in here.* Her nightmares showed her entire hilly landscapes covered in dead bodies. She woke up panting, with a scream thick in her throat. She refused to wake Scott. She let him sleep, even if she couldn't.

Margot's words snapped her out of her reverie. "Well, I guess it's that time."

"Time?"

"You have to take lunch to Ethel, like it or not."

Kaylan took the last bite of her burrito and followed Margot to the kitchen, carrying her plate. She placed the plate in the dishwasher and retrieved the covered plate from the warmer. She placed the entire meal on the cart and pushed it into the main hall.

The guard was waiting for her. He seemed surprised to see her.

"Where's Carrie?" he asked.

"She was not feeling up to her duties today. I offered to take over for her."

The guard showed no emotion as he led Kaylan down the hallway. She pushed the cart to the elevators and they descended to the ground floor. He glanced behind only a couple of times, maybe to be sure he wasn't outpacing her, and stopped at the infirmary door.

"If you wouldn't mind, I'll ask you to wait out here while I go get confirmation that you are allowed access to the prisoner."

"Whatever," Kaylan said.

She waited.

He returned and opened the door without telling her what the reply had been. She knew it wasn't necessary, really. Chris would have been the one to allow her access, and she already knew he had cleared her. She was glad the guard had the wherewithal to check into it, though.

She pushed through the entry to the infirmary and Dr. Jacobson looked up from her desk. She smiled at Kaylan and returned to her paperwork.

Kaylan felt the first twinge of nervousness as she watched the two guards converse. Her chaperone explained the situation to the on-duty guard. Then the guard pushed the door to Ethel's prison open and allowed Kaylan to enter.

Ethel sat at her table, smiling. When she spotted Kaylan, her smile turned instantly to a frown.

Kaylan own smiling face belied the crippling nervousness she felt inside.

"What's wrong with Carrie? What's happened to her?"

Kaylan's smile never faltered. "Nothing. She didn't feel well so I offered to take over her duties for the day." Kaylan took the tray of food from the cart and placed it on the table.

"You didn't bring me breakfast."

"I wasn't informed about having to take over for her until it was already too late to bring your breakfast. You survived."

Ethel stared at the covered dish. "What nasty surprise am I going to see when I lift that lid?"

"I don't know. I didn't look. It was prepared while I was elsewhere."

"It's poisoned." Ethel spat the word.

Kaylan shoved the tray across the tale at the woman. "Bitch, if I wanted you dead you wouldn't be handcuffed."

Ethel lifted the lid, sniffed the food.

Kaylan turned and headed for the door. "I'd have you dangling from the rafters already."

Kaylan walked through to the main room, preferring to wait out there for Ethel to finish her meal, not wanting—or willing—to make small talk while the woman ate.

Kaylan glanced around the room, her first visit to the infirmary. It was sparsely decorated, and the walls were painted a dull white. She thought she would go nuts if she had to look at those walls all day.

Her eyes came upon the door to the right of Ethel's prison. If she remembered correctly it was the door to the pharmacy, and somewhere inside there was the cold storage room. Chris had told them that the bodies were stored in there. She shuddered at the thought of Nora, Roger, Derek, and all the others being stored in there.

Then she was struck with the urge to look.

She tried the door, thinking it would be locked, but the knob turned and the door opened.

She closed it quickly and stepped away when the door to Ethel's jail cell opened. Her face reddened with embarrassment as the guard stepped out. He didn't seem to notice Kaylan's discomfort—or the reason for it.

He said, "She's finished eating."

Kaylan brushed past the guard and entered the room. Ethel's dishes were stacked up on the corner of the table, but Ethel still sat in the chair where she had been eating. Kaylan glanced at her briefly, but turned her attention quickly to the stack of dishes. Still, she could feel the woman's eyes on her.

Kaylan chanced a look at the old woman. Ethel's eyes pleaded to Kaylan, imploring her to give the old woman a moment of her time. Kaylan sighed and stopped collecting the used dishes.

Ethel offered Kaylan a tight-lipped smile. "I'm hoping you will do something for me."

"Ha." Kaylan barked a laugh. "Me do you a favor?"

Ethel's forced smile turned into a frown. "I'm serious. It's imperative that Chris speaks to me, and soon. Time is now of the essence. I need him to listen to what I have to say."

"No one wants to hear anything you have to say."

Ethel slammed her palms down on the table. The sound even made the guard jump. Ethel then settled back into her seat, calming herself.

She spoke in a calm voice. "I'm afraid you don't understand the situation. We're all in danger, and if Chris doesn't come see me soon we may all be dead."

"What did you do now, you crazy old bitch?"

"I didn't do anything. Believe me, if I could change the past I would. I had good intentions when I ordered all those people to die. I thought I was doing the right thing. I didn't mean for…"

"Doing the right thing? Did you forget I was one of those people you ordered to die? If I recall, you wanted to do me personally. Good people died because of you."

"And even more will die because of you."

Kaylan frowned. She placed a few of the dishes on the cart. When she reached for the rest, Ethel grabbed her by the wrist. She used the hand with the cuff attached to it, and the chain dragged across the table. Kaylan tried to pull away, but Ethel held tight.

The guard stepped forward and brought up a Billy club, intending to break Ethel's arm if she didn't let go.

Ethel did release her. Kaylan clutched her hand to her chest.

"I'm sorry. I'm trying to make you understand that if Chris doesn't stop letting you distract him from his true purpose we are all going to die. All of us." Tears formed in the old woman's eyes. "I want to tell him I'm sorry for my part in all this."

Kaylan sighed inwardly, but showed no compassion to the woman, otherwise. Instead she said. "I'll relay the message that you wish to speak to him. It's all I can do. But I'm sure he knows you are trying to get his attention."

Ethel wiped her eyes. "Thank you."

Kaylan finished loading the cart. "Don't thank me yet. He may not come see you even then. I think he plans to let you rot in here."

Kaylan exited the room, never to return.

8.

Kaylan told Chris about Ethel's request, but he ignored her. He was outraged when he heard Ethel had placed her hand on Kaylan. He almost marched in there then. Kaylan reassured him that the old woman had not harmed her, and that any rash action on his part would have been unfounded. He decided he would see her on his own terms, not hers.

But Chris did agree he had to meet with Ethel.

He made the decision to meet with her, but the crisis that arose regarding Nancy distracted him from that meeting, and it would be another month before he would finally have his consultation with Ethel.

Chapter Ten

1.

March 1. Seven thirty a.m.

"Hi Nancy," Chris said when her image came up on the screen.

She smiled, but she looked tired. Or sick.

Nancy had dark rings under her eyes and her lips looked chapped. *Is she getting enough water?*

"How is your water supply doing?" he asked.

"It's going great. I'm drinking a bottle of water a day. I've been drinking it sparingly, though I think I have enough to last the rest of the winter. It's really cold. There is no oil in the furnace and it kicked on for the last time about five days ago. I guess it was one contingency I hadn't planned for. But that's okay. The snow's beginning to melt and I feel warm sunshine hitting the house, heating it up. Spring's coming." She tried to smile, but it looked more like a grimace. "I just bundle up at night."

"Nancy, listen to me. You have to drink more water. At least three bottles a day. Can you do that for me? Can you drink more water? You're severely dehydrated. I'm concerned that your immune system will suffer if you don't drink more water."

"Okay," she said. "I'll drink more water."

"How is your supply of oranges? Do you still have some? Or something else with vitamin C?"

"I have a couple of oranges left. They are a little withered, but I think they are still edible."

She's running out of food. She's not going to make it if her supplies don't last until we can come for her.

She seemed to have expelled the last of her energy with her last comment, and she settled back in her chair. Chris could see she was wearing several layers of coats, and an electric blanket. *Apparently, the electricity is still running out there, but who knows for how long?*

"The epidemic has almost run its course, Honey." Brian sounded more cheerful than he looked.

Chris could see the worry for Nancy in the lines on Brian's face. Chris worried that Nancy wouldn't survive until the Ark was reopened. In order to confirm the contagion was extinct, a team of experts would have to be dispatched out into the world. And before they could be dispatched, Chris needed to believe no one exposed, and infected, still survived. Once the last sick person succumbed, only then could Chris send out the experts. Even then, it would take ten days from the moment the experts exited the Ark before they could report back. Chris was looking at mid-summer at the earliest before the doors would open. They had to be sure there was no chance of infecting the people inside the ark.

"The pond is booming. I had to hire three more lifeguards to overlook all the people coming." Brian talked, even when Nancy didn't appear to be listening. "Chris had to post a maximum occupancy notice to keep people from overcrowding. I now have a person at the doors to allow people in only when other people leave. There's a line down the hall of people trying to get in.

"It was a wonderful idea, to create Nora's Pond, Chris," Nancy said. "Good for you."

"Yeah, I was inspired." Chris's eyes glazed over as his mind turned back to the memories of Nora.

"You have to make sure the pond continues to thrive, Brian. No matter what." Nancy leaned forward again. "You have to promise me."

"I promise," Brian said. "I can't wait for you to see it."

Nancy opened her mouth to speak, but stopped mid performance. She stayed in that position, with her mouth open for several seconds. The seconds continued until they turned into minutes.

"Nancy, are you okay?" Brian asked. Panic caused his voice to waver.

"I think the screen is frozen," Chris said. Another minute passed and the screen went blank. Looking around, they saw that all the screens went blank.

Chris and Brian looked at each other.

Chris voiced what they were both thinking. "Maybe internet went down."

"How could that be? I thought we have internet in the Ark?"

"We do, but she's not on our internet. If the web went down out there, we won't be able to communicate with anyone outside the Ark."

They watched the screen for a moment more. Chris was about to reach up and turn off the monitor, but the screen blinked and Nancy came back.

"...think it's wonderful."

She doesn't know there was a glitch. She went on talking even when the screen was frozen.

Nancy laid her head down on her arm. The image was so much like Jeremy that Chris's blood went cold.

2.

March 1.

Eight a.m.

Margot looked up from her pot and let the shock show on her face. "What are you doing here so early?"

Carrie stood over the pot on the stove and looked in. She saw vegetables floating in boiling water. "What are you cooking?"

Margot furrowed her brow. "Vegetable broth for my soup. Why are you asking? And you haven't answered my question."

Carrie looked over at her sister. "I couldn't sleep so I thought I would come down and see what you do in the morning."

"I cook."

"I think you should teach me how to cook. In case something happens to you, I can keep the restaurant going."

"What's going to happen to me? What do you know?"

"Nothing. I'm just speaking in hypotheticals. I want to learn to cook."

Margot eyed Carrie with a suspicious glare. "Okay. Let's start with my world-famous hamburger vegetable soup. In this pot, I'm boiling carrots, celery, leeks and turnips. When the water starts to draw out the flavors of the vegetables, I'll strain it and continue cooking it while adding herbs and spices."

Carrie nodded. "Got it."

Margot led Carrie to a counter made of cutting board. She motioned to the array of vegetables spread out on the counter. "Here we cut up the vegetables going into my soup. When the broth is ready we'll put everything into a pressure cooker and slow cook it for about five hours."

"Sounds easy enough."

Margot deftly shopped potatoes into cubes, chopped carrots, and chopped celery as Carrie watched. Margot then moved to a pile of sugar snap peas.

"Here is the biggest chore on the ingredients list. This is what you do." Margot picked up a pea and snapped off the end. She pulled down and a thread pulled away from the pod. She then snapped off the other end. "Did you see what I did there? Pulling that filament away from the shell keeps the pea from becoming stringy. Try it." She stepped back.

Carrie picked up a pea pod and snapped off the first end. The thread did not come with the tip. She set that pod aside and picked up another. This time the trick worked and Carrie unthreaded the pea. "It's like unzipping a coat." Carrie smiled.

When Carrie had unshelled about one hundred peas, Margot led her to the large walk-in cooler.

"This is where we keep the hamburger. It's ground daily, so it's fresh. All the ingredients are fresh."

Margot picked up a tray with about twenty pounds of meat on it. Carrie held the door open for her sister.

"What's this bar for?" Carrie indicated a long steel pole next to the door.

"It's used to pry the door open if the door shuts while you're in here. The handle sticks and I'm not strong enough to open the door from the inside without leverage. Dad set it up when he accidentally locked himself in one morning."

They moved back out to the kitchen. Carrie watched—and sometimes participated in—the preparation of the soup. Once all the ingredients were ready, they were placed in a large stainless steel pot. The lid was clamped shut and the timer was set. Now, the food only had to cook. Margot moved on to breakfast.

Carrie helped with the preparation of the morning's breakfast orders by cracking eggs and buttering toast, but when people started arriving, she moved out to the dining area to take the orders. At around ten, the orders started to slow down, and Margot made a plate of scrambled eggs and sausage with French toast, and a glass of orange juice, for Ethel.

3.

March 30.

Ethel did what she always did. She paced. She sat on the bed. She paced again. She paced some more. When the door opened, she thought nothing of it. She assumed dinner was a bit early, but she had no way of knowing the time. When she looked up, she expected to see Carrie.

Ethel stood there in utter shock, staring at Chris in the doorway. The shock faded quickly and she returned to a more casual stance.

"Look who decided to show up," she said and dropped into the seat near the table. He took the seat opposite her.

"I'm not here because of any summons by you. I'm here because I need answers." He crossed his arms.

"I'll answer any questions you might have." Then she added, "Truthfully."

He leaned forward and clasped his hands in front of him on the table. "I want you to tell me what you believe. Am I the Chosen One in your eyes? And what does that mean to you?"

She thought about his barrage of questions before answering. She clasped her hands together, mimicking him. Her chains clattered. "You are the Chosen One. I never denied that."

Chris sat back again, waiting for her to continue.

"But your designation means nothing."

"What do you mean by that?"

Ethel thought about what she was going to say for several seconds. When she was ready to speak, she sat forward, leaning over the table as far as the chains would allow.

"The Dryad is not the only being at play here."

"What are you saying?"

She closed her eyes, as if calling up a memory. When she opened them again, she spoke. "I'm saying that Marbhdhraoi has awakened."

"What is that?"

"It is death. The bringer of the plague. Where the Dryad is the rebirth, Marbhdhraoi is the death of everything. It is a nasty thing. It's what we are truly fighting against."

Chris scowled. "Why am I just now hearing about all this?"

"I would have told you sooner, but…"

"Why wouldn't you tell me about this Mar… Mar-oo…Marb-ray-oy as soon as you entered the Ark?"

"To be honest, I didn't know if I could trust you. I wasn't sure how much you already knew. It would have been part of your training if Clarence had lived long enough to train you."

"Who is Clarence?"

Ethel laughed. "Clarence Brown. I'll have to start from the beginning. Will you indulge me?"

When Chris didn't protest, Ethel began.

"When we first started the search for the Chosen One, there were about 50 of us. Clarence and I were founding members. Gerard was just a baby then. But in the seventies, Clarence learned he was the ancestor of a merchant from the revolutionary period. One of the first victims of the Boston Massacre was Crispus Attucks. Clarence was informed that he was a distant relative of the Attucks's and had inherited a fortune from the estate. He legally changed his name to Crispus Attucks Brown. He moved into the house in the Adirondacks, which had belonged to his revolutionary hero ancestor, and he started his own branch of the foundation. He called it The Keepers of the Forest." She adjusted her position in her seat. "He was so proud of that name. His biggest mistake was to enlist the help of non-believers. Sure he had charisma, and could charm the pants off anyone, but in the long run, you need True Believers by your side. Crispus was a great man, but he was blinded by his own confidence."

"He was a murderer, and killed my guardians to kidnap me. There is nothing great in that. Go on with your story."

Ethel's smile faded. "Well, as it would turn out, he had been right all along. He found you. If things at the compound he created hadn't gone so horribly wrong, he would have groomed you properly to take over as the Chosen One. Instead that woman—Sherry—screwed everything up and he was killed by the very thing that he had brought into existence. He was blinded by his love for her."

"Sherry saved Scott and me, so I can hardly see where she was the problem. How can you possibly justify all the killing?"

Ethel spoke up quickly. "That's where Marb-oo comes in. He is the harbinger of death. It's his goal to destroy the human race, just as he did to countless species before us. Every extinction level event from the past was his work. Compared to him, what I've done—what any of us have done—is child's play."

"You keep saying 'he.'"

"He, she, it—doesn't really matter. Those are just useful pronouns to explain the unexplainable. Mar-oo is a grim reaper, of sorts, only he reaps entire species, not just one soul at a time. We're next on his—its—list."

"But we're safe in here."

She laughed. "Not for long. He'll find his way in here, and when he does, he'll put us on the list for extinction as well."

Chris's attention drifted. After a moment, he said, "the very first death inside the Ark was a man who had slit his own throat, but first he spoke to me. What was it he had said? Something about wanting the doors open. Did that man want to get out, or was he somehow already exposed to this Marbhdhraoi? Do you think I might have already spoken to this being?"

Ethel shrugged. "It's possible. But that's where you need to start tapping into the power of the Dryad. The Chosen One will lead the survivors into a new world, just as Noah did."

"How do I beat this…" Chris pronounced it the way he was hearing Ethel speak it. "Marb ray droy?"

Ethel sighed. A sad smile played across her face. "Unfortunately, that information died with Crispus."

"How am I supposed to protect everyone if I don't know what I'm protecting them from, or how to stop it?"

"I suggest you dig down deep into your subconscious and remember what is already inside you. You carry the seed of the Dryad. Perhaps there is something there that can help you. Remember what you lost over the years and use that knowledge to guide you. I'm sorry I wasn't there to assist with your training. Perhaps if Crispus had handled things a little differently, you might have grown up understanding what it means to be the Chosen One."

"I don't know how to do that. I don't know how to remember."

Ethel didn't respond. She didn't have to. She stared at him, studying him. He stared back until he could take no more of it and turned away.

"There is one more thing I have to tell you," she said finally.

He waited.

After a moment, she continued. "Beware of Marbh ag siul." She pronounced it slower for him when she saw the look of confusion on his face. "Marb-oo ix shue.

"What is that?"

"I don't know, but it came to me in a trance. I only know that it's Irish Gaelic. Perhaps you could look it up on the internet."

"The internet is spotty at best. I'm not sure how much time we have with it."

"You mean it's dying?"

"I don't like that word. Let's just say it's going defunct."

Ethel shrugged, indifferent.

"Say I take you at your word that this Marbhdhraoi is real, is there anything else you can tell me about it?"

"I have nothing else. I wish I did. Keeping those doors shut is your best defense against it right now, but if you think he may already have breached these walls, whether the doors are open or closed, we are in serious danger.

"What if I go out."

"Out?"

"Out of the Ark.

Ethel shifted again. "You would be putting yourself at risk. And I may not know much, but I do know this." She leaned forward to stress the importance of her words. "If you die, the human race dies with you."

"It doesn't matter. I can do no good in here. I'll have to go out there to look for the answers. If there are answers to my questions, that's the only place I'll find them. I have to go."

Ethel didn't try to argue. She knew he was right.

4.

March 31.

Brian continued to go about his business, but with one acceptation. He now dreaded his skype sessions with Nancy. He feared the moment when her internet went down. Every session was an exercise in terror. He spoke to her with his heart in his throat. If she took too long to answer, he would call out to her. She started to sense something was wrong, and it took everything he had to convince her all was okay.

"I'm so cold," she said to him on the morning of March thirty first.

Then the internet went down for good.

5.

March 31.

Chris entered the control room and sat down next to Toby. They stared at the screens without speaking. Nothing moved.

Everything—everyone—out there was dead.

Chris turned to Toby. "I want to send out an exploration party."

Toby nodded. "I think it's about time."

"I'm thinking of going out with them."

Toby turned to face Chris, stricken. He sputtered for a few seconds, unable to form words. Then, in a gasping spasm, he said, "You can't."

"I have to go get Nancy and bring her back."

Now Toby was alarmed. "She can't come in. She might…"

"If she's still alive, she didn't contract the plague. She's safe. We have to get her in here."

"We still have to do tests. We don't know if the plague has gone extinct yet. It could still be active. You bring her in here and you risk killing all of us. She can't come back here. You know all this Chris."

Chris's breathing grew erratic. His heartbeat quickened. "Then I'll go out and wait it out with her. Brian, too."

"No. You are needed in here. You are needed *alive*."

Chris relaxed. "The last I heard, you are not in charge, Toby. You have no say in the matter."

Toby blushed. "I'm sorry. I know that. I didn't mean to upset you. I—"

"I'm not upset. And my mind is made up. Begin preparations."

Toby stood as Chris headed for the door.

"I understand the implications here. I just ask you to wait until spring thaw."

Chris turned and faced Toby. He laughed. "This is Central New York. That might not happen till May."

"May is a good time." Toby grabbed Chris by the arm. "Just give me until May."

Chris stared at Toby's hand until he dropped it. He looked into Toby's eyes. "I know you don't understand this, but my friend is in pain. He won't be able to rest until his wife is safe. If I don't do this with him, he said he would do it alone. I can't have him do that. I have to go."

When Toby didn't respond, Chris exited the control room. He hopped onto the nearest golf cart and drove it down the central corridor, turned left.

He entered the infirmary, leaving the cart in the hall. He found Dr. Jacobson in one of the exam rooms counting supplies. When she looked up and spotted him, she stopped what she was doing.

"Hi, Chris. Need something?"

"As a matter of fact, I do. I'm going on an expedition outside the Ark." Chris paused and waited for her to respond.

Dr. Jacobson removed her glasses and placed them on the counter in front of her. She rubbed her eyes. After a moment, she spoke. "You can't really be serious. Outside of the Ark? Is it even safe to be out there?"

"That's what I plan to find out. We have to do it sooner or later. I chose now."

"But why you? Surely, you have people willing to do this for you. You are needed here."

"It is true that to really be sure, we should wait another month before going out. I have a group of experts I planned to send out to run tests, and conduct experiments. But something has come up and I have to forgo those plans. I'm leaving on this expedition instead, and the experts are not going."

"If you believe it's what you have to do, I guess I'll understand. I can't say I agree with this, but…"

"That's not all. I'm here asking you to join me."

She swallowed hard, having trouble understanding what he was saying. "You want me to leave the Ark?"

"I have a friend outside who could still be alive. I think the disease has run its course and we can leave without fear of contamination."

"But you don't know that for sure, though."

"No."

"I'm needed in here. I have…"

"You hand out headache pills and stomach remedies. There is nothing happening in here that requires your immediate attention. Hank can handle your duties while you're gone. I need you to go with me, into the world. We have to know what's happening out there. If there are survivors, they'll need your help. I'm not going to force you to go. But I truly need your help."

"I can't believe we're talking about this. I mean, I expected it to happen eventually, but I wasn't thinking it would be so soon."

"If my friend really did survive the epidemic, she's going to need medical attention. She's going to need your help. Time is of the essence."

Hellen nodded.

"We're leaving in the morning. I hope you'll be with us?"

"How many of you are there?"

"It's just me and my close friend Brian. And you if you'll come. We'll be wearing Hazmat suits."

"For all the good they will do."

Chris started to walk away. Hellen stopped him.

"I'll go," she said. "To be honest, I'm curious to know what's out there myself."

Chris took a deep breath of relief and exited the infirmary.

James McNally

Part Three: Living With the Dead

James McNally

Chapter Eleven

1.

Chris closed the door to the airlock with a resounding clang, and the telltale click of the hermetically sealed lock engaging told the trio that they were now locked out of the Ark. He turned to face the other two people in the room. Brian continued to pull on his hazmat suit, but Hellen had stopped to look at the door.

"I asked you if you were ready to do this. You said that you were."

"And I am."

"Okay, good. Because it's too late now. There is no going back that way."

Hellen resumed donning her hazmat suit.

Chris turned toward the door. *Scott had been so upset when I told him what I was doing. He was even more upset when I refused to let him come. He's still on the other side of that door, I know. He's over there, and he thinks he's never going to see me again. Probably, he's right.*

None of that mattered. They were going because the answers to all their troubles were out there. *Brian needs to get to Nancy. And I need to stop the annihilation of the human race.*

Hellen seemed distracted as she finished pulling on her hazmat suit. Chris helped her put her helmet in place, then he donned his own helmet.

He tried his two-way radio inside his suit. "Hellen, can you hear me okay?"

"Yes, Chris. You're coming in loud and clear."

"Good. Now tell me what's on your mind. Why do you seem like you're a mile away?"

Hellen paused. When she spoke, her voice was shaky. "I am fine with what we are doing. And I understand the reasons for it. I do. But you have to keep in mind that I don't have the same drive as you and Brian have. I have no real reason for being here."

"I get that. But your presence here is important."

She nodded, and inside the helmet, the action was exaggerated.

"I can here you loud and clear, too. If anyone cares," Brian said.

"Keep this line clear," Chris said. The laughter that ensued hurt Chris's ears.

Chris looked for breaches or leaks in Brian and Hellen's suits. They did the same for him. When they were sure their suits were good, they lined up near the door leading out to the world at large. Chris didn't reach for the door handle right away.

Although the three suits were linked to each other, only Chris, through the use of his wrist communicator, could speak to Toby in the control room. Chris spoke to Toby now. "We're about to open the door to the outside."

"Good luck, Chris. See you on the other side."

Chris's heavy breathing, intensified inside the suit, reminded him just how nervous he was. He supposed the others were going through the same thing. Chris spoke to them now, and his voice sounded tinny and hollow. "Here we go."

Chris turned the knob and opened the door. They stepped through the threshold and the door slammed shut behind them. Hellen turned back to the door, as if she planned to go back inside, but even if that had been her intention, she couldn't; there was no handle on the outside. The only way back into the Ark was through the front-loading doors, and they wouldn't open until Chris could confirm that there was no more danger from the disease.

The suits they wore were self-contained. A rebreathing apparatus inside the helmet converted their carbon dioxide back into oxygen, provided they didn't breathe too fast. There was a compartment in the back of the suit for holding waste, and each of the explorers had been fitted with catheters; male catheters looked like condoms with a hose running off the tip, and the female version was inserted directly into the urethra. A special one-way valve allowed them to empty their reservoir without contaminating their suit. This system could allow them months of

279

comfort. Their real issue was the food supply, which only lasted a week or two, depending on how often they delved into it. The food supply consisted of a thin paste, similar to baby food in taste and consistency, that passed through a straw-like valve near their mouth inside the helmet. A flip of a switch on their wrist toggled between water and the food paste. Being that the food wasn't that appetizing, Chris thought they would have no trouble making it last.

And in the long run, two weeks was plenty of time, because they would either know it was safe by then, or they would be forced to remove the suit and die from the disease anyway.

The trio rounded the corner of the building to the front. What he saw caused Chris's breathing to come in rapid pants, and his heartrate tripled.

Toby said, "What's the matter, guys? Your vitals just spiked.

Hellen spoke first. "All this death."

Chris turned away from the sight. *I knew this would be here. I saw it from the monitors.* But somehow, seeing it for real like this, was so much worse.

There were bodies piled up along the length of the wall. More bodies covered almost every inch of the ground around the Ark. The entire three hundred square yard length of property from the fence to the front of the building was littered with bodies. Some looked like they had been running to the Ark and had just collapsed, dying where they landed.

Chris had trouble stepping around the corpses, afraid to step directly on them. The three moved in single file, each stepping where the last one stepped. Chris was in the lead. Hellen followed up at the end.

The front of the building had so many bodies piled up, where people climbed onto the dead that had fallen before them, that it was clear some of those people died from being crushed.

As they approached the center of the yard, Chris saw the car Brian and Nancy had driven up in. It had been completely covered in the dead. Nearby, he saw the jeep Rick had driven up from the front gate in. Even if they could uncover either vehicle, they would have trouble navigating the bodies sprawled out across the yard.

Hellen leaned down to check one of the fallen bodies for any sign of life as she passed it until Chris stopped her.

"Don't," he said. "I'm sorry but there is no hope for any of them."

Hellen understood and stopped.

Brian said, "Oh, God."

Chris saw what he was looking at. Chris glanced over the helicopter accident, and the aftermath. He stopped to inspect the severed limbs, and the burnt bodies. He turned away when he saw that one person had been severed at the waste, but still had managed to crawl several feet before succumbing to the injuries. There was a line of blood and entrails marking his progress.

When Brian started running, Chris chased after him.

"Calm him down," Toby said. "His vitals are off the charts."

When he caught up to Brian, Chris managed to keep him still. Brian continued to hyperventilate inside his mask.

"Control your breathing, Brian. Otherwise, you're going to go into hypercapnia. There is too much carbon dioxide entering your bloodstream. Breathe slowly." Chris held Brian by the arms, guiding him. "Slowly, that's right. Good."

Hellen caught up to them and examined him. "Some of the blood vessels in his eyes have burst, but I think he'll be all right. Brian, you're going to have to avoid looking at the people around you. Keep your eyes on the trees above us, and we'll guide you out of the worst of it. Okay?"

Calmer now, Brian nodded.

When they reached the gate, Brian moved to put his hand on the fence to steady himself, but there was already a hand there, gripping the links, and he snatched his hand back. He crouched forward and put his hands on his knees instead. Chris unlatched the gate and they passed beyond the fence.

Like on the wall, there were bodies piled up on both sides of the fence. Some people had crawled to the top of the fence, and then died there, dangling on either side.

As they walked on, the dead around them began to diminish, and Brian felt comfortable looking down again. He simply didn't look directly at any of the people lying on the ground.

Chris looked down at a woman lying face up. Frost still clung to her pale, gray skin, and snow-melt covered her eyes like unfallen tears. Chris looked up to make sure Brian hadn't seen it.

As they walked down the dirt trail known as Ampersand Road, they saw openings in the tree line. Camp sites had been set up in these openings, with tents erected to offer their inhabitants some protection from the elements. Hellen checked some of the tents. She found no one alive. Chris looked into one tent and saw a woman dressed in heavy coats, and wrapped in blankets. There was a dead infant in her arms. Brian wasn't allowed to look.

As they came around the bend in the road (if you could call it a road), Chris turned and glanced back to where they had just been. He sighed at what he saw. Across the lake, the building known as The Ark stretched up and up, reaching into the clouds. It was so high he couldn't see the top of the building through the clouds.

"I used to live up there," Chris said, still straining his neck to look up.

The mountains behind the building looked like anthills in comparison.

He gave himself a moment to take in the scene with no dead bodies in sight. *This is our last chance to see anything so beautiful for a long time.*

2.

It took them three days to traverse Ampersand Road, and then Coreys Road, to get to the main road, Route 3. Brian stamped snow off his feet as he reached the solid and smooth blacktop of a real road.

Chris glanced in both directions, hoping to see an abandoned car, but there was nothing. "Looks like we are walking to town."

Brian pointed. "This way."

They began walking.

After about two and a half miles they reached the first intersection. When they travelled farther west, they began to finally see signs of human habitation. They entered a side road, hoping it led to a Day's Inn, or even a Motel Six.

It was a warehouse.

There were cars around, but none of them seemed to have keys in them. Nor did they have bodies, which was a plus.

"Anyone know how to hotwire a car?" Brian asked.

No one did.

"I guess we keep walking then."

Hellen sat on the hood of a blue car. "It's getting late. Shouldn't we find someplace here to crash for the night?"

"She's right," Chris said. "No sense stumbling around in the dark."

Brian looked back toward the road. "I want to keep moving."

Chris touched Brian's shoulder. "I know you're anxious to get to her, but if we show up exhausted and confused we'll be no help to her."

Brian's shoulders slumped, and he hung his head. He walked back to where Hellen waited.

They found lodging in the manager's trailer. There was a cot behind the officer's desk, a couch and a recliner. Hellen took the cot, and Chris took the couch. Brian wanted the recliner because he found it hard to sleep in the suit in a prone position. Even sitting up he slept very little. Chris had no trouble falling asleep.

Chris woke at the first sign of light.

Hellen woke next. She sat up and looked around.

Brian was nowhere around. *He went ahead without us.* Chris scrambled off the couch and staggered out into the morning sunshine. He squinted into the light, looking for Brian.

"Looking for me?" Brian came around the side of the building. "Had to empty out my reservoir."

They wasted no time heading out again.

As they walked, Chris began to lag behind. Brian spurred everyone forward, unencumbered by the weight of the suit he wore. Hellen held the middle position. She was tired, but not enough to slow her down. She waited for Chris to catch up, but Brian continued to move at the fevered pace he had set for himself.

"It's not a race," Chris said to Brian, panting.

"I can't stop. I have to get to Nancy."

"I know, Bud. I'm right there with you. But if I keep going at this pace I'm going to collapse. Are you going to leave me behind, or are you going to allow me to rest?"

Brian stopped. He waited for Hellen and Chris to catch up and they sat in the grass at the side of the road. Chris sipped at his water. *My water level is dangerously low. I have to conserve it. If I don't, I'm going to die of thirst.*

"I guess I should have prepared for this excursion. I'm Sorry, Brian. I wasn't thinking when I planned this. I just figured it would be a walk in the park. Boy, was I wrong." Chris puffed out an exhausted laugh.

"I appreciate your effort, Chris. If you hadn't authorized this trip we would still be inside the Ark, and that would have been that much longer Nancy would have spent alone. I don't mean to leave you in the dust, but I can't help but think she needs me, and the sooner I get there the better."

"I know," Chris said. "I curse my inadequacies."

Now all three of them laughed.

"Well, while you rest I'm going to go behind that tree and empty my reservoir." Brian said.

"Why the modesty?" Chris asked. "You're among friends…and a doctor."

"I'd like to be viewed as a friend as well." Hellen turned to face Chris, and then to Brian.

Brian said "you are" at the same time Chris said it. They all laughed again.

When the laughter ended, Brian broke the silence. "Anyway, if it's all the same…" He trotted over to the tree line and ducked behind a large maple.

Chris enjoyed the moment of rest, and then they were on their way again.

Chris's internal temperature gage told Chris it was sixty-eight degrees Fahrenheit inside the suit but felt like ninety-eight. An old-fashioned thermometer hung from the Marketplace Pub and Deli which read forty-one. He longed to feel that cool air as sweat dripped down the side of his face, tickling his skin. He had no way to wipe it away and the sensation was agonizing. He hadn't thought about those things, either. For what seemed like forever, his crotch itched unmercifully, and he couldn't hide a quick groin-scratch from Hellen. It didn't matter anyway, because he couldn't reach it. He wasn't sure when the sensation had stopped, but he was grateful, and he prayed it wouldn't return.

The next sign of civilization they came across was a large white building set far back from the road. There were trees scattered throughout the lawn between the road and the building, and a fence had been constructed around the perimeter of the property.

"I always wondered what this place was," Brian said as they approached.

"It's called Sunmount Hospital," Chris said. "We considered buying out this property for the Ark, but decided it wasn't big enough."

"A hospital?" Hellen's interest caused her to scurry to catch up. "Why does the fence have barbed wire along the top of it?"

"I don't know. This fence wasn't here before we entered the Ark. It's new."

As they came up on the center of the property, they began to understand why the fence had been erected.

"What the hell," Brian said.

Scattered across the lawn were dead bodies. Some were naked, and some wore pajamas. Still others wore hospital gowns. Most of the dead were barefoot, but a few wore slippers. The most amazing detail about the sight was the sheer number of dead littering the ground.

"There must be thousands of people in there." Brian stepped closer to the fence.

Hellen said, "careful."

Brian stopped and turned around.

"Do you see those white knobs located on the posts? That indicates the fence is electrified. I don't know if the electricity is still on, but if it is—if they have some kind of generator running it—the power could short out your suit. Then you would be trapped inside an oven. The sun would bake you into gingerbread."

Brian whistled. "Thanks for the warning."

"Don't mention it." She smiled through her face mask at him.

Brian turned back to the fenced in area. "What kind of hospital is this?"

Chris stood next to him and looked out at the sight in front of them. "In the past, it was a veteran's hospital, but then it was used as a place for the physically and mentally handicapped. By the looks, the military took it over and turned it into some kind of concentration camp for the sick. Looks like they tried to contain the sickness by rounding everyone up and putting them in here."

"Horrible," Brian said.

"The world was ending, and people were at a loss how to deal with it. Who knows what other atrocities were committed in the name of protecting the remaining population?" Hellen stopped talking when she noticed Chris and Brian were looking at her.

After a brief pause to consider her words Chris encouraged the group to move on.

Up the road only a few yards, from the Sunmount, they reached the first stoplight. The power was not on. There were two cars—a van and a four-door sedan—in the intersection that had smashed into each other. A quick glance into the vehicles showed that the riders in the vehicles had vacated.

They walked on, passing houses and businesses, but didn't stop to investigate. Chris wanted to, but he knew there was only one home Brian cared to check on. They came across more cars pulled over. Some still contained their drivers—all were dead. Chris expected nothing less.

They passed Park Motel, and just a short distance down from that was the Shaheen's Motel.

Many of the buildings had graffiti spray painted on them. Obscenities and lude drawings of penises. There were a few drawings depicting violence such as decapitations and hangings. Chris thought they were probably atrocities the artist had witnessed.

Brian showed no interest in any of the sights they passed, and after about a half a day walking at a good clip, they entered the heart of Tupper Lake. Chris peered into the restaurant identified as Little Italy. The business was closed, and there didn't seem to be any people—corpses or otherwise—inside, but he looked longingly at the prospect of eating something other than baby food that tasted like strained peas. After a moment, he gave up the dream and they continued on.

When they reached the Stewarts convenience store and gas station, they stopped. There had been some kind of catastrophic accident here, or massive vandalism. The streetlamp and the post holding the street light had been plowed over. The pumps had been smashed and the island's overhead had been knocked down. The ground around the pumps was charred, and several cars were burned-out wrecks. There were charred bodies as well. Hellen walked amongst the debris, and Chris thought she was taking mental notes on all the victims she saw. When she finished, she moved on down the road. Chris and Brian followed her, saying nothing.

Chris took note of the old-time movie theater called the State. The two-screen theater boasted the movies P N and The Ma tian. The missing A and R littered the sidewalk below the marquee.

Further down the road the Community Bank's electronic time and temperature banner sat black and dark. After that they reached the end of park street and started down Wawbeek Avenue, Chris took note of the unfinished construction at the intersection. *Work that will never be finished.*

"This way," Brian said and directed them to the left.

As they passed by the Wawbeek gas station, Hellen stopped. As Brian continued walking, Chris stopped to see what had Hellen's attention. He stood next to her and looked in the direction she was looking. He saw the open door at the gas station, but nothing else.

"I think I saw movement," Hellen said with a voice filled with awe and shock. "I'm sure I did."

She took a step forward, but Chris stopped her.

"Wait."

Brian had stopped and returned to stand with the them.

She turned to Chris. "We have to check it out. If there are other survivors…" She didn't have to finish her thought.

Chris walked beside her. Brian followed slowly behind them. When they were a couple of feet from the building, they learned that the door wasn't open; the glass was smashed out. In fact, all the windows were smashed out. The place had been ransacked. The damage was extensive.

Movement from the darkness inside the building caused them all to stop moving forward. In the space of a few breaths, the mysterious intruder revealed itself.

An animal—the ugliest dog any of them had ever seen—pulled a dead body through the opening of the door. It dropped its prize and stared down the newcomers. Chris realized that in this world he and his travel partners were the intruders. After a few seconds of stillness, the animal snarled. A sound, low and gruff, rumbled up from its throat. Its lip curled and it barked a warning.

None of them dared to move until Chris finally stepped forward and put himself in the way of Hellen and Brian.

"Chris, no," Brian said in a whisper.

"Move backward very slowly, without turning." Chris kept his eyes on the monster in front of them.

Without warning, a second coy dog leapt through the smashed window and landed near the first. The two coy dogs turned on one another snarling and biting, with slather flying off blood-caked muzzles, and landing in the muddy earth.

All three humans turned and ran.

The coy dogs stopped their fighting and gave chase.

Chris pushed the others along, but running in their bulky suits was nearly an impossible task. The dogs caught up to them without difficulty. The animals leapt into the air.

From between two houses, several domesticated dogs raced out and attacked the wild dogs. The humans stopped and turned, watching as the animals rolled and snarled at each other. Mud flew up around the animals, and sprays of blood flew out, landing on the frozen ground.

As the animals fought, the humans took opportunity to slip away unnoticed. When they were several blocks away, they turned and headed down another street. They cut through a few yards until they were far enough away to be out of danger from being seen by whichever animals had won the fight.

In another hour and a half, they had arrived at the house Brian and Nancy had shared for the entire length of their married lives together.

Brian ran toward the house.

3.

"Nancy." Brian shouted the name. And again. "Nancy."

Chris said. "She can't hear you through the suit, Bro." He chased after his runaway friend. Hellen followed.

When they caught up to him, Brian was pushing at the door, trying to open it with brute force.

All around the house, dead bodies lay in heaps like piles of leaves. Snow and frost still clung to the corpses. They were the would-be looters and intruders that had died before they could get into the house. The windows had been well boarded, on the outside, and on the inside. Nancy had been very thorough. Chris tried to use his gloved hands to pry the boards loose.

"Careful," Hellen said. "You could puncture the suit."

Chris stopped. "How do we get inside?"

Brian pounded heavily on the door, hoping to draw Nancy's attention to the little window imbedded in the door. She could look out and see…

See what? The aliens invading her home?

Hellen walked around the perimeter looking for a weakness, but she found none. Brian continued his useless hammering at the door, throwing his weight against it. He even tried kicking at it, but the suit wouldn't allow him the movement to get a good swing at the door with his feet.

As Chris continued to look through the windows, he came across one window where there was a gap in the wood. He could see into the house. He used one finger to reach through and tap on the glass. It was a feeble attempt, but he had to try. As he peered in and changed his angle, he thought he saw Nancy sitting in a chair. She wasn't moving.

"I see her," he said into his intercom link. Brian raced over and shoved him out of the way.

Brian peered in. It took him a moment to get situated to the right angle. "I see her, too." He gripped the boards blocking his way and pulled with all his strength. He leaned into the board and then whipped himself backward, trying to force the board loose. At one point, Chris thought he heard a creaking sound as a nail gave up a bit of its hold. He tried to help, but couldn't repeat the success.

Brian collapsed against the side of the house with his gloved hands covering his face mask. If he was crying, he made no sound.

"Think man," Chris said. "There has to be a way into this house."

Hellen walked off the porch and headed around the side of the house. Chris had watched her leave, but didn't ask where she was going. He turned back and focused on Brian. He placed an arm around Brian's shoulders for comfort. After a moment, Brian jumped up and began battering at the door again, with renewed vigor.

His efforts were as useless as the other attempts.

He slammed his fists into the wood covering the windows. Some of the panes of glass shattered, but he was no closer to getting inside.

He returned to window that showed him a view of his wife. He peered in. "Is she moving? I think I see her moving."

Chris looked. He saw no movement, and she seemed to be in the same position as the last time he looked.

"I think I saw her moving, too." Chris cursed himself for the lie.

Brian walked out to the road. He looked in both directions. "If there was a car we could drive through the front door."

"It won't work."

Brian ignored Chris. "A four-wheel-drive vehicle could climb the porch steps. We could cinch a chain to the door knob and pull the door right off the hinges. That could work, couldn't it?"

But there was no car.

Brian returned to the house, defeated. He stared at Chris and Chris stared back. He didn't know what to tell his friend to make him feel better.

"She needs our help," Brian said.

"I know."

"She's alone in there."

"I know."

"I need her, Chris. I need to be with her."

This time Chris didn't respond. They both turned back toward the house and, with a combined effort, slammed their weight into the door.

The door held.

Chris stood staring at the door, impressed with Nancy's ability to hold off attackers. Brian stood next to him silently staring at the door as well. When Chris saw movement in his periphery, he turned and saw Hellen. She was holding an axe.

"Found it in the neighbor's shed," she said.

It was a long, red-handled axe, like the one firemen used. She held it out to them. Brian flew at her and snatched the axe from her hands.

"Thank you." He said it in a breathless rush.

He returned to the door and swung the axe down in an arch from above his head, hitting the door knob with the dull side. After a second swing, the knob broke loose. But it did not fall. He hit it again.

The knob came off and fell to the floor. They were deaf to the clatter it made when it hit the wooden deck.

He then butted the axe against the door where the lock engaged the frame. He hit several times in the same spot with all his might, but the door did not give.

"The hell with this," Brian said and began slamming the blade of the axe into the door.

He hit it again and again. When the axe got stuck in the wood, he wiggled it free and hit the door again.

Chris thought of the movie The Shining and almost said, "here's Johnny," but refrained.

Brian's effort finally began to bear dividends, and he opened a hole in the door the size of a basketball. He stopped, panting. He dropped the axe, blade side down, and reached into the hole. He fumbled around for a bit, and then located the object of his dissatisfaction. He removed a large two-by-four from the inside of the door and it swung inward without any effort.

Chris gaped. *Come on in; sit a spell.*

Brian dropped the axe and pushed through the door. Chris followed. Hellen picked up the axe and brought it into the house with her. She set it against a wood-paneled window.

Brian raced over and dropped down in front of Nancy.

The woman in the chair stared out with dead eyes, seeing nothing. Her lips were blue, skin pale and gray. Brian dropped his head into her lap. Chris could hear his sobs, but tried to give him privacy.

This was when Nancy's eyes flicked to the left.

4.

"Brian, she moved." Chris spoke with the excitement of a kid on Christmas day.

Brian jerked his head up. He looked into Nancy's face. Her eyes moved again but she didn't look at anyone in the room. She muttered something that they couldn't hear. Her head lolled, as if she had trouble keeping it up. She continued to look around, almost as if she was trying to avoid looking at Brian or the others.

"Honey, it's—" He cursed, annoyed by the helmet.

He waved a hand in front of her face but she didn't look at the hand either.

"What's wrong with her?" Brian pounded his fists into the chair's arms on either side of her.

"I think she's in shock," Hellen said. "Or perhaps she's suffering from anxiety...Cabin fever, if you will."

"What do we do for her?"

"There isn't much we can do, unfortunately. All we can do is keep her warm, comfortable. Hope she snaps out of it."

"That's not very comforting," Brian said.

Hellen flashed a penlight in Nancy's eyes. "Fascinating."

"What?" Chris asked.

Hellen continued to flash the light in Nancy's eyes. "Her pupils are hyper-dilated. Her irises are nearly non-existent. She must have superior night vision in this state. I guess it's the shock causing this."

"I think she's cold."

Chris found blankets in a nearby closet and they draped them over her. Brian tried to use his bulk to warm her, but the suit made it too awkward. Hellen used the equipment stored in the pack she had brought with her to monitor Nancy's vitals. She tried to take a blood pressure, but was unable to get a conclusive result. She tried to take Nancy's temperature, but that garnered the same result.

"I can't effectively examine her inside this suit." Her voice was filled with irritation, tempered with restraint.

Brian tucked the blankets around her tighter.

"She looks..." Chris didn't finish his thought. He wanted to say she looked bad—her lips were cracked and dry, and her eyes looked hollow—but he didn't want to upset Brian.

At the sound of Chris's voice, Nancy turned her head and looked into Chris's eyes. She even held his gaze.

"She's looking at me. She sees me."

She continued mumbling to herself—or was she trying to talk to Chris? —as she stared deeply into his eyes.

Brian picked up one of Nancy's hands in his gloved fists, but she continued to stare at Chris, oblivious to Brian's touch.

"This is killing me. We have to do something."

Hellen moved to the oversized sofa and said, "Can you lift her, and bring her over here?" She shook out some blankets and laid them over the cushions. Brian and Chris worked together to lift Nancy out of the chair. They worked in tandem to carry her over to the sofa.

"She feels like dead weight." Chris immediately regretted his words.

They situated her in a supine position on her back, with throw pillows under her head. They covered her up with extra blankets and tucked them snugly around her slight frame.

"Is there any way to make a fire? We need to heat water and get warm liquids into her. She looks like she hasn't had anything to drink or eat in days. We also need to warm her up more than what the blankets can do."

Brian looked around the room. "We don't have a fireplace in the house, or a wood stove. The house runs — ran — on oil heat. We own a couple of electric heaters, but they're useless."

Brian stopped. He stared at Chris. Chris stared back, suddenly chilled to the bone. *What terrible plan is brewing in that head of yours, buddy? Whatever it is, it isn't good.*

Before Chris had a chance to voice his concern, Brian reached up and pulled the release on his helmet. The helmet came away from the rest of the suit with a hiss, and steam rushed out as the warm air inside the suit hit the cold air in the room. The helmet came loose.

"Brian, what have you done?" Hellen's words came out in a breathy rush.

Brian removed the helmet and tossed it aside. He pulled his hands out of the armholes and reached down to his groin. He carefully removed the rubbery adhesive holding the catheter to his penis and rolled it off. It felt good to be free of that thing, and he sighed. He stripped out of the rest of the suit and kicked it away.

"It is freaking cold." Brian wrapped his arms around his bare chest.

He stood in the middle of his living room wearing nothing except a pair of boxer briefs. "Now I wish I had thought to wear long johns."

Chris could still hear Brian, but barely. The helmet was picking up sounds in the room and transmitting them.

"Watch her for a minute." Shivering, Brian ran to his bedroom. His bare feet slapped at the cold, hardwood floor. Moments later he returned wearing jeans, a flannel shirt and heavy white socks. He scurried over and climbed under the blankets with Nancy.

Chris and Hellen stared at each other. They looked down at Brian as he cuddled under the blankets with his wife. He was saying something, but he had moved out of range of the helmet microphone. Brian shivered.

Chris said, "Bloody hell." Then he pulled the release on his own suit.

5.

Brian groaned as Chris stripped out of the hazmat suit. *Just because I did it, doesn't mean you have to. What have I started?*

Chris stood in the middle of the room in his boxers, shivering and hugging himself, and asked, "G-got any extra clothes ff-for mme?"

"Second room on the left, left side of the closet," Brian said.

Chris headed off in search of warmer wares. When he returned, he wore several layers of clothes that were baggy on him. But he was smiling.

"Better," he said.

Chris crawled under the blankets to add his warmth to the mix.

As the three of them cuddled close, Brian said, "Thank you, man. I'm sorry. I just didn't know what else to do."

"It'll be fine," Chris said. "I'm sure the plague has run its course. It has a short incubation period. Once the last sick person died, the plague died with him. I'm sure of it."

Nancy whispered something.

"Could you hear what she said?" Chris asked. "I didn't catch it."

"I didn't, either. What did you say, Honey?" Brian placed an ear close to her mouth. After a long pause, she whispered again. Brian shook his head, discouraged. He couldn't understand her.

They lay quietly together for several minutes. Hellen had taken a seat in the chair Nancy had vacated when they moved her. She turned it so she could face them, even if she couldn't hear them—or them her. She watched them with a patient determination. Chris almost forgot she was there.

To Brian, Chris said, "She doesn't seem to be warming up. In fact, she's making me cold."

Brian sighed. "I know. It's like her cold is pushing our heat away. The warmth is escaping out instead of being drawn in."

Chris lay shivering under the blanket until exhaustion finally let him fall asleep. Brian could feel his friend's body heat, but he felt nothing from Nancy. She smelled bad, too. As Chris slept, he draped one leg over Nancy, and over Brian, as well. Chris had stopped shivering. He mumbled something incoherent and slipped an arm over them. He was practically straddling Nancy. Wake up, kid. *You're practically humping my wife.* Hell, he was humping both of them. Though, Nancy did feel warmer than she had the night before, so Chris was doing something right.

In the morning, when Chris opened his eyes, Brian was staring at him. They were practically nose to nose. "Good morning."

Chris smiled. "Morning." His voice croaked. "Cozy."

"Yea, you've been like this all night."

"Is that your breath I smell, or hers? Someone needs to brush their teeth."

Nancy lay calmly beneath the two men, though she stared up at Chris.

"Why is she staring at me like that? It's freaking me out."

Nancy whispered something.

Brian and Chris shared a look. Brian shrugged. *I didn't catch that.*

Chris said, "I'm sorry, Nancy. I didn't hear you." Chris placed his ear to her lips.

She whispered again.

"Marbh ag Siul."

Chris scrambled to get away from her. He knocked the covers away, and his feet sank into the cushions. He tripped and fell backward. He slammed his lower back into the sofa's arm and rolled onto the floor.

Brian jumped up, startled. He looked around and found Chris sitting on the floor against the wall. "What the hell?"

Chris stood. His face had gone as pale as Nancy's, and his eyes were wide, frightened.

Hellen had been dozing in the recliner, jumped up and rushed to Chris. She looked him over. She motioned for Chris to pick up one of the discarded helmets. He understood and lifted a helmet and placed it on his head. He could hear her frantic questions, but they sounded far off...as if from down a long tunnel.

"What happened? Are you all right? I thought something was attacking you."

"I'm ok," Chris said. "Can you hear me?"

Hellen nodded.

"I didn't mean to startle you. I'm sorry."

Chris removed the helmet and tossed it aside.

Brian sat Nancy up and put an arm around her shoulder. He couldn't understand her fascination with Chris. She watched intently as Chris walked over and stood over them.

Brian fixed her hair. "She's doing better. She's warming up."

"Brian step away."

Brian looked up at Chris, puzzled. "What?"

"Step away. It's not Nancy."

"What are you talking about? Have you gone nuts? Why are you saying that? It's Nancy."

Chris gripped Brian under the arm and pulled him away from Nancy. Brian rose, but then angrily pulled away and dropped back down beside his wife.

"What the fuck, Man? Have you gone crazy?" Brian turned away from Chris to focus on Nancy.

Chris said something that sounded like, "Marble-ray-droy."

Brian studied Nancy's mouth as it stretched into a hideous semblance of a grin. Her eyes never left Chris.

"As the Chosen One, I demand that you step away from her Brian. Now."

Brian turned an incredulous eye up at Chris. "Really? That shit doesn't work on me. I'm not one of your true believers." He returned to doting on Nancy.

Chris picked up the helmet again and backed away from Brian. He motioned for Hellen to follow. He pulled her out to the kitchen, Brian would not be able to hear him.

Brian held Nancy's hands. They were warmer, but still not warm enough. She was still staring at Chris. *What is it about Chris that had her so captivated?* Brian looked out at the two in the kitchen. *Are they out there plotting against us? It sure looks like they are.*

Chris looked like a bobble-head with the helmet rattling around on his head like that. Brian would have laughed if he hadn't been so pissed about their sudden conspiratorial attitude.

Hellen seemed upset about whatever Chris was saying to her. She kept stepping away from him, and he would grab her arm and pull her back. Her gloved hands continually shot up to her facemask, as if she was appalled, and wanted to cover her mouth. *What are you telling her…buddy? What lies are you filling her head with about my wife?*

Brian had never felt so out of touch with everything as he did at that moment. *This is how Nancy felt all along. She was the troublesome outsider looking in. And now that's me. No, that's both of us.* He leaned in closer to Nancy.

Hellen turned away, and Chris touched her arm, willing her to turn and look him again. There was a pause, and neither of them moved, until Chris turned to walk away. Now Hellen pulled him back. She had questions. She moved her hands u and down, using her body to express her concerns. When her hands dropped back to her sides, Chris removed the helmet and carried it back into the living room under his arm.

"Are you two finished discussing my wife?"

Chris set the helmet down. He turned to Brian.

Brian glanced through the doorway to the kitchen where Hellen paced.

"She seems upset. What did you say to her?"

"I told her I'm leaving."

"What?" Brian felt like the earth just opened up beneath him. "Where are you going?"

"I have a mission to fulfill. I have to go in search of the answers to a few questions that have been chasing me lately. I won't find those answers here. Hellen is staying with you and Nancy."

"She doesn't seem all that thrilled to be staying. What was all that nonsense about Nancy not being Nancy?"

"I was disoriented when I woke up. I didn't know what I was saying. I'm sorry about all that. I'm stupid." Chris smiled from the side of his mouth like he always did. Brian missed that expression. "Forgive me?"

Brian stood and they hugged, tightly. He was afraid to let his friend go.

Brian stepped back and returned to his post on the sofa. "Nothing to forgive."

"I'll be back as soon as I can." Chris turned away from Brian and waved goodbye to Hellen.

Hellen came out of the kitchen, but still was not relaxed enough to sit. She paced. She seemed to be silently begging to go, too. Brian couldn't shake the feeling that Chris, his oldest and dearest friend, was hiding something from him.

Chris stepped out the door and was gone before Brian could question him any further.

6.

Brian saw that Hellen was staring at him from behind her facemask. He smiled nervously back at her then turned to Nancy. He pushed her hair behind her ear and wrapped an arm around her shoulder. She had begun to get cold again. He didn't know what else to do, so he simply hugged her.

After a moment, Hellen walked around the room opening drawers and cabinets. She found what she was looking for in the Armoire. She approached Brian with a pad of paper and a pen. She couldn't hold the pen in the traditional position, so she wrapped a fist around it and scrawled her note in large, sprawling childlike print. Brian read what she had written.

HOW IS SHE?

He took the pen and replied.

SHE'S GETTING COLD AGAIN.

Hellen nodded her understanding and pulled a blanket around Nancy's shoulders. She placed one on Nancy's lap. Once done, she stepped back quickly.

She acts like she's afraid of Nancy.

Nancy continued to stare at nothing, muttering nonsense occasionally. Brian pulled her into an embrace and Nancy didn't resist. He held her, resting her head against his shoulder. He prayed Chris would come back soon. He didn't understand what Chris thought he was going to find to prove the plague was over. Only time could do that, or at least that was what Brian was led to believe from the discussions he had overheard. He closed his eyes and gently rocked his wife in his arms. When he opened his eyes again he saw that Hellen had gone back to searching the room again. When she saw that he was looking at her, Hellen walked over and picked up the paper and pen again. She scrawled another note and handed him the pad.

He read what was written there. *I'M GOING TO SEARCH THE HOUSE FOR SUPPLIES, OKAY?*

He nodded and dropped the pad on the coffee table. As Hellen went off to search the house, Brian closed his eyes again.

He must have dozed off, because when he snapped them open again Hellen was kneeling in front of him holding something in one fisted hand, and a bottle of water. He reached out and she dropped two white pills in his hand. She also handed him the water.

"What's this for?" His own voice startled him in the eerie silence.

Hellen must have read his lips, because she picked up the pen and paper and began writing.

He read. *SEDATIVE. HARMLESS.*

Brian wasn't so sure about that, but still he tilted Nancy's head up to administer the meds. She moved easily under his direction. He placed the pills in her mouth. He put the water to her lips and guided her to drink. Water spilled over the corners of her mouth but he could see her throat moving as she swallowed. When he gently opened her mouth, he saw that the pills were gone. He dabbed at her wet face with the corner of a blanket. He lay back with her again, cradling Nancy in the crook of his arm. She felt so frail in his arms, so helpless. It broke his heart to see her like this.

When he looked around, he saw that Hellen had gone off again. He wondered what else she would find. As he closed his eyes and tried to sleep, it occurred to him that maybe the sedatives had been meant for him. He thought of asking Hellen for his own sedatives the next time he saw her, but it turned out he didn't need them after all.

Brian dropped into a fitful sleep.

7.

Hellen felt like a trapped rat. One in a space age bio-suit, but a trapped rat, just the same. She had investigated every inch of the house, and had learned that the master bedroom locked from the inside. She thought she could lock the door, jam the wooden chair to the desk under the doorknob, and maybe she would be able to get some sleep. She dared not sleep out in the open. If that wasn't Brian's wife on the sofa—and Chris had been pretty sure it wasn't—she didn't want to let her guard down anywhere in the vicinity of her…or it…

Or whatever.

In the kitchen, Chris had told her that Nancy was not Nancy, not anymore. He mentioned that she was not to be trusted. In the same breath, however, he had assured her that Nancy was not dangerous. She didn't know if she believed that. When Bill had been possessed, he had taken a knife and slit his own throat. Who was to say Nancy's possession wouldn't result in murder instead of suicide?

Hellen emptied her urine bag into the toilet and flushed. She replaced the bag and zipped up its little compartment in the suit. She returned to the living room and took a seat in the chair. Brian was asleep. The thing in his arms stared out of dead sockets, seeing nothing, or so it seemed. Whatever it was harboring inside Nancy, Hellen figured it had to be planning something. That dumb, empty stare had to be a ruse. Chris could see through it, and so could she.

When Brian woke, he motioned for Hellen to hand him the note pad. She stood and handed it over. Brian wrote something quickly then handed it back to her. She read what he had written.

CAN YOU WATCH OVER NANCY WHILE I GO TO THE BATHROOM?

Reluctantly, she nodded that it was okay. He saluted his appreciation and headed off. Hellen paced back and forth in front of Nancy, studying her face. She was trying to get some kind of reading from whatever resided inside that shell. Was it an act, or wasn't it? She didn't realize how close she had gotten to Nancy until the woman's eyes darted to look directly at her. Hellen jumped back. Then the eyes stared forward again.

Hellen didn't dare get close again. When Brian returned, she was sitting in the chair. As far as he could tell, nothing had happened while he was gone. She didn't bother to tell him.

She started planning her escape about three hours after the woman had looked at her. She didn't care what she promised Chris; that woman's dead, glassy eyes locking on hers had shaken her to the core. Her hands still shook. She didn't know how she would get away, or where she would go, but she couldn't stand to be there any longer than necessary. The going plan was to light out for the Ark in the morning.

When she looked up, she noticed that Brian was looking at her. When she looked back he gave her a tired smile. He pointed to the pad. She reluctantly stood and retrieved it. She passed it to him and he awkwardly scribbled his note with the thing balanced on one arm. Its head bobbed as he wrote, but it showed no discomfort—no emotion at all. When he finished, he passed the pad to Hellen.

I'M SORRY YOU HAVE TO BABYSIT US, the note said.

She wrote back. *It's fine.* She then tried to offer him a smile to back up the lie. She thought of something else to write, but instead of writing it, she dropped the note pad on the table and picked up Brian's helmet. She held it out to him. He took it and placed it over his head.

"Would you mind if I sleep in your bedroom tonight? That chair is killing my back."

He removed the helmet and nodded his approval.

In truth, she doubted if laying prone with the equipment she wore was even possible.

She picked up the pad again. *THANK YOU.* Then she wrote, *IF YOU DON'T MIND, I'LL HEAD UP NOW. I'M EXHAUSTED.*

Brian nodded again. He looked as tired as she felt.

She hated deceiving him like this, she liked him; and Chris, too, was counting on her, but she couldn't take looking into those dead eyes anymore. If he wanted to continue believing that this was his wife, he would have to do it without her. She waved and walked up the stairs. She stopped and turned to look back down the stairwell. When she was sure no one was following her, she entered the room.

She latched the door, hoping the click of the lock didn't alert Brian to what she had done. She carefully pinned the chair under the doorknob. She didn't know if that trick worked, but she would have shoved heavy furniture in front of the door if there had been any in the room. The desk was one of those small, personal desks and wouldn't stop an infant from entering the room. Other than that, the only other piece in the room was the bed.

She laid down on the bed. It took her several tries to get in a position that was even slightly comfortable. She tried to sleep but couldn't. She wished she had stayed at the Ark. She hated the suit, and really hated the food it pumped into her. Though she couldn't smell herself, she was sure she smelled bad.

She looked toward the door. In the gloom, it was hard to make out shapes, but she thought the door was still shut, and the chair was still in place. Her eyes drooped. She yawned.

The bed was more comfortable than she thought it would, and she fell asleep quickly. She dreamed of Chris. She dreamed that he returned and gave her permission to leave. In the dream, Nancy was alive and healthy. Hellen was out of the hazmat suit and heading back to the Ark. She was with Brian, Nancy and Chris, and they were all heading back to the Ark. There were no dead bodies littering the ground.

It was a beautiful sunny day.

Then things in the dream turned bad.

The coy dogs returned, and the day turned dark. They were running. When Hellen turned to look back, she saw Nancy had been taken down and ripped to shreds by a pack of the vile-looking wild beasts. When Brian stopped to help her he, too, was swarmed. Hellen called out for Chris to come with her, but he wanted to go back for his friends. She grabbed his arm and wouldn't let him go. *No*, she cried out. *You can't you must come back.*

But her hazmat suit was back on, and he couldn't hear her. Her panting breath filled her ears.

Chris turned back to her. She read his lips.

Save yourself.

Save…

Hellen woke with a gasp. Something was wrong inside the room. She looked toward the door, and even in the inky darkness she could see that the door was open. It was open. The chair was gone and the door was open.

She lifted her head and looked at the foot of the bed.

Nancy—or what passed for Nancy—stood at the end of the bed looking at her. Its preternatural eyes glowed with an inner light. She felt something inside her let go. It was hope.

The Fortress

The Nancy thing tilted its head as it looked at her. With a speed almost too fast for Hellen to see, the thing jumped at her. It had a cat-like grace as it landed on the bed, straddling her.

Hellen screamed, but the scream only filled the inside of her helmet. It reverberated throughout the small space around her ears until the sound seemed to split her head. The thing swiped at her with its nails, shredding the suit. The fabric ripped, and Hellen heard air hissing from the torn suit. She slapped at the thing that had her pinned to the bed until she managed to roll to the side and slip off the edge. She scrambled toward the door, but the thing pursued her. It gripped her suit and pulled her back into its embrace.

Hellen reached up and unlatched the suit from the helmet. She struggled out of the suit. A painful ripping sensation from her groin told her the internal catheter had been ripped from her body. She didn't care. She lifted the helmet over her head and threw it at the thing.

It laughed, a grinding, cancerous sound, and batted the helmet away harmlessly. It came at her again.

Hellen's hand found the chair and she lifted it. She was ready to swing the chair down on its head when the thing stopped coming at her. In the hesitation, she felt the chair being torn from her grip as if by a magical force.

"What the fuck is this?" Brian held the chair in his hands. He looked over at his wife standing frozen in place, as expressionless as ever, then looked at Hellen. "Why were you going to hit my wife?"

"*She* attacked me."

"Attacked you? She's an invalid. She's sick."

Hellen backed away from both of them. She didn't trust Brian, either now. "You don't have to believe me, but it's the truth." Hellen ripped open the closet door and found a sweatshirt and pants. She spoke as she put them on. "I'm leaving. I'm not safe here. I'll return the clothes once I get some of my own."

306

Brian set the chair down. "You don't have to worry about that. Come back downstairs and we'll sort this out. You don't have to leave. And help yourself to whatever you want. It's fine. I'm sorry. We're all wound pretty tight. I'm sorry."

Brian guided his sick wife out of the room and shut the door.

Hellen fell against the door and shook. She hugged herself, trying to calm herself. She took a few deep breaths and regulated her heartbeat. It was a trick she learned from a yogi in India.

She stood and took a look at herself in the mirror, then wished that she hadn't. Her hair was in tatters. Her skin was waxy and pallid, with a sheen of cold sweat covering it. She longed for hot water.

Once she was as calm as she could manage, she did the thing she dreaded the most, and exited the room.

On the first floor, Hellen saw that Brian had returned to the sofa. Nancy lay on the cushions next to him with her head turned away. There was that much to be thankful for; Hellen never wanted to see those horrible eyes ever again.

"I'm…" Hellen cleared her throat. "I'm going."

"Are you sure? I think you should stay here and wait for Chris—"

Her response was curt. "No." She realized she had gone tense and relaxed her muscles. "I can't. I have to go."

"Where will you go?"

"I don't know." She struggled to keep her voice steady. "I can't stay here. I can't make you believe me, but your wife attacked me. I can't stay."

"What if I say I believe you, would you stay?"

Hellen leveled her gaze at him. "If you believed me, you wouldn't ask me to stay."

Brian lowered his eyes. "Look, I'm not saying she didn't attack you. I think we should look at reasons why she might. Perhaps she had a moment of lucidity and thought you were an intruder. If she comes to again, I'll be sure to explain the situation to her. You'll be safe."

Hellen said nothing, but her mind was made up.

"What do I tell Chris when he returns?"

Hellen looked toward the door, willing Chris to walk through it. She turned back to Brian. *You won't have to tell him anything; he will already know.* What she said was, "Tell him I headed back to the Ark early. Tell him that."

"Is that where you are going?"

She shrugged.

"Will they let you in?"

"Eventually, maybe. I don't know. Maybe they will when they see I'm not getting sick."

"I'm sorry," Brian said again.

Hellen stared at him with sadness in her eyes. "I know."

She walked out the door without saying another word. She closed the door behind her before he had a chance to say anything that might have convinced her to stay.

8.

Brian watched the door close behind Hellen. Why was everyone abandoning him when he needed them most? When Nancy needed them? He turned and looked at the beams of sunlight pouring through the cracks in the wooden slats covering the windows. It was looking to be a nice spring day. He wondered if it would do Nancy some good to be out in the sunlight. She had been cooped up in the house for months. Maybe it was time for her to see the sun.

When Brian took her by the hands and lifted her off the sofa she offered no resistance. She shuffled along as he led her to the door. He dropped one of her hands in order to reach behind him and open the front door. Holding her by one cold hand, he guided her out the door and sat her down in one of the three patio chairs they kept on the porch. She stared out at the lawn, but Brian could tell by the blank expression she wasn't really seeing anything out there. He wondered what it would take to snap her out of this funky state. How could he pull her out of this inner shell she seemed trapped in?

Brian looked around at all the corpses littering the ground around his home. The thermometer on the side of the house read fifty-two degrees. Any warmer, and these bodies are going to start stinking. He decided it was time to clean them up. He stepped off the porch and walked out to the road.

At the end of his road, the unfinished road work left a hole that had been dug, and then abandoned. The digging equipment had also been abandoned. Brian saw that hole now as a huge, empty mass grave.

Brian walked through the side yard to his neighbor's property. The house belonged to Old Man Thorp and his wife Mary. He wondered if they were inside their home right now, curled up together in a death embrace. He hoped their passing had been peaceful, but looking at the shape their house was in, he thought it more likely the looters had murdered them. He would go in there later and see, but first he had to take care of his own problem.

He walked around to the back of the Thorp house and, as he had suspected, just as Hellen had found the axe, their shed door was open, and Old Man Thorp's lawn mower waited there. He started it, drove out of the shed and attached a wagon to the back of it. He then drove it to the front yard.

He stared down at the pale and thawing corpses, not wanting to touch them. He doubted garden gloves would do much good here.

Brian looked toward the house. Nancy relaxed in the chair, staring. She hadn't moved. If he didn't know better, he would have thought she was dead. She didn't even seem to blink.

But ignoring her for the time being, Brian looked past her into the open front door. He remembered something that might be useful in his present situation. He hurried up the porch steps and ran into the house. He saw what he was after scattered on the floor of the living room. He slipped into his hazmat suit and zipped it up. He looked down at Chris's hazmat suit. When he left, he had even taken off his magic bracelet. Brian picked it up and tapped it, unsure of how it worked.

"Chris is that you?" Toby's tinny voice burst forth from unseen speakers. His voice sounded frantic.

"Hi, Toby. No this is Brian. We've all removed our suits. Even Hellen."

"No kidding. Why?"

"It's a long story."

"Where is Chris. I need to know what's going on."

Brian said, "I'm home with my wife. She survived the plague. I think the threat of contagion has passed. Will you be opening the doors soon?"

"Not without Chris's approval."

"Oh, well, if I see him again I'll tell him you need to talk to him."

"Where did he go?"

"He said he went to find himself. Whatever that means."

"Where is Hellen? Can I speak to her?"

"She's gone, too. We had a bit of a disagreement."

"What kind of disagreement?"

Brian didn't want to go into the specifics, so he just said, "I think my wife is living proof the plague is gone. She was disturbed by my wife's present state. She left because she thought my wife attacked her."

"Did she? Your wife, did she attack Hellen?"

Brian hesitated. "No. Well, maybe. Nancy is very confused. She doesn't know Hellen. She might have thought Hellen was an intruder. Hellen said she was coming back to the Ark."

Toby released and audible sigh into Brian's ear that clearly expressed his frustration to Brian. "I don't know why she would do that. Without Chris's approval, I can't let her back in."

9.

Hellen knew well enough that she wouldn't be allowed back into the Ark. So, she had no real plans to go back there. When she left Brian and Nancy, it was to find someplace to lay low, and out of danger from Nancy until Chris returned. If and when she decided to go back to the Ark, it wouldn't be with Chris. The Ark towered over everything, and could be seen for miles away. She merely had to head toward it and eventually she would make it back.

That would have to come later, though. After the doors were opened.

For now, she walked down one street after another until she found what she was looking for: a house far enough away from Brian as she could get, and feel safe.

The house she chose had a chimney, which meant it had a fireplace. The yard had very few corpses around, which told her the house had not been bothered by looters. She could understand why; the house was as far away from everything as a house could get. She entered it through a side door that opened easily when she pushed her hip into it. She slipped quietly inside and closed the door behind her.

"Hello?" Her voice echoed in the stillness. There was no response. She walked further into the house. "Hello?"

Still nothing. She explored the home and found it empty except for two elderly corpses—a man and a woman—in an upstairs bedroom. She didn't bother closing the door. She returned to the first floor and entered the den, where the fireplace had been built into a stone wall of the room.

A more thorough search of the house yielded a pack of stick matches, and several pieces of furniture that could be broken up and burned in the fireplace. She found a bin of old newspapers in the recycling bin on the back porch, and used them as kindling to start a fire. Within minutes, she had a blazing fire to keep her warm. She felt confident that the house was far enough away from Brian's house that the smoke bellowing out the chimney would not be seen by him, or—more precisely—by his wife.

Hellen found a copy of The Great Gatsby in the old couple's library. With that, and a can of creamed corn from the cupboard (which she found uncomfortably close to the consistency of the food from the hazmat suit), she sat down by the fire, wrapped up in a blanket to eat and read.

Before long, she fell asleep.

She woke with a start, and almost jumped out of her seat; but after a quick scan of her surroundings, she knew she was in no immediate danger. She laughed at herself for being so jumpy.

The fire had died down, so she added more broken furniture to the glowing embers. The fire licked hungrily at the new fuel, and a new blaze was burning in a matter of seconds. She was warm, so she stripped out of the blanket covering her. The windows showed darkness had approached while she slept. The room was lit by the flickering radiance from the fireplace. The constantly changing shadows gave the illusion of things moving in the room. This unnerved her, and she felt an uncontrollable shiver up her spine. She didn't know if she could ever feel safe again. She recalled the attack she had endured from Nancy, and she shivered. She went to the door and made sure it was still secure.

But that didn't stop the Nancy thing in the bedroom. The thought made her shiver again.

She moved her chair to the side, so she could see if anyone came through the doorway. She also had a clear view of the only window in the room. She picked up the book and read some more. She wanted to sleep, wanted to get into the habit of sleeping at night again, but she wasn't the least bit tired. She hoped that common practice would come back to her in time.

She was a doctor, and dead bodies didn't bother her, but knowing those two corpses were above her head did give her pause. She thought that, eventually, those bodies would have to be removed. She was just hoping Chris would return before the bodies started stinking. And, even if she didn't smell them, their very presence posed the threat of disease. Not the plague, but common diseases spread by rotting flesh. She grew more and more confident that the plague had been eradicated with every day that passed and she didn't get sick. Still, each day that passed and Chris didn't return depressed her. By mid-summer the entire land was going to turn into a stinking, festering land of new potential diseases. They would have to plan some kind of cleanup if they were going to return to anything resembling normal life.

Halfway through The Great Gatsby, Hellen set the book aside and headed off in search of more food. She found food she hadn't noticed during her first raid. There was shelf after shelf of canned and boxed foods in a pantry. Most of the boxed stuff was useless without a cooking fire, but much of the canned food was perfectly fine right out of the tin. She opened a can of Spaghetti-O's, and ate it straight from the container. When the meal was finished, she tossed the can in the sink. Later she would wash it out and toss it into the recycling bin. She doubted an act as mundane as recycling was necessary anymore, but she decided the less mess she made, the less danger of drawing bugs. Better safe than sorry.

She exited the kitchen and walked toward the door to the den. Halfway through the atrium, Hellen froze. She looked toward the door she had used to enter the house. The door was wide open. She remembered closing it.

Didn't she?

She headed toward the door to close it when a sound from the stairway stopped her. She looked up the stairs. She stopped in her tracks.

The coy dog dropped the corpse it had been dragging down the stairs and growled. Its muzzle was pulled back in a snarl, and its teeth were covered in gore. It had been feasting on human corpses for months, she surmised. How long before they decided living bodies tasted better?

Hellen held out her hands in a placating gesture. She bowed her head, showing the animal deference. She stopped when she backed into the wall. The coy barked and she flinched. She chanced a glance up. The thing picked up the corpse it had been dragging—the old woman—and finished carrying it out the door.

After a moment, a second coy dragged the old man down the stairs and out into the night.

When the animals were gone, Hellen rushed to the door and slammed it shut. The door no longer latched because of the damage she had done to it, so she dragged a heavy, waist-high bureau in front of the door. No animal would be able to move it, she concluded, and returned to the fire in the den, appreciative of the animals for taking care of one matter for her.

Nature takes back its own.

10.

Cleaning up the yard had taken two whole days, and most of a third. But the task was done, and Brian was glad to have the nasty business done. He celebrated by taking a sponge bath and donning fresh clothes. He bathed Nancy as well this way, and dressed her in clean clothes, also. She didn't show any acknowledgement of the attention, but neither did it do anything to draw her out of her shell. He hoped, if anything, it would alleviate her horrible body odor.

After five days, Chris still hadn't returned, and Brian felt the first stirrings of agitation at his situation. Would he be forced to take care of his invalid wife in complete solitude forever? Was there no one who would help him?

Brian stared at Nancy, and wondered what he could do to help her? She seemed perfectly content to continue doing nothing, but Brian was restless. He decided that she would be fine on her own for short stretches of time, and he started going for walks. Mostly, he was trying to get a sense of the neighborhood. He was also secretly hoping he would run into someone — anyone. He would give anything to have Hellen back. He also wished Chris would return. He wouldn't even mind running into a stranger. Surely, there were other survivors out there, wasn't there? The plague couldn't possibly have killed everyone on the planet. Were the survivors in the Ark the only people left on the planet?

No, he refused to believe that. Nancy survived, so surely others had, too.

So, he walked and he searched.

Upon returning home after his walks, he saw that Nancy never moved. He wanted badly to come home and find that she had moved on her own. She had apparently done just that when Hellen had accused Nancy of attacking her. The idea that Nancy had done such a thing was absurd—clearly. Hellen had been mistaken. But, dream or reality, Nancy had gotten up the stairs somehow. Maybe Nancy had gone up there out of memorization. Brian could drive himself crazy trying to understand it all.

After fifteen days of solitude, Brian decided it was time to go farther than he had gone on previous walks. He headed South down Wawbeek Ave, past Lakeview Lanes bowling alley, to the stretch of highway where the road headed out over the water. He walked faster, almost as if he was trying to run away from his new life. He recalled that it had been on this road where Brian had nearly lost Chris, then an eleven-year-old boy, to the creature known as the Dryad.

The creature had been made entirely of parts of trees, bushes and vines. It had attacked him, nearly killing him. Chris had saved his life.

Chris had saved *his* life.

But had he really saved Chris that night? The creature—the Dryad—had taken Chris into the water. Brian had gone after them, but Chris had drowned before Brian could get him out of the water. Chris had been dead. Brian performed CPR on the boy, but nothing seemed to be working. It wasn't until Brian had given up hope that Chris miraculously revived himself. Chris woke, but seemed to have no memory of anything that had happened prior to the drowning.

And the boy seemed different somehow. Chris seemed more sure of himself. He had taken on the role of a leader. Brian remembered how the new and improved Chris had unnerved him somehow. Brian had been afraid of the boy. That was partly why he and Chris had lost touch over the years. Well, that, and the fact that both of them had lives to live. Brian went on to marry Nancy, and begin a life with her; and Chris had gone back to where he lived with his family in southern New York.

Now Brian was once again on this road, heading toward that place where the Dryad had—in all manners of speaking—taken over Chris's life.

Brian was flat out running, he realized. Running so fast he was in danger of tripping over his own feet. He slowed down. As he approached a building on the left, Brian stopped. This was the Trail's End Bar.

A bar.

Alcohol.

Brian could use a drink.

He was a recovering alcoholic, but if there was ever a time to have a drink, it was now. It was here.

The door was open. Brian entered the bar.

The interior was dark, and there were no corpses in sight, which was a good thing. There were several bottles of liquor on the shelves behind the bar. Brian took a seat in one of the barstools and swiveled it. How many times had he sat in a chair much like this one, while Nancy—a then part time bartender—served him beer after beer. By marrying him, she had helped him kick the habit. He swore never to touch alcohol again. He had kept that promise.

Until now.

He hopped over the counter and examined the bottles. He picked up a bottle of Grey Goose off the top shelf and removed the cap.

"Bottom's up," he said and took a long swig from the bottle.

The liquor went down smooth and hot, warming his veins as it hit his system. He moaned.

Brian looked at the table to the right of the cash register and furrowed his brow. He saw a set of keys. He picked up the keys and studied them. One of the objects on the keyring was a fob. The buttons were marked with the symbols of a locked padlock, an unlock symbol and a trunk release. At the bottom was a big red button: panic mode.

Out of curiosity, Brian pressed this red button.

From outside, an alarm blared, loud and threatening.

Brian rushed out the door to the parking lot, and around the side of the building. He spotted the vehicle to which the button belonged. He almost screamed in delirious joy.

The alarm on the big yellow Hummer continued to bleat with angry abandon. Brian laughed, and hit the red button again, stopping the alarm. He used the fob to unlock the doors and climbed into the driver's seat. The vehicle started up with ease, and Brian drove away.

He returned to his house and hopped out of the vehicle, leaving it running. *No one is around to steal it.* He laughed, maybe a little drunk. He entered the house and stood over Nancy.

"Baby," he said. "Pack your bags, we're leaving."

He lifted her up and carried her toward the door. As he reached the exit, he stopped and looked back. He reached down and scooped up Chris's wrist watch. It would be handy to be able to speak to the people in charge of opening the doors when he arrived at the Ark.

He placed Nancy in the passenger seat, and climbed back in behind the wheel. He put the gear in drive and headed off, with the looming shape of the Ark directly in his path.

Chapter Twelve

1.

Chris had no idea where he needed to go. He started out just walking aimlessly down one street after another. Before long, he found himself on Wawbeek Ave. He headed south on that street, with only a slight knowledge of where that road led.

After a day of travelling, he reached a small side road that seemed familiar to him, but he wasn't sure why. After travelling the road, he realized it was the road that led to the house where he and Scott had been held as children. Though it frightened him to think about going back to that place alone, he figured it was his best chance at finding the answers to his questions.

If there were even any answers to be had.

But the place seemed to be calling to him, so he went.

He wasn't sure if he would remember where it was; the place was very well secluded, and was almost impossible to find. But as he reached each intersection, he simply had to close his eyes, and the path opened up to him. Each road he took became more and more remote. Soon he was on a road that was nothing more than a dirt trail, and he knew he was on the right track.

By nightfall he reached his destination.

As he stood in the shadow of the place that had been his childhood torment, Chris questioned the validity of his plan. If Ethel had been correct, and the answers Chris sought were out here to be found, this was where he would find them.

He remembered very little about the place, and what he did know mostly came from the tour Brian had given him before entering the Ark. He recalled that the back yard had been where the old man, Crispus, had been killed. Chris walked around the house to the back yard.

A memory surfaced then. He saw the back door open and a tall figure ran from the house and jumped onto the hood of a car, a station wagon. The car had belonged to his Aunt Virginia and Uncle Ed. When they had been murdered, the killers commandeered the vehicle for their own use. Brian had used that vehicle to drive Chris away from the house.

Chris recalled the tall man's name: Ted.

Ted had jumped on the hood, and Brian had driven away with the maniacal man clinging to the hood. Chris recalled that Brian had managed to fling the man from the car, and then had run him down, killing him.

Chris felt another memory surface. He saw the man known as Crispus holding the dead body of a woman on the platform at the edge of the property. That man had been Crispus. The woman was Sherry.

Sherry. He remembered now that he had been there when she died. She who had managed to get Scott away from the house, had been captured by the thickly muscled man known as….

Mason.

Mason killed Sherry. The man had used those exceptional muscles to pry apart the flexible bars that made up the torso of the wicker man and shoved Chris inside the opening. From inside his wooden prison, Chris watched as Mason placed a noose around Sherry's neck. She was still unconscious from the blow she had sustained when Mason punched her.

Mason waited until Sherry had regained consciousness, and struggled to get the rope off her neck. He cut a line, and a set of pulleys and gears worked to fling Sherry into the air. She kicked and jerked for several seconds until she died. Then her dead body just hung there, limply swinging from the rope.

That was when Mason began calling out for Crispus.

"Old man." He had shouted over and over. "Old man. Come out and see what you have done."

Another memory surfaced, they were rushing back like a video in rewind. In this memory, Brian was fighting with a giant tree. But this wasn't a tree, this was the Dryad, and it was trying to take Chris. Brian fought hard, but it was a losing battle. The Dryad was as relentless as time itself, and it would not leave without its prize.

Chris was taken by the Dryad, and darkness enveloped him. Darkness and cold. He was in the water. The Dryad dragged him deeper and deeper until…nothing.

Nothing.

Then there was something. It was light. Chris was floating in the water, and Brian had ahold of his foot. A light flooded in from above. Chris could see everything. He could see the Dryad floating like flotsam at the edge of the light. He could see Brian dragging Chris by the foot back to the surface. Chris could breathe. He was underwater, but he could breathe.

Then Brian was at the surface. He dragged Chris back to shore. He started CPR. Chris was lying unconscious on the ground, but he was there in the air above them, too. He was looking down at the unconscious boy and the distraught man. There was a light shining all around but it was a light that only he could see. All at once, the light entered the floating Chris. And in an instant, too fast for the human mind to calculate, the light and the floating Chris entered the unconscious boy.

And the unconscious boy opened his eyes.

Chris opened his eyes, abandoning the vision, and looked around the yard with new eyes. The Dryad had become the light. The light had entered Chris. Chris had become the Chosen One in that instant. He had the power, residing within him, to destroy the enemy that threatened his people. He knew this, but still he didn't know how to use that power.

At the house, the screen door swung open and slapped shut. Chris looked up. He saw the old black man with the white beard walking down the porch steps to join him in the yard. This wasn't a memory. This was happening.

The old man stopped in front of Chris and smiled.

He spoke in a gravelly voice that reminded Chris of someone who had smoked too many cigarettes in his youth. "You finally remember what you needed to know to stop Marbhdhraoi."

Chris shook his head. "I still don't know anything. I don't even know what Marbhdhraoi is."

The old man smiled again. "Marbhdhraoi. The Necromancer. He who manipulates death. Only the Dryad can stop him. And the Dryad is you, my boy."

"I still don't understand. I thought I was the Chosen One."

"You are. You are the Chosen One. The Chosen One is you. The Dryad is the Chosen One, and you are the Dryad."

Chris shook his head again, not understanding. "You're talking in riddles. None of it makes any sense. I don't understand."

The old man laughed, a gravelly sound like boulders rubbing together. "Learn to unleash the power and all will make sense." The old man motioned for Chris to walk with him.

"How do I unleash the power?" Chris asked as they walked.

The old man led Chris to the wooden platform and they sat with their feet dangling over the side. "It will come in time."

"That's just it. I don't have time. People are dying and I need to know how to save them before it's too late." Chris's voice reflected the desperation he felt.

"The Necromancer fears you. He mocks you, but he fears you."

Chris admitted to a fear he had. "I'm worried that the Necromancer resides inside the body of one of my friends."

Crispus nodded. "You are correct. The female died several hours before you arrived. She died of exposure, not from the disease. The Necromancer took over the body in an attempt to hide in plain sight."

"Some hiding place. I saw through him right away."

The old man glanced around, almost as if recalling his own memories of the place. What he recalled seemed to please him, because he smiled. He returned his gaze to Chris. "He's not hiding from you."

"Who is he hiding from then?"

"The others. The people who don't believe in him, or who don't know he exists."

Chris seemed more confused than ever. Something else occurred to him. "I think I also saw a glimpse of him in another person. I saw a man kill himself right in front of me."

"Yes, your building is quite safe for the moment. As long as the doors are closed, the Necromancer cannot get inside. Defeat him before the doors are opened and all your people will be safe."

"But what about the man I saw kill himself. If he was possessed by the Necromancer, then he had already been inside the Ark."

The old man shook his head. "What you saw was a harmless attempt to gain entry. The man had a diminished mind, and the Necromancer used him to get a peek inside. That man was nothing more than a periscope for the Necromancer to peer through. The man killed himself in an attempt to stop the Necromancer from using him to see inside. The man broke the connection, and stopped the enemy from seeing anything useful. The man sacrificed himself for the cause."

"He was also talking about opening the doors."

"It was the will of the Necromancer being spoken."

"So, in order to free my friends inside the Ark I have to kill the Necromancer. That's why I'm here. I need to learn how to do that. And if I defeat the Necromancer, does that mean I have to kill Nancy, my friend?"

"You have to remember that the woman is already dead. You are not killing her; you are freeing her."

Chris took a moment to digest this news. Although it was something he already suspected, hearing it being confirmed caused an ache in his heart. The sadness was compounded because he knew how Brian would feel after learning his wife never stood a chance. This was news Chris was reluctant to share.

But then something else occurred to Chris. "Is Brian in danger? He thinks that thing is his wife. And Hellen. She's there, too."

"The Necromancer will bide his time until the doors to the bastion are opened and he has gained entry, once that happens, no one is safe. Until then, the thing will continue to leave well enough alone."

"So, we're good there because the door won't be opened without my permission. I destroy the Necromancer, and then we can open the doors."

"That is correct."

"So now all that I need is the knowledge of how to kill him."

"The Necromancer isn't a real man, and can't be killed; he can only be rendered impotent. Only the power of the Dryad can do that."

"Are you saying that chopping the body up into little pieces isn't enough?"

"I'm afraid not. The body is just a vessel. Kill the body and he will simply choose another vessel to possess."

Chris sighed. "And in this world, there are a lot of vessels to possess."

The old man stayed quiet as Chris grasped the implications.

"That means all I have left to learn is how to control the power of the Dryad."

The old man jumped down to the ground with a deftness that belied his age. "Then let's begin, shall we?"

2.

Chris's first two attempts to control the power ended in complete failure. Actually, that was too kind; it was embarrassing. He went at it with all his being and soul, and nothing at all happened. He tried swinging his arms, and throwing his hands out in front of him. Nothing happened. The apparition of Crispus laughed at him, with that gravelly, irritating laughter. It infuriated Chris, and in that second attempt, he tried to use that anger to stir up something within him.

Nothing happened.

When the laughter died down, Crispus said, "I think you need to meditate. This should come as easily to you as your own voice, a wave of your arm. You need the power to work in the blink of an eye. If it does not, you will be dead before your body hits the floor. Do you understand?"

Chris nodded.

"Rest, and we'll try again later."

Chris paced. "I don't have time to rest. My friends are in danger now. I have to do this now, not later."

"Rest your mind, and the answers will come to you."

Chris shook his head. "It's impossible. Maybe I don't have control of the power. Did you ever think of that? What if the Chosen One isn't meant to save anyone? What if it's all a lie?" Chris looked at Crispus. "Can you control the Power? Can you use it to save my friends?"

"My boy. I'm going to let you in on a little secret. I'm not really here. I am a figment of your imagination. You conjured me from the deepest darkest recesses of your mind. The power to control the Dryad comes from that same place from which I came. Figure out how you conjured me and you will find the power you seek. Just remember, it's already in you."

"If I conjured you, couldn't I make you tell me what I need to hear?"

The old man shrugged.

"This is ridiculous. I may as well have conjured my mother. You're no help."

When Chris turned back to face the old man, he was gone. In his place, Chris saw his mother standing there.

"Do not say 'ain't' in this house again, you little puke." His mother's face was twisted into a grimace. This wasn't so much a conjuring, as it was a memory. His mother had said those very words to Scott. Her look of anger and…yes, hatred…toward Scott had affected both boys that day. Chris remembered how bad he had felt for Scott. And Chris's pity only angered his older brother. Scott would not tolerate Chris feeling sorry for him. Chris had forgotten that moment, until now. Chris recalled how hurt Scott had looked when his mother said those words, called him that name. Tears formed in Scott's eyes that he refused to shed. After that day, Scott had treated Chris like the enemy. Scott was angry at their mother, but took it out on Chris. That didn't change until after the abduction, and all the pain and horror they had gone through together during the time the Keepers of the Forest held them prisoner.

When Chris's mother was gone, Sherry took her place.

"You helped Scott and I escape," Chris said, as if telling her something she didn't already know.

"Yes, I did."

"Are you going to give me more information on how to control the power of the Dryad?"

Sherry walked over to Chris and placed a hand gently on his face. He could actually feel her touch. What a vivid vision.

"You already provided yourself with the answer. You want to rest. You should rest."

When she was gone—right in front of him, she simply blinked out of existence—Chris realized that he was in need of rest. He had tried to tell himself, first through Crispus, and then through Sherry. They had spoken the words, but it had all come from him.

Chris entered the house. He headed up the steps to the third door on the left. It was here he had been kept during the abduction. The room still held all the same furnishings it did when he had stayed there. Or, perhaps, it was just his imagination conjuring it to look this way; either way, it didn't matter. Chris climbed up on the dusty, mildew-laced bedding and lay his head on the pillow. He fell asleep almost instantly. He didn't recall having any dreams when he woke, but he did feel refreshed and well-rested. It was something he hadn't experienced in a very long time. *Really? I needed to come back here in order to experience the best sleep of my life? I must be totally messed up in the head.*

Whatever the case, it didn't matter. After a full night of rest, Chris's third attempt to conjure the power was a success.

3.

Brian tried not to drive over any of the dead bodies during his ride back to the Ark, but at times the corpses were so thick, he had no choice. He cringed as he heard the squishing sound of flesh splitting, and the crunch of breaking bones. He whispered heartfelt apologies to the bodies that he ground under his tires. The car bumped and jostled from side to side as the four-wheel-drive made quick work of the terrain—and its obstacles.

The Ark's silhouette loomed larger and larger as they drew nearer, and Brian grew excited to think he would soon be back inside the safety of its walls, where his wife could finally recover with some success.

Brian hoped Chris had already returned to the Ark, and ordered the doors opened. If not, he would use his negotiation skills to convince Toby that the plague was gone, and the doors could be opened. Perhaps even Hellen—Dr. Jacobson—had gotten Toby to open the doors.

Brian followed Coreys Road through the trees, until he reached the archway announcing Ampersand Road had begun. He moved slowly through the narrow entrance to the lake view road. He noted that his aversion to running over the bodies had slackened the closer he got to his destination. He only wanted to get there as quickly as possible now. He was sorry that those people had died, but he needed to get his wife under the protection of the Ark as soon as possible.

He drove with abandon, spinning out around corners and skidding on icy patches, but he didn't care. He barely noticed the lake as he drove along its border. He reached the length of road where the biggest curves ended and he could speed up.

He glanced over at Nancy, and though he couldn't be sure, he thought she looked excited to reach the Ark as well. He placed his hand on her hand but she didn't react to the touch. The slight smile touching her lips didn't falter.

"Soon," he said to her. "We'll be there soon."

No response from Nancy.

"That's okay." Brian squeezed her hand. You'll talk when you're ready. He leaned over and kissed her cheek. The Hummer swerved, but he recovered. "Woah. I got this." He laughed.

The gate loomed ahead. He stopped in front of it and stepped out of the vehicle. He used a hammer he found in a tool box behind the driver's seat of the Hummer to break the lock, and shoved the gate open. He had to drag a few dead bodies out of the way, but he stopped caring about diseases a long time ago, and it didn't bother him to touch them anymore. He climbed back behind the wheel and drove the Hummer up as close to the main bay doors as he could get, but the helicopter wreckage, his old car, and about fifty dead bodies stopped him from getting too close. He snatched up the helmet and stepped out of the Hummer once again. He slipped the helmet over his head.

"Toby, Ole Buddy," he said into the wrist band.

4.

When the big yellow Hummer came up to the fence, he first grew anxious that survivors had made their way to the Ark; but then Toby saw Brian get out and move the gate, and he became immediately excited that Chris was on his way back. Toby called for Scott. Within minutes, Scott was next to Toby watching the vehicle approaching the front of the building.

"You saw my brother?" Scott asked.

Toby struggled to maintain his enthusiasm. "No. I just figured they wouldn't come back without him."

Scott put his arm around Toby's shoulder. "He'll be there then."

Toby leaned toward Scott. *Please be with them Chris.*

Kaylan walked into the control room and stood next to Scott. He placed his other arm around her. He pulled her close to him. "Chris is back?" She kissed his cheek.

He turned and they kissed. "We hope," he said as he turned back to the monitors.

The Hummer stopped and Brian climbed out. They watched as he put the hood on his head.

"Toby, Ole Buddy," Brian's grainy voice came over the speaker. "We're here. You going to open the door?"

"Sure." Toby inserted his key into the lock for the casing over the big red button that opened the bay doors. He flipped up the covering. "Where's Chris put the helmet on him so he can give me the word."

Brian chuckled. "Chris, uh…Chris isn't here."

"What do you mean? Who is with you?"

"It's me and Nancy, my wife. We need to be let in. Please."

"Brian, I need Chris's word. The doors can't be opened until he gives the word. I'm sorry. I really am."

Brian was silent for a moment. Then he continued with his plea. "Nancy needs help. I have to get her inside and stabilize her environment. This is important. It's life and death, here."

"Is…is she sick?"

Brian was quick to clarify. "No. No, she's not sick. She doesn't have the plague. It's shock. Hellen said she's suffering from severe shock."

"Where is Dr. Jacobson?" Toby asked.

"She said she was coming here. She left us days ago."

"She left you? If your wife is as bad off as you say, why would she leave you? That doesn't sound like her at all. Brian, I really need Chris's permission. Please go back and get him. That will clear all this up."

Brian's voice grew desperate. "He left us. He left us and Hellen left us. We're alone out here. Please let us back in. Please."

Toby said, "No."

"God damn it, Tobias. We're cold. We're tired. Let us in." Brian's voice wavered, perhaps with sorrow, but Toby thought it was anger.

"No, Brian. I'm sorry. Your wife denied our hospitality, and chose the death of the plague instead. She was never a part of us in here."

"Is that what this is all about? You're butt-hurt because my wife's morals didn't allow her the luxury to sit on the bones of the dead? She hurt your feelings, Toby? Is that why you are willing to let us die out here?"

"That has nothing to do with my decision. Chris, himself, made the rule that no one but him is allowed to give the command to open the door. I have the lives of seven thousand people to think about."

"I've always thought of you as a friend, Toby. Now I'm starting to believe you're no different than Ethel."

Toby clenched his jaw. "That's not fair. You're chastising me for doing my job. I'm doing what Chris asked of me. Why can't you understand that?"

Brian's voice returned to a compassionate tone. "Please just let us in. We're fine. The plague is gone. It's been eradicated. We're free. It's time to return to the real world, Toby. Open the doors. You can clearly see my wife is fine." He turned back to the vehicle and they clearly saw Nancy sitting placidly in the passenger seat. "She beat the plague. Chris will confirm this as soon as he returns. But right now, we need help or we're going to die from exposure."

"No." Toby was stern, talking to a willful child. "Not until Chris returns. It's as simple as that. I—"

Scott leaned over and hit the button.

A claxon blared and red lights flashed. A grinding moan filled their ears. The doors were opening.

Toby turned to Scott. "What have you done?"

Scott was unapologetic. "They are my friends and they need our help."

"Scott, no." Toby collapsed back in his chair, defeated.

"They are my friends. I watched you people kill all my friends, and my family. Your people wanted to kill my wife. Now someone who means as much to me as my own brother does is asking for my help. I helped. It's as simple as that."

329

"No, it's more than that." Toby's voice softened. "You may well have just killed us all."

5.

The doors started their slow crawl away from each other, and the opening began to form. Brian put his hand to his head, praying he had gotten through to Toby. He took a step toward the doors, but stopped when he heard the car door open and slam shut. He looked over and saw Nancy walking toward the entrance. He smiled, but the expression faded quickly. Her movements seem too rushed, too desperate. How had she gone from nearly catatonic to practically running toward the doorway?

As she broke the threshold, she stopped and lifted her arms, looking much like a marathon runner breaking through the finish line. She spun and looked back toward Brian. She pointed at him.

Then she just dropped to the ground.

Brian took a few steps toward the door, worried about his wife, but movement around him caused him to stop.

He froze in place and looked around, gaping at what was happening.

The bodies were struggling to stand. Some took a few tentative steps toward the Ark. Some stopped and looked at him. One woman with a smashed face reached for him. He backed away, tripping. When he saw what he had tripped over, he crab-crawled away quickly.

The legless man crawled after him.

Brian scrambled to his feet and worked his way around the Hummer to the driver's side door. As he opened it and squeezed in, a woman reached out, gripping his coat, trying to pull him back out of the car. He worked her stone-hard fingers off his sleeve and pulled the door closed. He engaged all the locks. The woman slapped at the glass leaving bloody streaks.

Brian stared into her face, seeing something Hellen had pointed out in his wife. The woman had enlarged pupils. She bit at

330

the glass like an animal not understanding there was a barrier between it and the food source it craved.

His attention was drawn away from the woman at the window when he saw movement in the rearview mirror. Coming from the open gate, he saw more marchers staggering forward.

Hundreds of them, and they were all heading toward the open doors.

Brian thought his heart had stopped beating, but in actuality it was beating faster. Too fast. Dangerously fast, and he was heaving. He didn't realize he was crying until he tasted the salty tears on his lips.

6.

Kaylan moaned softly and the two men stopped arguing to look at her. She pointed to the monitor.

Toby made a choking sound.

"Oh my God," Scott said.

They turned to the large observation window that looked out at the bay floor. Several dozen of the intruding force had already entered the Ark. Some continued their slow march into the depths of the structure, but a few stopped and turned toward the control room.

Toby dashed across the floor and bolted the heavy steel door. He backed away slowly as the first clumsy thumps hit the door on the other side. Toby slipped into his seat and flicked a switch on the control panel. He lifted a microphone to his mouth and spoke slowly and clearly.

"If you can hear my voice, you must leave where you are. Go to the top floor—to the main hall on the top floor. Once there, lock the doors. I repeat, make your way to the top floor and lock yourselves in. This is not a drill. The Ark's defenses have been breached and an enemy is inside. Please save yourselves and make your way to the main hall on the 400th floor."

Toby repeated his warning over and over until his voice went hoarse. Then Scott took over for him.

7.

Carrie pushed the cart into the infirmary as her guard held the door for her. The guard outside Ethel's room waved to them as they approached. "Breakfast time at the zoo." Carrie giggled.

The guard smiled as he held the door open for them. When Carrie's guard passed through to the room, the guard closed the door.

Ethel stood from where she had been laying on the cot and sat down in the chair to eat. "What do we have today?"

Carrie placed the tray on the table in front of Ethel and lifted the cover. She screamed and dropped the steel lid. It clattered onto the table and rang like a bell as it hit the hard, concrete floor. Ethel stood and backed away from the table, knocking over her chair. The guard rushed over to protect Carrie. He looked down at the tray.

A dead rat lay curled up on the plate.

"What the fuck is this?" Ethel ran forward and pushed the plate, and the dead rat, onto the floor. She turned an angry eye at Carrie. Her lip pulled back in a scowl. "Why would you bring that to me?"

Carrie shook her head, violently. She struggled to control her hysterics. "No, I didn't. My sister—"

"Fuck that. You should have checked. I don't deserve to be treated like this." Tears of anger formed in Ethel's eyes.

"I...I'm sorry. I'll—"

"Oh, my god." Ethel paced. "I'll never be able to trust anything you bring me again. I won't be able to trust any of you. I'll starve." She kicked her upturned chair. She screamed. She balled her hands into fists and shook them at Carrie.

"I am truly sorry. You can trust me. From now on I'll check everything. I'll watch her make the food. I won't let her tamper with your meals ever again. I promise."

Ethel slammed her hand down on the table. "If Chris doesn't do something about this, I'll—" She stopped.

Outside the room, they could hear the faint, muffled voice of someone talking over the loudspeaker, but inside the room they couldn't hear what was being said. The guard stepped closer to the door.

"What's that?" Ethel asked.

The guard turned to her and shrugged. "Can't hear."

"Well, go out there and listen, dumbass." Ethel flicked an impatient hand at him.

The guard ignored her, but stepped closer to the door. He reached for the knob, but stopped when a loud thump caused the door to shake in its frame. The sound of a struggle carried through the cracks.

The guard opened the door.

They all leaned in to peer out at the main room of the infirmary. What they saw confused them.

The guard on the outside of the door lay on the floor. There was someone leaning over him. As they watched it became clear what they were seeing.

Derek leaned back and turned toward the door. In his teeth was the guard's throat. The guard lay bleeding and twitching beneath him. Derek spit the wad of meat out of his mouth and stood.

Carrie screamed.

The door opened wider and Nora entered the room. She fell on the guard. He struggled to get her off him, but she was too strong. She bit into his neck. Derek entered and tore into the guard as well. All three went down. The man screamed until he lost too much blood.

Then his screams stopped.

Carrie backed away from the door, closer to Ethel. The old woman rattled her chain at Carrie. She indicated the lock on the bracelet.

Carrie shook her head and pointed to the guard; she didn't have the key, he did. They both stood in shocked horror as more of the dead walked through the door.

Gerard entered, as did Patty and Roger. Derek and Nora stood and joined the others as they fell on Carrie and Ethel.

Carrie cried as Derek and Nora pulled her down to the floor.

Ethel reached out and touched her son's cheek. She smiled up at him as he leaned over, as if to give her a kiss.

He ripped out her throat with his teeth instead.

No one could hear their screams.

8.

When Scott could no longer send out the warning with any effectiveness, Kaylan took over for him. He and Toby walked over to stare out the bay windows. More of the intruders had arrived. They had begun to get stuck against each other. There were too many in the space of the docking bay. The things that had gathered at the observation window were pushed up against the glass.

"Can they break it?" Scott asked.

Toby shook his head slowly. "I don't know. It's thick—very thick—and was made to withstand the crushing depths of the deepest parts of the ocean, but…to be honest…I just don't know."

They stared at the window as faces were pressed so tightly against the glass that the flesh tore. Some heads burst against the window in a spray of bone fragments, brain matter and blood. As the things slid down the glass they left muddy streaks in the gore. After a few minutes the entire area had gone opaque with blood. Occasionally, a hand or a shoulder rubbed up on the window, leaving behind a clean streak, but those spots filled in quickly as more blood, thick and crusty, continued to coat the glass. Those in the room had no way of knowing how bad things were getting out in the main hub of the Ark.

9.

Brian, had a front row view of it all. He watched as the dead continued to march through the doors by the hundreds. They were so thick that some were pressed down underfoot and trampled. His wife was under there, too. He knew now that she was dead—had been all along. Chris had tried to warn him, as had Hellen, but he wouldn't listen.

The dead march on, moving past his vehicle as if it wasn't there. The crowd was so thick that all he could see out the windows were their slack, emotionless faces. Their skin looked as white and pale as the undersides of mushrooms. Some had damage, some looked to be intact, but frost clung to them like moss. They moved slow, but they moved steady. And they were relentless. They just kept coming. First by the hundreds, and then by the thousands.

He prayed the people inside the Ark could make it to safety.

10.

Margot thought that her sister should be returning soon, pissed off by the dead rat, no doubt; but damn it, she was tired of that old woman getting the royal treatment after everything she did. Margot already had the real breakfast ready to go as soon as Carrie returned.

As Margot chopped cilantro, she heard something coming over the loud speakers, but in the kitchen, she couldn't hear it clearly. She wiped her hands on a cloth and walked out to the dining room.

"…not a drill." It was a woman's voice. She thought it was Kaylan speaking. "If you can hear the sound of my voice, make your way up to the four-hundredth floor. Go up to the main hall and lock yourselves in."

Margot thought that Ethel had broken her chains—or gotten loose somehow—and was causing more havoc. She hoped her little stunt hadn't driven the crazy bitch over the edge.

Paul came into the dining room from the hall. "What's going on?"

"I don't know. I guess we better do what they say. Sounds serious."

"It's crazy. I've never heard of them sending out warning like this before. Make sure the ovens are off, and let's get going."

Margot turned to go back to the kitchen, but the door to the main entrance opened and she heard her father talking to Carrie.

"Here we go," Margot mumbled under her breath as she returned to the dining room. She stopped when she realized something was wrong.

"Carrie, my God. What's happened?"

Her sister was covered in blood.

And Carrie wasn't alone.

The pale and lifeless bodies moved with purpose and determination, but by no means could be described as being in a hurry. The first to arrive fell on her father with a vicious ferocity. They took him screaming to the floor. The one she thought was the mentally ill man, Derek, reached into her father's stomach and pulled out handfuls of entrails, even as her father continued screaming, and commenced cramming them into his mouth.

Carrie was messed up. Her throat was gone, as was most of the right side of her face—torn away...no, bitten away. Carrie stumbled toward Margot. The sisters locked arms.

Margot struggled out of her sister's tight grip and tumbled back. She almost fell, with Carrie on top of her, but she caught herself on a wall and used it as leverage. She ducked out from under her sister's grappling hands, and away from her snapping mouth. Margot ran to the cooler and shut herself in. She used the metal bar that would normally be used to unstick the door if it jammed, and shoved it through the handle and behind a metal shelving unit.

As the being outside the door began to slam into it, the bar rattled but stayed in place. With the bar in place she doubted they could get in. But then, she couldn't get out, either. And it was cold in there. She could see her breath? How long would she be trapped in there?

Margot found the sweatshirt her father had placed inside the cooler for people who had to spend more than a few seconds in the in it. Thank goodness for her father's resourcefulness. Without the sweater, she would surely freeze to death. Then, she still might if she spent too long in there.

Her father.

She had watched that man, who she had been told was dead, kill her father, eat him. She closed her eyes to try to force the memory out of her head. Tears froze to her lashes. Her father was dead.

And so was Carrie.

That was a dead girl attacking her. Carrie was dead, but still had somehow walked. She had attacked Margot. She had intended to kill Margot.

She slid down a wall and wrapped her arms around her knees. She rocked herself. As the door continued to rattle, Margot pressed her hands to her ears like a child trying not to hear her parents fight. Her hands moved off her ears and covered her mouth. She breathed into her hands, trying to warm them.

She thought of Chris.

She missed him. She hoped she would get to see him again. The thought of him returning to the Ark and finding her frozen to the wall in the cooler caused her to start crying all over again.

But thinking of Chris gave her hope. She needed that right now.

She thought of Chris. And she hoped.

11.

Hellen heard a vehicle rumbling in the distance, something with a large motor, and she thought it might have been Chris. She wanted to go out and see if she could find him, but she was too worried that it was Brian, so she didn't go. She stayed near her fire and hoped—if it was Brian—that he didn't see the smoke. If it was Chris, she hoped he did see it. She couldn't remember if smoke was more visible during the day, or at night. She thought daytime was the dangerous time to be making a fire.

But several hours passed and no one came to the house.

Hellen dozed and woke with a start several times during the day. When she couldn't sit anymore, she searched through the cupboards and found a can of soup. She poured it into a pan and set it on the fire. She took it off the fire when it started to boil and used a dish from which to eat it. The soup warmed her up from the inside, but it did nothing for her hunger.

The meal was a serious breach of her vow not to dirty any dishes. There was no water to clean it with — barely enough for her to drink. Dirty dishes also attracted unwanted guests. But the soup was good, and it made her feel thawed out. So she risked doing the dishes.

As night started to fall, Hellen found herself pacing. She didn't know how much longer she could go on like this. She would need to go out soon. She would need to go back to the Ark. She had been stupid to agree to come on this mission. She hadn't been any help at all.

She heard movement outside and stopped moving. She thought it could be more coy dogs. Maybe they wanted fresh meat. She crept quietly to the window and looked out.

What she saw shocked her. There were people out there. People were walking through the field toward the house. As they grew closer she felt apprehension filling her up inside. These were not ordinary people. They were pale, and walked with an odd gait. She compared it to how a person might walk on Thorazine. Some of the more unethical healthcare workers referred to it as the Thorazine Shuffle. She found that kind of talk counterproductive to the patient's recovery, however, and would never have stooped to that level.

But these were not escaped patients from a mental ward. As they moved closer, she could see their pale skin. They seemed to grow more numerous as they moved through the fields around the house. She watched as they passed by the house and continued on, moving toward the Ark. The crowd continued moving. She thought there had to be thousands. What did they want with the Ark? Once the horde of travelers slowed, and the scenery was once again devoid of movement, Hellen found herself heading out to follow the people. She stayed close, never wanting to fall too far behind the exodus. But she was afraid to get too close. She didn't want them seeing her. She had no idea who they were or what they were doing.

As the horde moved out of the trees and into a clearing, Hellen found herself out in the open. She wanted to stay close enough to see them in the fading light, and that meant moving out of the tree line as well. Vulnerable now, she kept pace, staying low to the ground and as invisible as possible. Her breath puffed out in fluffy wisps, but she couldn't help that. Between the exertion of keeping up with the travelers and her terror, her breath was coming in raspy pants.

She watched as more of them came in from different directions and joined the main group. None of them spoke to each other, or even acknowledged the one next to them even existed.

There was something else that concerned her.

None of them seemed to have a cloud of breath coming from their mouths. Unless they had the ability to hold their breath indefinitely, she thought that she should surely see the plumes of their breath. She was that close.

As if sensing her presence, several members of the group turned and looked her way. This smaller group, maybe twenty or so, broke off from the main group and started coming her way. The rest continued on their way as if they had no concern about what the smaller group planned.

She froze. They moved slowly, but they could catch her easily if she didn't head back.

Since her cover was blown anyway, Hellen stood and turned to run in the other direction.

There was another group that had been coming up from behind. She ran into the arms of one of these. She staggered and fell backward. The first two in the group that had been behind her reached down for her. Their mouths opened and snapped shut, as if chewing…or biting.

As close as she was, she could now see they were not just people, but corpses of people. They had those large pupils, and their skin was as pale and waxy as fish bellies. There was some rot, but it looked like the cold had mostly preserved them.

She slapped away their hands as they reached out for her. She wanted to scream but her fear and confusion mixed to make her unable to do anything more than grunt and pant.

She tried to squirm out of the grasp of the thing holding her, but its grip was more powerful than her. At this point, the few that had been coming back toward her had joined the group that had surprised her. Together, they numbered at least fifty. She placed her arms over her head and curled into a fetal ball. She felt their hands touching her, tugging at her; and she thought they were probably trying to get at her tasty parts. She fought against their groping hands as best she could. But her strength was waning, and they were going to win the battle. They didn't get winded or care if they were hurt. They were as relentless as death itself.

Something grabbed her hair and whipped her head back. Hellen looked into the thing's milky white eyes, its pupils huge. She pulled her eyes away from its gaze and she looked at its pale, blue skin. A bite on its cheek had torn away a chunk of flesh, exposing moist red muscle that glistened inside the open wound. White bone protruded from the red flesh in stark contrast. It opened its mouth.

Snapping teeth filled her vision, and she watched as the mouth moved toward her throat. She closed her eyes and prayed for a quick death.

Hellen opened her eyes when she heard a strange whipping and whirring sound. The thing attempting to bite her was yanked violently back. Now Hellen could see more clearly, and she saw what looked like a hurricane blowing all around her. The things surrounding her were being pulled, one by one, into the swirling mass of tree limbs and debris. Soon she was the last one standing. But still the violent winds didn't touch her. She turned around, and then turned again. It was all around her, but her hair wasn't even being blown.

After a moment, she started seeing what had happened to her attackers. Torn body parts dropped onto the ground around her. There was nothing left of them.

She saw movement from the corner of her eye and turned.

Chris stepped out from the swirling storm and stood smiling at her. Once she had overcome the worst of her shock, she took a step toward him. He held out a hand to her and she fell into his arms, sobbing wildly.

Chapter Thirteen

1.

Scott's eyes burned from the need for sleep, but there would be no sleeping. Not now, and maybe, not ever. There was a deep, low rumble passing through the Ark. It was the marching feet of the invading horde. They watched on the monitors—when they could stand to look—as thousands of dead continued to come. They had crammed together so tightly that some were crushed, but even if they were rendered immobile, there was always more to replace them. They numbered in the hundreds of thousands now, Scott imagined.

Sometimes the door to the control room bulged, and they all held their breath; and so far, the door had withstood the pressure, but Scott expected it to crack down the middle at any moment.

They had no way of knowing if anyone had heeded their pleas to retreat to the top floor of the Ark, but Scott was hopeful.

"This is all my fault," Scott said suddenly. Kaylan pushed up against him and placed an arm around his shoulders. "I opened the doors and let them in."

Toby looked the most tired of all of them. He had told them he was going on his third shift in the control room, and hadn't slept in two days. He blinked at Scott. "No, you're not to blame. I left the button exposed. I should have closed the guard cap. I could easily have accidentally pressed it myself. Hell, I was about to press it myself. I hated the thought of leaving them out there."

Scott shook his head. "No. You were holding firm. I had no business touching the button. I'm to blame."

"Enough," Kaylan said. "Fighting over who's to blame isn't going to solve anything. Hell, we're all to blame. I could have stopped you, Scott. Brian brought it here. He gets some of that blame. We can blame Chris for leaving us here. The truth is none of us knew what we were in for. We didn't know what was going to happen. Let's come up with a solution."

Scott pointed to the crowd outside the doors. They were so thick they couldn't see the yellow Hummer Brian had retreated to. They had no idea if he was still alive. "How do you propose dealing with that?"

"We could close the doors again, couldn't we?"

"No." Toby pressed the button. "No power. It won't have power again for another forty-eight hours. Takes seventy-two hours for the power to recharge."

Kaylan shrugged. "It was worth a try."

Toby walked into Chris's office and found three bottles of soda in his pint-sized fridge. He shared with Scott and Kaylan. There were others in the room with them, but they were huddled in the far corner, too terrified to do anything but cover their heads and block out the sound of the invaders.

They could see the bodies brushing up against the window even though the blood and gore covering the glass had dried to a crusty paste. Every now and then, one of the things reminded them that they were out there, and a hand slapped heavily against the glass. The thickness muffled the worst of the sound, but they knew the things were out there just the same.

Scott had a thought. "What if we opened the door and let a few in? Killed them. Let a few more in and killed them?"

"Bad idea." Toby rolled his eyes. "We open that door and a flood is going to pour through it and never stop. We would be done for."

Scott nodded. "Yea, bad idea."

Kaylan snorted. "What would we do anyway? Kill all two hundred thousand of them? And do you even know how to kill them?"

"I said it was a bad idea."

Her eyes widened. "The worse one yet."

"No stupider than closing the door. Even if we could, that would be locking them in here with us."

Kaylan punched him in the arm.

Scott leaned in and she kissed him.

"I'm sorry," Scott said.

Something heavy hammered against the door and they all stopped fooling around and waited to see if this was the moment they all dreaded. With each thump a woman in the back of the room screamed.

Scott wanted to scream for her to shut the hell up, but he couldn't take his concentration away from the door long enough to breathe, never mind speak . He exhaled when the thrashing stopped.

Toby turned away from the door and glanced at the monitor. He leaned in. "What the…"

Scott and Kaylan moved over to look at what had his attention. He pointed to the screen.

They saw it, too. At the periphery of the advancing horde a storm was brewing. It was a strong one, too. It whipped and tossed debris into the air. They watched in shocked silence as the bodies were flung into the air. None of them were coming back down.

2.

Brian sat in the driver's seat staring at nothing. He had learned to ignore the faces pressed up against the glass. He didn't care if they got in anymore. Nancy was dead, and so was he…inside. He replayed that moment over in his head. She had walked into the Ark, turned and pointed at him—as if to say, your fault—and then she just collapsed into a boneless heap. Dead.

It was his fault. He did this.

If he had thought to grab the helmet, he could have talked to Toby in the control room. Toby might have known more about what was happening. But he didn't want to talk to Toby, anyway. He couldn't bear hearing the condescending tone in his voice that said *your fault. Your fault. Your…*

Sudden movement outside the vehicle pulled Brian out of his self-deprecating stupor and he turned to glance out. He watched, confused, as the bodies out there flew into the air and disappeared from sight.

A body slammed into the windshield and its head cracked the glass, but then it, too, flew up and away. Brian leaned forward and looked up at the sky through the windshield. Bodies flew into the air so high that when they came back down they were turned into crushed meat as they hit the ground. Some seemed to be shredded right in front of him. The debris in the swirling storm cut through them, leaving nothing but ground meat in the wake. Within minutes, the area around the Hummer was clear of the dead. Brian risked getting out of the vehicle. He watched as the maelstrom kept working its way toward the Ark. Bodies were obliterated in its path.

The ground was littered with body parts—millions of harmless tiny little body parts.

"Who's going to clean up this mess?"

Brian spun around to look for the source of the voice. He stared at Chris standing near the back bumper of the Hummer. Hellen stepped around and stood with her arms crossed.

"Chris, I…" He couldn't say the words.

"It's okay, Brian."

Brian stuttered, unable to come up with the words, because it wasn't okay. "Nancy…she…"

Chris went to Brian and hugged him. He whispered into Brian's ear. "I'm sorry for your loss, my friend. Because it's my loss, too."

"She's dead." Brian managed to gain some composure. "She was always dead. I didn't know. I didn't want to know. You knew, and you warned me; but I didn't want to believe it."

As Hellen stepped closer, Brian looked at her.

"I'm so sorry. I…" Brian wasn't allowed to finish. Hellen pulled him into a hug. She kissed his cheek.

She pulled away and looked into his eyes. "I can't imagine what you're going through."

Brian shook his head as if to clear it. He looked back at the storm which was now sweeping into the Ark through the open doors. There wasn't a body to be seen anywhere in the yard.

Not a whole body, anyway.

"What's happening?" Brian asked.

"Cleanup," Chris said.

3.

"I've been on a quest to learn how to control the power of the Dryad," Chris said as he, Hellen and Brian, strode into the Ark. "At first, I could barely move a twig, but as more and more of the knowledge came to me I was able to blow entire trees apart and control the debris. It's that power I'm using to sweep through the dead, destroying what the Necromancer wrought on us."

The three of them walked into the Ark and examined the damage. The bay was littered with body parts, but the danger had passed. They knocked on the door to the control room but when no one answered, Chris feared the worst.

"Open up in there." He shouted at the door.

"Hold up." Brian returned to the front of the Hummer, searched the ground and seemed to find what he was looking for. He ran back to Chris. "Your wristband. I dropped it during my scuffle with the legless dead man. The face was cracked, but otherwise it seems ok."

"Hey, can you hear me?" Brian said into the microphone.

"Brian?" Toby's voice was tentative, disbelieving.

"Open the door. I have company."

He waited with Chris and Hellen for the door to open. After a long moment, they heard the click of the lock and the door creaked slowly open. A terrified face peered out. It was Toby.

"Chris." Toby flung the door open and dragged Chris into the control room. Scott and Kaylan rushed over to throw their arms around him. They greeted Brian and Hellen as well.

Toby spoke to Hellen. "Brian said you had come to the Ark days ago, but when I didn't see you, I feared the worst."

Hellen laughed. "I was…hiding out. Chris found me. I was almost torn apart by those things. If he hadn't come when he did with that—" She made a whooshing sound. "I'd be dead now."

Chris looked away when everyone turned to him. "We have to see who made it out alive." He headed for the door.

Kaylan followed him. "We sent everyone to the top floor, like an inverted fire drill."

Chris's expression lightened. "I'm impressed. Hopefully, it worked."

"It was Toby's idea." Kaylan allowed Toby to take up the space to Chris's right. Scott didn't want to be undone, however.

Scott slid in at Chris's left. "But we all helped."

The floor was littered with dead body parts and debris from the storm that had decimated the enemy horde. Once it had completed its task the power had just stopped. The storm ceased and the flotsam just dropped out of the air. It looked like a tornado touched down inside the Ark.

They rode the elevator to the top floor. The floor was clean up here. The dead had not found their way to this floor, it seemed. Chris used the keypad and opened the door. A collective gasp of thousands of people filled the room. Some people screamed. When they saw Chris, there was an audible sigh of relief. Some cried with joy. He assured them the danger was over.

"I was running," one woman said to him. "And the people around me were taken down. I looked back, and the people who were killed, stood and came after me. I don't know how I made it up here."

A man said. "Thank goodness for the announcement. Though they were saying it wasn't a drill, I thought they were playing some kind of gag. But you trained us well, Chris. When we're told to do something, we do it."

Chris listened to many of their stories. He was happy for them—all of them—but there was one he had yet to see.

"I'm looking for Margot. Has anyone seen Margot?"

"I think she was trapped in the restaurant." The man looked apologetic as he spoke.

Someone else agreed. "I'm sorry, Chris. I don't think she made it."

Chris turned and ran from the banquet hall. He stabbed a finger into the call button on the elevator, but didn't want to wait. He raced to the stairs and flung himself down flight after flight until he reached the Jungle Café's floor. He rushed into the dining hall. He stopped.

Carrie and Paul wandered aimlessly around the café. The sound of jungle cats and ape screeches, putting an eerie tingle down Chris's spine. When the two creatures spotted Chris, they staggered toward him, reaching out. Their mouths worked with a hunger that could never be satisfied. Chris closed his eyes and grieved for their loss. As they reached him, the doors behind him blew open and a humanoid creature made entirely of broken tree limbs, branches and vines stomped in. The tree-thing came apart and flew like cannon fire into the two creatures. Carrie and Paul came apart and ceased to move. The tree-thing reformed and stayed close to Chris, protecting him. Chris moved to the kitchen. He took tentative steps, expecting to see Margot as one of the creatures, but praying he didn't.

She was not in the kitchen.

He was about to leave the restaurant, but something about the cooler door caught his eye. He motioned for the tree-thing to open the door. It obeyed. Under the strength of the Dryad's power, the door crumpled like tin foil. It tore the cooler door off the hinges. Chris entered the cooler.

Margot sat huddled on the floor, unconscious. Her skin had turned blue. Chris scooped her up and carried her out of the cooler. He laid her down on the counter and checked her vitals.

Her heart was beating, barely. But she wasn't breathing.

Chris started rescue breathing. He covered her with table clothes and helped her warm up. After a few minutes, Margot opened her eyes. She tried to focus on Chris. She reached up and touched his face.

"You found me." Her voice was a strained whisper.

"I found you."

Chris carried her to the elevators and placed her in his bed. He made her hot tea and kept her wrapped in blankets. He stayed long enough to ensure that she would be okay, and then he left her there to rest.

He still had one more place to visit.

4.

Chris rode the elevator to the ground floor and strode rapidly to the infirmary. He entered Ethel's prison room. Behind him the Dryad reformed.

Chris stared at the thing straining against the chain holding it in place. Ethel had been ravaged. Flesh hung from her bones in strips. Most of the skin on her face had been torn away. It reached for him, but he was out of its range. He studied it for a moment.

He said. "I'm talking to the thing inside the body of Ethel."

The thing that had been Ethel showed no sign of understanding his words.

"Speak to me, you bastard. I know you can. You have before. Talk to me."

Ethel's bloodless eyes turned and focused on Chris. He stepped closer, studying the huge pupils, looking beyond that for the intelligence behind the eyes.

"Is that you?" he asked. "Is that the Necromancer in there?"

The ruined mouth opened and words spilled out. "You…task…me."

"You task me, as well." Chris sat on the edge of the table, still out of the creature's reach. "You killed a lot of my friends."

"It is what…I do."

"Why?" The question was a demand. "Why do you have to kill my friends."

"Not your friends. Everyone."

"Your intention is to kill everyone in the Ark?" He motioned around him. "Everyone inside this structure?"

"I kill everyone…everywhere."

Chris took a deep breath. He closed his eyes to settle the thumping in his chest. "You plan to kill everyone on the planet? To what end? What do you get out of that?"

"It is what I do."

"Well, what I do is stop you."

"I will seek out survivors and finish what I started."

"And where there are survivors, I will be there as well, protecting them. I will keep you down until you crawl back into whatever hole you came from. I will stop you from causing the extinction of the human race. Do you hear me? I will beat you."

"You will try. But you will fail."

"We'll see about that." Chris stood and exited the room. He left the Dryad behind to do what it wished to Ethel's talking corpse.

5.

Of the more than seven thousand members of the Ark, only eighty souls were lost to the invasion. Toby's quick thinking saved thousands of lives. It helped that Chris had worked out an efficient routine for the people of the Ark to follow when they are sent to the top floor. The people wanted to do something special for Toby, so they gave him a day. On his day, they would cater to his every need, every whim. He was modest, but he didn't deny that he loved his day.

Chris organized a memorial for the lives that were lost inside the Ark, including the victims of the massacre during the New Year celebration.

The body parts were burned with flame throwers, then raked into the earth. After a month of non-stop cleaning, there was no trace of death inside the Ark, or out. Margot recovered completely, and she assisted in the clean-up. During the eulogy, she said a few words on behalf of her sister and father.

Brian spoke on behalf of Nancy.

Nancy's trampled body was recovered, and Brian buried her in a separate ceremony that only he was a part of. He stayed by her grave for most of the night, talking to her. When he was finished, he was ready to rejoin the living.

Chris was happy to have him back.

When Scott, Kaylan, Margot, Brian and himself were alone, Chris looked at each of them directly before speaking.

"I can't help but believe there are more survivors out there. I think not everyone died of the plague, and there are people out there who are alive, and having to fight these walking monsters to say alive. I plan to go out and look for them. I need to help them if I can."

"You're needed here," Kaylan said.

"No. Toby is more than capable of handling things around here. The being known as the Necromancer is out there hunting the survivors and killing them. It plans on eradicating the human race from the face of the earth, and I can't let that happen. I'm heading out in the morning."

"*We're* heading out," Margot said. He hugged her.

"I'm going, too." Scott stood and sat down next to his brother.

"I go where he goes." Kaylan giggled.

Everyone turned to look at Brian. He shrugged. "I'm fine here."

"Really?" Chris chuckled.

Brian tried to ignore their stares for as long as he could. Finally, he smiled. "Fine, I'll go, too."

"Damn right, you will." Kaylan punched his arm.

He laughed. "I had every intention of going along. I was just kidding around."

6.

The next morning, Chris informed Toby of his plan. They said their goodbyes, and he left it to Toby to break the news to everyone else. They headed out in the Hummer, and the first thing they did when they reached Tupper Lake was wash the blood and gore off the vehicle. Then they hit the hardware store and collected weapons.

Once they were geared up, and the Hummer was packed with supplies, they drove south out of town.

Brian said, "Let's go bust some zombie ass."

Laughter filled the inside of the vehicle.

Chris said, "Technically, these aren't zombies. A zombie is a living person who has been rendered subservient through ritualistic brainwashing, and drugs. These are reanimated corpses."

Brian chuffed. "Yeah, but saying 'let's bust some reanimated corpse ass' doesn't have the same ring to it."

Chris agreed.

Then he thought of something else.

"Marbh ag Siul."

"What now?" Brian scowled.

"That's what the Necromancer calls them. It's an ancient Irish word for them."

"What does it mean?" Margot leaned against him.

"It means 'dead that walk.'"

No one spoke. The car grew silent for a time.

Scott broke the silence. "Ugh, who farted?"

Brian laughed.

The tension was broken and the warriors traveled on to the next town in search of survivors, and the Marbh ag Siul who sought to kill them.

James McNally

Epilogue: Survivors

James McNally

About an hour ago, night had fallen. The yellow Hummer drove slowly down the street, headlights searching.

"Slow down." Chris tapped Scott's arm. Scott slowed the vehicle even more. Chris never diverted his eyes from what he was looking at outside the window. The Hummer rolled up to the curb and stopped, but Scott didn't turn off the motor. Chris climbed out of the car, and behind him, Brian did the same.

On the other side of the vehicle, Margot and Kaylan climbed out. They came around to stand with the others.

Scott waited in the driver's seat.

Chris glanced around at his backup. "I think I can handle one by myself."

Chris took a hatchet from Margot and broke away from the group. He walked up behind the dead boy. He raised the hatchet. The stumbling dead boy stopped and turned to look behind it. *This one seems different than the others.* It looked up at the hatchet in Chris's hand. Chris had one more thought before he started to swing the hatchet toward the dead boy's neck: *it seems more aware than the others.*

A blond man materialized from nowhere, and he placed a katana in the path of the hatchet, stopping the weapon from connecting with the dead boy's neck. With a flick of the sword, Chris was disarmed.

The others flew into action.

Brian and Margot were at Chris's side in an instant. The blond man shoved the dead creature behind him and protected it with the sword. In another moment, two black wolves appeared beside the blond man, snarling and slavering. A young woman came out of a nearby house and lifted a bow, arrow nocked.

What hornet's nest did we just step on? Chris put out a hand out to the sword-carrying blond man, and raised a hand behind him to his comrades. "No one do anything rash," he said. "We were just doing our jobs here. We're out to eradicate the reanimated dead.

Why are you protecting it?" Chris didn't lose eye contact with the man.

"He's not what you think he is," the blond man said. "He's with us."

"You're protecting that thing? It's out to destroy humanity." Margot stepped up and stood beside Chris.

The woman with the bow and arrow strolled up from her position at the house and stood with the blond man. "He's not out to destroy anything. His name is Jake, and he's harmless." She looked down at the boy and winked at him. "For the most part, that is."

The blond man lowered the katana and Chris relaxed his stance. He silently ordered his group to stand down. *They have no idea they didn't stand a chance against the power of the Dryad.*

Now that he wasn't vibrating with the energy of the Dryad, Chris was able to examine the blond man more closely. There was something different about him. When the creature peeked out from behind the blond man, Chris's eye was drawn to it.

The thing waved at him.

"I'm David," the blond man said.

"Chris." Chris was too stunned by the walking corpse to say anything else.

David sheathed his sword.

"Uh, can you call off Mutt and Jeff now?" Kaylan said from her position behind Chris. Scott had come out of the vehicle when the confrontation turned deadly, and now stood beside Kaylan.

Chris glanced down at the two, nearly identical wolves. They stared back at him with uncanny eyes, decidedly *human* eyes. They studied him with distrustful malice.

"You're hunting the dead things?" David placed a hand on the head of the wolf Chris had determined was a female. The other wolf was a male, he deduced.

"Yes. As a matter of fact, we are."

A young girl of seven or eight walked over from behind a tree carrying neatly folded clothes. In Chris's estimation, they looked to be a complete set of clothes for one man and one woman. "Clothes for my Nanna and Daddy."

What an odd thing to say. Chris studied the girl. *Shouldn't she be in bed? Who are these people?*

David pulled the girl to him. "We're hunting them, too."

Margot pushed forward and looked into David's face. Something about him intrigued her. She was almost face to face with him. Chris placed a hand on her arm.

We can't trust these strangers, but no need to act rash; the Dryad will protect us.

David smiled.

Chris yanked Margot back to him, but she came back willingly.

"He has fangs," she said in a breathless rush.

As Chris and his friends drew together into a tight clump, something miraculous happened. The two wolves shook and vibrated. Their forms melted away and began to reshape. In an instant, the wolves were replaced with a woman and a man, both nude.

Chris shuddered. We're in the presence of something as supernatural as my Dryad ability. If we don't team up with these people, they would make dangerous adversaries.

The woman and the man, a boy, really; took the clothes from the little girl and commenced dressing in them.

When the woman finished dressing, she stepped forward and introduced herself. "I'm Maggie. This is my son, Gardner. You already met my husband, David." Maggie turned to Margot. "And yes, those are fangs. He's a vampire."

Chris stepped closer to Margot.

As she turned and walked away, Maggie continued speaking. "There are more of us around. We have friends—fellow werewolves—named Kenyon and Simone."

As the other group followed Maggie, so did Chris and his group. He felt he was running to keep up. She stopped moving and turned back to Chris.

"We'd be happy to team up with you, if that is what you would like to do. We seem to have a common goal, after all."

Chris's friends turned to him, eager to hear his answer.

Chris stepped forward. He nodded. "We'll join you. And you should know that we don't come without a few tricks of our own."

Eager to show off, Chris raised a hand. He called to the Dryad and it came to him.

The End.

James McNally

Afterward

In the Fortress, as in the previous novel Keepers of the Forest, there were some artistic liberties taken in the description of Tupper Lake. Mostly, there are subtle changes, but one major change was the pool where Brian worked. Although the pool exists, it will not be found in Tupper Lake. The pool is one I frequented often as a kid, but it is in the nearby town of Oneida, NY. I moved it for two reasons: I liked that pool and wanted to use it in my story, and because the town of Tupper Lake did not have a pool of its own.

Ampersand Lake is privately owned, and the owners will be glad to know that no one plans to come along and grab their land in a bid of eminent domain...at least, not as far as I know.

Thank you for reading

Made in the USA
Middletown, DE
02 July 2017